MAUPASSANT
AND THE
AMERICAN SHORT
STORY

Richard Fusco

MAUPASSANT AND THE AMERICAN SHORT STORY

The Influence of Form at the Turn of the Century

The Pennsylvania State University Press
University Park, Pennsylvania

Library of Congress Cataloging-in-Publication Data

Fusco, Richard.
   Maupassant and the American short story : the influence of form at the
turn of the century / Richard Fusco.
      p.   cm.
   Includes bibliographical references and index.
   ISBN 0-271-01081-9
   1. Short stories, American—History and criticism. 2. Maupassant,
Guy de, 1850–1893—Influence. 3. American fiction—French
influences. 4. Literary form. 5. Short story. I. Title.
PS374.S5F87   1994
813'0109—dc20   93-20350
                                                          CIP

Published by The Pennsylvania State University Press,
Barbara Building, Suite C, University Park, PA 16802-1003

It is the policy of The Pennsylvania State University Press to use acid-free
paper for the first printing of all clothbound books. Publications on uncoated
stock satisfy the minimum requirements of American National Standard for
Information Sciences—Permanence of Paper for Printed Library Materials,
ANSI Z39.48–1984.

For Lou Budd

Lo duca e io per quel cammino ascoso
  intrammo a ritornar nel chiaro mondo;
  e sanza cura aver d'alcun riposo
salimmo su, el primo e io secondo,
  tanto ch' i' vidi delle cose belle
  che porta 'l ciel, per un pertugio tondo;
e quindi uscimmo a riveder le stelle.

Contents

Acknowledgments   ix

Abbreviations   x

Introduction   1
    A Theory on *Conte* and Structure   4
    Maupassant and Short-Story Structure   7

1   Maupassant and the Simpler Structures of the
    Short Story   11
    The Linear Short Story   11
    The Ironic Coda   17
    The Surprise-Inversion Story   21
    The Loop   33

2   Maupassant and the More Complex Structures
    of the Short Story   45
    The Descending Helical   49
    The Contrast Story   63
    The Sinusoidal Story   84

3   Maupassant and the American Mainstream   99
    Maupassant and Bierce   103
    Maupassant and O. Henry   118

4   Maupassant and Chopin   139
    The Early Stories   146
    The Translations   154
    Descending Helicals and the Later Stories   159
    Sinusoidals and the Later Stories   166

5   Maupassant and James   173
        The Reluctant Disciple   174
        James and the Contrast Story   188
        James and the Descending Helical   204

Afterword   217

Works Cited   221

Index   227

Acknowledgments

I wish to thank those who contributed significantly to this book. Of course, the lion's share of my gratitude goes out to Louis Budd (professor emeritus at Duke University), whose imagination, example, thoroughness, and patience (which I tried to extraordinary limits) bestowed a legacy that this book can only partially repay. I thank Buford Jones (also of Duke) for our conversations on the short story, which had a seminal impact upon my thesis. Wallace Fowlie (professor emeritus at Duke) closely read the Maupassant chapters and made several kind suggestions for their improvement. Martha Turner isolated a number of argumentative inconsistencies in my manuscript and offered keenly reasoned alternatives. B. F. Fisher IV (of the University of Mississippi) and Kathryn Lawry both attentively combed through portions of my manuscript and offered substantive recommendations. Cathy Davidson, Kenny Williams, and Thomas Ferraro (all from Duke) offered comments that helped clarify difficult points in my argument. Philip Winsor (senior editor at Penn State Press) offered much encouragement and many practical suggestions. Burton Raffel (of the University of Southwestern Louisiana), Thomas Bonner, Jr. (of Xavier University), Cherene Holland (of Penn State Press), and Betty S. Waterhouse all helped to shape the final draft.

My aunt and uncle, Josephine and Joseph DeMayo, provided stability in my life during the difficult process of composition. Also, I would like to thank John Fedorko for his last-minute technical assistance. And finally, I owe more than just a financial debt to my sister, Joann, who provided me with an unofficial loan during the lean years: the money has since been repaid, but I still owe a deeper measure of gratitude.

Abbreviations

B1   Bierce, Ambrose. *The Collected Works of Ambrose Bierce*, vol. 2: *In the Midst of Life: Tales of Soldiers and Civilians*. 1909. Reprint. New York: Gordian, 1966.

C1   Chopin, Kate. *The Complete Works of Kate Chopin*. Ed. Per Seyersted. Baton Rouge: Louisiana State University Press, 1969.

H1   Henry, O. [William Sidney Porter]. *The Complete Works of O. Henry*. Garden City, N.Y.: Doubleday, 1953.

J1   James, Henry. *The Novels and Tales of Henry James. New York Edition*. 24 vols. New York: Charles Scribner's Sons, 1907–9.

J2   ————. *Henry James Letters*. 4 vols. Ed. Leon Edel, Cambridge: Harvard University Press, 1974–84.

J3   ————. *Henry James Literary Criticism: French Writers, Other European Writers, The Prefaces to the New York Edition*. Ed. Leon Edel and Mark Wilson. New York: Library of America, 1984.

J4   ————. *The Complete Notebooks of Henry James*. Ed. Leon Edel and Lyall H. Powers. New York: Oxford University Press, 1987.

J5   ————. *The Complete Tales of Henry James*. Ed. Leon Edel. Philadelphia: Lippincott, 1964.

M1   Maupassant, Guy de. *Contes et nouvelles*. Ed. Louis Forestier. 2 vols. Paris: Gallimard, Editions de la Pléiade, 1974 and 1979.

Introduction

When Guy de Maupassant, syphilitic and insane, died in a Passy asylum on 6 July 1893, the literary corpus he bequeathed enriched a world unwilling to appreciate it fully. During the nineteenth century, France had witnessed the emergence of giant luminaries in fiction and poetry: Hugo, Baudelaire, Flaubert, Mallarmé, Zola. Against this constellation, Maupassant seemed a star of inferior magnitude. Beyond France, where more puritanical sensibilities sometimes prevailed, the rumors about his fiery life, fanned by the overt sexualities in his *contes*, *nouvelles*, and *romans*, often consumed any chance for honesty in assessment. Furthermore, although he was a splendid craftsman of the short story, the form itself damaged his reputation. Considered a pathetic pretender to the novel's throne, short fiction (and its practitioners) had been exiled from high art. Consequently, critics at the turn of the century seldom entertained the possibility that a writer such as Maupassant could ever have had an influence as pervasive as contemporary novelists. The impact exists, however, and it was felt keenly by, among others, American short-story writers of the 1890s and early 1900s.

Appreciation of Maupassant in the United States ostensibly began with Henry James's 1888 biographical essay on his French friend, whom he had met in Flaubert's salon a dozen years earlier; the essay appeared first in the *Fortnightly Review* and then was collected in James's *Partial Portraits*. True, Lafcadio Hearn had already published (as much as five years earlier) translations of Maupassant's *contes* and critiques of his importance in the New Orleans *Times-Democrat*, but aside from the impact on Hearn himself, his efforts had little effect on the course of the American short story beyond the hermetic culture of Louisiana. James's essay, however, inspired his young friend, Princeton graduate Jonathan Sturges, to publish through Harper and Brothers thirteen translated *contes* under the title *The Odd Number* in 1889, with James himself penning the introduction.

The ripple from the critical stone cast by James soon became a tidal wave, washing over the provincial shores of the American literary marketplace. Sturges's volume inspired others to translate more *contes*, which found their way into periodicals as diverse as the stalwart *Cosmopolitan*, the humorous *Puck*, and the fledgling *Short Stories*. Newspapers across the country reprinted excerpts and complete stories from Sturges's book. Soon, contemporary reviewers and observers of American fiction displaced Frank Stockton's "The Lady or the Tiger?" as the paragon of short-story artistry and substituted Maupassant's "The Necklace."

During the 1890s, many influential editors of American magazines, such as H. C. Bunner of *Puck*, used their interpretation of Maupassant's principles as a measuring stick by which to judge submissions. The character of Bunner's own output in fiction changed as his stories began to imitate more and more the Maupassant model, especially his short-story sequence *Short Sixes*, first published in *Puck* and then collected in an 1891 volume. The success of this collection prompted Bunner to try his own hand at translation by "Americanizing" a series of Maupassant texts, again printed in *Puck* before being collected in book form in 1893.[1]

Bunner's example attracted the notice of other writers, including the local colorist Octave Thanet (pseudonym for Alice French), who in a 10 February 1894 fan letter to Bunner praised the translator for capturing and exceeding the spirit of his model:

> You are yourself and De Maupassant (whom I admire as much as you do!) too. . . . You rendered his soul into American and his words into English and kept (*How* did you do it?) the indefinable sorcery of his style. . . . Guy, himself, never did

1. See *Short Sixes: Stories To Be Read While the Candle Burns* (New York: Keppler and Schwarzmann, 1891); *Made in France: French Tales Retold with a United States Twist* (New York: Keppler & Schwarzmann, 1893). Not all of the translations in the latter are so divorced from Maupassant's original texts as Bunner's title suggests. Although Bunner does relocate several stories to the United States, he retains French geography, customs, and manners in others.

anything finer [than *Short Sixes*]. And the humor is kinder and gentler than his always was.[2]

As the century came to a close, the Maupassantian *conte* became a blueprint for marginally popular writers such as Thanet. In his only volume of original short stories, even Sturges tried to imitate the models he had translated.[3]

The inspiration of Maupassant's work also infused new life into short fiction by major writers of the 1890s, such as Stephen Crane, Frank Norris, and James himself. Even noted conservative critic Brander Matthews, Bunner's literary confidant, came to concede the refreshing centrality of Maupassant's influence in American letters. In the original version of his landmark essay, "The Philosophy of the Short-Story" (1885), Matthews had tersely dismissed the Frenchman: "In the *contes* of M. Guy de Maupassant there is a manly vigor, pushed at times to excess." In the essay's final version, published in book form in 1901, the critic amended his assessment, yielding to the current of popular opinion:

> Here I cancel a casual sentence written in 1885, before Guy de Maupassant had completely revealed his extraordinary gifts and marvellous craftsmanship. His Short-stories are masterpieces of the art of story-telling, because he had a Greek sense of form, a Latin power of construction, and a French felicity of style. They are simple, most of them; direct, swift, inevitable, and inexorable in their straightforward movement. If art consists in the suppression of non-essentials, there have been few greater artists in fiction than Maupassant. In his Short-stories there is never a word wasted, and there is never an excursus. Nor is there any feebleness or fumbling. What he wanted to do he did, with the unerring certainty of Leather-stocking, hitting the bull's-eye again and again. He had the abundance and the ease of the very great artists; and the half-dozen or the half-score of his best stories are among the very best Short-stories in any language.[4]

2. Cited in Gerald E. Jensen, *The Life and Letters of Henry Cuyler Bunner* (Durham, N.C.: Duke University Press, 1939), 149.

3. *The First Supper and Other Episodes* (New York: Dodd, Mead, 1983).

4. See "The Philosophy of the Short-Story," *Lippincott's Magazine* 36 (1885): 374; *The Philosophy of the Short-Story* (1901; New York: Peter Smith, 1931), 67–68.

The wave induced by James had flooded American letters to its horizon.

In the selections made by Maupassant's translators and in stories analyzed by commentators and reviewers at the turn of the century, Americans seemed attracted by *contes* that placed the significant point at the end, often called a "trick ending" by critics. Within the context of the history of the short story, this unduly selective response in America had profound consequences worldwide. Eventually, these end-oriented texts popularized by English-language translations of the Frenchman's *contes* inspired a generation of overly predictable American writers—concluding conspicuously with O. Henry, who has become a pivotal figure in the twentieth century if for no other reason than that later artists of merit, especially Sherwood Anderson, Gertrude Stein, and Ernest Hemingway, rebelled against his structural dogma for the short story. These modern writers, many of whom would acknowledge Chekhov's works as the source for their structural approach, adopted the American misreading of Maupassant in fashioning their own aesthetic framework. Consequently, they lumped and condemned Maupassant with O. Henry.[5]

A Theory on *Conte* and Structure

Tales that end with tricks invariably arouse aesthetic dismissals by twentieth-century critics. We easily recognize the plot formula in such works: at the end of a text, the author uncorks a surprise for the reader. Do other short stories—ones without such tricks—have structures of their own, ones designed to inspire different intellectual responses in the audience? If so, a systematic approach to story structure could distinguish patterns between forms. In the past, taxonomies for short fiction depended upon impressionistic assessments of the presence or absence of some traditional conception of plot. One often-revived scheme attempted to divide short fiction into two categories: (1) the overly plotted, hence inferior, tale and

5. Artine Artinian has sampled responses to Maupassant by many twentieth-century writers in *Maupassant Criticism in France, 1880–1940* (Morningside Heights, N.Y.: King's Crown, 1941).

(2) the more subtle, hence superior, lyric short story.[6] In his *Anatomy of Criticism*, Northrop Frye offhandedly proposed an interesting variation. Treating the short story as a bastard cousin to the novel, he suggested that his fourfold matrix for classifying long fiction (novel, confession, anatomy, and romance) had counterparts in short fiction (story, familiar essay, colloquy, and tale).[7] Useful as they are in some critical contexts, these taxonomies lack precision in distinguishing nuances in fictive form.

A small body of criticism, hitherto generally ignored, attempted to apply Aristotelian techniques to the study of the short story. Buford Jones suggested that Poe's famous concept *unity of effect* could be understood in light of two terms from *Poetics: anagnorisis* and *peripeteia*. Poe believed that in a true tale "there should be no word written, of which the tendency, direct or indirect, is not to the one pre-established design."[8] If this maxim concerns plot, the unity of a text then relies on a "turning point," characterized by the protagonist's self-discovery and change of fortunes, which would make most modern stories function like the third act of five in a Shakespearean play. This notion may, by implication, constitute a limited definition for the genre: a plot complicated by more than one turning point would cease to be a short story.

6. As recently as the 1970s, critics associated with *Studies in Short Fiction* have tried to standardize the terms *lyric* and *tale* into short-story criticism. For one example, see Eileen Baldeshwiler, "The Lyric Short Story: The Sketch of a History," in *Short-Story Theories*, ed. Charles E. May (Athens: Ohio University Press, 1976), 202–13.

7. *Anatomy of Criticism: Four Essays* (Princeton: Princeton University Press, 1957), 303–14.

8. From "Review of *Twice-Told Tales*. By Nathaniel Hawthorne," *Great Short Works of Edgar Allan Poe*, ed. G. R. Thompson (New York: Harper and Row, 1970), 522. The essay originally appeared in *Graham's Lady's and Gentleman's Magazine* in May 1842. I wish here to thank Buford Jones for outlining his approach to the short story during several conversations in 1983 at Duke University, Durham, North Carolina. Several critics have attempted to apply Aristotelian concepts of drama to the short story. For example, Cay Dollerup's critieria for a viable short story includes a single pivotal revelation (Aristotle's anagnorisis) that produces significant change (peripeteia). He also cites the classical representation of tragedy: complication, turning point, denouement; see his "The Concepts of 'Tension,' 'Intensity,' and 'Suspense' in Short-Story Theory," *Orbis Litterarum* 25 (1970): 317–18, 323. Other concepts defined by Aristotle have also influenced some short-fiction critics. For example, in *The Modest Art: A Survey of the Short Story in English* (London: Oxford, 1968), T. O. Beachcroft treats the pre-nineteenth-century sources for the modern short story in light of Aristotle's aesthetic value of mimesis; see 6, 10, 19, and 43.

The range of the short story in the nineteenth and twentieth centuries, however, spills over the perimeters of these limiting criteria. In my study of the genre, I have found that the usefulness of peripeteia as an interpretive concept is problematic at best. Particularly in the fictional explorations of ennui and alienation so popular after the Franco-Prussian War, many authors have carefully structured their plots so that a protagonist's lot does not materially change. Occasionally, a hero has been so intellectually blinded by his life or is so dimwitted that he cannot even gain significant insight into his plight. Poe never suggested, however, that the cohesiveness of a story centers upon a character's significant realization. In a brilliant clarification, Charles May points out that the unity of effect originally centered on abstract concepts—truth, beauty, horror, terror—rather than a single plot incident, as Poe's later students tried to redefine the concept.[9]

Nevertheless, anagnorisis is a useful tool in categorizing short stories. However, I focus not upon how the plot steers a character into self-discovery but how it manipulates an audience toward insight. Often in a short story our appreciation and a character's awareness of the importance of an incident coincide, but this shared vision is not a requirement. Sometimes, by the grace of an author's textual clues, we may be intellectually ahead of the protagonist, which heightens dramatic irony. At other instances we may ascertain a truth that a character could never fathom. Although a majority of stories contain only one threshold into insight for the reader, a text may occasionally contain more than one and still qualify as a short story if we view all these points from a common frame of reference.

Although loose, this definition inspired me to devise an alternate scheme to classify various manifestations of the short story. I separated texts according to the placement and number of discovery points for the reader.[10] In doing so, I noticed that works by writers of even different nationalities fell into similar patterns. When O. Henry placed a significant point at the end of a tale, he elicited a response in his audience similar to that when Maupassant employed the same plot device. In all, I saw more than fifteen differing plot

9. "The Unique Effect of the Short Story: A Reconsideration and an Example," *Studies in Short Fiction* 13 (1976): 289–97.

10. Since its properties depend upon its relationship with story form, I shall amplify my definition of "discovery point" in Chapters 1 and 2.

structures and variations in my reading of nineteenth-century stories. In each category of form, the position of the discovering moment controls our vision and, hence, interpretation of a text. For
example, we react differently when an author centers a significant
point in a work as compared to when he concludes his story with it.

Maupassant and Short-Story Structure

By 1880, the year he first considered himself a professional writer,
Maupassant had already had the benefit of exploring six decades of
modern short-story writing.[11] As the better stories were, generally,
the more economical, he extrapolated this principle from stylistics
and applied it to plot construction. Initially, he tried his hand at the
least complicated forms, notably, the linearly developed plot. Born
from concepts of journalistic simplicity, these early efforts seemed
to pursue a naive notion of mirabile dictu, involving implicit confidence that the story itself needs little adornment. Joseph Conrad
believed that economy along such lines in Maupassant's work was a
virtuous form of self-denial.[12] On the surface, such stories seem to
follow the principle of economy best; if so, these simple patterns
best represent the ideal short-story form. With "Boule de suif" (Ball
of tallow), however, Maupassant committed himself very early in his
writing career to more complex constructions.

   Although simple plots were easier to compose, they were not
necessarily easier to read or, more important, to remember. He
immersed himself more and more in the reader's perspective and, in
doing so, discovered the paradoxical principle that carefully and

---

11. Sullivan notes that while Maupassant did address aspects of novel theory in
his essays, he seldom discussed short-story techniques. Sullivan therefore concludes
that Maupassant was an instinctual *conteur* who used this natural ability as a
foundation to develop an affinity with the novel; see his *Maupassant the Novelist*
(Port Washington, N.Y.: Kennikat, 1972), xiv–xv.

12. *Notes on Life and Letters* (Garden City, N.Y.: Doubleday, Page, 1921), 25. Conrad
later writes: Maupassant "refrains from setting his cleverness against the eloquence
of the facts. There is humor and pathos in these stories; but such is the greatness of
his talent, the refinement of his artistic conscience, that all his high qualities appear
inherent in the very things of which he speaks, as if they had been altogether
independent of his presentation" (27).

complexly arranged story lines contributed significantly to a story's overall economy, especially in its suggestive powers. On one level, then, economy in the short story involved the coordinating of all events, descriptions, and symbols to a significant point, one designed to arouse a sense of discovery in the reader. Obviously, during a text's composition, all that was not closely relevant had to be identified and excised.[13]

In his experiments with more complex plots, he saw that two or more focal points could coexist within a single work. Two incidents may compete for the reader's attention. A key event does not necessarily coincide with a character's moment of insight. A reader may fathom the truth of a situation in a story long before a character does. These compounds of significant moments do not violate the aesthetics of economy if the author's essential thrust depends upon the reader's linking competing impressions by comparing two or more phenomena.[14] Thus, Maupassant's conception of the short story became not so much a meticulous adherence to some formula but instead an intuitive pursuit of a principle of reduction—confining a short story as much as possible but never constraining it.

13. André Vial has systematically applied such an apparatus to Maupassant's work. He distinguishes short stories from longer fiction forms by an author's intention "d'isoler, dans la multitude des traits qui constituent un événement ou le destin d'une personne, un élément et de déblayer au profit de cet élément unique" (to isolate one element from among the many traits that make up an event or the destiny of a person, and to clear away the rest for the benefit of that unique element [italics in original]). Vial then adopts short-story theory from Poe and others: "tous les traits se subordonnent à cet trait privilégié" (all traits are subordinated to this privileged trait). He later extends his definition to include interpretive purpose: "L'objet du conte est d'humaniser et parfois d'intellectualiser à l'extrême l'événement" (The object of the story is to humanize and sometimes to intellectualize the ultimate event [italics in original]). See his Guy de Maupassant et l'art du roman (Paris: Librairie Nizet, 1954), 442, 443 and 466. In his introduction to a 1904 English translation of the Frenchman's stories Yvette and Other Stories, Conrad had found this same trait in Maupassant's work: "His is the power of detecting the one immutable quality that matters in the changing aspects of nature and under the ever-shifting surface of life" (31).

14. Vial sees a similar tendency in the progression of Maupassant's novels: "Ainsi s'établit . . . avec une économie d'artifices de plus en plus grande, avec des moyens qui se renouvellent non par substitution, mais par approfondissement et spiritualisation de ceux qu'une pratique ancienne avait éprouvés, la cohésion du roman, la solidarité d'une multitude d'éléments et d'épisodes divers" (533; Thus . . . with an economy of bigger and bigger artifices, with devices that are repeated not through substitution but through profundity and spiritualization of those devices tested by long-standing customs, the cohesion of the novel, through the interdependence of a multitude of elements and various episodes, is established).

Perhaps, then, more so than traditional criteria such as word counts or vague definitions of the *unity of effect*, this impulse to limit serves to distinguish the short story from the novel in the works of Maupassant and his literary ancestors and progenitors.

He garnered formulas from many sources. Poe's meticulous tracings of a psyche's descent into madness have plenty of grandchildren in Maupassant's canon. Turgenev fathered the practice in the modern short story of coordinating the beginning and ending of a plot around a single phenomenon, a principle his disciple found very fruitful. The Frenchman's debts to his literary ancestors have countless other examples. In fact, with only a few exceptions, Maupassant refrained from radical innovation in form. He chose instead to foster new directions with his experimental hybrids of two or more forms within one text. With his growing commitment to more intricate patterns and to kaleidoscopic combinations of them, he would still occasionally return to a simpler form if it appeared apropos for a particular story, but he never retreated to simplicity. With every year Maupassant increasingly explored the more subtle recesses of his craft to produce stories sufficiently economical to impress memory indelibly.

Overall, I composed this argument with the historical progression of the short story foremost in my purpose. For me, understanding story structure and measuring the growth of the short story are reciprocally rewarding endeavors. Among the complex array of reassessments needed for a better appreciation of the short story's place in the study of literature, I believe that Maupassant's exercises in form need more attention. I contend that his influence on the twentieth-century story rivals that of Chekhov's, but it has remained, for the most part, unrecognized or disavowed by artists and critics. Even Henry James's precious self-assessments often failed to admit all the invasive nuances of the Maupassantian *conte*. The enormity of this impact upon world fiction precludes any study confined to a single volume; thus I have restricted myself to a sequential juxtaposition that addresses Maupassant's influence upon the concerns for structure among turn-of-the-century American short-story writers.

Therefore, I have arranged this book to highlight an efflorescent moment of literary influence. The first two chapters sample the heterogeneity and development of seven short-story forms in the Maupassant canon:

1   linear
2   ironic coda
3   surprise-inversion
4   loop
5   descending helical
6   contrast
7   sinusoidal

In Chapter 3, I have selected two writers at opposite ends of a literary generation—Ambrose Bierce and O. Henry—whose works typify America's selective response to the Maupassantian *conte* at the turn of the century. Heavily influenced by the selections offered by contemporary translators, both men favored fictive structures that depended on last-second, ironic reversals in the reader's perception. The final two chapters deal with two writers who cut through American literary prejudice in order to see Maupassant's artistry in fuller aspect. Kate Chopin encountered Maupassant's work while she was mastering the craft of fiction writing. Consequently, Chopin felt his influence more keenly and perceptively than any other American writer of her day. Unfortunately, when her own work lapsed into relative obscurity for more than sixty years, so disappeared the potential for her clearer reading of Maupassant to have a resounding direct impact upon American letters. Finally, Henry James knew Maupassant personally and wrote the most sensitive and perceptive essays on his friend's works among contemporary critics. The expatriate American had his aesthetics firmly in place before he delved into the Frenchman's *contes*. During the 1890s, however, in the throes of his temporary self-doubt, James turned to models by Maupassant as one path toward literary survival. His appreciation and, hence, his incorporation of Maupassantian structural principles in his own work, though, existed on a level too fine for his peers or the succeeding generations of writers to realize. Chopin once suggested that a sincere and discerning appreciation for Maupassant evokes strong allegiances that disciples are not willing to share.[15] She may have been right.

15. See *C1*, 700–701. This passage is cited in Chapter 3.

1

Maupassant and the Simpler Structures of the Short Story

The Linear Short Story

Quite naturally, Maupassant gravitated to the simpler literary forms in his early writing. The simplest of these was the linear short story, a text almost free from an omniscient narrator's intrusions and a plot unadorned by authorial manipulation. Most often, the story is presented in its proper chronological sequence, stripped of all irrelevant happenings in the lives of the characters so that the reader sees the story in terms of a causal chain in which no one cause or effect dominates the text. Such a choice in form suggests the writer's implicit belief that the story possesses in itself sufficient qualities to impress his reader.

Early in his career, a naive and, perhaps, egotistical Maupassant, believing in his ability to ferret out those incidents of human reality that most entertained men, trusted that linear presentations would suffice. "Le Donneur d'eau bénite" (1877, The bestower of holy water), for example, presents a parent's horror: a child that vanishes mysteriously. Rather than employ literary devices, Maupassant relies upon a reader's sympathy with the plight of the protagonists, a wheelwright and his wife. In theory, if such stories reached primal emotional levels, a reader could even project himself into the parents' situation. Each succeeding plot element competes for the reader's attention with the result that neither the loss of the child Jean, the parent's patient remorse, nor their joy in rediscovering the adult Jean dominates the story. Calculated to arouse one's awe of the curious whims of providence, "Le Donneur" has the underlying assumption that both misery and happiness are products of chance. With the aid of religious faith, symbolized by the old and destitute wheelwright's position as "le donneur d'eau bénite," chance led ultimately to happiness, an ending very uncharacteristic of Maupassant's later stories. Perhaps the outcome of "Le Donneur" suggests why linear patterns seldom dominate his later work: left to chance, situations could resolve themselves happily, a consequence that an increasingly pessimistic Maupassant recoiled from accepting.[1]

Another early story, "Le Papa de Simon" (1879, Simon's Papa), also concludes happily, but Maupassant qualifies this perspective by readjusting the reader's role from sympathy to observation. He accomplishes this not by altering form but by increasing the functional weight of the title.[2] Unlike "Le Donneur d'eau bénite," which merely stresses symbolically a religious conviction never explicitly stated, the title "Le Papa de Simon" serves as a barometer against which a reader can compare Simon's various contentions with real

1. In his textual notes to Maupassant's stories, Louis Forestier notes the role that probability plays in "Donneur"; he suggests that the motif manifests itself throughout Maupassant's work. See Louis Forestier, ed. *Contes et nouvelles* by Guy de Maupassant, 2 vols. (Paris: Gallimard, Editions de la Pléiade, 1974 and 1979), 1:1285. While I do agree with Forestier that Maupassant remained interested in questions about destiny, I believe that through more sophisticated structures he learned to control the tendency of such a theme to appear an awkward succession of events. In discussing the story, Forestier himself notes: "Maupassant n'a pas encore trouvé l'art de réduire sa nouvelle à un seul sujet" (1:1284; Maupassant has not yet found the art of reducing his short story to a single subject).

2. In *Guy de Maupassant et l'art du roman* (Paris: Librairie Nizet, 1954), 442, André Vial notes correctly: "lorsque le récit porte pour titre le nom de son personnage, ce nom a été imaginé pour suggérer *la* singularité de son destin ou de son caractère" (when the short story bears a protagonist's name for its title, that name has been conceived to suggest *the* uniqueness of his destiny or his character [italics in original]).

and imaginary father figures.[3] Initially, "Le Papa de Simon" focuses the reader's attention on the child's inability to understand what his illegitimacy means socially and, consequently, to explain his situation to his schoolmates. When a good-natured blacksmith volunteers his services as a surrogate father, Simon thinks that he has met all the requirements set by the children and thus has ended his ostracism. He finds out, however, that in the eyes of his peers, and consequently society, he still has no father because as one child taunts, "si tu en avais un, il serait le mari de ta maman" (M1, 1:30; if you had one, he would be your mama's husband). Maupassant then presents a third meaning to the title when the blacksmith proposes marriage to the boy's mother and thus becomes the boy's foster father, after having promised to protect the boy by physical force from slurs; this turn of events apparently wins social approval.

By the end of the story Simon secures happiness, but closer examination reveals it to be a precarious sort.[4] First of all, it is a child's happiness, based on relatively uncomplicated and short-term criteria. In fact, Maupassant permits his readers to see only through Simon's eyes. We as readers do not know the detail of the mother's relationship with the child's biological father, only that her "reputation tombée" (fallen reputation) fuels local gossip. The smith's offer comes as a surprise to both the woman and the reader. In truth, Maupassant reveals so little of each adult's motivation that he leaves open the possibility, albeit remote, that the blacksmith may be Simon's true father. These questions, although interesting, are beyond Simon's inexperienced view of the world; consequently, they do not enter in his formula for determining his emotional state. To achieve happiness he fixes upon social acceptance. He sees a single conclusion: having a father would stop the taunts of his peers. As in "Le Donneur," whimsical providence seems to control "Le Papa."

3. Many of Maupassant's subsequent fictional works have substantive or symbolic titles that attempt to ease the reader's transition into the circumstances of a story. His practice anticipates Susan Lohafer's examination of how a text's opening passages (including its title) bridge an ontological gap between reality and fiction; see her *Coming to Terms with the Short Story* (Baton Rouge: Louisiana State University Press, 1983), 52–55.

4. In *Maupassant: The Short Stories* (London: Edward Arnold, 1962), 28–29, Edward D. Sullivan finds the happy endings of both "Le Donneur d'eau bénite" and "Le Papa de Simon" sentimentally implausible and, consequently, unacceptable.

Chance made Simon a bastard. While contemplating suicide by a river, he unexpectedly meets the smith. On the surface the blacksmith's offer to act as the boy's father and his subsequent marriage proposal appear to be caprices. Culminating in procuring for Simon a father whom the schoolchildren accept, providence restructures the boy's life so that he gains a sense of security, but again it is based upon a child's perspective. Thus, his newly found happiness promises to exist only for the moment of his youth. In presenting his story linearly, however, Maupassant risks that his readers will miss this implication. Without more suggestive structural clues, the story depends upon readers surmising that this restriction in Simon's perspective has interpretive significance.

"Le Donneur" and "Le Papa," published less than two years apart, demonstrate the darkening of Maupassant's vision. By 1880 his pessimism firmly ensconced itself in his fiction. Even his linearly constructed stories succumbed to the new perspective. In "Le Papa" the weight of social morals influenced to a significant degree Simon's sense of self-worth. In "Une partie de campagne" (1881, A country outing), however, Maupassant raises the impact of this morality to the level of an intervening and invariably counteracting variable between providence and the possibility of happiness. The constriction of social values upon individual men virtually eliminates the possibility of self-fulfillment, even through chance.

In "Une partie de campagne," like many Maupassant stories, chance has placed a potentially ideal lover before Henriette Dufour, but her social inhibitions impede her impulses. Maupassant suggests that, prior to the action of the story, self-control and tempered expectations ruled her life. The picnic itself seemed to be a metaphoric reconstruction of her existence: a long-considered and meticulously planned elaboration of the bourgeois dream. Within the normal progression of this carefully mapped-out picnic, however, providence interjects Henri, whose masculinity simultaneously attracts and threatens the girl. Even his name suggests that he is more the soul mate of Henriette than he who is her fiancé, whom Maupassant dismisses in terms so unflattering that the man all but recedes from Henriette's and the reader's vision. As Henri presses his advances upon the reluctant woman, sexual tensions mount, overwhelming Henriette's young conception of decency. She finally yields, but we witness her seduction only vicariously through sexually suggestive metaphors, which Maupassant draws from nature. In the story's coda, Henri accidentally meets the girl's mother. We perceive his wistfulness, but our glimpse of Henriette's does not come until their chance meeting a year later. Thus, the linear progression of events during the picnic, constituting but a few hours in the life of each, tints the color of their existence with the somber hues of regret. The effects are not devastating but do reinforce a sense of feeling "fort triste, sans trop savoir pourquoi" (M1, 1:254; very sad, without really knowing why).[5]

In order to demonstrate the changing role of fate in Maupassant's linearly plotted stories, I chose to stress only one aspect of "Une partie." More properly, it ought to be classified as a *simultaneous* plot because Mme. Dufour's pleasant seduction by Henri's friend provides the reader with an interesting counterpoint to her daughter's unsuccessful attempt at self-denial.[6] The story does indicate, though, how unadulterated linear plots became rarer in the Maupassant canon, being subsumed by more complicated forms. In his later work, however, Maupassant used this simple form in a few of his Normandy stories. Following the precepts of local color, Maupassant believed that simple chronological accounts best expressed the inherent fallacies of the Norman and, hence, his own life-style.[7] The social interaction that creates the malaise of pessimism becomes the focal point of Maupassant's attack. By presenting acts of cruelty, avarice, and other vices, he conveys an impression that man's immanent nature undercuts decency in human intercourse. Thus, in essence, Maupassant's Normandy stories provide case studies of how much behavior became institutionalized in one region.

5. Forestier comments: "En fin de compte, une vie médiocre ne s'éclaire pas d'un souvenir heureux; c'est, au contraire, l'instant de bonheur entrevu qui ronge et anéantit chaque jour d'une existence irrémédiablement terne" (M1, 1:1358; At the end of an account, an indifferent life is not lightened by a pleasant memory; to the contrary, it is the half-seen moment of happiness that gnaws at and prostrates each day of a lackluster, irremediable existence).

6. In an otherwise excellent treatise on his personal reaction to Maupassant, Tolstoy mistakenly claims that in "Une partie" "only one side of the subject is presented, and that the most insignificant one, namely, the pleasure taken by the scoundrels." See "Guy de Maupassant," *The Novels and Other Works of Lyof N. Tolstoï*, trans. Aylmer Maude et al. (New York: Charles Scribner's Sons, 1900), 20:479. A careful reading of the story provides insight into all four of the principals.

7. For a discussion of Maupassant's local color techniques, see John Raymond Dugan, *Illusion and Reality: A Study of Descriptive Techniques in the Works of Guy de Maupassant* (The Hague: Mouton, 1973), 12–18.

That Maupassant occasionally employed simple plots in the Normandy stories indicates his trust in their inherent entertainment value.[8] To the cosmopolitan Parisian, the Norman peasant and his world probably appeared as a distant and alien being and place. Maupassant presumes that readers will judge his attack upon such a social environment as justified because of their instinctual conceit of superiority. The Normandy stories usually aim to evoke sympathy, not empathy. Ultimately, we laugh at, we disapprove of, we pity such characters, but we do not see ourselves in them or in their plight. Rustic humor in "Farce normande" (1882, Norman farce), for example, comes off as coarse, the product of imaginations stifled by a stagnant social environment. In "Coco" (1884), Maupassant traces the successive cruelties a stableboy inflicts upon a horse. The author presents only this one case, but through it he conveys a communal attitude toward old age in both beasts and men.[9] "Le Diable" (1886, The devil) continues this theme as the community's symbolic resentment against a dying old woman culminates in her nurse's frightening her to death. Although Maupassant does share bonds with these people, the linearly plotted story permits him to let them convict themselves of hypocrisy and meanness by their own desires and actions: no method of authorial stressing can highlight an inhumane act more than the deed itself.[10]

These situations often had undertones of irony, but one dilemma of linearly plotted stories is that this undertone may remain an

8. Perhaps influenced by friend William Dean Howells's notion of the importance of local color in contemporary fiction, James proposed in 1888 that Maupassant would ultimately be remembered for his tales of the "Norman peasant"; see *Partial Portraits* (1888; reprints, Ann Arbor: University of Michigan Press, 1970), 268.

9. Michael G. Lerner notes that after 1883 Maupassant explored more intense and perverse forms of human violence in his fiction, which reflected both his personal frustrations in coping with life and his audience's greater tolerance of bizarre plots; see *Maupassant* (New York: George Braziller, 1975), 218–19.

10. Forestier points out how Maupassant's precision succeeds in the story: "c'est l'économie des moyens employés par Maupassant. Cette farce . . . converge inexorablement vers l'apparition finale, burlesque et fantastique" (M1, 2:1570; Maupassant employs an economy of means. This farce . . . inexorably converges toward the final burlesque and mysterious apparition). In *The Paradox of Maupassant* (London: University of London Press, 1967), 65, Paul Ignotus discusses Maupassant's wavering empathy with the Normans, noting that he "loved his Norman brethren not for being better than the rest of mankind but for being so very strikingly like them. . . . What he saw [in them] most often was awkwardness, boredom, cruelty, but he found comfort in portraying them precisely."

undertone in interpretation. Irony was perhaps the strongest of Maupassant's impulses in his fiction, but simply constructed stories, for example, of local color or the Franco-Prussian War or human duplicity, often failed to elicit insights of such subtlety in readers. One could easily miss the symbolic paradox of a lone civilian successfully defending patriotic honor in the aftermath of a French military defeat in "Un duel" (1883, A duel).[11] In "La Dot" (1884, The dowry) Maupassant hints that a young woman finds a better prospect in love through the perfidy of her bridegroom, who absconds with her dowry; but the very construct of the story, which follows a simple episodic chronology, unintentionally downplays the irony. We have reasons for such speculations, but the clues Maupassant provides are among his most tenuous. Therefore, since irony became his most potent literary weapon—it conflated his pessimism with his humor—Maupassant had to incorporate linear progressions in more complex forms in order to portray life more as he saw it. The absence of literary devices that stressed irony made his stories more difficult to interpret properly. Thus, economy paradoxically demanded complication.

The Ironic Coda

The simplest development of the linear story employed by Maupassant was to add a brief coda. Most often these codas take place after the time frame of the primary story, long enough so that characters can view a significant event more reflectively than emotionally. These codas do not force the reader to reinterpret the story; rather, they serve to highlight some irony. If anything, their existence suggests the possibility that the author is somehow dissatisfied with the primary body of the story. Believing that a linear plot cannot stand alone, he risks disunity by breaking the chronological flow of the text in order to buttress its ironic thrust. Whether it exists as a tagged section, paragraph, or even a sentence or two, however, the ironic coda often seems no more than an afterthought; thus it is

11. In *Guy de Maupassant* (Boston: Twayne, 1973), 94, A. H. Wallace proclaims that the dueler's challenge is vain, "late and meaningless." I submit, however, that the linear construction of the story fails to support any such decisive interpretations.

perhaps the weakest of Maupassant's organizing devices, tenuously integrating text and interpretation.

Although ironic codas do appear fairly early in the Maupassant canon, they were not sequentially the next step in his experiment with form. Instead, he alternated among several schemes as he explored the nuances of the genre. Ultimately, as he matured as a writer, ironic codas appended to linear plots appeared less frequently. When he chose to direct the reader's attention toward the ending of a text in his later work, he usually opted for stronger plot devices.

Nevertheless, codas do serve to illustrate how Maupassant strived for interpretive economy by manipulating form. In "Une Partie de campagne," for example, the linear progression of the picnic episode stresses impermanent experiences such as sexual frustration and fulfillment. Standing alone, the main body of the text would permit readers to contemplate a significant moment only within its own temporal confines. By adding two separate codas, however, Maupassant expands the vision of his audience, permitting them to see the enduring effect the rendezvous had upon Henriette and Henri. For him, the remembrance of that day has become a fixation upon a lost sexual and spiritual treasure; for her, the basis for a fantasy lover against whom her drab groom pales. In essence, the codas redirect our memory of the story from clinically observing sexual passion to considering the poignant implications of regret. By contrast, the unencumbered tryst Mme. Dufour has had with Henri's rowing partner and her fond memory of the encounter (hinted at in the first coda) reinforce our insight into her daughter's situation. The coda does not force us to reanalyze "Une Partie de campagne" but to realize a little more deeply its implications—especially within a temporal framework.

Rather than using extended and elaborate episodes, Maupassant more often reduced codas to a terse sentence or two, constituting a last paragraph. He found this form and style particularly suitable for his war stories. He primarily intended to render faithful impressions of the events of 1870, and so linear exposition, which usually conveys to the reader a sense of immediate presence, created the illusion of validity in each account. Yet he had a secondary, almost extemporaneous, purpose. Writing a dozen years after the French defeat, Maupassant saw French society reshaping history to fit its ego. Individuals elevated their common duties in war to acts of extraordinary patriotism and heroism.[12] After the main text dispassionately dissects the events and motivations in a war incident, the coda briefly and ironically exposes how French society of the 1880s has twisted its memory of the past. In a sense, Maupassant shows his offhanded preparedness to laugh at and to dismiss any personal yarn of patriotism. Overall, the war fiction promotes a notion that (rare) true patriotism produces silence either because an authentic hero tries to forget or because he is dead.

Perhaps no work illustrates the nature of the literary coda so well as "L'Aventure de Walter Schnaffs" (1883, Walter Schnaffs' adventure). Essentially, the text linearly traces the misadventure of a war-wearied Prussian soldier who resolves to surrender himself to the French at the first opportunity. At one point the famished Schnaffs enters a castle, whose tenants imagine an enemy invasion and flee the premises, leaving a sumptuous supper behind them. After much ado, the local militia take the satiated and now somnambulant Schnaffs prisoner. Amid victory cries, the officer-in-charge records in his log that

> [a]près une lutte acharnée, les Prussiens ont dû battre en retraite, emportant leurs morts et leur blessés, qu'on évalue à cinquante hommes hors de combat. Plusieurs sont restés entre nos mains. (M1, 1:800)

> (after a fierce battle, the Prussians were forced to retreat, carrying their dead and wounded, which I estimate to be fifty casualties. We hold several prisoners.]

The coda adds the following to the history of the soldier who almost could not surrender despite his willingness:

> C'est ainsi que le château de Champignet fut repris à l'ennemi après six heures seulement d'occupation.
> Le colonel Ratier, marchand de drap, qui enleva cette affaire

---

12. Wallace notes that Maupassant's "brief and unillustrious service" (100) during the war had a disproportionate effect upon his writing, which suggests the possibility that the author subconsciously included himself among the war's braggadocios.

> à la tête des gardes nationaux de La Roche-Oysel, fut décoré. (M1, 1:801)

> (This is how the chateau at Champignet was recaptured after only six hours of enemy occupation.
> Colonel Ratier, a draper, who commanded the national guard of La Roche-Ossel during this incident, was decorated.)

The last sentences do not surprise the reader; in fact they echo the comic self-importance of the national guard so evident in the text. The passage does, however, attack the blind acceptance of a military decoration's meaning. It is not the primary thrust of the story but instead an ironic offshoot, slightly undercutting the main text in a manner similar to how contemporary society's memory undercuts the truths of the past. The reality of Schnaffs' fear and desperation is gone; only a tall tale of a battle with a phantom Prussian military expedition remains.

"Les Prisonniers" (1884, The prisoners) explores identical themes.[13] Through rustic cunning, a peasant woman, Berthine, traps a lost Prussian troop in her cellar and keeps them prisoner until the local militia arrive; the sly heroism of Berthine is eclipsed, however, by the comic efforts of the French townsmen to force the prisoners from the cellar. At one point, ascertaining if the Prussians really exist turns into a game of leaping over the open cellar door, until a corpulent and buffoonish baker receives the proof in the form of "une balle dans le gras de la cuisse, tout en haut" (M1, 2:418; a bullet in the upper flesh of the thigh). After finally flushing the Germans out, the Frenchmen return to the town marching triumphantly. The coda records that the commander

> fut décoré pour avoir capturé une avant-garde prussienne, et le gros boulanger eut la médaille militaire pour blessure reçue devant l'ennemi. (M1, 2:419)

> (was decorated for having captured a Prussian scouting patrol, and the fat baker received a medal for wounds inflicted by the enemy.)

---

13. Forestier briefly discusses the analogies between "Les Prisonniers" and "L'Aventure de Walter Schnaffs," noting the similarities of each story's conclusion; see M1, 1:1436, 1439.

It is an ironic tag that the reader has come to expect because of Maupassant's swift yet deft caricatures in the main body of the text. Berthine's practical nature succeeds in imprisoning the six Prussians but simultaneously inhibits her from parading her daring. In contrast, the militia face little danger from the already entrapped soldiers but still usurp credit for their capture. The coda merely extrapolates further into time this ironic dichotomy between truth and history. Through humor, through irony, the Maupassant coda invites us not only to challenge the memory of our fellow men but also, perhaps, to question our own. For Maupassant, consequently, history itself, especially oral history, falls suspect in his assault upon human vanity. All the writer need do is portray an event honestly and then dismiss in a brusque conclusion modern society's exaggeration of it; no more elaborate fictional device could better prick the pretentious balloon of memory.

The Surprise-Inversion Story

In 1881, only a year after he began publishing regularly, Maupassant first experimented with the form with which most associate him. In analyzing the aesthetics of such stories, critics in the late nineteenth and early twentieth centuries (as well as a few students of the short story in later years) often ascribed a pejorative term to them: the surprise or "trick" ending.[14] A more descriptive and apt label is the surprise-inversion story. Essentially, an author leads his readers along what appears to be a linear plot; but at the end of the story—often in the last paragraph and sometimes in the last sentence—he unexpectedly introduces a twist that forces his audience to invert

14. Artine Artinian cites many examples of this erroneous association in his *Maupassant Criticism in France, 1880–1940* (Morningside Heights, N.Y.: King's Crown, 1941). For example, Sherwood Anderson wrote the Artinian in 1938: "At one time I read and liked [Maupassant] a very great deal but later my admiration rather waned. I came to feel that Maupassant had asserted a tremendous influence on the American short story, that for example, our Mr. O. Henry stemmed directly from him but that on the whole the influence was not good. I have felt that what I think of as the plot short story—I almost said the trick short story—came from this influence. It seemed to me that Maupassant was very, very insistent upon technique and that in this insistence upon technique, the human element pretty much got lost" (129–30).

its perspective of a character or of a circumstance. He seldom carries the story line any further, a literary tactic that forces our attention upon the surprising reversal.[15] Although it invites speculation about how characters will cope with their dramatic change in fortunes beyond the time frame of the story, such endings more strongly direct a reader to reconsider the events in the text he has just read. Often, he will find upon reexamination that incidents, character traits, and symbols take on altered meanings in the light of now knowing where they lead. The inversion is perhaps the most potent of plot forms for the short story. Used judiciously, as by Maupassant, it shocks us out of our aesthetic doldrums, imprinting a memory more indelible than its sister forms because such endings graft our emotional response as readers to the events in the text.[16] Curiously, used indiscriminately, as does Maupassant's denying disciple O. Henry, an author weakens our response: if we come to expect the surprise because a writer employs it with formularized regularity, it loses its power to startle us.

Given that we remember the emotions of a moment more vividly than its facts, the properly played twist of an inversion story threatens our self-confidence as readers more than most literary devices. Whereas in linear and ironic-coda stories Maupassant directs his acerbity toward spotlighting the foolish manners of only his characters, in inversions he escalates his attack to include his audience— suggesting that as he experimented more and more with form, he discriminated less and less in selecting and challenging potential objects for ridicule. He recognizes our propensity to anticipate and feeds our expectations by withholding vital elements of the story until its conclusion. In addition he presents us with incidents and symbols that direct our attention one way but that ultimately prove to have alternative significance. In his battle with his reader, the author attempts to defeat his opponent through tactics designed to deceive. When the trap is successfully sprung, the magnitude of the

15. Mistakingly assuming that most stories follow this pattern, Cay Dollerup cites Elinore Mordaunt's graphic sketch of surprise-inversions—a triangle with "a long base, one long side, and a short drop," the latter side representing the "catastrophe" at the end of the text; see "The Concepts of 'Tension,' 'Intensity,' and 'Suspense' in Short-Story Theory," *Orbis Litterarum* 25 (1970): 324.

16. In *Maupassant: A Lion in the Path* (New York: Grosset and Dunlap, 1949), 205, Francis Steegmuller theorizes that Maupassant's desire to shock readers was adolescent and betrayed a "mild expression" of sadism.

victory over the reader's pride is likely to be overwhelming, for the author has duped him. The point of inversion becomes the moment that the reader awakens to his own perceptual follies. His ego occasionally attempts to defend itself by attempting to dismiss the experience as a cheap literary trick, but the perceptual shock lingers, simultaneously introducing an element of self-doubt in his intellectual confidence and imprinting an emotional memory so vivid that it likely stands out from his other reading experiences. Perhaps this tendency suggests why critics, particularly those of Maupassant, tend to gravitate toward the inversions in an author's short-story canon. No other form so threatens us with intellectual defeat—and our reaction to such a stimulus dominates our memory of a writer's work. As readers, though, we sublimate the author's victory by substituting our appreciation or our disapproval of his plot trick, an assessment that endures in our literary values.

Maupassant's inversion stories had three stages of development. From 1881 to 1883, they seem part of his experimentation with and his struggle to master literary techniques. Stories that employ such manipulative devices constitute less than a tenth of the work written during this period.[17] One early effort was the boatman's tale in "Sur l'eau" (1881, On the water).[18] The story employs several plot structures, but the one that dominates is the inversion at the conclusion.

Ostensibly, "Sur l'eau" begins in the guise of a local color tale and progresses as a folk character's apparent superstitions symbolically imbue the Seine. In a prologue Maupassant employs his favorite device to distance reader from story: a first-person narrator acts as mediator between the reader and the principal character, a rural boatman.[19] This literary tactic achieves several effects: (1) it "establishes" the author's possession of the facts of the story, projecting an illusion of truth upon the account; (2) by detailing the events that led to his acquisition of it, the narrator suggests that only he—and

17. Steegmuller defends Maupassant's reputation on this point. He suggests that critics who maintain that trick endings dominate the Maupassant canon expose their ignorance of it; see 205–6.

18. This story should not be confused with an identically titled autobiographical essay Maupassant wrote later. Also, the story "Sur l'eau" was a substantially revised version of "En canot" (1876, In a dinghy), which Maupassant published under a pseudonym; see M1, 1:1281.

19. Vial calls such a passage a *preambole* (*Guy de Maupassant*, 466ff.). Sullivan prefers *cadre*; see *Maupassant: The Short Stories*, 12–19.

not his readers—could happen upon such a story, which somewhat pre-empts any challenges to the potential unreal excesses of the plot; and (3) Maupassant further distances his original audience, the cosmopolitan society of Paris, by setting the scene outside the city along the river, which, though only a few miles from the capital, symbolizes a gulf between life-styles. Dugan extends the power of this mediator even further: "For the reader hears it told, he does not witness it directly. It is in itself an organization, a selection of circumstances, details and events, a fact of which the reader is conscious. Structure thus becomes an essential of narrative, and form is so closely interwoven with fact that the two cannot be disunited."[20] All these facts lead the reader's subconscious to anticipate a novel perspective on something, some type or some circumstance to which he has previously paid little attention. The boatman asserts: "Vous autres, habitants des rues, vous ne savez pas ce qu'est la rivière" (M1, 1:54; You outlanders, street-dwellers, you do not know what the river means).

The boatman's tale proceeds in a manner characteristic of many Maupassant short stories: an abstract, often rustically philosophic summation of a character or his experience often precedes his account of his "singulière aventure." The boatman's love for the river fosters his discriminating insight:

> [La rivière] est la chose mystérieuse, profonde, inconnue, le pays des mirages et des fantasmagories, où l'on voit, la nuit, des choses qui ne sont pas, où l'on entend des bruits que l'on ne connaît point, où l'on tremble sans savoir pourquoi, comme en traversant un cimetière: et c'est en effet le plus sinistre des cimetières, celui où l'on n'a point de tombeau. (M1, 1:54)

> (The river is a mysterious, deep, unknown entity, the region of mirages and surreal images, where you can see the unreal things of night, where you hear strange noises, where you tremble without knowing why, as when you cross a cemetery: and it is, indeed, the most sinister of cemeteries, the one that has no tomb.)

20. *Illusion and Reality*, 142.

The boatman's philosophy grafts gothic horror with poetic delight. This curious filter controls the reader's vision before he enters the story proper, forcing him to abandon his previous symbolic associations with rivers and to accept the sailor's interpretation.

The boatman's tale recounts a night-fishing excursion when his anchor snagged on the river bottom, forcing him to wait alone amid eerie circumstances. Perhaps inspired by the rum he drank, he experiences a creeping anxiety as if a genius of evil ruled the locale. His imagination exacerbates his terror, a pattern of human behavior that Maupassant explored extensively in his later stories. Unlike these later stories, where self-illusion would lead a character into madness, the inversion point of "Sur l'eau" rescues the boatman, in the manner of deus ex machina, from the brink of insanity. With the aid of two passing fishermen, the sailor finally drags aboard the mass that held his craft dead-in-the-water: "C'était le cadavre d'une vieille femme qui avait une grosse pierre au cou" (M1, 1:59; It was the cadaver of an old woman with a large stone tied to her neck). That one sentence alters the reader's perspective on the boatman's tale. We now entertain the possibility that anxiety was not induced by rum but was instead the product of an empathic response to the surroundings of a murder scene. Earlier sentences—such as "[l]a rivière n'a que des profondeurs noires où l'on pourrit dans la vase" (the river has only black depths where someone rots in the slime)— have their significance transformed from the idle and dismissible musings of a queer character to a more integral part of our appreciation of the boatman's conception of the river (M1, 1:55). Like our experiences with all inversion stories, examining "Sur l'eau" again does not produce a reaction that duplicates our first reading. Instead, we judge each sentence anew by comparing its contribution to the surprise we now expect. In effect, we have read a different story although we have reread the same text.

"Sur l'eau" typifies, however, some of the imprecision of Maupassant's technique in his early efforts. Even Vial qualifies his acceptance of the ending's plausibility: "la précision finale . . . confère une sorte de justification rétrospective et mystérieuse aux angoisses antérieures du héros" (the final point . . . confers a kind of retrospective and mysterious justification of the protagonist's earlier distress).[21] The body of the murdered woman has no integral meaning

21. *Guy de Maupassant*, 452.

in the boatman's life; it merely represents a chance encounter that serves only to reinforce his gothic interpretation of the river. Sullivan suggests that the denouement actually interferes with the tale's atmospheric qualities.[22] Still immature in his use of inversion structures, Maupassant valued more the dimension of surprise in the discovery of the corpse rather than its potential to complement more explicitly the boatman's vision.[23]

Other inversion stories contemporary to "Sur l'eau" have similar inelegancies in their cohesiveness. "Denis" (1883), for example, ends with a joke that strains credulity. Stopping his attack upon his master only after discovering that he could not profit by it, a repentant and trepid servant, Denis, nurses his victim back to health. Oddly, the wounded master does not dismiss Denis. Nevertheless, when the local police later apprehend the servant for petty theft, he stupidly blurts out the details of his murder attempt. In response to a magistrate's query as to why he kept Denis in his service, the master replies: "on a tant de mal à trouver des domestiques. . . . je n'aurais pas recontré mieux" (M1, 1:868; it is so much trouble to find servants. . . . I could not have discovered a better one). Similarly as the inversion point in "Sur l'eau," the ending of "Denis" does provide the reader with an unanticipated key to interpret the story that merely adds another superficial dimension to a character rather than increasing the depth in his portrait. The master's odd logic does amuse us, but we dismiss both him and his servant as caricatures because the joke that binds then strikes at best a faint and discordant note of reality. In essence, the circumstance of the story seems contrived for the sake of humor rather than for that of mirroring life. Although it exists to challenge our vision, the misused inversion point becomes mere artifice, losing its structural potency because we as readers cannot intellectually or empathically identify ourselves with the story's ironic denouement.

By 1884, however, Maupassant mastered the intricacies of the inversion story and employed it repeatedly throughout the year. That year proved to be among his most productive, his published output totaling nearly sixty stories. With such demands upon his creativity, he found it necessary to repeat themes, symbols, and

22. *Maupassant: The Short Stories*, 27.

23. René Dumesnil suggests that Maupassant's tale was an early, thorough imitation of Edgar Allan Poe; see his *Guy de Maupassant* (Paris: Armand Colin, 1933), 178.

forms often, particularly those that were artistically and commer-
cially successful. The surprise-inversion tactic probably appealed to
Maupassant's sense of the dramatic. Recognizing its potential effect
upon and appeal to his audience, he began to invoke it time and
again throughout the year. Not yet concerned with the problems of
amalgamating differing and, at times, conflicting literary forms, he
produced stories that were thematically unified, relatively simpli-
fied, yet psychologically complicated, the result being perhaps the
best examples of the subgenre ever written.

Certainly, the most famous of all these efforts was "La Parure"
(1884, The necklace). The surprise in the conclusion so overwhelms
the reader that often he tends to obliterate in his mind any other
Maupassant story he has ever encountered. In nineteenth-century
America, the literati seized upon it as an artistic blueprint. The
author probably would have been amused and, in his strange way,
gratified by the response the story would evoke: the same artistic
devices would ultimately elicit both praise and censure.

Published early in 1884, "La Parure" demonstrates how the author
had improved his technique. Unlike earlier efforts, Maupassant has
intimately tied the surprise with the complication of the story. The
bulk of the text explores the themes of pretension, vanity, and pride.
Although Maupassant presents the protagonists in an irritating light,
we can still sympathize with their plight, and consequently at least
partially identify with them. The ending attacks these human traits
and, therefore, attacks our own values. By knitting these various
elements together with a finer stitch, then, he creates a stronger and
more vivid fabric, capable of enduring in our literary memory.

At the heart of the short story is Mathilde Loisel's bourgeois
aspiration. Choosing the easiest of all human foibles to attack—
pride—Maupassant manipulates his audience so that it finds her
yearnings at first as insipid and selfish, later as tragic and possibly
heroic. Pride exacerbates her supposition of poverty. It forces both
material and psychological concessions from her acquiescent husband. He sacrifices his savings for a hunting weapon so that his wife
may have a new dress for Minister Ramponneau's ball. But the overly
expensive dress symbolically pales before the elaborate diamond
necklace she borrows from a wealthy friend. The jewelry piece
encapsulates her pretension and pride, masking reality with her
dream of what should have been. The party reinforces her delusion

in that for one night everyone accepts her for what she pretends to be.

The loss of the necklace restores reality but does not end pride; it merely redirects it toward seemingly more productive ends. The Loisels secretly replace the lost jewels with a duplicate necklace, incurring an oppressive ten-year debt in the process. The repayment of these loans—yet another act of pride—reduces the couple to physical and emotional hardship. Mme. Loisel realizes true poverty by sacrificing the few luxuries she had but never appreciated fully. Regardless of our misgivings about her hauteur, we now pity her, rejudging her pride a virtue.

Maupassant subtly reinforces such sympathy through his characterization of M. Loisel. The husband is not only the victim of or the unwitting catalyst to his wife's pride; he too falls victim to the deadly sin. Although not directly responsible, he certainly contributes to the circumstances surrounding the loss of the necklace. It is he who suggests to his wife that she borrow the jewels from Jeanne Forestier, the wealthy friend. Come the crisis, however, his pride proves commensurate with that of his wife, for he is the one who resolves to replace the jewelry, a decision to which his wife accedes. By attributing the resolution to the more sympathetic husband, Maupassant manipulates us into believing that the couple's solution was indeed correct, especially since it complies with our Christian ethic.

Unlike earlier efforts when the surprise seemed divorced somewhat from character development, "La Parure" unites the inversion with the main theme by repeating that theme. Pride determined the decision to replace the necklace; it placed upon the couple a self-imposed vow of silence until they paid every debt. Once they had extricated themselves from their plight, however, pride once again inspires Mathilde to boast of her heroic sacrifice to her friend Jeanne upon their accidental meeting. Only then do we and Mme. Loisel discover that the lost necklace was composed of only false stones, that ten years of dissipating toil and pecuniary hardship were the product of a vainful miscalculation, that our vision itself was incorrect because it had been filtered by uninformed presumptions. In essence Maupassant has attacked our conceit about comprehending the perimeters of reality.

Granted, a good deal of Maupassant's small victory depends upon contrivance—most inversion stories do. Even sympathetic critics such as Steegmuller have some difficulty in resolving such awkwardness.[24] These artificial circumstances are, however, more acceptable in a short story than in longer fictional forms. For example, the situation hinges upon the complementary personalities of the Loisels, which seem to conspire in aggravating their dilemma. Artistic economy dictates that the writer reveal only those traits of his characters that further the plot. Consequently, these characterizations may appear rather curt, approaching caricatures and leaving themselves subject to our dismissal as mere artifices designed to deceive.

Even the harshest of Maupassant's critics will admit, however, that the machinations in "La Parure" are tolerable amid the total impact of the story. Because of its brevity, we subconsciously permit the short story more leeway in achieving its artistic goal. Thus, we grant Maupassant's restricted portrayals of the Loisels as concessions toward unity.[25] Nevertheless, the unreality of their isolated pride paradoxically leads to our questioning our own assumptions about the wisdom of pride. By concentrating the story's impact at its conclusion, the surprise-inversion forces us to deal with the issue. Vial suggests that the absurdity of the Loisels' fate overwhelms our inclination to pity them.[26] "La Parure" does not end with Mme. Loisel's reaction to her friend's revelation. Such a passage would have risked directing a reader, through his empathy with the protagonist, toward a precise answer. By ending with the surprise, Maupassant forces his audience to contend with its own perceptual folly. Indeed, the form elevates the importance of the inversion's effect upon the reader over that of any character. The resolution of our uncertainty continues the action of the story within our mind beyond the boundaries of the text.[27] It thus imprints a stronger

24. *Maupassant: A Lion in the Path*, 204.

25. Sullivan would add that Maupassant scrupulously avoided assuming mystical powers of insight in his writings: "In a world where falsity masquerades as truth and blind chance rules, not even the clarity of the artist's eye is any guard against the deceptions and risks of life; all one can do is expose again and again the drama of deceit" (*Maupassant: The Short Stories*, 20).

26. *Guy de Maupassant*, 452.

27. For example, Dugan interestingly assumes as fact a reaction that Maupassant never described: "That moment of nothingness which the Loisels experience upon the discovery of the truth about the necklace serves to reduce to futile meaninglessness the long tragic passing of years between the loss of the jewels and the revelation

image, so strong in the case of "La Parure" that it becomes for many a frame of reference by which to compare similar fiction.

Given the frequency that Maupassant used this story structure in 1884, it seems probable he recognized not only its potential but also that he had mastered it. Although each story deals with a differing subject, they all follow the same pattern. Unlike his earlier efforts, the 1884 inversion stories are so artfully constructed that every paragraph, every sentence, almost every noun and verb leads deceivingly to the surprise ending. Thus the significant moment becomes a target in the plot as well as a standard by which the author can determine the relevance of a description or characterization.

Above all other benefits, though, such a structure permitted Maupassant to attack whatever aspects of human behavior or of the human condition that his whimsy disliked—and to include his audience as the victim of his attack. For instance, "Idylle" (1884, Idyll) investigates the complexities underlying a seemingly simple incident. On a train, a bucolic peasant wet nurse, portrayed disparagingly and comically, begins to feel discomfort because she has no child with her to suckle. To relieve her distress, she asks a young stranger, also traveling in the carriage, to suckle her milk. The reader immediately recognizes the humor and the sexual aspects in the situation, but despite Maupassant's clues to the youth's poverty we do not see the irony and pathos of this chance encounter until the last sentence of the story. When the woman thanks him for doing her "un fameux service" (a great favor), the man replies: "C'est moi qui vous remercie, madame, voilà deux jours que je n'avais rien mangé!" (M1, 1:1197; It is I who should thank you, madam; I have not eaten anything for two days!). Tragedy coexists with superficial comedy and prurience. The shock of the unexpected last sentence again alerts us to our perceptual inadequacies.

Other 1884 stories present similar challenges to the reader. "Châli" astounds us with the notion that an act considered benevolent in Western civilization can be misunderstood by foreign cultures, in this case leading to the execution of an innocent girl. By tracing in "Un lâche" (A coward) a fop's twisted logic in choosing suicide over participating in a duel he instigated, Maupassant ex-

---

of their worthlessness" (Illusion and Reality, 158). In essence, the inversion has inspired Dugan to project his own response onto his perception of the Loisels.

poses the archaic pretensions of chivalry and, in doing so, causes the reader to doubt his ability to fathom the eccentricities of human thought. Wallace correctly notes that the story "is a typical Maupassantian attack on the myth of male courage and resolve."[28] Each of these stories seeks its own hermetic niche in our memory through the didacticism inherent in being surprised, but often we remember such fiction begrudgingly.

Maupassant may have realized the potential for such an attitude in the reader. Used too often, the surprise-inversion structure could burden his audience in that if it began to expect such endings from him, the shock would be diluted. Interestingly, after 1884 Maupassant used the form sparingly, and he often disguised it by fusing it with other short-story structures. With one structure competing with the surprise-inversion, these fusions devitalized the shock potential of each ending, suggesting that he no longer valued such absolute effects. Stories such as "La Parure" had secured a minor place for him in French letters, but his artistic drive compelled him to leave behind such simple formulas and to seek instead the more complicated as well as the more subtle.

By 1890 Maupassant had substantially altered the role surprise plays in a short story. He retained the target-inversion structure but planted more overt symbolic and psychological clues for the reader to lead him to that ending. Such intentions demanded sophisticated mixtures of form. In "Le Champ d'oliviers" (1890, The olive orchard), for example, the plot proceeds along a psychological decrescendo, preparing the reader for Abbot Vilbois' suicide. Prior to reading the story, a nineteenth-century Frenchman would have believed the clergyman's act to be unrealistic and almost inconceivable given the tenets of the church. The first scene of the story supports the stereotype of an honored country priest. Symbolized by the olive orchard, Vilbois' placid life seems inviolable.

"Le Champ d'oliviers" is, however, one of Maupassant's random challenges to religious dogma. The possibility of a priest's suicide in itself shocks us; but if Maupassant presented such an incident in a surprise ending (in the manner of an 1884 story), he would have risked his readers dismissing the philosophical attack as mere literary artifice. The author himself apparently believed that without the

---

28. *Guy de Maupassant*, 118.

insight provided by the third-person narrator, suicide would be an implausible conclusion. In dealing with the case, the town officials assumed that their priest had been murdered; Maupassant ends the story: "car l'idée ne serait venue à personne que l'abbé Vilbois, peut-être, avait pu se donner la mort" (M1, 2:1204; for they never entertained the notion that someone like Abbot Vilbois had possibly taken his own life).[29]

Maupassant wants us to accept such an occurrence as plausible, so he imposes a second structure upon the story that establishes how human concerns can engulf religious principles. Vilbois tries to contend with discovering the truth of his lover's deception after twenty-five years. He faces the prospect of falling subject to the whims of a dissolute son that he had never known. Each new revelation places him deeper into the well of his calamity. Thus the ending confirms rather than surprises, and we now entertain what we once hesitated to consider. Micheline Besnard-Coursodon suggests that the clergyman's inevitable downfall is part of Maupassant's bleak view of man's role in the universe:

> Or, l'étouffement, la gorge coupée représentent concrètement l'effet du piège et consacrent l'impuissance de l'individu devant la nature. La révolte contre le lien ne peut . . . qu'aboutir au suicide.[30]

> (Therefore, the suffocation and slit throat clearly represent the effect of the trap and sanctify the impotence of the individual before nature. The revolt against the bond [with nature] can only . . . end with suicide.)

In essence, Maupassant's new conception of the inversion story transfers the time when we contemplate implications: whereas the 1884 story forced us to consider its import after reading the text,

29. Interestingly, Maupassant's original manuscript continues the plot beyond the cleric's suicide, following the son's inevitable fate. The most notable authority on Maupassant texts, Forestier, does not address the problem of whether Maupassant or an editor excised this five-hundred-word passage. Whichever the case, the effect is unmistakable: "Le Champ d'oliviers" was deliberately edited into an inversion story. For the text of this passage, see Forestier, 2:1706–7.

30. Etude thématique et structurale de l'oeuvre de Maupassant: Le piège (Paris: A.-G. Nizet, 1973), 78.

hybrid inversion stories thereafter demanded that we weigh consequences while in the initial act of reading.

The Loop

In sum, Maupassant seemed more and more inclined to make his
readers aware of how the act of reading a short story can alter their
perception. He shied away from using surprise-inversion structures
because his audience began to anticipate them. In addition, he had
already experimented with other story configurations that better
suited his purpose. In fact, with one form he already had by 1882 an
alternative at hand.

Coterminous with his mastering the inversion form, Maupassant
began employing a parallel technique—the structural progression of
which can be described as a *loop*. The loop resembles the inversion
in that both place stress points at the end of the text. Thus, like its
counterpart, the loop treats the story's climax as a target toward
which the rest of the text aims. It differs from the inversion story,
however, in that the author has included a subsidiary stress point at
the beginning of the text. This secondary key moment presages the
significance of the target. Consequently, by providing a clue to the
resolution of the plot, Maupassant deliberately pre-empts the story's
potential to surprise the reader totally. Not only that, he has also
given us an indicator by which we may recognize the interpretive
value of every nuance of symbol and meaning immediately upon
encountering it.[31]

The loop by no means precludes the possibility of inverted perception. What it avoids, though, is the compressed tumult inherent
in surprise. By focusing attention on salient elements right from the
beginning, the author dilates the reader's awareness of the change.[32]

31. Dugan's concept of the *cadre* story shares some similarities to my definition of
the loop. He recognizes the Maupassant approach of the present reflecting upon a
meaningful instant of the past, but he fails to point out how the author coordinates
the opening and closing passages in the "framework structure"; *Illusion and Reality*,
158.

32. In Lohafer's coined terms, the loop defers cognitive closure. Intervening between the inital stress point and its counterpart at the end of the text, the explanatory
story changes meaning by changing the context, thus altering the reader's ability to
perceive the "intensity" of a significant moment (*Coming to Terms*, 43–46).

Thus, Maupassant interjects a stronger note of psychological plausibility in the plot, but he does so at a price: readers respond less emotionally to a story, diminishing the likelihood that the twist will affect them profoundly.

In contrast to the surprise-inversion story, which attempts to mask causation, the loop story seeks to emphasize each step of a fictional syllogism. The author proclaims his conclusion at the beginning of a text and then circles back to the past to retrace the sequence of events that led to that end. Often, the reader's return to this significant point challenges his initial perception; but unlike the trick ending, which compresses his realization to a single instant, the loop expands his awareness of ironic reversal over the length of the text.

In employing such a form, however, Maupassant does not abandon the notion of attack. After he had mastered the form, he would usually describe the first appearance of the significant point in terms that tended to make his audience overlook or dismiss it. The rest of the text then seemed dedicated to questioning the reader's presumptuousness. Maupassant's stance was quite simple: we instinctively draw conclusions even from superficial observations, but without insight we inevitably fail to deduce true motivations and consequences. In essence, we play the role of a befuddled Watson who listens to omniscient Holmes as he struts and presents the verities of human experience. More than any other structure in fiction, the loop points out the importance of retrospection in insight. Known ends shape and color our interpretation of their causes.[33]

Thus, given his penchant for choosing story lines that unsettled his audience, Maupassant hinted, perhaps more subconsciously than knowingly, that irony underscored human experience. In confining himself to the economizing principles inherent in the short story, the artist demands that his readers see how the unexpected colors the salient moments of life. By focusing upon these highlights

33. Among his various treatments of the theme of entrapment in Maupassant's fiction, Besnard-Coursodon deals with an intellectual one: "Et nous arrivons à ce paradoxe: la faculté propre à dissiper le mystère (et à éviter ou surmonter les dangers), est elle-même un mystère, et peut-être un danger. . . . l'impuissance à voir est aussi impuissance à connaître" (Etude thématique, 93; And we arrive at this paradox: the faculty suited for dispelling the mystery (and for escaping or surmounting dangers) is itself a mystery, and perhaps a danger. . . . the inability to see is also the inability to know).

and eliminating all competing plots, the short-story loop not only challenges the vision of the careless reader; by its existence it also threatens longer fictional forms. A novel may belabor irony through misdirection or inflated explication, or mask it within other interpretive contexts. In contrast, the short-story loop proclaims that the ironic moment alone deserves our attention, our remembering, our esteem.

Curiously, although it would be reasonable to presume that Maupassant developed it as a literary corollary to the surprise-inversion story, he in fact mastered the loop a full year before the other form. From late 1882 to the end of 1883, Maupassant employed this retrospective structure more than any other. The most plausible explanation for this anomalous progression concerns his friendship with Ivan Turgenev. The Russian had successfully developed the loop story thirty years earlier in his landmark collection *Sportsman's Sketches*, the most notable example among which was "Yermolay and the Miller's Wife." Whether the young Maupassant was profoundly influenced by Turgenev or so desperate for ideas that he borrowed what was at hand, the Frenchman imitated the themes and forms of the Russian throughout his career.[34]

Consequently, Turgenev's artistic insights hastened those of Maupassant to the extent that he was able to handle a relatively complicated form before he mastered simpler story structures. In *Sportsman's Sketches* Turgenev refrained from surprises such as those in inversion stories. Possibly, then, Maupassant did not feel comfortable with the surprise-inversion story until 1884 because he had few acceptable examples to mimic and so had to rely upon experimentation in realizing the form's potential and limitations. Of the two parallel forms, though, Maupassant would favor the loop after 1884. He frequently superimposed it over other fictional frameworks, suggesting that he eventually found it more useful because its repeated use among short stories does not, unlike its counterpart, dilute its

---

34. Critic G. Hainsworth offers a different source for Maupassant's concern with circular movement in his work. He believes that the Frenchman was trying to imitate Flaubert's interest in the drab, repetitive elements of human existence; "Pattern and Symbol in the Work of Maupassant," *French Studies* 5 (1951): 2, 4. Although Maupassant's debt to Flaubert was substantial, I conclude that he owed more to Turgenev in this one literary matter. His loop stories resemble Turgenev's more than Flaubert's. Also, Maupassant's interest in circle motifs grew after the death of Flaubert and during his strengthening friendship with Turgenev.

effect. Its shock value may be less and so single stories may tend to fade to the further recesses of memory; but our consciousness of the pattern of the loop, produced by the aggregate of Maupassant's fiction, becomes in itself a continual reminder of our perceptual inadequacies. Only the artist can explain what we see yet fail to understand.

In the score of stories he published prior to 1882, Maupassant usually turned to forms other than the loop. Only "Suicides" (1881) manages to capture any semblance of the technique's desired effect. As was characteristic of most of his early work, though, the flaws produced by youthful arrogance and the heavy-handed tactics of an immature writer enervate the potential of the structure to inspire self-doubt in the reader. One significant problem in "Suicides" arises from Maupassant's mishandling of form. After teasing the reader with a "newspaper account" of a suicide, he belabors the first stress point of the text:

> Quelles douleurs profondes, quelles lésions du coeur, déses-
> poirs cachés, blessures brûlantes poussent au suicide ces gens
> qui sont heureux? On cherche, on imagine des drames d'a-
> mour, on soupçonne des désastres d'argent et, comme on ne
> découvre jamais rien de précis, on met sur ces morts, le mot
> "Mystère." (M1, 1:175)

> (What deep sorrows, what heartaches, hidden despair, burn-
> ing emotional wounds drive seemingly happy people to sui-
> cide? You seek, you imagine tragedies of love, you suspect
> financial ruin, and, when you find nothing concrete, you
> superimpose on these deaths the word Mystery.)

The tone of the passage prematurely reveals that these common assumptions will prove not to be the norm. The author then uses a ploy he often invoked to trick his audience about the truth-value of a fictional account: the narrator of "Suicides" announces that he possesses a letter that will unveil the mystery behind such desperate acts. What follows is a cliché-filled account of one man's ennui, culminating in his reevaluation of the futility of life as he ponders the significance of his old correspondence. Plagued by an overabun-dance of philosophical musings that point too directly to the author's intention, "Suicides" squanders our effort in reading it. Throughout the text Maupassant maintains such strict control over the possibilities for interpretation that our participation becomes more casual than active. Consequently, the likelihood that the story will produce a perceptual revolution in us seems remote.

In the loop stories of 1882, however, Maupassant applied a more delicate brush upon an increasingly intricate canvas. The righteous voice of the moralistic narrator in "Suicides" has fewer and fewer echoes in Maupassant's later work. In "Fou?" (1882, Mad?), for example, a crazed husband recounts, in a narrative reminiscent of Poe's tales, his descent into maniacal jealousy. He unwittingly taunts us with his first words, a rhetorical supplication that reappears as a refrain in the text and that ends the story upon an ironic note: "Suis-je fou?" (Am I mad?) The question alerts us immediately to the interpretive crux of the text. Thus, despite the narrator's rationalizing tone, we notice every nuance of his confession that supports an answer he himself cannot accept. We need no intervening voice to interpret the text properly; the madman himself betrays the truth:

> . . . la femme de tout cela, l'être de ce corps, je la hais, je la méprise, je l'exècre, je l'ai toujours haïe, méprisée, exécrée; car elle est perfide, bestiale, immonde, impure." (M1, 1:522)

> (. . . but the woman of all [the things I love], the corporeal being, I hate her, I scorn her, I loathed her; I have always hated, scorned and loathed her because she is treacherous, bestial, foul, impure.)

Note how through tone itself Maupassant suggests that hate has gone beyond rationality. The staccato rhythm, the successive surge of virulence in each adjective expose the instability of the husband's psyche. Consequently, when we encounter later in "Fou?" the transference of his hate to his wife's horse, the potential humor of this turnabout is qualified by our already-formed perception of the story's central effect: horror. We may still laugh at him, but it is an uneasy laugh. The nature of the loop has forced us to see beyond the superficiality of such humor. Each action, each sentence, each thought fails to bring relief to the narrator. Thus, when after ambushing the horse and murdering his wife he asks once again, "Suis-je fou?" we now possess enough insight to surmise that his conscious mind replies "no," but his subconscious knows the answer is "yes." The story's assault upon the reader's security takes a curious turn. It begins with a question that all intelligent men and women ask themselves when confronting the inevitable irrationalities of life; it ends with the same question to suggest that no man, including the reader, can judge his own sanity.[35]

For the most part, though, Maupassant's attacks that employed loop structures assumed more subtle forms in 1882. He found that the form especially suited his artistic purpose in his local color stories. In his role as interpreter of rural France (particularly Normandy), Maupassant often directed a chastising tone at his cosmopolitan readers' propensity to dismiss everything not Parisian as quaint and superficial. Looping structures permitted him to play upon this tendency in that typical readers often fail to surmise the significance of the first stress point of the text. The author abets this erroneous perception by various techniques designed to misdirect. In "Ce Cochon de Morin" (1882, That pig Morin), for example, Maupassant apparently repeats the device he employed in "Suicides." This time, however, the refrain does not focus our attention upon the narrative crux of the story.

When Labarbe, a government official, offers to explain the origin of a curious local phrase—ce cochon de Morin—to his companion, the narrator, the reader anticipates a bucolic (and perhaps ribald) tale. Given such tepid expectations he hopes for a moment's diversion, perhaps even amusement, but little insight. Initially, the tale fulfills this preconception. Morin, a draper from La Rochelle, becomes infatuated with a young woman while traveling by rail to Paris. With the impatience of a bumpkin he surprises the woman with a kiss, which results in his arrest and social ostracism. At this point Maupassant starts to challenge his reader's predilections and values. In an attempt to have the charges dropped, Labarbe and a colleague act as intermediaries between the woman's family and Morin. Upon seeing the woman, however, the mediator begins to pursue his own sexual interests. He succeeds where Morin has failed because his manner is more practiced and urbane, qualities with

---

35. Wallace suggests that the presence of a question mark in the title "is most significant in revealing Maupassant's reluctance to judge a man mad"; Guy de Maupassant, 109.

which a Parisian reader might identify. Maupassant obviously wishes his audience to compare the clumsy but honest Morin with the skilled but sly Labarbe. The former becomes the butt of a catch phrase, repeated so often and so long that it fades into a cliché. On the other hand, Labarbe ironically earns communal respect in his handling of the matter, which ultimately wins him a seat in the Chamber of Deputies. In fact, long after the incident the woman's new husband—ignorant of what occurred between his wife and Labarbe—thanked the deputy for his part in "l'affaire de ce cochon de Morin."

The repetition of the shibboleth serves to remind us how insubstantial our initial impression of the story was. The story proved to involve more than just a curious incident from a remote corner of civilization; Maupassant has unexpectedly slipped into the text a barometer by which we can ascertain the social worth of our own vagaries of character. The seemingly empty phrase that we wanted to dismiss in the beginning becomes at end the centerpiece of a complex parallel, designed by the author to challenge the values of every sophisticated cynic—including himself.

In Maupassant's 1882 stories, the initial stress points in a looping plot donned even more cunning guises. In the latter half of the year he began to employ with greater frequency a variation that threatened the confidence of his audience to read intelligently. Maupassant underplays the initial revelation in these stories so well that readers tend to miss recognizing its significance. Basically, he follows Poe's principle from "The Purloined Letter": the best hiding place is in open view. A crucial sentence is placed amid a battery of expository sentences—descriptions of the setting, the time, or a character—that readers normally expect at the beginning of a story. The purpose of the remaining text becomes then to flaunt before the reader that what he had valued as just the ornamental façade to a literary arch was actually the interpretive keystone. The direction of Maupassant's attack is obvious: in encountering a person or a circumstance, we face a similar problem in discerning the few objects of significance amid the myriad of trivial details. Without being privy to an authoritative voice or vision, we should find the dilemma insurmountable. Nevertheless, being creatures of prejudice we arrive at solutions regardless of the poverty of evidence. Through this development of the loop story, which demonstrates our proclivity to overlook the significant, Maupassant parades before us the perceptual folly that is socially ingrained in all of us.

The most successful of the 1882 stories that follow this variation is "Le Loup" (The wolf). The first four paragraphs seem typical of any story: they identify the setting (a dinner party at Saint-Hubert), the key character (the marquis d'Arville), and the topic of conversation (hunting). In describing the group's activity prior to the party, the author sneaks in one seemingly irrelevant clause:

> On avait forcé un cerf dans le jour. Le marquis était le seul des convives qui n'eût point pris part à cette poursuite, *car il ne chassait jamais.* (M1, 1:625; italics mine).

> (Someone had forced a deer into the open. The marquis was the only one of the guests who had not taken part in this pursuit, *because he never hunted.*)

Only when the marquis begins his dinner-table tale by reiterating that he never hunts do we realize the significance of the earlier clause, but even that fails to prepare us for the family legend that follows. As is typical with most loop stories, the marquis directs the attention of his listeners toward the past.

In the eighteenth century his great-great-grandfather, Jean d'Arville had a brutal passion for hunting. The marquis recounts in extraordinary detail Jean and his brother's hunt of one particular quarry: a white wolf to whom they ascribed supernatural powers. In pursuing the wolf on horseback at night, Jean accidentally is struck and killed by a low branch. Contemplating his dead brother, François migrates emotionally from fear through anger to hysteria. Pursuing revenge maniacally, he corners and strangles the wolf. The marquis ends his narrative with "[l]a veuve de mon aïeul inspira à son fils orphelin l'horreur de la chasse, qui s'est transmise de père en fils jusqu'à moi" (M1, 1:630; the widow of my ancestor instilled in her orphaned son a fear for hunting that has descended from father to son down to me). The marquis' listeners, who beforehand likely dismissed his reticence as a reaction to some unpleasant personal experience while hunting, have some initial difficulty in accepting the explanation. One even questions: "Cette histoire est une légende, n'est-ce pas?" (M1, 1:630; That story is a legend, isn't it?). The inquisitor's doubt mirrors the reader's in that the story forces us to accept a formerly untenable proposition: sometimes a person's behavior is the product more of his ancestral past than of his own present. We could not entertain such a prospect at the first stress point in the story because we lacked the imaginative ability to conceive of it. In transforming the superficially trivial into a significant insight on the possibilities of causation, Maupassant thus reminds us of our intellectual limitations.[36]

In sum, Maupassant gravitated from the blatant to the subdued in 1882. Within his growing artistic awareness he realized that luring his audience into a story with too strong an initial clue toward its interpretation ultimately voided its potential to move anyone intellectually or emotionally. Disdaining the slightest hint of literary amateurism, he learned not to reveal too much prematurely; yet in loop-structured stories he still planted a seed that at first appears to be insignificant but later grows both to control the text and to challenge our conservative expectations in understanding that text. In essence we initially see only the mundane or trivial surfaces of a situation or a character; the author then manipulates us to appreciate its marvelous depths.

In the sixty-plus stories of 1883, numerically his most productive year, Maupassant employed the fruits of his newly mastered structure often and well. In "La Ficelle" (The piece of string) a peasant spies a length of string on the ground at a Norman marketplace and pockets it almost out of instinct. This originally innocuous event launches a bizarre causal chain that culminates in his social ostracism and death. The loop technique forces us to notice how, even when braced with truth, man sometimes loses control of his reputation and, therefore, his life. "Mademoiselle Cocotte" follows a similar pattern. In the story the narrator, who comes upon an insane coachman in an asylum, learns that he was driven mad by drowning a dog. The inherent absurdity in this happenstance almost elicits a dismissive laugh in the reader, but the narrator reminds him that "[l]es choses les plus simples, les plus humbles, sont parfois celles qui nous mordent le plus au coeur" (M1, 1:758; the simplest and humblest of things are sometimes those that gnaw most deeply at

---

36. Curiously, Dugan dismisses the significance of the opening and closing passages, suggesting that they "offer us nothing but a brief outline of the basic situation which inspires the story"; *Illusion and Reality*, 15.

our heart). He then discovers those circumstances that made the coachman's plight not only plausible but inevitable.

In looping the structure of "Le Père Milon" (1883, Father Milon) by mentioning the protagonist's execution early in the text, Maupassant redirects our attention toward assessing the motivational roots of the patriotism manifested by Norman peasants during the Franco-Prussian War. In "Le Modèle" (1883, The model), Maupassant offers a touching initial glimpse of the devotion between an artist and his crippled wife, but then the story retreats into the tortured foundations of that devotion, strongly suggesting that the husband acts more out of guilt than love. Again the author attacks our propensity to romanticize a cursory impression through revealing its sordid depths.

Upon mastering the surprise-inversion technique in 1884, Maupassant refrained somewhat from employing loop structures. After his disillusionment with trick endings, however, he returned to the loop. Perhaps he recognized that such a form was an expedient remedy to his artistic disenchantment: pre-empt the surprise by presenting it early in the text. In his movement toward more complicated plots, however, he yoked the loop with other, more sophisticated structures in stories such as "Fini" (1885, End), "La Baptême" (1885, The baptism), and "Boitelle" (1889). This practice suggests that he mistrusted the affective power of the loop alone. He probably associated it with his naive and experimental literary past. To retreat was unthinkable.

Nevertheless, the initial stress point of the loop still served an artistic purpose: it mediated between conflicting impulses in Maupassant. Toward the latter half of his writing career, he seemed to avoid simple stories. Convoluted histories, bitterly ironic circumstances, and daedal, often hypocritical motivations were interwoven in rich brocades of growing pessimism. Such intricacy, though, threatens the very holism of the short story, its fundamental artistic principle. Given this dilemma, Maupassant probably returned to the loop because of its power to unify a text. In essence, it frames the central thesis of a story, giving readers a reference by which they may coordinate those elements that are more taxing to interpret properly.[37]

37. The pictorial suggestiveness of the structure of the loop tallies with Kurt Willi's notion of the omnipresence of circle imagery—symbolizing "la monotonie de l'exist-

Given this potential, then, it is not so curious that Maupassant favored the loop over the inversion story in the latter half of the decade. After all, while the trick ending has the greater potential to upset the reader, it ultimately portrays a false conception of the human condition by failing to stress the historical context of a significant moment. In fact, the shock of the surprise seems to isolate the event in time. For Maupassant, to draw a reader's attention to such a moment might superimpose a simple solution on a complicated fictional circumstance. In addition, a well-wrought surprise-inversion ending would likely overwhelm all other plot structures in a text.

Curiously, critics contemporary to Maupassant as well as to us sometimes injudiciously confuse Maupassant's loop stories with the inversions. Because of the reputation of "La Parure," critics want to see it as the blueprint for the essence of Maupassant's writings. Americans especially are prone to shove as many of his texts as possible into that one interpretive pigeonhole. Whether arising out of selective inattention or just careless reading, this inability to differentiate has contributed in part to the twentieth-century tendency to dismiss his work as formulaic and, consequently, inferior. Had Maupassant built stories using only simplistic structures, such a view might have validity, but he found more challenging forms that better suited his shifting perspective toward art and life—a view colored by a darker pessimism, resignation, and a sense of disintegration. As Henry James wrote of Maupassant's literary metamorphosis and its effect upon the reader: "Such a gift may produce surprises in the mere exercise of its natural health. The dogmatist is never safe with it."[38]

---

ence" (the monotony of existence) and "l'étroitesse de la destinée" (the constraints of destiny)—in Maupassant's fiction; *Déterminisme et liberté chez Guy de Maupassant* (Zurich: Juris-Verlag, 1972), 61–65.

38. Henry James, preface to *The Odd Number*, by Guy de Maupassant, trans. Jonathan Sturges (New York: Harper, 1889), xvii.

2

Maupassant and the More Complex Structures of the Short Story

On the surface, Maupassant's "complex" forms appear no more taxing to decipher than a linear or inversion story. They involve, for the most part, logical variations in the deployment of the stress point. To avoid his conclusion-dominated constructions, for example, he shifted the significant point to an earlier position in the text. Occasionally, he would interject two points in a story that were invariably mirror images of each other. Even with end-oriented forms, he sometimes borrowed a tactic from Poe in deemphasizing the outcome by incrementally preparing the reader for its inevitability. Like simple story structures, Maupassant's complex forms had many precedents among the works of nineteenth-century short-story masters—and they were still practiced by his peers, domestic and foreign. Thus, again, their existence did not lie in Maupassant's ability to innovate but in his impulse to intensify his convoluted vision.

Rather than from any inherent intricacy in form, then, these complexities derive from the artistic and philosophic import of such impulses. First, they demand more astute analytical skills from readers. Loops and surprise-inversions tend to offer limited interpretive possibilities. Usually, such forms spell out what the author wishes us to ponder. In contrast, Maupassant's complex variations force us to ferret out more subtle comparisons of circumstance, character, or belief to appreciate a text properly. The artist is thus faced with a curious situation: by moving the significant incident to an earlier part of the text, he dilutes its impact; but its very prominence is, ironically, the key to the capacity of his readers to frame their response. Consequently, the potential of such a story to survive within the reader's collective literary memory depends upon his ability to interpret and the writer's skill in making legitimate interpretation possible. In the latter case, the author must make the turning point noticeable enough so that his readers take it into consideration.

In essence, each time he used a plot that invited complexities in its analysis (which twentieth-century disciples of Chekhov sometimes called the *lyric* short story), Maupassant risked creating an entity that might not survive amid all the literary pieces that competed for the public's attention, a defeat his ego could never comfortably accept. Evidently, considerations other than his reputation came into play. For one, his threshold for ennui was forever curiously low. His continual pursuit of the outrageous and the untrodden in life and art seemed designed more to allay his own fear of boredom than to shock friends and the public. However successful, the repetition of only a few models would not support his compulsion to push the limits of human existence. Had his intellect only been able to comprehend inversions and the like, I suspect that Maupassant's interest in writing would not have survived beyond a year or two. Thus, even "Boule de suif," his early masterpiece, unexpectedly has a sophisticated sinusoidal structure, suggesting that the combined influence of Flaubert and Zola accelerated (at a miraculous rate) their common disciple's artistic insight. Other early works likewise indicate that from 1880 on, Maupassant sought extensively for formal alternatives.

Nevertheless, he still wanted to startle readers into recognizing the pretensions of society and those within themselves. If the diversely complex forms of the story could not produce such an effect, then the topic of the story must. Thus, at times Maupassant pursued aspects of human behavior, especially sexuality, that stretched the perimeters of literary naturalism. Confronted by a public that had already dealt with Zola's Darwinian rebellion, Maupassant surpassed his mentor by supercharging human motivation with convoluted irony. Thus, in "Le Lit 29" (1884, Bed 29), for example, he could present a woman's hauteur in infecting Prussian soldiers with syphilis, an act she proclaims commensurate with any French patriot's deed on a battlefield. A complicated structure must abet the capacity of such subjects to provoke rather than dominate them so heavily that the essential thrust becomes lost.

Given this integrative subservience to theme and subject, a multifarious form necessarily becomes involved with larger contexts than simpler structures do. In simple plots, the implicit irony in the ending often dominates our recollection of a character. We seize upon Mathilde Loisel's discovery of the ultimate meaninglessness of her sacrifice, although other aspects of her life fade in our memory. The significant point in such stories encapsulates life itself. It takes advantage of our inclination to stereotype whenever possible. We find it easier to react to someone if our image consists of only one conspicuous event in her life, for we are not taxed to place that happening amid the total personality or the progression of a life.

With complicated forms, however, Maupassant diffuses turning points within less restrictive perimeters. Compared with its prominence in a loop or inversion story, the significance of one incident now fails to dominate our total perception of a character. Complex structures generally necessitate more detailed accounts of a character's development; and since the plot has no terminal surprise to overshadow the rest of the text, we tend to elevate the importance of these accounts in our critical analysis. For the most part, then, the significant point functions as a partition that invites us to compare two or more parallel phenomena, often marking interesting changes in a protagonist's situation, behavior, or insight. Consequently, a complicated form generally makes concessions toward depicting continuity in life at the expense of dramatic effect. Such a structure does not end with insight but dwells upon the consequences of that insight. As qualified by Maupassant's pessimism, these repercussions often betray a more insidious irony that all must face: apperception seldom brings about any meaningful improvement in one's lot. Instead, it perversely intensifies suffering, for it robs the victim of his blind hope that relief would someday be possible.

Maupassant thus forces readers to contend with the unresolvable disparity between life as it ought to be and life as it is, leading them to admit the inevitable duality of most perceptions. This power to create simultaneous, often conflicting, visions within the reader is perhaps what best distinguishes complex story forms from more contrived structures. A surprise-inversion story, for example, would often only displace one interpretation of a circumstance with its ironical counterpart. On the other hand, the significant point in a complex plot usually serves to weave competing perspectives so inextricably that readers must vacillate among them. Ultimately, based upon our prejudices—literary, philosophical, or personal—we accept one of them, but we can never discount the plausibility of alternative explanations.

In effect, Maupassant frames for us an analytical dilemma that Gestalt theorists have termed *cognitive dissonance*. Throughout Maupassant's work, this dual vision becomes the most persistent, subtle, yet far-reaching of his attacks upon the self-images of an audience. Usually, the author provides us with sufficient criteria to gravitate toward a credible perspective, but our interpretation sometimes depends upon first assumptions that the text may not support. Maupassant forces our imaginations to supply them as well as to create the seed for their possible annihilation. In the famous Gestalt illustration, we successively see the white vase, then the two black profiles, and then again the vase. Likewise, in "Le Horla" (1887), we entertain at one moment the possibility that the narrator is mad and in the next the chance that the specter really exists.

Through this multiplicity of vision, Maupassant's sense of intricate forms attacks our confidence in our own ability to know.[1] The author parades before us every relevant detail, but we still fail to comprehend with any self-conviction. Isolated by the gulf that separates one man from another, we cannot discern total truth. This egocentric alienation parallels Maupassant's own, betraying perhaps

1. In "Maupassant and the Motif of the Mask," *Symposium* 10 (1956): 36, Edward D. Sullivan agrees with such a reading: "In a world limited to sensation and matter, as Maupassant saw it, each man lives in solitary confinement, relying on his imperfect senses for his knowledge of the world and of other men. Most men do not even use properly their own instruments of perception."

his frustration at the world's inability to understand him. Therefore, he bequeathed to us stories that are philosophically impossible to juxtapose against each other: the sexism underlying "Mouche" (1890), for example, seems inconsistent with the overt feminist approach in "L'Inutile Beauté" (1890, Beauty without Purpose).[2] In a sense, then, complex structures permitted Maupassant to sketch via the microcosm of the short story a viciously circular vision that symbolized the sound and fury of his entire canon.

The Descending Helical

The most salient of Gestalt effects contained in Maupassant's work appears in the supernatural-madmen narratives. Through Baudelaire and other translators, the patterns established by Poe more than thirty years earlier had grown popular. In "The Tell-Tale Heart," for example, Poe had tantalized his audience with a narrator of dubious sanity. By the conclusion of the tale, we little doubt that the narrator is indeed crazy. With good cause we presume that his diseased mind created the noetic heartbeats that drive him to confess his perfect crime, but a tremor of possibility remains that they were the physical manifestation of a supernatural avenger who wanted him to go mad. "Ligeia," "The Cask of Amontillado," and other gothic monologues pursue similar circuits, all of which established Poe's approach as a prototype for most fictional treatments of dementia in nineteenth-century France.

The structure of these stories can be viewed as familiarly simple. In fact, they often apparently follow the linear patterns of loops and surprise-inversions. They are end-oriented in that each successive incident or statement serves an ultimate purpose: to fuse the horror and fascination in surreptitiously witnessing the human mind in decay. Like Poe, though, Maupassant forestalls any chance that readers will be surprised. The beginning of the text suggests that the

---

2. A. H. Wallace defends Maupassant from those critics who see his "behavior paradoxical to such a degree that they could see little but hypocrisy in his defense of woman." Such charges, Wallace asserts, ignore the impulse that dominates a story such as "L'Inutile Beauté": Maupassant's "scorn" for the male ego. See Guy de Maupassant (Boston: Twayne, 1973), 56–57.

narrator may be mad. The balance traces step-by-step every stage as he succumbs to insanity. Unlike the loop, which tends to retreat into the past, these madmen narratives usually adhere to a traditional chronological sequence.

If anything, these stories approximate a true linear structure, but a reader senses a double direction in their conceptual impact, which Maupassant's simpler techniques cannot in themselves achieve. Two music terms provide a good analogy to picture this complex effect. In one respect, the course of the narrative mimics a crescendo: each successive sentence portrays a situation more desperate, a narrator acting more frenzied, a mind one step farther removed from normality. At the same time, the reader detects a decrescendo, a sinking spirit within himself. Maupassant extends a character's initial behavioral quirks, with which we may sympathize or even identify, to an apparently inevitable conclusion that arouses our horror at the bizarre capacity of the human mind.

Poe himself provides an apt metaphor for this pattern in "A Descent into the Maelström," in which he incrementally transforms dilated, meticulously painted observations into a furious and fragmented sketch of horror. The *descending helical* structure of the whirlpool parallels a schizophrenic's inability to free his perception from its egocentric orbit as he spirals always from hope and truth while moving toward psychic chaos and death.[3]

Why, then, did Poe and Maupassant sometimes undercut the reader's desire for certainty in dealing with these psychological issues by suggesting that the supernatural may be at work? First, this ambiguity imbues their portrayal with a mystical element that perhaps betrays a subconscious distrust about their own conceptions of the human mind. More important, the cognitive dissonance between the real and unreal in these stories poses an interpretive puzzle that can only be resolved after carefully reading and analytically manipulating the text. The difficulty in arriving at a completely satisfactory understanding of Maupassant's intent compels us to dwell upon the individual facets of the plot more than we do with other story structures. Properly accomplished, the helix story paradoxically

---

3. In *Maupassant et les autres* (Paris: Editions Ramsay, 1981), 14, 16, Jacques Chessex sees a similar pattern for the entire Maupassant canon. The growing fatalism in coping with "les terreurs des fantasmes et des rêves" (the dread of fantasies and dreams) expands the importance of death as a theme in his work.

secures its place within our memory by our dissatisfaction with our own inability to react confidently to it. In essence, its absolute irresolution prevents us from dismissing it.[4]

During his ten-year reign, Maupassant's development of helical stories shifted increasingly inward in vision. Early in his career, he showed interest in dyadic sensory moments, when events force two incompatible emotions to coexist. Although not necessarily confined to such stories, the significant moment in helixes captures this duality. In his early work, Maupassant confined us solely to witnessing such a moment, impressing us with the extent human behavior indulges in excess. Eventually, though, he constructed plots so that we empathize with the tortuous ambivalence experienced by the protagonist; and as a result we suspect dissonant undercurrents within ourselves.[5]

The whirlwind pattern of the typical helix portrays a character's self-destruction. Perhaps reflecting his harbored meditations about his growing anxiety regarding syphilis, Maupassant often ends such stories with the protagonist's suicide as an inescapable response given his inability to resolve the perceptual complexities of a situation. Again, a shift is apparent between early and later helical stories. During the first half of the 1880s, Maupassant often presented a suicide's necessary reaction to a predicament under the guise of temporary insanity. With his subsequent burgeoning fears about the intellectual consequences of his disease, Maupassant seldom dealt with the momentary consequences of someone's trying to cope with the futility. Instead, he depicted the cumulative and enduring effects that maddening events impose upon men and women.

Examples of descending helical stories in Maupassant's oeuvre appear as early as 1881. "La Femme de Paul" (1881, Paul's woman),

4. Ross Chambers proposes that the reader empathizes with and thus experiences within himself the obsessive nature of such narratives; see "Le Lecteur comme hantise: Spirite et Le Horla," Revue des sciences humaines, no. 177 (1980): 105–17.

5. In a Freudian reading of Maupassant, Nafissa A.-F. Schasch suggests a five-stage pattern in the author's use of the supernatural: (1) a precocious pessimism in his early stories, (2) a period dominated by fear about syphilis, (3) a psychologically turbulent time marked by both hope and physical suffering, (4) the initial stages of madness signaled by a sense of alienation, and (5) absolute nihilism. Although somewhat interesting, Schasch's interpretation relies too exclusively upon biographical parallels and antiquated psychiatric principles. See Guy de Maupassant et le fantastique ténébreux (Paris: Librairie A.-G. Nizet, 1983), 19–20.

for one, traces one man's intensifying anxiety over the sexual realities of his circumstance. Maupassant's choice of narrative voice betrays some of the crudities in his first experiments with such structures. Instead of centering the text upon protagonist Paul Baron's first-person account, which would enhance the psychological thrust of the story, the author employs a third-person narrator. Consequently, this objective technique inordinately shifts the balance of the reader's attention toward the external phenomena that impinge upon Baron's fragile vanity and away from the internal reshaping of his vision.

Nevertheless, "La Femme de Paul" contains many earmarks of helical structures. Foremost among these is Maupassant's adroitness in preparing us to accept why Baron cannot resolve his plight. In essence, we see all the machinations of his cognitively dissonant moment. He must juxtapose his bourgeois past against a sexual arena unconventional in his eyes. On the one hand, Maupassant emphasizes that Baron is a senator's son, bearing an air befitting the staid customs of his class. Even his affair with Madeleine accentuates his adherence to a conservative tradition rather than representing a departure from it. Initially, his only deviation is, perhaps, that he loves her too much.

Tacitly opposing Baron's fixed sexual mores is the lesbian society at La Grenouillère, a spa on the Seine. Using helical principles, Maupassant details how this world engulfs Paul Baron's. After establishing the milieu—"toute l'écume du monde, toute la crapulerie distinguée, toute la moisissure de la société parisienne" (M1, 1:294; all the scum of the world, all the distinguished villains, all the mold from Paris society)—and the circumstances for Baron's presence there, the text traces his descent into despair as he confronts each new assault upon his masculine self-image. When four women in a canoe paddle by, they are jeered by the locals, which incites Baron's own indignation. Even Madeleine's embarrassment and anger about his protestations fail to quiet him. Only his sensibility has been frightened so far. His inability to read the true import underlying Madeleine's retorts indicates that he perceives a threat only to a world seemingly forever foreign to his own.

Subsequently, after the police question and dismiss the four women, Madeleine recognizes one as her friend Pauline.[6] Despite

---

6. Obviously, Maupassant intended to establish criteria for us to compare "Paul"

(and because of) Baron's insistent forbiddance, Madeleine renews her acquaintance with the woman. The attack thus becomes more personal for Baron. Consciously, he can see only Madeleine's defiance; he cannot yet admit her bisexuality to himself. The situation rouses an indefinite sensation of jealousy that prompts him to realize for the first time the depth of his love for his mistress, symbolized by one of Maupassant's most heavy-handed analogies: Baron's identification with a fish as he sees it gutted.

Each successive event suggests more strongly Madeleine's other sexual self, revelations that induce increasingly frantic responses in Baron. He attends Pauline's party solely because of Madeleine's threat to end their relationship otherwise. His suspicions about his mistress's unfaithfulness are reinforced by her disappearance from the festivities and are confirmed when he discovers her embracing Pauline. Unable to cope with the loss of her love, with the inability of his male ego to compete with a woman, with circumstances that exceeded his imagination, Baron becomes locked within a perceptual circle:

> Alors il eut une envie immense de fuir, de ne pas voir, de ne pas savoir, de se sauver pour toujours, loin de cette passion furieuse qui le ravageait. Il allait retourner à Chatou, prendre le train, et ne reviendrait plus, ne la reverrait plus jamais. Mais son image brusquement l'envahit, et il l'aperçut en sa pensée quand elle s'éveillait au matin, dans leur lit tiède, se pressait câline contre lui, jetant ses bras à son cou, avec ses cheveux répandus, un peu mêlés sur le front, avec ses yeux fermés encore et ses lèvres ouvertes pour le premier baiser; et le souvenir subit de cette caresse matinale l'emplit d'un regret frénétique et d'un désir forcené. (M1, 1:305)

> (Then he had a strong urge to flee, blindly, unconsciously, saving himself forever, far from this intense, devastating passion. He had to return to Chatou, take the train, and never return, never think about her again. But suddenly her image invaded his thoughts, and he thought about the moment each

---

Baron to "Pauline," which suggests interesting thematic parallels with Poe's "William Wilson," adding to it a feminine principle.

morning when she awoke, snuggling against him in their warm bed, throwing her arms around his neck, with her hair strewn, her bangs slightly tangled, her eyes still closed, and her lips opened for the first kiss; and the sudden memory of that morning embrace filled him with frenzied regret and mad desire.)

This violent debate within himself obliterates all other facets of existence for him. Fueled by ever-diminishing hopes, the insanity of the moment compels relief at any price; consequently, young Baron drowns himself in first self-pity and then the river. Entrapped by its noetic limitations, his spirit progresses realistically from security to despondency. Whether or not we accept Baron's suicide as an appropriate response to his dilemma, the structure of the story justifies its psychological inevitability. In sum, Maupassant challenges the timeworn notion that the human intellect has an inherent ennobling quality because of its potential. In Maupassant's view, given sufficient provocation the mind remains powerless to resolve any meaningful spiritual crisis. Instead, such quandaries threaten to dash all pretension, to limit vision itself, to regress a soul into illusions of infinite despair.

Several stories published in 1884 demonstrate Maupassant's tighter handling of descending helical structures. In "Un lâche" (A coward), for example, he superimposes a minute account of the Viscount Signoles's psychological tumble into despair in order to stultify the audience's surprise over the fop's ultimate suicide. Written early in the year, the story retains Maupassant's early reluctance to employ first-person narrators. Unlike "Le Femme de Paul," however, "Un lâche" devotes itself almost exclusively to the succession of fears in Signoles's contemplations on his plight.[7] In "La Femme," we saw a battle of wills among Baron, Madeleine, Pauline, and, at times, society itself. Consequently, the bitterness in Baron's spiritual descent is diluted when set within a social context. In "Un lâche," after a brief exposition to establish the circumstances that prompted the challenge to a duel, Maupassant devotes the rest of the text exclusively to revealing the subcurrents of Signoles's para-

7. In his textual notes for Contes et nouvelles, Louis Forestier records that Maupassant's first title for the story (published in La Gaulois on 27 January 1884) was the suggestively ambivalent interrogative "Un lâche?" (1:1625).

noia. As a result, the limited omniscience of the narrator provides us with an uncensored account of the protagonist's deliberations.

Signoles's periodic outbursts confirm the accuracy of the descriptive sentences, but the narrator tacks ironic portents to his subject's anguished statements. For example, after first ignoring his fear of death through his subliminal defenses, Signoles finally apprehends the heart of his anxiety:

> . . . tout d'un coup cette pensée entra en lui à la façon d'une balle:
> "Après-demain, à cette heure-ci, je serai peut-être mort."
> Et son coeur se remit à battre furieusement. (M1, 1:1163)

> (. . . suddenly this thought entered his brain like a bullet:
> "The day after tomorrow, at this hour, I shall perhaps be dead."
> And his heart again began to beat madly.)

In emphasizing a mirror in this scene, the narrator reinforces the dominant pattern of self-contemplation in helicals. When hypochondriac Signoles sticks out his tongue to check its coat, the act reminds us that he himself instigated the duel by taking offense over a trifling event. Consequently, his own actions threaten to strip off his social mask, which would leave only the true cowardice of his inner being for all to view. The image *balle* metaphorically predicts his future. And his own premonition of death will be carried out not by his opponent but ironically by his own hand.

Trapped within its own confines, his mind alternates between contemplating the social disgrace of not fulfilling the challenge and the possibility of death if he does. As is typical in helical stories, his reason becomes engulfed by an unresolvable infinite circle of meditation. In lieu of normal mental processes, Signoles develops a pseudologic, which ultimately compels him to choose suicide. Curiously enough, the bullet he fires into his head assures his death and social opprobrium, the two outcomes he professedly wanted to avoid. Without the psychological insight provided by the text, we would be as mystified by Signoles's death as his peers must be, who have only the abortive, blood-spattered note for an explanation: "Ceci est mon testament" (M1, 1:1166; This is my will).

Maupassant improved his handling of helical patterns with subsequent stories, including "Un fou" (1885, A madman).[8] Among
other features, "Un fou" demonstrates his newfound ability to infuse
first-person narratives with a changing personality. Unlike "Un
lâche," where the omniscient narrator highlighted the quirks in
Signoles's behavior, "Un fou" depends upon the protagonist's be-
trayal of his own murderous proclivities. The narrative succeeds in
vivifying the intensity of psychological portraiture. Essentially, in
"Un lâche" the narrator functions as a teacher in our attempt to
fathom the darker recesses of the mind; in our glimpse of a madman's diary in "Un fou," Maupassant permits our illusion that we
observe and theorize alone. And since it is usual for the casual critic
to celebrate mimesis above all other literary values, the text of the
journal, although fictional, still strikes us as authentic. Within only
two years, Maupassant rediscovered that Poe's marriage of a madman's monologue with a helical structure was the best of unions,
maximizing the impact of a tale upon the reader's literary sensibility.

"Un fou" does have a brief third-person preface that addresses
several of Maupassant's habitual concerns in presenting monologues. First, he often felt the necessity to "justify" how thoughts so
private, obviously never meant for public consumption, have found
their way into print. The very fallacy that we are privy to an
uncensored noetic truth augments our belief in the account's inherent realism. On another level, Maupassant often employed such
prefaces to establish the sound psychological plateau from which
the protagonist fell. Generally, the monologue would fail to set up
this initial point adequately because the madman cannot convinc-
ingly brag about his sane past. With the necessity of psychological
descent in helical patterns, then, Maupassant would often frame a
monologue with sparse passages that permit us to discern the cognitive dissonance in human personality.

The dual perspectives in "Un fou" consist of the public versus the
egocentric image of a jurist. The preface paints a respectful portrait
of a high-court judge, whose funeral elicits lofty eulogies nation-
wide. Against this superficial backdrop, the narrator presents a
document found secreted amid the judge's personal files, kept sug-

8. "Un fou" should not be confused with a story published in 1884 similarly
entitled "Un fou?"

gestively with his case histories of great criminals. Titled with a cryptic "Pourquoi?" the manuscript details in annalistic form the protagonist's increasing mania to commit murder for its own sake. In almost two dozen entries recorded within a year's time, the diary traces how the judge's very intelligence creates the discordant seed that in the end alienates his inner self from his social renown.

The seed proves to be the judge's initial inability to explain one of his cases, that of a man who killed his five children. Over the following week, this contemplation sprouts into philosophical musings about the biological origins of man's aggressive intincts. Adhering to offshoots of Darwinian theory especially prevalent in the works of his naturalistic peers, Maupassant has his judge reflect how the impulse to kill appears to be universal among beasts, men, and man's institutions. This sprout matures over the next several months into increasingly cynical perspectives that parallel the judge's unquenchable thirst to commit murder. He first yields to his monomania by slashing his servant's pet bird. His crimes soon flower into random homicidal acts, impulsively strangling a child and clubbing a fisherman. Ironically, he presides over the trial of the person accused of killing the fisherman, which allows him to commit another murder by sending an innocent man to the guillotine.

The helical pattern of the judge's descent into madness starts and ends with his executing his legal responsibilities. He has regressed, though, from idle musings of killing as a creative act to malignant delight in satisfying maniacal compulsions. Before the jurist's death the public respected his disposition of both cases. Only after his journal was found could they (and we) comprehend the complex meshing of a warped spirit with social respectability. If we accept the validity of this possibility, Maupassant has planted in us a propensity to mistrust the motivations of anyone who appears altruistic, dignified, or self-righteous. Essentially, we now must entertain the chance that curious and wicked thoughts may underlie acts for the public good, thus threatening our very faith in man's foundation for progress.

After his many experiments during 1884 and 1885, Maupassant perfected his own conception of helical patterns with "Le Horla" (1887).[9] Superficially, the story resembles "Un fou." The text con-

___

9. A shorter and substantively different version of "Le Horla" had appeared earlier in Gil Blas on 26 October 1886. Comparing both works beyond the superficial changes,

sists of four months' worth of journal entries recorded by a man as he lapses into deepening paranoia. This time, however, Maupassant felt comfortable enough with the monologue not to frame it with an omniscient voice to expose circumstances. By limiting our vision to the narrator's testimony, Maupassant finally achieves the irresolvable supernatural-insanity dichotomy that Poe had employed repeatedly. Although the text manipulates us into believing the diarist suffers from progressing mental dissolution, we cannot establish conclusively whether the spectral Horla exists in fact or fantasy. In essence, the Horla exists as two parallel but different interpretive story lines that amazingly depend upon a single text.[10]

The span of "Le Horla," about treble the length of "Un fou," suggests the growing sophistication of Maupassant's insight into mental illness, a product of both clinical and personal observation.[11] For example, the rate of mental disintegration is not so uniform as

---

Micheline Besnard-Coursodon correctly assesses the major difference between them as a profound shift from an exterior point of view on madness to an interior one. See *Etude thématique et structurale de l'oeuvre de Maupassant: Le piège* (Paris: A.-G Nizet, 1973), 192–95. Forestier suggests that Maupassant moves from a social context to a physiological and psychological egomania; see M1, 2:1619–20.

10. Besnard-Coursodon (*Etude thématique*, 272) suggests that Maupassant's use of the supernatural does not necessarily exclude him from the realm of literary realists. He proposes, in fact, that the spectral phenomena in Maupassant's work may have composed a new prospectus for symbolic realism.

11. There has been much controversy over the extent to which Maupassant's syphilis affected the quality and drift of his fiction. Michael G. Lerner documents testimonial evidence from Maupassant's valet in order to assert that the writer was not mad when he composed "Le Horla." He concludes that the "story indicates not Maupassant's insanity but his closer conformity to the taste of his sophisticated readers, who sought new sensations and new pleasures in the increasingly amoral climate of wealth and self-indulgence." See *Maupassant* (New York: George Braziller, 1975), 220. In a typical biographical reading of "Le Horla," Wallace sees a progression ending with the horror tale: "The notoriety of *Le Horla* tends to dazzle us so that we do not see all the works behind it and of which it represents the perfect culmination. In the beginning he had treated madness as someone else's problem; *Le Horla* treats madness as his own problem" (104; see also 137–38). As one might expect, Schasch proposes even a stronger biographical parallel (*Guy de Maupassant*, 92). Chessex suggests that the insidious spread of the disease tallies with Maupassant's growing cynicism (*Maupassant et les autres*, 23–24). I take a somewhat middle ground. On the one hand, I cannot see syphilis as the controlling metaphor throughout the Maupassant canon. On the other, his illness led to external and internal observations that proved on occasion to be rather useful in challenging his audience's sensibilities or expectations. Also, the symbolic discourse of fiction permitted him a conscious and subconscious outlet to relieve a little of the psychological stress he faced almost daily.

in previous helical monologues. Unaware of the applicability of his words to his own case, the narrator offers the reader several appropriate metaphors that describe the variable pace of decaying intellects:

> [Les fous] parlaient de tout avec clarté, avec souplesse, avec profondeur, et soudain leur pensée, touchant l'écueil de leur folie, s'y déchirait en pièces, s'éparpillait et sombrait dans cet océan effrayant et furieux, plein de vagues bondissantes, de brouillards, de bourrasques, qu'on nomme "la démence."
> (M1, 2:927–28)

> (Madmen converse quite clearly, easily and profoundly, but suddenly their thoughts collide with the reef of madness, dashing them to pieces, scattering and submerging them in a terrifying and furious ocean, full of billowing waves, fogs and squalls, which we call "insanity.")

The Horla apparently takes up residence as the evil genius of the narrator's ancestral home along the Seine near Rouen. Consequently, the *ebb* and *flow* of his fits of anxiety coincide with his travels and his return to home.[12] In a sense, then, Maupassant found that his redesigned approach to helical structures, more than any other short-story form, tallied with his darker personal experiences.

This sustained cycle of surging and receding madness represents one of Maupassant's few true innovations in form itself. With it, he confirms that no single incident, change, or revelation qualifies as a significant moment in descending helical texts. In fusing dual perspectives, Maupassant concedes that the decisive moment that tips our vision one way or another must be made according to our individual prejudices. The helix, then, differs from loops or inversions in that the entire text dilates one significant event: the transition of a mind from reason to self-delusion. Through form, then, he asserts that radical changes in behavior are not the product of instantaneous responses to a personal crisis but of agonizing refor-

---

12. In *A Woman's Revenge: The Chronology of Dispossession in Maupassant's Fiction* (Lexington, Ky.: French Forum, 1986), 72, Mary Donaldson-Evans notes the suggestiveness in the narrator's temporary recovery when he is *"away* from his home" (italics in original).

mations in philosophy, perception, or intellect itself under the threatened assault by external realities.

The gradations among the levels of the narrator's sanity are deliberately and precisely wrought. No leg of his metamorphic journey into madness ever risks falling into a precipice. To establish his protagonist's sane past, Maupassant begins the tale with a journal entry replete with blissful musings about a spring day. The narrator misinterprets the only discordant note to the scene: the passage of a Brazilian frigate that he will later blame for importing the Horla, which perhaps signifies the xenophobic roots of his malady.[13] For now, though, caressed by desultory euphoria, he salutes the vessel as an apotheosis of a rare moment's ocular and emotional splendor.

His mysterious fever and anxiety during the following days prompt the first of his philosophical meditations on the possibility of a world invisible to our own. The growing involution of these sophistries directly corresponds with the progression of his mental dissolution. In developing the narrator's theory from a vague conception of something unfathomable interacting with tangible existence to the precise embodiment of the Horla and its specific threat to his character's sanity, Maupassant evinces how rationalization accompanies perceptual transfigurations. The victim's invariable intellectual skepticism when first confronted by a human enigma dilates his philosophical conversion into horrific belief in the supernatural. Even during his remissions while vacationing away from Rouen, he encounters phenomena and explanations that he will eventually incorporate into his radical reinterpretation of man's lot. A chance meeting with a monk, who knows of local legends about demonic possessions, subsequently fuels the narrator's fiery digressions. In a sane respite, he witnesses the ability of a hypnotist to manipulate a relative. Long after this episode he draws despondent conclusions about the violability of human will, making him fear the inherently superior Horla all the more. In truth, his phantasmophobia does counterpoint his intellect's inability to incorporate exterior phenomena within its hermetic confines.

Nuance by nuance, then, Maupassant prepares the reader to accept

13. There has been much critical ink spilt over the etymology for Maupassant's coining of the name *Horla*. In advocating the traditional and most plausible explanation—that Maupassant corrupted *hors-là*—Chambers stresses the exteriority (or the foreign nature) of the apparition ("*La Lecture comme hantise*," 111).

the penultimate manifestation of his character's compulsive rejection of reality: in his apocalyptic struggle with the unseen enemy,
he torches his ancestral home, symbolically severing ties with his
heritage and physically killing his servants through his failing to
warn them. Whether it be a true ghost or the symptom of a diseased
mind, the Horla survives the holocaust, forcing its quarry to admit
the futility of the battle. In fragmented sentences that betray his
weariness, the narrator ends his journal with his decision to escape,
continuing his struggle against possession (by either the Horla or
insanity) through killing himself. His suicide completes the final
twist of the helix. The ruined landscape that constitutes his last
glimpse in life is his ironic physical and allegorical reinterpretation
of the same Edenic garden he treasured four months earlier.

Helical stories do not always map out such precipitous psychological cliff-dives. Maupassant's last significant employment of this
pattern, "Allouma" (1889), deals with more subtle shifts in moral
perspective on several levels. The primary focus of the text concerns
the mutable relationship between expatriate Auballe and his Arabian
mistress, Allouma. The first-person narrator prefaces his host's monologue with a history of Auballe's rakish past in France, which
dissipated his fortune and forced him to settle in Algeria. Responding to a query about how he copes with cultural isolation, Auballe
notes the incremental manner of his social acclimation

> . . . on se fait à ce pays, et puis on finit par l'aimer. Vous ne
> sauriez croire comme il prend les gens par un tas de petits
> instincts animaux que nous ignorons en nous. Nous nous y
> attachons d'abord par nos organes à qui il donne des satisfac-
> tions secrètes que nous ne raisonnons pas. L'air et le climat
> font la conquête de notre chair, malgré nous, et la lumière
> gaie dont il est inondé tient l'esprit clair et content, à peu de
> frais. Elle entre en nous à flots, sans cesse, par les yeux, et on
> dirait vraiment qu'elle lave tous les coins sombres de l'âme.
> (M1, 2:1098).

> (. . . you grow accustomed to this country, and then you end
> up loving it. You cannot believe how it possesses people
> through arousing a lot of small animal instincts that we ignore
> in ourselves. At first, we become attached to it through our

senses, which nurture secret and ineffable satisfactions. The air and climate conquer our flesh, in spite of ourselves, and the intoxicated light that floods [the land] effortlessly keeps our spirits clear and clean. It continuously streams into us through our eyes, and I can truthfully say it cleanses all the dingy corners of the soul.)

His understanding of sexual realities in his new world progressed at a similar rate. His initial meeting with Allouma is complicated by his European expectations and his uncertainty about Arab values. At the heart of his anxiety lies his inability to decipher his servant's motivation or emotion in ceding Allouma to him. But the unfathomable woman herself symbolically encompasses all his frustrations.[14] Allouma's periodic, mysterious disappearances continually vex Auballe, but his old cosmopolitan view of women fades a little more each time she returns. Even when his mistress finally runs away with a shepherd, Auballe responds under his revised dual perspective. His European past mandates that he feel anger at yet another instance of Allouma's infidelity, but his Algerian present superimposes his desire for her return. Together the two attitudes mesh into a philosophy of fatalism that strives toward stoicism.

The Auballe we understand at the conclusion of the text is an ironic reversal of the man we first encounter. In France, Auballe controlled all the factors in his dealings with women. In Algeria, Allouma usurps what he once considered male prerogatives. Despite Auballe's attempts to dominate, Allouma is the one who determines the depth and duration of their affair. She, not he, has the freedom to pursue other lovers and to return to Auballe at her whim. Perhaps befitting the usual reaction to a descending helical structure, "Allouma" must have elicited in the 1889 French audience a sensation that Auballe's final attitude was tainted slightly by madness in that his exposure to a differing moral system had irrevocably alienated him from "pristine" European values.

What makes the foreignness of Auballe—which he himself fails to realize—more palatable to us is the narrator's role as a mediator

---

14. Donaldson-Evans sees the character Allouma as just one of several Maupassantian women who have each "become an isolated microcosm, basically unpossessable, sufficient unto herself, vain and egotistical [whose] conduct is often motivated by her vanity" (A Woman's Revenge, 117).

between the reader and the anecdote. Unlike earlier efforts, the prefatory material in "Allouma" actually extends the helical pattern. As the lost narrator wanders through the countryside of Algeria, his symbolically rich descriptions immerse us within a relatively barbarous world.[15] Maupassant obviously expects the narrator's readjustment to initiate a temporary suspension by his cosmopolitan readers of their own ethical considerations. The narrator's awe of his new vista provides us with a reference point by which we can later accept the dual motivations underlying Auballe's behavior.

Interestingly, Maupassant's last major employment of the helical pattern detailed perceptual shifts still confined by reason. The sophisticated structure of "Le Horla" has counterpoints in "Allouma." The rhythm of Auballe's relationship with Allouma parallels the undulating lapses of the narrator of "Le Horla" into mental decay. Xenophobic elements comprise the seed of these declines through the Horla's Brazilian-ness and Allouma's Arabian-ness. At the close of his writing career, Maupassant applied his insight into madness on a smaller scale. Life itself had become a continuous struggle for sanity. If one escapes the fate of a schizophrenic, he must still cope with a regressing vision against an intrinsically maddening existence. The extrinsic will always threaten the intrinsic, and the threat itself disheartens even the most buoyant of spirits.

The Contrast Story

Helical structures permitted Maupassant to distend a psychological turning point over the length of a text. As its essential movement entails the passage from truth to fantasy, no single incident forges its way past any other within the reader's perception. Consequently, we seldom witness a detailed account of a protagonist's life before

15. In "Beginning to Understand the Narrative 'Come-On' in Maupassant's Stories," *Neophilologus* 68 (1984): 37–47, Mary Donaldson-Evans traces Maupassant's personal development in constructing such "preambles"; that is, a passage that appears at the start of a story, permitting the reader to fix scene, time, character, circumstance, etc. She concludes, quite perceptively, that during the course of his career, Maupassant exhibited greater and greater control over an introduction, enabling him to invoke more meaningful metaphors and to tighten the passage's integrative position vis-à-vis the main body of the text.

or following the bloated significant moment. Maupassant usually tosses off his subject's sane past in a few tersely summarizing paragraphs. Since helical paths often end at death, he seldom continued a narrative beyond the character's demise; at most he provided a cursory sentence or two on the community's wonder in uncovering the secrets of a decaying soul.

In opposition to these analytical effects, a *contrast* structure reaffirms the interpretive integrity of a condensed significant moment. A contrast text resembles a helical pattern in that both deal with the mutable foundations of insight, but a contrast story shifts our focus away from the change itself to the consequences of that change. Such texts demand more analytical energy from the reader. The author expects us to compare beliefs, circumstances, or behavioral responses occurring before a critical point with a parallel phenomenon that follows such an event. Through the surreptitious manipulation of the writer, who depends on our human instinct to assume superiority, we link the differences we detect to the significant moment. With false pride, we praise our own insight into causation. In truth, Maupassant tricks us into adopting his interpretive position. Adhering to the rules of short-story economy, he reduces the text to a phenomenological account, allowing our creativity to bridge the hermeneutical gaps.

More than any other form, the contrast story became the dominant structural pattern in what twentieth-century writers and critics would call the lyric short story. Most of these men and women declared themselves disciples of Maupassant's contemporary Chekhov, evidently ignoring the scores of such stories in the Frenchman's canon. Outnumbering surprise-inversions by at least a factor of three, contrast stories were still eclipsed in popularity by their textual cousins. In some ways, contrasts can be seen as extensions of inversion stories, repositioning a vital revelation from the end of a text to its middle, diluting the perceptual shock. One dimension of the "superiority" of the lyric, its greater ability to develop character, owes its subtlety to the author's digressions upon the consequences of change, which suggests that the differences between the "trick" and the lyric text are not so profound as short-story theorists would like us to believe.

In his quest to diversify his artistic sensibilities, Maupassant soon found that contrasts sparked the central impulse of his literary experience. During his most fruitful years, he explored this form more than any other. In his later work, some interpretive aspect of the contrast invariably underlies the theme of a story. By 1883, most of his notions about other short-story forms apparently became variations of the contrast, which toyed with the significant event's placement, dimensions, and number. In that contrasts almost always invite differing perspectives toward similar episodes, cognitive dissonance thus became the controlling artistic direction in the Maupassant canon, betraying his early skepticism that truth or even vision itself can ever be conclusive.

Maupassant gathered the concepts of the contrast form from no single source. Most of his primary and secondary mentors practiced it at one time or another. It was popular among his realist and emerging naturalist contemporaries in France, including Zola's artistic school to which Maupassant pledged himself early in his career. In fact, though, the contrast seems to owe its origin to a genre older than the modern short story. While other short-fiction forms make use of Aristotelian theory, the contrast depends upon a conceptual abridgment of the notion of the turning point in classical tragedy. Beside his direct interest in the theater, Maupassant also demonstrated his knowledge of drama in his fiction. Several of his stories read as if they were synopses of formulaic five-act plays.[16]

Aside from the pyramidal movement of such texts, the contrast story of the 1880s takes several liberties with Aristotle's observations about form. First, complication and denouement may play a factor, but a successful text may omit melodramatic progressions of plot. Instead, the contrast depends upon descriptions of scene, character, circumstance, or human reaction. The significant point, placed between depictions of parallel phenomena, permits the reader to compare. The spatial shift of focus to midtext (when compared to loops and inversions) reduces its potential to dominate the reader's memory of the plot. By elaborating on its effects, Maupassant makes the turning point less monstrous, suggesting that significance does not arise from within its own perimeters but is a product of its context.

In a second important liberty, Maupassant's contrast stories vary

16. For example see "Histoire d'une fille de ferme" (1881, Story of a farm girl) and "Le Père" (1883, The father).

the application of Aristotle's definition of the turning point in his *Poetics*. The traditional concepts of anagnorisis and peripeteia do not always coexist in the Maupassant contrast text. In addition, the changes in fortune may be slight or even nonexistent. Characters may be incapable of perceiving any change in their plight. If they discover some elemental truth about their own lives, they often cannot alter their behavior in response. Faced with the rigidity of diurnal life, a protagonist now feels that his suffering intensifies with his deeper insight into the bleakness of existence.

Whether or not these effects occur, Maupassant still depends upon classical notions, but he reroutes their impact more emphatically toward the reader. The essential consequence of the contrast's significant event is that it arouse our own sense of discovery. This intellectual stimulation should not hang upon our empathic link with a central character. Often, Maupassant demands that we see ramifications that are beyond the perceptual capabilities of the victim and his fictional peers. Relying on our analytical astuteness, the author expects us to recognize the significant point, to bifurcate the text, to compare similar phenomena from each half, and to gain insight. Given the product of such cognizance in his fiction, however, I suspect that Maupassant believed that despite its aura of enlightenment, our proper recognition of truth will ultimately lead us to grimmer assessments of the human condition. In a sense, a continual reading of contrast texts might evoke an incremental degeneration of spirit, paralleling the psychic descent Maupassant detailed in helical stories. As we expand our knowledge of human nature, we ironically imprison ourselves in despair.

In itself, Maupassant's extensive employment of contrast structures refutes the modern assessment of him as a writer prone to trick endings. True, his admirer Chekhov would perfect the form. ("The Kiss" is one of the finest examples of a contrast story in the genre.) On the other hand, Maupassant's playfulness with textual organization allowed him to explore side paths never traveled by the Russian. With rather inspired artistry Maupassant would occasionally relocate the temporal coordinates of a significant point outside the time frame of a narrative. We do not necessarily need a diptych text to excite our analytical proclivities. Skillfully coordinated parallel incidents can produce similar observations, leading to similar conclusions. Despite such experimentation, the contrast story tended to reflect Maupassant's imprecise resignation to Schopenhauerian nihilism. Properly arranged, the contrast elements in the Maupassant canon possibly isolate numerous spiritually regressive responses to his own life. If helical texts permit us our illusion about how Maupassant saw the broad patterns of his life, then contrasts fix the individual moments of his sobering bathos over man's lot.[17]

Before 1885, these moments seemed more often stimulated by external sources than generated exclusively by some internal impulse. These early stories provide evidence of Maupassant's eclectic and broad interests in intellectual fads, particularly in any new philosophic, biological, or political theory that attempted to fathom human behavior. "Aux champs" (In the country), for example, is on one level a thinly disguised social-Darwinist treatise. At issue is the effect environment plays upon the well-being of two boys, Charlot Tuvache and Jean Vallin. Unlike his scientific contemporaries, however, Maupassant wished to measure perceptual more than material differences.

On the surface "Aux champs" is a typical local-color story of Normandy. We can see Maupassant waver between idolatry of rustic simplicity and mean-spirited depiction of avarice. At first, the Tuvaches' fatalistic acceptance of their poverty has a blissful tinge of innocence about the possibility of a better life. Simple meals suffice for daily subsistence, and a modest addition of meat on Sundays is treasured as a feast. Throughout the first half of the text Maupassant carefully draws a prelapsarian existence with deft strokes of psychological insight.

Into this Eden, though, slithers an ironically inverted symbol of the serpent, a childless couple, M. and Mme. d'Hubières, who wish to adopt Charlot. Heroically, the Tuvaches rebuff Mme. d'Hubières' offer of a sizeable pension for them and her promise to make their son a rich man. This incident proves to be the crux of the plot, for the couple subsequently adopts one of the three Vallin boys, Jean, whose parents, like the Tuvaches, seem repulsed at first by the idea of selling their son but whose Norman greed ultimately drives them to haggle over his price.

17. Marie-Claire Bancquart sees similar fragmentation in Maupassant's vision and concludes that this tendency to isolate contributed to his "dégradation du Moi" (degradation of the Self). See her *Maupassant conteur fantastique*. Archives des lettres modernes [63] (Paris: Minard, 1976), 70.

In overview, Mme. d'Hubières randomly chooses between identical commodities, two boys who probably would have lived and died as poor farmers like their fathers. Early in the text, Maupassant suggests through their parents' symbol-laden confusion that we think of both children in the same terms:

> Les deux mères distinguaient à peine leurs produits dans le tas; et les deux pères confondaient tout à fait. Les huit noms dansaient dans leur tête, se mêlaient sans cesse; et, quand il fallait en appeler un, les hommes souvent en criaient trois avant d'arriver au véritable. (M1, 1:607)

> (Both mothers hardly recognized their own offspring in the brood, and both fathers confused them completely. The eight names danced in their heads, always in a dizzying whirl; and when they had to call for one, the men often shouted three times before finding the right name.)

Obviously, Maupassant wants to set up the fictional ingredients for an ideal social experiment. Two socially equal beings have their destinies separated by accident. The results of the experiment—that is, each other's perception at maturity of the quality of his life—invite us to compare.

The irony in the denouement is that the family that exhibited nobler sentiments in the situation, the Tuvaches, suffer for not taking a bite of the apple. Since they refuse to allow Charlot to leave their Eden, the garden disintegrates around him, not materially but perceptually. Through the years, the security that the pension provides for the Vallin family instills only resentment in Charlot over his own poverty. When the adult Jean returns to visit his family, parading all the advantages of wealth and status, Charlot's latent jealousy erupts as he rebukes his parents for not giving him away years ago. He ends his tirade by leaving into the night, calling them "Manants" (hicks). The life-style that decades ago amply fulfilled marginal expectations for contentment now only inspires hopelessness and envy. Serving its purpose, the significant point that divides the text recedes in the reader's memory, leaving us with a strange syllogism: not maternal devotion but cupidity led to happiness. Based upon a momentary reflection amid his whimsical sampling of liberal ideas, Maupassant illustrates how the laws of survival in an economic jungle have consumed Christian ethics in the modern world, an insight that permits us to fix the coordinates of one early moment along the curve that traces the degeneration of his spirit.

The capriciousness of Maupassant's convictions becomes apparent in subsequent publications. For example, whereas in "Aux champs" Maupassant uses contemporary socioeconomic theory to attack Western traditions of family values, he reverses circumstances in "Les Bijoux" (1883, The jewels): the successful pursuit of economic survival leads the protagonist beyond the brink of emotional ruin. The two texts parallel each other in that their characters move from comfortable innocence to uneasy awareness. But Charlot Tuvache frets over alternative possibilities for his past while M. Lantin of "Les Bijoux" must reinterpret the past he thought he knew. For Maupassant, however, "Les Bijoux" does not signal a thorough artistic, philosophical, or political refutation of "Aux champs"; it just details some transient impression of ennui directed against bourgeois materialism.

The key point in this contrast story divides Lantin's two perspectives of his first wife as well as of her apparent costume jewelry. In fact, his accidental discovery of the true worth of her jewels formulates the inflection points of his vision and the text. One interesting variation in the story, which Maupassant occasionally employed in his fiction, is the tactic of permitting the reader to see in advance of the dense Lantin. Thus, although the husband treasures the memory of his dead wife, we see all the clues to her double life: her inordinate love for costume jewelry; her ruse of going to the theater; her management of her spouse's finances, which permitted luxuries beyond his means. Although Lantin's happiness blinds him, our suspicions are soon confirmed that Mme. Lantin supplemented the couple's income as either a mistress or a prostitute: after her death, Lantin struggled to live alone on an income he thought had sufficed for two.

Essentially, Maupassant has placed disparate discovery points in the text for his audience and for Lantin. In preparing us to expect the revelation, the author compels us to continue reading the text through the ordinary technique of suspense. We wait for Lantin's understanding to match our own. Driven by poverty he tries to sell his dead wife's "false" gems. When apprised by a jeweler of a necklace's true value, the husband seeks another opinion.[18] Because of Maupassant's manipulation we react with frustration at Lantin's slow-witted comprehension of the realities of his past, which sets him up as an object to be ridiculed. Thus, in the denouement of the story, we are more prone to accept Maupassant's position as he broadens his attack to other sociological phenomena.

This attack depends upon layers of interpretive contrasts that the author builds in the text. The objects that Lantin once had playfully chided his wife for admiring now become the means for his economic survival, but he pays an emotional price. He can no longer remember his wife with the same blissful ignorance. Meanwhile, as in a fish story, he continually inflates the worth of the entire jewelry collection to each passerby, betraying his subconscious difficulty in substituting ever-increasing fictions of material wealth in the place of a pleasant illusion about the past. As many other Maupassant characters do, Lantin reacts complicatedly; he simultaneously values the financial significance of the jewels and resents their symbolic import. He subsequently marries a "très honnête [femme avec] un caractère difficile [qui] le fit beaucoup souffrir" (M1, 1:771; a very honest, demanding woman who made him suffer very much).

In essence, Lantin represents what we might have seen in "Aux champs" if Maupassant centered the story on Jean Vallin. We assume that Vallin is happy because our limited vision is governed by Charlot Tuvache's assumptions. We find, however, that elsewhere Maupassant criticized the efficacy of wealth (in "Les Bijoux") and of avarice (in "Première neige" [1883, First snow]). Consequently, the choice made by Mme. d'Hubières damned not only the child she left behind but also perhaps the one she adopted. The bulk of the pre-1885 contrast stories likewise attack both sides of competing social, cultural, and artistic assumptions. Maupassant did not advocate a clearly conceptualized view of nihilism, though. Often, he found one theory to be momentarily serviceable enough to attack another. Nevertheless, truths for him had only vestigial validity, gratifying intellectual whims but satisfying no single creed.

18. The obvious contrast between the real gems believed to be false in "Les Bijoux" and the fake necklace believed to be genuine in "La Parure" has prompted several critics to treat them as thematically complementary stories. The most detailed discussion is Mary Donaldson-Evan's "The Last Laugh: Maupassant's 'Les Bijoux' and 'La Parure,' " French Forum 10 (1985): 163–73.

Eventually, though, Maupassant's contrast stories began to refrain from mere cursory societal or even cosmological nihilism. Starting in 1883, he seemed to sublimate his vague sense of universal decay. This movement did not reflect a naturalistic shift from environmental to biological determinism. Maupassant's frustrations had more personal sources. The contrast structure allowed him to project his nebulous yet perpetual self-dissatisfaction into more definable fictional dilemmas. Characters heroically but ludicrously struggle for personal dignity. The shift in vision created by a central contrast inflection denies the possibility of a protagonist's succeeding psychologically. More and more, the contrast stories mark the continual failure of Maupassant to retain a stable self-image. Thus, interspersed amid his idle attacks upon contemporary thought, we find that Maupassant occasionally used the contrast form to question himself. He only indirectly targets us in such fiction through our sympathy or perhaps empathy.

No doubt one component of his inward futility arose from his battle with syphilis. He probably interpreted the temporary paralysis in one eye during 1883 as yet another manifestation of his disease.[19] On 5 February 1883, under the pseudonym Maufrigneuse he published "Deux amis" (Two friends), ostensibly a testament to the capriciousness and the animalistic brutality of war. The controlling metaphor—several netted fish—suggests a more private symbolic import for the narrative. As his intellectual boutades sporadically invaded his fiction, so did his momentary anxieties over the progression of his venereal disease.

Superficially, the contrast point in "Deux amis" occurs when a Prussian patrol captures two French soldiers on an impromptu country holiday.[20] The incident fuses two apparently disparate perspectives. Initially, Maupassant portrays the hardships that Morissot and Sauvage, the two friends of the title, have to endure in Paris. Meeting by chance on the street, they resolve to relieve their hunger by setting out on a fishing excursion, an activity that revives their friendship and triggers their nostalgia for pre-war France. Finding

---

19. Forestier notes the symptom in his chronology of Maupassant's life; see M1, 1:lxxvii.

20. Morissot and Sauvage are national guardsmen in uniform because of the crisis, not soldiers in the regular army.

their old fishing spot, they successfully resume their once habitual pastime, which arouses a long-dormant sense of pleasure:

> Et une joie délicieuse les pénétrait, cette joie qui vous saisit quand on retrouve un plaisir aimé dont on est privé depuis longtemps. . . . ils n'écoutaient plus rien; il ne pensaient plus à rien; ils ignoraient le reste du monde; ils pêchaient. (M1, 1:735)

> (And a delicious joy overwhelmed them, a familiar sense of rediscovering a long-deprived pleasure. . . . they no longer listened to anything; they thought about nothing; they ignored the rest of the world; they fished.)

The second section of the text, which follows the capture of Morissot and Sauvage, consists of a Prussian officer's interrogation of the two and their subsequent execution. Compelled by the mandates of their military code, the Parisians refuse to reveal the password, thus protecting the security of the French advance guard.

Awaiting the inevitable, Morissot notices his catch lying in the grass: "Et une défaillance l'envahit. Malgré ses efforts, ses yeux s'emplirent de larmes" (M1, 1:737; And he felt faint. Despite his resolve, his eyes filled with tears). The parallels are obvious: like the fish he and his friend were also seized by chance and were now subject to the bidding of a more powerful entity. During his years of fishing Morissot only pursued his own edification, never giving much thought to his catch.[21] The ironic reversal in the status of the Frenchmen reinforces Maupassant's notion of the self-consuming element in man's brutality. As he orders the bodies of the two French soldiers thrown into the river, the Prussian officer sarcastically notes that "[c]'est le tour des poissons maintenant" (M1, 1:738; It is the fishes' turn, now). Interestingly, Maupassant ends the story with the officer's command to his orderly to fry "ces petits animaux-là pendant qu'ils sont encore vivants" (M1, 1:738; these small animals

---

21. Chessex believes that the exposition of "Deux amis" is transparently perverse; (*Maupassant et les autres*, 15). I maintain that such a viewpoint is unlikely during a first reading. We must have the benefit of knowing the entire text before we can appreciate the dualities in symbolism during the first half of the story.

while they're still alive), which completes the theme of helplessness before an omnipotent force.

This sensation of futility in all likelihood paralleled Maupassant's attitude toward a new outbreak of his degenerative affliction. As his eyesight deteriorated during his battle against syphilis, his frustration on a physical level affected his aestheticism. For an artist who preferred to observe others rather than reveal his innermost self, Maupassant likely found himself in a quandary. A contrast structure allowed him to reinsert some distance between himself and his reader. Through it he could evaluate by proxy the perceptual shift brought about by physical pain. Just as his new empathy with the fish forces Morissot to view negatively a once pleasurable diversion, Maupassant's war with syphilis possibly inspired continual melancholic reinterpretations of his own past.[22]

One recurring motif that arose out of young Maupassant's premature contemplations of his own death was the lost possibilities in life. The contrast structure provides the framework for an interesting reversal of the significant moment in the text. Rather than representing a tangible watershed in a character's life, the turning point hinges upon a protagonist failing to seize an opportunity. In the archetypal story of this thematic subgenre, "Regret" (1883), the missed moment involves a sixty-two-year-old man's poignant remembrances of a possibility in his past: an afternoon picnic decades ago when he had the chance to seduce the wife of a friend. Maupassant provides us with ample clues that if M. Saval had pressed his advances upon Mme. Sandres, his infatuation would have been consummated. Out of a turbulent combination of friendship, fear, and propriety, however, Saval yielded to the safety of discretion and accompanied the wife back to her physically and symbolically sleeping husband.

Haunted his whole life by his nostalgia for that one day, the now old, emotionally burnt-out Saval resolves to ask the woman for the truth. The woman informs him that she had always known of his passion for her and thought he was silly to think he could hide it. Had he pursued his desire, "[j]'aurais cédé, mon ami" (M1, 1:1052; I

---

22. In fact, several of Maupassant's war stories manage to yoke syphilis and battle on a variety of analytical levels. In "Le Lit 29," for example, a woman on her deathbed pridefully proclaims that she used her infection as a soldier uses a bullet. This allegorical association may explain the dearth of war themes in Maupassant's later stories, that is, those written after his suffering intensified.

would have yielded, my dear). Occurring late in the text, this discovery assumes the interpretive elements characteristic of a surprise-inversion. Indeed, within Saval's perspective, her revelation does shock his sensibilities. On the reader's level, however, her last statement merely confirms what the author has already strongly hinted, evidence that Saval's egocentric blindness had poorly interpreted during an entire lifetime. Thus, on our level, the revelation cannot shock us; it fades in relative significance, becoming just one more element to compare between contrasting halves of the text.

Maupassant often yoked various structures together, a technique that created his favorite illusion: the reader's appreciation of the proper significance of events proceeds in advance of the limited vision of the characters in a story. Because he deliberately evokes our natural proclivity to feel intellectually superior (in this case, our self-delusion that we are more insightful than the figures we encounter in a text), Maupassant obviously does not target any explicit defect in our analytical vision. Instead, a multiply structured text attacks the depth of quality in that vision. More than any other form, the contrast story permitted Maupassant to set up two parallel though emotionally descending levels of human insight. In other words, the turning point in midtext usually does not represent a momentous shift in the quality of a protagonist's life; it marks only a notable increase in comprehension, invariably pessimistic in nature, about the tragedy underlying each individual reality. Such opinions eventually tap into our subconscious foreboding about the inutility of the human race amid the universal scheme of things. For Maupassant, man may bungle his way into oblivion.

The contrasting parallels in "Regret" illustrate one man's way to void a more propitious destiny. The essential passage in the story's exposition details Saval's despondent summation of his lifelong emptiness:

> Il songe à son existence si nue, si vide. . . . Si encore sa vie avait été remplie! S'il avait fait quelque chose; s'il avait eu des aventures, de grands plaisirs, des succès, des satisfactions de toute sorte. Mais non, rien. Il n'avait rien fait, jamais rien que se lever, manger, aux mêmes heures, et se coucher. Et il était arrivé comme cela à l'âge de soixante-deux ans. (M1, 1:1047–48)

(He reflected upon his wasted, empty existence. . . . If only his life had been more full! If he had done something; if he had experienced adventures, great delights, success, any sort of satisfaction. But no, nothing. He had done nothing more than get up, eat—always at the same times—and go to bed. And with [such monotonous habits] he turned sixty-two years old.)

These contemplations lead inevitably to notions about a lonely death. Conceding his own propensity for indifference, especially in his relationships with women, he cannot imagine any alternative to his grey existence.

During his self-commiseration, he remembers the picnic incident, the one event that colors his memory. Confronting Mme. Sandres, he finally learns the truth, but this discovery does not change his life materially. Entrapped by his own prejudice about the limits age places upon him, Saval never considers trying to recapture her love. As in the beginning, he remains alone, but with a crushing perceptual difference:

> Saval ressortit dans la rue, atterré comme après un désastre. Il filait à grands pas sous la pluie, droit devant lui, descendant vers la rivière, sans songer où il allait. . . . Ses vêtements ruisselaient d'eau, son chapeau déformé, mou comme une loque, dégouttait à la façon d'un toit. Il allait toujours, toujours devant lui. Et il se trouva sur la place où ils avaient déjeuné au jour lointain dont le souvenir lui torturait le coeur.
>
> Alors il s'assit sous les arbres dénudés, et il pleura. (M1, 1:1052)

> (Saval went out again into the street, shattered as if he had been struck by a disaster. With long strides he ran downhill toward the river through the rain, without thinking about where he was going. . . . His clothes were drenched; his misshapen hat, limp like a dishrag, dripped water like rain off a roof. Onward he walked and walked. And he found himself where they had dined so long ago, the memory torturing his heart.
>
> Then he sat under the leafless trees, and he wept.)

Nature anticipates and encourages his tears. We pity not Saval's reticence or his life but his profounder understanding of the disheartening irony that governs human existence. His diurnal routine will continue as before; now, however, he will be haunted by one discarded chance for personal meaning.

The significance of this theme for Maupassant was perhaps double-edged. On one hand, Saval's experience mirrored the author's own regret over missed opportunities during his young life. On the other, Maupassant justifes in a way his social daring. For him, taking chances, whether they ended successfully or in failure, was better than remaining a spectator. Moreover, the contrast structure of such stories produces a similar effect upon his audience. As readers we indulge our inclination for passive observation, sitting silently as the writer conjures his tale. Latently, then, Saval's plight must approximate something fundamental in our own existence. Thus, we at least subconsciously identify with Saval, succumbing by proxy once again to another whimsical attack engineered by Maupassant.

In "Promenade" (1884), Maupassant reiterates how recognizing one's own insidious complacency can drain the will to live. During an impromptu stroll, a bookkeeper named Leras recapitulates his monotonous life. Maupassant painstakingly details how regimented a routine the clerk followed:

> Les jours, les semaines, les mois, les saisons, les années s'étaient ressemblé. A la même heure, chaque jour, il se levait, partait, arrivait au bureau, déjeunait, s'en allait, dînait, et se couchait sans que rien eût jamais interrompu la régulière monotonie des mêmes actes, des mêmes faits et des mêmes pensées. (M1, 2:128)

> (The days, the weeks, the months, the seasons, the years looked alike. At the same hour every day he arose, left for work, arrived at the office, breakfasted, left for home, dined, and went to bed without anything ever interrupting the regularity of these monotonous events, monotonous facts, and monotonous thoughts.)

At first, Leras's dissatisfaction with his life remains vague and rather stoical. Rather than deal with its true causes, he places the blame upon his limited income.

Chance meetings during his excursion force Leras to reevaluate his experience. Along the avenue du Bois-de-Boulogne, he observes a long parade of lovers and is propositioned by several prostitutes. Both events trigger his realization that love never entered his life. Materially nothing changes, psychologically everything explodes:

> Et tout d'un coup, comme si un voile épais se fût déchiré, il aperçut la misère, l'infinie, la monotone misère de son exis-tence: la misère passée, la misère présente, la misère future: les derniers jours pareils aux premiers, sans rien devant lui, rien derrière lui, rien autour de lui, rien dans le coeur, rien nulle part. (M1, 2:131)

> (And suddenly, as if a thick veil had been torn in half, he saw the misery, the infinite and monotonous misery of his life— the misery of the past, the misery of the present, the misery of the future; the last days were like the first, with nothing before him, nothing behind him, nothing around him, nothing in his heart, nothing anywhere.)

After this inflection point in the text's structure, Maupassant parades before us how the shaken Leras reinterprets each facet of his mundane past. His apartment and job, while never luxurious, had formerly been sufficient. Now they seemed lamentable. Every vibrant symbol of Paris itself now reminds Leras of his imprisoned solitude. Even the bookeeper's anagnorisis had to remain noetic. His one profound moment has little meaning for the world that surrounds him, as Maupassant slyly notes: "Le défilé des voitures allait tou-jours" (M1, 2:131; The procession of carriages continued on as always).

Devoid of hope, Leras impulsively hangs himself, yet his death does not surprise us in the manner of an inversion story. The turning point at midtext and the subsequent comparisons it forces us to make prepare us for such an eventuality. Maupassant places before us what no external investigation could reveal: the wondrous con-spiracy of psychological musings that can lead a man rashly to suicide. Again, the contrast structure transforms apparently bizarre phenomena into the raw material for acute insights into human motivation.

Maupassant did not originally constrain his notion of the contrast story to loose diptych structures alone. During his prolific formative years, he experimented with several variations, probably more to avoid the ennui of repetitiveness than to stretch his artistic range. Most of these attempts were derived from popular, almost timeworn, fictional conventions. The modification always lay in Maupassant's transformation of the significant point, usually involving its omission from the text.

In some instances, a quasi-contrast short story manages to avoid addressing individual change. Often, Maupassant intends us to compare two static characters, whose juxtaposition in a single text tends to illustrate both more vividly. Inevitably, such stories unfold the author's attitude of damning both houses. Maupassant's targets are occasionally political. In the humorous "L'Ami Joseph" (1883), for example, a couple loyal to the Royalists must suffer the renewed acquaintance with the husband's college friend, who boisterously supports the Republic. No one changes his or her political beliefs during the friend's stay; in fact, the couple go to the extent of abandoning their summer home, leaving it in the hands of the friend, rather than succumbing to his proselytizing. The confrontation only exposes the personality foibles of both: the couple's incredible reticence and indulgence versus the friend's jovial though tyrannical arrogance. Obviously stereotypes representing political factions, they all come across as buffoons.[23]

In such a story there can be no isolatable turning point in the traditional sense. The contraposition of irreconcilable forces itself constitutes a sort of significant event, one which, given the intransigence of the characters, can never influence their self-perceptions. Instead, the reader—especially Maupassant's Parisian audience during the 1880s—becomes the exclusive recipient of any benefits accrued through such fictional comparisons. Commentaries such as "L'Ami Joseph" cannot effect change in our beliefs, but they do invite self-qualifications in that political fervor seems to generate its own ridicule.

A second common variation of contrast structures stems from an implied rather than an explicit turning point. Again, rather than

---

23. Maupassant's perception of the absurdities in the Royalist-Republican conflict would resurface from time to time in his comic short stories, for example, "Un coup d'État" (1884).

using the single entity of the typical contrast text, Maupassant divides between characters the parallel experience he wants his reader to compare. Frequently, the peripeteia that explains the perceptual disparity between figures over a shared experience involves the gulf dividing generations. Thus, Maupassant projects cognitive dissonance by having characters with differing outlooks analyze one aspect of the human dilemma.

Through various literary devices, the opinions of an older character usually dominate those of a younger one. Sometimes, Maupassant effects such matriarchal superiority (for these dialogues often involve confidences between women) by simply using the techniques and ramifications of a debate within the confines of an epistolary contrast structure. For instance, in "Correspondance" (1882, Letters) a young socialite, Berthe de X., writes to her aunt, Geneviève de Z., complaining among other matters about the pervasiveness of ill manners among the men of her day. In her response the aunt takes the counterposition: "que si les hommes ne sont pas toujours polis, les femmes, par contre, sont toujours d'une inqualifiable grossièreté" (M1, 1:530; that if men are not always courteous, women, by contrast, are always downright vulgar). Assuming the air of one more experienced and thus more wise, although qualified by a bemused cynicism, Geneviève patronizes her niece, attacking Berthe's hasty generalization and insinuating that such views on men betray inelegance.

As in a debate, the aunt benefits by the order of the argument. Competently dismissing each of her niece's points, her rebuttal stands unchallenged, thus leaving the stronger impression upon the reader. Speaking last allows her to presume and assert an authoritative voice, which hints to the niece that in time she will accept her aunt's comments.[24] Consequently, the inversion point of the story exists simultaneously before and after the events covered by the text. Geneviève has already arrived at her distaste for the manners of her own sex; she implies that life will force Berthe toward acknowledging the same.

"Correspondance" and its companion stories offer clues for interesting speculations about Maupassant's theory on the relationship

---

24. Forestier believes that the structure of the text in itself supports Maupassant's nihilistic and pessimistic philosophy; see M1, 1:1455.

between age and belief. He accepts the truism that years must precipitate psychological change. Unlike the typical contrast story, however, the implied turning point in these variations does not depend upon a precipitous event. Rather than shouting "eureka," we gradually recognize some truth about our condition. Such discoveries are often the product of minute psychic reorientations. In "Correspondance" change depended upon the aunt's accepting a more negative interpretation of femininity in order to explain the petty annoyances of life. She rejects her niece's external reason—the intrinsic vulgarity of men—and substitutes a belief that has internal implications: by damning her sex, she tacitly implicates herself in the universal social crimes committed by women.

Obviously, Maupassant uses Geneviève as a mouthpiece for one of his egocentric, masculine attacks upon feminine pretenses, a prejudice that often emerged among his early and middle stories. "Le Baiser" (1882, The kiss) continues the generation themes of "Correspondance." The format is still epistolary, the aunt is now named Colette, but the tone of chastising the naiveté of the young remains the same. If anything, Colette controls our attention more. Maupassant omits her niece's letter, so our understanding of what caused the separation between the young woman and her husband depends solely on what Colette chooses to reiterate.

She asserts that the reason for the estrangement lies in her niece's excessive and inappropriate affection, which prompts a philosophical, at times cynical, diatribe on the judicious use of the kiss. With humor she compares its romantic illusion with the reality of the sensory experience. For instance, she cites François Coppée's verse— "Oh! les premiers baisers à travers la voilette!" (Oh, the first kisses through the veil!)—and notes the popular interpretation of it: "Toutes celles qui ont couru au rendez-vous clandestin, que la passion a jetées dans les bras d'un homme, les connaissent bien ces délicieux premiers baisers à travers la violette, et frémissent encore à leur souvenir" (All those who have kept a secret rendezvous, whom passion has thrown in a man's arms, know well the first delightful kisses through the veil, and quiver in remembering them). Then she proposes the farcical counterpart of the event:

> Il fait froid dehors. La jeune femme a marché vite; la voilette
> est toute mouillée par son souffle refroidi. Des gouttelettes

d'eau brillent dans les mailles de la dentelle noire. L'amant se précipite et colle ses lèvres ardentes à cette vapeur de poumons liquéfiée.

Le voile humide, qui déteint et porte la saveur ignoble des colorations chimiques, pénètre dans la bouche du jeune homme, mouille sa moustache. Il ne goûte nullement aux lèvres de la bien-aimée, il ne goûte qu'à la teinture de cette dentelle trempée d'haleine froide. (M1, 1:633)

(It is cold outside. The young woman has walked rapidly; her cold breath has moistened the veil. Little streams of water shine in the lace's black mesh. Her lover hurls himself toward her and presses his burning lips to that condensed vapor.

The wet veil, discolored and pungent because of the dye, invades the man's mouth and saturates his mustache. He never tastes the lips of his beloved, only the lace's dye after it has been diluted by her cold breath.)

With each premise, each illustration, each criticism of her sex's practices, Colette advises that practical considerations must take precedence over feminine romantic impulses. Her experience permits her to see the dualities in love and engenders her patronizing tone in writing to her niece. Once again, Maupassant tilts the perceptual balance of cognitive dissonance toward world-weary knowledge, cynical insight, and ironical condemnations.

Although most of Maupassant's variations of contrast structures involve the splitting of symbolic importance among two or more characters, his most interesting experiment in form altered temporal elements instead. Unlike the derivative origins underlying most of his contrast texts, Maupassant found a rather inventive and, in retrospect, surprisingly self-evident approach that distilled the perceptual and emotional ambivalences inherent in all men and women. A protagonist simultaneously deals with two aspects of a recurring progression. Often, the end of one relationship coincides with the start of a similar pattern in another. In Maupassant this usually involves the demise of one love affair and the beginning of a new liaison. As before, we do not see the turning point in the text. Maupassant details not the causes but only the manifestations of the decline, and he does not project the new encounter far beyond its initial stages.

In essence, the juxtaposition of end with beginning manipulates the reader into considering the cyclical nature of human behavior. In a positive light, this renewal of sexual passion suggests both the resilience of the human spirit and its psychological tendency for *kainomania*, the intense pursuit of novelty. Negatively, such a structure dooms man in a sense to repeat behavior destined to end in failure. The most tragic of implications in these stories is that the protagonist usually does not recognize the parallel. That duty is left to the reader. Thus, we arrive at a curiously ambivalent response to such fiction: we sense ironical humor in these double experiences, yet our insight gives way to our frustration over man's inability to free himself from a vicious circle that traces a socially deterministic path. Consciously, we laugh at such human folly in fiction; subconsciously, we fall victim to Maupassant's obvious message that we all fail to deal with the repetitive parallels that limit our lives.

The best of the end-beginning contrast stories is "Le Rendez-vous" (1889). The limited omniscient text reveals the misgivings of Jeanne Haggan as she travels to meet her extramarital lover, the viscount of Martelet. Maupassant does not recount the turning point of this relationship; he instead concentrates on its death throes. Mme. Haggan's reluctance to keep the appointment grows out of her boredom, after two years, with the affair and with the man. Initially, her resistance manifests itself in a variety of delaying tactics to avoid the rendezvous: impulsively, she leaves her cab to contemplate the trees in Trinité Square. Later, she kills time by staring at the moving hands of a clock. Her ennui has become so acute that she no longer remembers what attracted her to Martelet. For her he now symbolizes a staid and vapid habit. Every meeting with the unimaginative viscount had followed the same agenda. Ironically, Mme. Haggan realizes that her chief motive for meeting him that day was because "elle en avait pris d'habitude" (*M1*, 2:1120; she had taken it for granted).

Occurring simultaneously with the cessation of one union is the germination of another. Amid her infuriated self-assessment of what her affair with Martelet has and can cost her, Haggan compares him with an idle acquaintance, a baron named Grimbal, judging the latter to be far more worldly and keen-witted. We find out shortly the psychological origin for her choice of a standard. When she encounters the baron seemingly by chance, we learn that he had been watching her during her ruminations in the garden square. Obviously, although her conscious had not noted him, her subconscious did so and interjected him as a factor into her considerations. After briefly feigning reluctance, she agrees to accompany Grimbal to his apartment to see his "collections japonaises." In one sense, the impromptu liaison with the baron represents yet another tactic to avoid Martelet, to whom she dispatches a hasty telegram pleading illness. Ironically, her desire to end one affair apparently launches the beginning of another.

If we fail to discern the cycle of Jeanne Haggan's behavior via the perimeters of the circumstances themselves, Maupassant provides us with supplementary and, at times, blatant interpretive clues. For instance, despite her lengthy tirade on her horror that the adultery will be revealed publicly, the risk involved in her first rendezvous with Martelet had heightened the thrill: "quelle émotion, quelle crispation, quelle peur horrible et charmante à ce premier rendezvous, suivi de tant d'autres, dans ce petit entresol de garçon" (M1, 2:1120; what emotion, what agitation, what terrible and delightful fear in the first tryst, followed by so many others, in the bachelor's second-story apartment). Now, however, her memory of that day is more intellectual than emotional; time and habit have dulled the event's initial luster. Grimbal symbolizes the possibility of recapturing such an intense experience—to begin the cycle anew. The parallels suggested by this contrast variation are necessarily pessimistic. By reason of her temperament, Mme. Haggan's affair with Grimbal will likely run the same course as the one with Martelet. For Maupassant, in their greed to escape monotony human beings selectively ignore the lessons of their past and so repeat absurdities, which ironically fosters an eventual relapse into tedium.[25]

25. Yet another variation of a contrast structure would be what Angela S. Moger calls a "framed" story. An essential, "contained" story is framed by usually a first-person narrator telling it as one or more listeners are affected by it. She notes the cognitive dissonance created by such a form: "We see, finally, that the cleft that the reader encounters in the syntax of the narratives—containing story and contained— and the compulsion to build in a dual perspective on the contained narrative— [narrator] and listener—may be the 'reflection' of the conflict between the exigencies of truth and the exigencies of stories." Using my approach to Maupassant, the central story usually marks a perceptual change in the storyteller's audience between their initial "innocence" (that is, before hearing the tale) and their subsequent reaction.

The Sinusoidal Story

In a sense Maupassant's most complicated short-story structure derives logically from the more simple contrast form. Rather than hinging plot or character development upon a single pivotal incident, Maupassant would interject a second inflection point within midtext, thus delineating another section for the reader to consider in his comparative analysis. In such a tripartition, the purpose and often the handling of the first and last passages (that is, the text before the first significant point and that after the second) remain the same as in the simpler contrast techniques. Parallel episodes occur in each segment, prompting us to correlate and to note relevant perceptual differences.

The more interesting passage is the interlude suspended between both significant points. In Maupassant's work, it often depicts a protagonist's momentary escape from the realities of his existence. Such a character seeks a romantic alternative and sometimes does succeed fleetingly in achieving an ideal. In a way, the interlude qualifies as a mystical experience: (1) it ultimately provides the central character with a transcendent grasp of his plight; (2) the ineffability of the insight confirms its noetic nature; and (3) his euphoria cannot be sustained.[26] Occasionally, the protagonist even deludes himself that he will benefit by the turn of events symbolized by the first critical point. Heralded by the second inflectional event, however, a grimmer reality reasserts its presence, returning its dispirited victim to an existence now made even more difficult to accept.[27]

Graphically, the course of such a text resembles a sine wave: the first and last dark passages plot out as the negative values of the

Moger first treated Maupassant's "Une ruse" in "That Obscure Object of Narrative," *Yale French Studies* 63 (1982): 129–38. She later expanded her theory in "Narrative Structures in Maupassant: Frames of Desire," *PMLA* 100 (1985): 315–27 (above quotation on 324), this time explicating "En voyage" (Traveling) and "La Rempailleuse" (The upholsterer).

26. I derive my terms and definitions for mysticism from William James's *The Varieties of Religious Experience* (1890; reprint, New York: Dolphin, n.d.), 343–44.

27. Although he uses it in a different context, Hervé Alvado's insight on one trend in Maupassant's fiction applies here: "Le réalisme a tué le rêve" (Realism has killed the dream); see his *Maupassant ou l'amour réaliste* (Paris: La Pensée Universelle, 1980), 94.

curve; the Romantic interlude, the positive arc; each turning point marks where the line crosses the axis. This *sinusoidal* structure reconfirms Maupassant's notion of the ephemeral nature of happiness, especially when challenged by the continual onslaughts of diurnal exigencies. Thus, a protagonist's return to his normal life in the final section of the text damns him doubly. First, he has briefly tasted of a better but untenable alternative. Consequently, he now has a standard by which he must always condemn his present and future life. Second, at least latently he now recognizes parallel circumstances between past and present, verifying the circularity of existence and thus the futility in dreams of escape.

Given the convolution in sinusoidal structures, it is surprising that Maupassant frequently used them to construct his earliest fictional efforts (see, for example, "Le Docteur Héraclius Gloss" [1875–77?] or "En famille" [1881, At home]), which suggests he borrowed the technique from well-established literary conventions. Possibly, he was inspired by the writings of Prosper Mérimée, who on occasion framed short stories using similar principles (examine, for instance, "Le Vase étrusque" [1830]). Maupassant's precocious mastering of double turning points in "Boule de suif" (1880, Ball of tallow) suggests, however, that Zola and his Medan colleagues accelerated their disciple's growth as an artist. His fluent treatment of character and metaphor as well as of structure represents a profound leap in ability, likely the consequence of his liaison with French naturalism.

The critical points in "Boule de suif" are readily apparent. Ten men and women from various strata of French society attempt to flee from the threat of Prussians occupying Rouen during the war in 1870. The first change occurs when a Prussian military unit in Totes forces them to disembark from their carriage. The second inflection point is a mirror image of the first: after the prostitute Boule de suif yields to their captor's demands, the voyagers embark again on their journey to Havre. These incidents split the text into three distinct sections. A major portion of the first and the entirety of the last take place in the carriage's cabin, thus reminding readers to compare and assess the significance between these episodes. The interlude, detailing what befalls these Frenchmen at the hands of their enemy, provides us with enough insight on human behavior to interpret these cognitive mutations properly.

The first section of the tripartite text establishes the shallow intentions of the travelers in undertaking this trip. They had survived the panic brought by the defeated French army as it retreated through Rouen; they weathered the initial shock of subjugation. After occupation has settled into an acceptable routine, however, the

> vainqueurs exigeaient de l'argent, beaucoup d'argent. Les habitants payaient toujours; ils étaient riches d'ailleur. Mais plus un négociant normand devient opulent et plus il souffre de tout sacrifice, de toute parcelle de sa fortune qu'il voit passer aux mains d'un autre. (M1, 1:86)

> (victors demanded money, a lot of money. The inhabitants always paid; they could afford it. But the richer a Norman dealer becomes, the more he suffers in surrendering part of his fortune to the hands of another.)

Pecuniary interests motivated three wealthy men with their wives to regain control of their business assets by going to Le Havre. Obviously, Maupassant sets them up as unsympathetic characters. Given the surrepitious violence of some of their neighbors who resist Prussian rule, their attempt to escape in itself attests to the hypocrisy of their professed patriotism. In fact, one of the three expected to profit by the war by selling his wine to the enemy.

Basically, these three couples—the Carré-Lamadons, the de Brévilles, and the Loiseaus—symbolize the political, aristocratic, and mercantile manifestations of a laissez-faire society and economy. Their actions usually pursue the path of weakest resistance: to maximize the gain or minimize the loss of the moment. Maupassant uses the changing image of a prostitute as a barometer to measure their philosophy of self-interest. Because of her corpulence, Elisabeth Rousset is nicknamed "Boule de suif" by the third-person narrator, yet the sobriquet's alternative meaning suggests the malleableness of her perceived worth.

During the coach ride, her fellow travelers initially view her with disdain and hatred. Unusual circumstances bring about a small social revolution, however. All had forgotten to bring food for the trip—that is, all save the prostitute. To quell their hunger they abate their rude insinuations. All eventually reshape their image of Rousset under more positive light, and one by one each man and woman partakes of the prostitute's offer of food, quickly devouring the contents of her well-stocked basket. In the forced intimacy of this isolated little world, Rousset can, for the moment, earn a respect that would never be possible in a larger social arena. The passengers' subsequent behavior toward the prostitute never rises above pleasant condescensions. They dutifully applaud her patriotic reason for fleeing Rouen. (She attacked a Prussian soldier.) Yet their new attitude intoxicates Boule de suif, for she never experienced such good treatment from people of their social caste. Nevertheless, as Wallace writes, it "is a world where her refusal to accept the defeat the others took for granted both sets her apart from the common herd and brings her into conflict with it."[28]

The first turning point details the end of their illusory safety and signals their reimmersion in the uncertainties of war. A Prussian outpost troop waylays the passengers at a coach stop. The officer-in-charge of the detachment refuses to allow anyone to proceed on the journey until Rousset and he copulate. Fresh from her brush with respectability, still fired by her nationalism, she refuses the Prussian's proposition. Although passive, her resistance assumes heroic proportions, especially considering the circumstances.

Had she been a solitary traveler, she would likely have persisted in not complying with her captor's demand. The pressure applied by her newfound peers forces her to succumb. Acting upon their self-interests, her fellow passengers again judge her worth by her profession: "Puisque c'est son métier à cette fille, pourquoi refuserait-elle celui-là plus qu'un autre?" (M1, 1:111; "Since it is her trade, why should she refuse one man more than another?") Through their combined manipulations and because of her desire to promote the good of the group, she compromises her stance and goes to bed with the Prussian, while the rest revert to snide jokes at her expense.

The second turning point returns the prisoners to their haven from the war: the carriage. Maupassant sprinkles this final section of the text with obvious analogies to the first. Their contempt for the prostitute resurfaces. Her sacrifices already made, Rousset can offer them nothing more of material value. Maupassant uses subsistence again to symbolize the rewidened gulf between the prostitute and

28. *Guy de Maupassant*, 49.

the rich. Whereas in her haste to depart Rousset had forgotten to procure food and drink for the rest of the trip, all the others had remembered their hunger during the first leg of the journey and so brought provisions for the second. Unlike Boule de suif's earlier generosity, no one offers to share with her. With its foundations of self-interest, the rebuilt social wall cannot be breached.

On a superficial level every passenger views the prostitute as he did in the beginning. The interlude with the Prussian guard, however, attacks the ease with which all perceive the justice of their behavior. In effect, the parallels between the different legs of the journey promote cognitive dissonance. On one hand, her fellow travelers regard her vulgar, beneath the dignity of associating with their class. On the other, she has been generous, and her act freed them all. When a fellow traveler, a sarcastic Republican named Cornudet, whistles and then sings "La Marseillaise," its patriotic words prick the conscience of all but inspire no one to rectify the injustice suffered by the sobbing and hungry and alienated woman.

The sinusoidal structure of "Boule de suif" hints that even with insight, people cannot overcome their own prejudices. The illusion that a society, even one in microcosm, can improve interrelationships must end as soon as circumstances permit, for man's egotism ultimately pursues its own expedience rather than the common good. The transient attainment of respect between Rousset and the rest only imprisons each irredeemable soul within its hypocrisy.

Because of the detail necessary to construct such extensive parallels between scenes and to capture every nuance of a subtle transformation, Maupassant's sinusoidal stories tend to be long, sometimes approaching novella length. By 1884 he apparently discovered that the size of this sort of story permitted him to experiment via complex structural combinations. Having command of most short-story forms by 1883 and seeking new outlets that would end artistic inertia, he naturally toyed with compounds, finding that the dual inflection of sinusoidal stories dominated other patterns. In effect, the tripartition of the overall text allows for three subtexts, each with its own structure. Maupassant's new challenge thus became how to blend all without parading a story's convoluted design before the reader.

His first meaningful success was with "Yvette" (1884). The two turning points of the sinusoidal do dominate the plot's structure. The first occurs when Jean de Servigny, a cynical suitor to the young and naive Yvette Obardi, confronts her with the social truth that limits her fate: that he (and, by implication, any "respectable" man) would never seriously entertain the notion of marrying a woman with her background. This discovery divides the first and second sections of "Yvette," marking the end of the different intentions each lover has for the potential relationship and the beginning of Yvette's effort to deny the realistic possibilities for her future. Her failed attempt at suicide, the second significant point, signals the end of her romantic quest for escape and heralds the third major portion of the text, which apparently returns both characters to their initial perceptions of each other.

Maupassant manages to impose other short-story forms in both the first and second sections. The purpose of the first is to establish the cross-purposes of Yvette and Servigny, which Maupassant effects by utilizing a contrast substructure. A change in geographic setting from a Parisian party attended by Yvette and her courtesan mother to the Obardis' villa in Bougival demarcates a shift in the sexual dialogue between the prospective lovers. In Paris we find a procession of suitors, all of whom desire to be the daughter's first lover, none of whom contemplates marriage. Mistaking their interest for honorable intentions, however, Yvette plays the role of the belle, pleasantly inciting competition among them.[29] Because of his glibness, Servigny emerges from the pack in her calculations for marital bliss, while he imagines that he has accomplished the first step toward seducing her.

Whereas in Paris circumstances limit the liaison between Yvette and Servigny, in the country the sexual implications in their banter intensify. Freed from the necessity to compete, Servigny takes advantage of his isolation with the daughter to press the relationship. The earlier repartee in Paris assumes a more insistent tone, finally erupting into a comical divergence of perceptions about a conversation's topic. While he presses here for a sexual relationship, she mistakingly believes that he is proposing marriage.

29. Besnard-Coursodon sees initial innocence in Yvette: "Mais Yvette n'est redoutable que pour qui ignore sa vraie nature. Sa duplicité féminine cache sa candeur, alors qu'en général elle cache le mal. Il n'y a pas en elle volonté mauvaise" (Yvette is frightening only for those who ignore her true nature. Her feminine duplicity hides her ingenuousness, whereas in most cases it hides evil. There is no evil will in her") (Etude thématique, 24).

The argument ends when Servigny finally clarifies his position:

> finissons cette comédie ridicule qui dure depuis trop long-temps. Vous jouez à la petite fille niaise, et ce rôle ne vous va point, croyez-moi. Vous savez bien qu'il ne peut pas s'agir de mariage entre nous . . . mais d'amour. (M1, 2:269)

> (stop this ridiculous comedy which has gone on for too long. You act like a silly little girl, and, believe me, this role does not suit you. You certainly must know that there could be no question of marriage between us . . . only love.)

This declaration triggers the interlude of the overall sinusoidal pattern, in which Yvette tries via Romantic ideals and action to stay a procession of sordid revelations about her circumstance. Unlike the first section, the structure of the interlude resembles a descending helix. Each incident seems to drive Yvette to more desperate considerations and behavior. When she first learns of her mother's profession, she tries to deny it to herself. Nevertheless, her mother's relationship with Servigny's friend, Leon Saval, confirms the allegation. Later, the marquise chides her daughter for not appreciating how this manner of life provided Yvette with luxuries.

One after another, every Romantic pretense fails, but Yvette persists in balancing untenable perspectives between the subconscious and consciousness. On the one hand, she undergoes a mystical awakening, which allows her to transcend her naiveté. On the other, she continues to disbelieve the validity of such insights. Finally, rather than accept the logical consequence that goes with the impracticality of escape—a destiny that demands that she follow in the path of her mother—Yvette opts for one final Romantic act, the definitive ploy to flee her fate: suicide by inhaling chloroform.

By chance her rescuer proves to be Servigny. The import of the final sinusoidal section, which follows, is replete with possible interpretations, all of them ironical. The bulk of this third part consists of ambivalences in the conversation between the lovers. Servigny's words are qualified by his guilt; she still thinks under the euphoria of the drug. It is quite possible that Yvette again misinterprets Servigny's kindness as a prelude to a marriage offer. He likely sees in her conciliation that she now accepts her lot in life and so will yield to him sexually. In effect, they both resume the fantasies that constricted their vision during the first part of the text. Even if both do retreat to earlier hopes, however, each must still contend with a new perspective of the other: the woman must now recognize that sexual instinct motivates Servigny to deceive her; the man has to admit to himself that her social ambition constitutes part of her charm.

The cluster of images surrounding each of these small visual filters tends to dull the luster of an idealized mate—whether sexual or marital. Nevertheless, the more complex response each has toward the other conflates a variety of emotions that ironically increase desire in both. Yvette's realization (during the interlude) of the limits her mother's status places upon them both cannot bring about any social regeneration; it merely measures the difference between actual and quixotic life. In essence, the sinusoidal story traces the undermining of reality by hope, creating oppressive and omnipresent dissonance in our cognition of the extent of the human dilemma.

Maupassant's most daring mixture of sinusoidal and other forms occurs in one of his last published works, "L'Inutile Beauté" (1890, Beauty without purpose). Although other stories have achieved higher critical acclaim, "L'Inutile Beauté" has the most interesting structure in the Maupassant canon. While the first and third sections of the text follow the usual precepts of the form, the interlude challenges the narrative boundaries of the literary tradition that Maupassant himself accepted and nurtured. In essence, he interjects a metaphysical treatise that comments upon the story line yet is almost divorced from its progression.

The circumstance that frames the text is the deteriorating relationship between the count of Mascaret and his wife, Gabrielle. Given Maupassant's satyric reputation, many would find rather surprising that the implications of the marital conflict advance feminist ideas.[30] The husband becomes jealous and sexually aroused at the sight of his wife's hauteur as she sets out in her chauffeured carriage to drive through Paris. The countess rebuffs him, proclaiming herself the victim of his "féroce égoïsme." She confronts his confusion by

30. The first substantive discussion of Maupassant's ambivalence toward women in his fiction is in Chantal Jennings, "La Dualité de Maupassant: Son attitude envers la femme," *Revue des sciences humaines*, no. 144 (1970): 559–78. With *A Woman's Revenge*, Donaldson-Evans established her authority on the subject in 1986.

parading his offenses before him. Because her parents' poverty forced them to defer to his wealth, she had always felt purchased rather than joined in marriage. She accused him of jealousy, which he allayed by making her unattractive to other men by consigning her to "une existence de jument poulinière enfermée dans un haras" (an existence like a brood mare trapped on a stud farm). For Gabrielle, her seven children represent her husband's abuse of his privileges:

> Et comme vous ne pouviez pas m'empêcher d'être belle et de plaire, d'être appelée dans les salons et aussi dans les journaux une des plus jolies femmes de Paris, vous avez cherché ce que vous pourriez imaginer pour écarter de moi les galanteries, et vous avez eu cette idée abominable de me faire passer ma vie dans une perpétuelle grossesse, jusqu'au moment où je dégoûterais tous les hommes. . . . Vos enfants, vous les aimez comme des victoires et non comme votre sang. Ce sont des victories sur moi, sur ma jeunesse, sur ma beauté, sur mon charme, sur les compliments qu'on m'adressait, et sur ceux qu'on chuchotait autour de moi, sans me les dire. (M1, 2:1208, 1209)

> (And since you could not prevent me from being beautiful and comely, from being recognized in salons and newspapers as one of the prettiest women of Paris, you racked your imagination for a way to keep away my admirers, and you have had this vile idea to make me spend my life in perpetual pregnancy, until the day when I would disgust all men. . . . Your children, you treasured them as victories but not as your progeny. They are victories over me, over my youth, over my beauty, over my charm, over the compliments directed toward me, and over those who whispered among themselves about me.)

Surviving such a life for eleven years, she vows not to spend the next ten in confinement.

The infrastructure of this first section resembles a contrast story. The turning point hinges upon the wife's confession of infidelity in order to quell her husband's sexual assault upon her youth. She angrily tells him that one child is not his, but she refuses to tell him which one. Later, we find out how desperate her ploy was as she arms herself, anticipating that he may respond violently to the revelation. Unable to deal with the new circumstances created by her admission, however, the count alienates himself from both his wife and the children by embarking on a long journey alone. The contrasts established in this first section validate Gabrielle's claims. As his jealousy once motivated him to impregnate his wife periodically, it now estranges husband and wife because his subconscious fears have been realized. Since she refuses to divulge details, his imagination allows her planted seed of discord to blossom, spreading his anxiety to all his children rather than focusing it upon one. Thus, instead of "victoires," all of them symbolize his wife's successful revenge upon him.

After the count informs his wife by letter of his departure, the plot deviates from a conventional progression. Rather than presenting another direct glimpse of the couple, Maupassant shifts the time to six years later and our perspective to two opera patrons who idly inspect the audience during an intermission. More than any other sinusoidal story by Maupassant, the conversation between these men, Roger de Salins and Bernard Grandin, confirms the metaphysical purpose underlying the interlude. Prompted by their admiration of the still beautiful Gabrielle, whom they spot in the crowd, the two gossip about her relationship with her husband.

With the countess for inspiration, Salins launches into a prolonged meditative monologue on our necessary rebellion against God's biological control over us. Our chief weapon in the battle is our capacity to appreciate beauty aesthetically. Calling man's intelligence an accident, Salins postulates its portent for humanity: "Et plus nous sommes civilisés, intelligents, raffinés, plus nous devons vaincre et dompter l'instinct animal qui représente en nous la volonté de Dieu" (M1, 2:1219; And the more we are civilized, intelligent, refined, the more we must conquer and subdue the animal instinct that symbolizes the will of God in us). Gazing upon the bejeweled and costumed elegance of Gabrielle, he concludes rhetorically: "Regarde cette femme, Mme de Mascaret. Dieu l'avait faite pour vivre dans une grotte, nue, ou enveloppée de peaux de bêtes. N'est-elle pas mieux ainsi?" (M1, 2:1220; Look at that woman,

Mme. Mascaret. God has made her for living in a cave, naked, or wrapped in animal skins. Isn't she better off now?).

In a sense, her beauty triggers a mystical episode for Salins, inspiring him to clarify his formerly vague notions about the human experience.[31] The countess of Mascaret is not privy to his thoughts; only we the readers are. Thus, Salins's philosophical musing sanctifies her behavior for us. Maupassant effectively employs a physical and metaphorical "between the acts" device (some four decades before Virginia Woolf's masterpiece), which allows him simultaneously to paint in broad strokes the terms of Gabrielle's ideal existence in sustained beauty and to cultivate a seldom used story form. Occasionally, he would pursue philosophical themes, generally derivative of Schopenhauer, in lieu of plot (see for example "Auprès d'un mort" [1883, Next to a dead man]). Such stories usually failed because they retreat into the purpose of the expository essay, possessing only the thinnest veneer of fiction.[32] With "L'Inutile Beauté," however, such a passage succeeds because of its placement between sections of conventional narrative. It justifies the legitimacy in appreciating supererogative beauty (that is, beauty beyond that meant to attract men for the sole purpose of procreating the species).[33]

In the final phase of the plot, Maupassant returns our attention to the couple. After years of self-torture and self-exile, the count asks

31. I agree with Donaldson-Evans's defense against André Vial's charge that the opera scene hinders the continuity of the story. Citing Maupassant's own positive assessment of "L'Inutile Beauté," she writes that the passage is not "merely a heavy-handed attempt at philosophical enrichment, but rather an integral part of the whole story" (A Woman's Revenge, 99).

32. Because of the paucity of such stories in the Maupassant canon, I will treat the philosophical monologue only briefly here.

33. Besnard-Coursodon suggests that this aspect of "L'Inutile Beauté" constitutes a late Maupassantian attack upon naturalism, both literary and othewise (Etude thématique, 92, 98–99, and passim). The critic later cautions, however, that despite the inherent ambiguity in Maupassant's stance, his attack upon the notion that women must fulfill their reproductive function does not mean he advocated some sort of nihilism for the species (161).

Lerner believes that "L'Inutile Beauté" is a story and a philosophy half-told. He proposes that Maupassant continued the symbolic import of Gabrielle de Mascaret in Michele de Burne, the central figure in his novel Notre Coeur (1890), who represents "the supreme product of [her] sophisticated civilisation" but in the process "falls into an unproductive dilettantism" (Maupassant [New York: George Braziller, 1975], 258). Rather than the novel supplanting the interpretation of the short story, I believe that the almost coterminous publication of Notre Coeur and "L'Inutile Beauté" suggests that Maupassant toyed with and so pursued both sides of the issue.

his wife to name the child that is not his. Gabrielle tells him that she had lied in order to avoid continuing "cette vie odieuse de grossesses" (this vile life of pregnancies). Immediately, he recognizes the perceptual dilemma that will haunt him for the rest of his life:

> . . . je vais retomber en de nouveaux doutes qui ne finiront plus! Quel jour avez-vous menti, autrefois ou aujord'hui? Comment vous croire à présent? Comment croire une femme après cela? Je ne saurai plus jamais ce que je dois penser. J'aimerais mieux que vous m'eussiez dit: "C'est Jacques, ou c'est Jeanne." (M1, 2:1222)

> (Again I am plagued with new incessant doubts! When have you lied, before or today? How can I believe you now? How can I believe any woman after this? I will never know again what I ought to believe. I would rather you had told me: "It is Jacques, or it is Jeanne.")

Later, he subliminates his doubts and accepts her word, which inspires in him an admiration for her that parallels what he had felt six years ago. Now, however, his love is imbued with an appreciation of the aesthetic and emotional complexity underlying his wife's superficial beauty. Although he cannot articulate it so well, Mascaret now views beauty more like Salins, giving rise to a perceptual revolution within him: "Puis il sortit, en la regardant toujours, émerveillé qu'elle fût encore si belle, et sentant naître en lui une émotion étrange, plus redoubtable peut-être que l'antique et simple amour!" (M1, 2:1224; Then he left, still looking at her, amazed that she was so beautiful once more, and sensing a strange new emotion in himself—more formidable, perhaps, than venerable and simple love!).[34]

Upon the count's reconciliation with his wife, the text ostensibly restores matters to what they were before the rift. But the husband must now entertain a new perspective of his marriage that taxes his ego; the wife must abide once again her husband's presence, which

---

34. Besnard-Coursodon notes that the wife's welfare ironically lies in her ability to rival nature (Etude thématique, 76–77).

may affect her beauty and independence. For Maupassant, however tenuous and self-compromising our ability to handle human intricacy, we should still treasure our illusion that we can cope, for it provides us with a brief respite from the travails of life.

In contrast to America's monocular dismissal of it, the Maupassant canon presents readers with a panorama of form. In most instances Maupassant borrowed these forms from past masters of the short story. The nature of his talent did not involve foundational innovation: for example, his philosophical stance was invariably an extension of Schopenhauer's pessimism. Maupassant's deft use of language was born with his introduction to the clever sparseness of the Flaubert sentence and nurtured by his contact with the sensory realism of the Zola school. Likewise, in the matter of form, Maupassant borrowed extensively from nineteenth-century French and foreign fiction, thus stressing his inclinations to develop, to react, to comment, rather than to create.

In essence Maupassant approached his fiction more in the role of an intellectual critic than artist. Ultimately, he felt uncomfortable in linking pretensions of art with himself or his fiction. As Benedetto Croce has remarked, Maupassant "made no transcendental ideal of art, in the manner of other artists, his predecessors and contemporaries; nor did he even direct a curious glance at the nature of art or engage in any kind of inquiry or criticism relating to it, having little taste for theorizing, discussions or polemics."[35] Occasionally, he even attacked artistic figures in his short stories. His superficial reason for doing so involved his association of artists with the lack of virility. Unlike Schopenhauer, who saw the arts as a refuge from the futile tragedy of human experience, Maupassant could recognize few exceptions in a foredoomed world. In his art the poet mimics the horrible vicissitudes of diurnal existence but also succumbs to them. Consequently, in his wish to create an alternate order for the purpose of leading men toward insights that will better them, the artist becomes the most foolish of vain men, instinctively seeking utopias that a hostile universe will not permit.

Unlike the Romantic artist, Maupassant saw no redemptive powers

---

35. *European Literature in the Nineteenth Century*, trans. Douglas Ainslie (New York: Haskell House, 1967), 352.

in insight. For him the discovery of truth was at best entertaining; more often, however, it further exacerbated the intensity of misery. Its only didactic effect was to reinforce the bleak determinism of human history and destiny.[36] Thus, the challenge to Maupassant as writer was not to create parallel realities in light of one artistic theory or another, but to report life as it was. As a critic rather than creator, he could select, isolate, focus, and dilate only those aspects of life that interested him for the moment without excessive concern about how they belonged in any larger philosophical context. The nature of his intellect did not predispose him to construct such a context with precision, and so he refrained from overt philosophical statements and instead trusted that his fiction would somehow support his Schopenhauerian perspective.[37] In his short stories (save for the half-dozen that purposely pursue philosophic themes) Maupassant rarely resorted to authorial intrusions to elaborate some intellectual point—invariably negative in character—or social criticism. At best, such points were quickly dismissed in a sentence or a short paragraph.

During his decade of writing fiction, Maupassant used such devices less and less frequently each succeeding year, which suggests on one level that he thought such omissions a refinement of technique. More fundamentally, he may have come to realize that undisguised attacks against human folly in fiction, however brief, could produce consequences he did not intend. Direct attacks in the form of authorial intrusion often suggest that the writer advocates the opposite of that which he criticizes. But Maupassant took no firm

36. Besnard-Coursodon describes Maupassant's philosophical view in Platonic terms: "Les conditions de notre vie, fixées par Dieu, ou la nature, dont l'immuabilité rend éternelle la nécessité de la lutte, ne répondent pas à nos besoins" (Etude thématique, 91; Fixed by God or by nature, whose immutability makes the necessity for struggle eternal, the conditions of our life do not respond to our needs).

37. In his introduction to The Portable Maupassant (New York: Viking, 1947), 1, Lewis Galantière comments: "He had of course emancipated himself from certain conventions, and he possessed a sharp intelligence of a skeptical and negative kind; but his pleasures were without distinction and his opinions without originality." In his 1888 verbal portrait of Maupassant, Henry James professed an attitude that many later American and English critics would emulate: "I may as well say at once that in dissertation M. de Maupassant does not write with his best pen; the philosopher in his composition is perceptibly inferior to the story-teller. I would rather have written half a page of Boule de [s]uif than the whole of the introduction to Flaubert's Letters to Madame Sand"; "Guy de Maupassant," Partial Portraits (1888; reprint, Ann Arbor: University of Michigan Press, 1970), 244.

intellectual stand; at best his fiction betrayed an uncommitted and flawed understanding of Schopenhauer's principles. Galantière suggests that Maupassant's vision of the omnipresence of evil was his chief spur to creativity.[38] His attacks, then, were for the sake of attacking, not promoting coherent causes or consistent ideas. Thus by pretending to let the story tell itself with minimal authorial intrusion, Maupassant sought to lessen some of the intellectual burdens of writing fiction.

If Maupassant's temperament inhibited him from asserting an opinion either directly or through attacking its opposite, it did permit him to hint at notions he thought curious and to underscore circumstances with irony—particularly those of his favorite target, society.[39] Such possibilities obviously relieved him from acts of affirmation and, in consequence, from the obligation to adhere perfectly and consistently to any epistemological truth.[40] Thus, the Maupassant canon epitomizes the turn against didacticism in nineteenth-century fiction, particularly in the short story's divergence from the essay through sophisticated techniques in form. Writers less and less propelled readers along any turnpike toward moral betterment but instead structured stories to direct them through labyrinths of doubt and speculation.

38. See *Portable Maupassant*, 2.

39. Maupassant's critics since Henry James have bemoaned the absence of theory in his work. In his introduction to an English translation of thirteen Maupassant stories, James writes: "His strong, hard, cynical, slightly cruel humor can scarcely be called a theory" (*The Odd Number* [New York: Harper and Brothers, 1889], xv). In *Maupassant the Novelist* (Port Washington, N.Y.: Kennikat, 1972), 9, Edward D. Sullivan maintains that Maupassant's nonfiction writings do contain sufficient ideas to constitute a literary credo, but he concedes that there are "contradictions and conflicts, since each article represents to some degree the preoccupations of the moment when it was written." Biographer Michael G. Lerner adds: "such subjects allowed Maupass[a]nt to poke a critical finger in an ironically humorous and amusing way at the hypocrisy and superficiality of the established social system of conventional habits and respectable morality of the world about him" (*Maupassant*, 153).

40. For a brief discussion of Maupassant's refusal to ally himself with a literary school and of his dismissal of the practicality of any literary principle, see Sullivan, *Maupassant the Novelist*, 12–14.

3

Maupassant and the
American Mainstream

Up until 1889 America's cognizance of Maupassant remained faint
at best. In a New Orleans newspaper during the mid-1880s, Lafcadio
Hearn published translations and aesthetic critiques of the Frenchman's short stories. Louisiana existed, however, on the rim of America's literary galaxy. Fashions radiating from New York could alter
Southern tastes, but no comparable influence counterflowed to the
east. Ironically, then, the most extensive and technically superior
renderings of Maupassant into English done in the nineteenth century were read as idle divertissements, quickly forgotten and consequently entombed in the yellowing tattered pages of a newspaper
file.[1] The only other likelihood of a small American audience for
Maupassant existed among the literati of French-speaking commu-

1. Lafcadio Hearn published more than fifty translations of Maupassant short
stories in the New Orleans *Times-Democrat* during the mid 1880s. Twenty-three were
republished in *Saint Anthony, and Other Stories by Guy de Maupassant* (New York:
Boni, 1923). More were reissued in *The Adventures of Walter Schnaffs, and Other
Stories by Guy de Maupassant* (Tokyo: Hokuseido, [1931]).

nities in the major Southern ports along the Mississippi River. As for the rest of the United States, Maupassant existed only as a name occasionally cited by critics who paraded laundry lists of contemporary French authors. When one singled out Maupassant for comment, he often dismissed the writer as an insubstantial luminary, destined to be extinguished as soon as the next trend ignited itself.[2]

The publication of Jonathan Sturges's translations ended this obscurity. In 1889 Sturges was twenty-five years old, well traveled, a Princeton graduate, a journalist, an occasional fiction writer, and somewhat a dandy. As a correspondent for the New York Times, he had been among the early American admirers and promoters of Ibsen. Long invalided by a childhood bout with polio, his energy in the face of his own frailty won him devoted friends, particularly among artists. He and Henry James shared a loyal and sustained, caring friendship.[3] When Harper and Brothers issued thirteen of Sturges's translations of Maupassant under the title The Odd Number in November 1889, an essay by James prefaced the collection, obviously lending the prestige of his reputation to excite public awareness of the volume.

Perhaps James's auspices had more of an impact on the public than he himself would have believed (especially considering the poor reception of The Tragic Muse the following year). Perhaps the publication was conveniently timed with the initial wave of popularity enjoyed by neogothic texts during the 1890s. Perhaps Maupassant's stories clarified an already extant but still vague trend in American literary tastes. Perhaps The Odd Number simply became a convenient stocking-stuffer for Christmas. Whatever the cause, the volume conquered the linguistic provincialism of Americans, whose ignorance of French no longer proved an impediment. Throughout 1890 the name of Maupassant rippled through American literary circles. Across the country, newspapers reprinted selections from Sturges's volume. In published discussions of the short story, Maupassant entered the critical vocabulary as a revered standard.[4] During the rest of the decade, various major and

2. One example of Maupassant's mercurial literary reputation in the United States can be found in the writings of critic-author-educator Brander Matthews; see the Introduction for how Matthews revised his opinion in the various editions of The Philosophy of the Short Story, (New York: Peter Smith, 1901).

3. The most substantive discussion of Sturges's life is Leon Edel's "Jonathan Sturges," Princeton University Library Chronicle 15 (1953): 1–9.

4. Fred Lewis Pattee notes how immediately Maupassant's influence was felt; he

ephemeral periodicals commissioned more translations. Sturges himself offered two more stories in *Modern Ghosts*, published by Harper
and Brothers in 1890.[5]

For the most part, Sturges selected stories with climactic endings,
structurally ranging from the surprise-inversion ("The Necklace" / "La
Parure") through the loop ("The Wolf" / "Le Loup") and descending
helical ("A Coward" / "Un lâche") to the ironic coda ("Happiness" /
"Le Bonheur").[6] The two stories in *Modern Ghosts* followed the same
pattern. Sturges's choices and the popularity of "The Necklace" in
particular focused American literary values upon one plot device that
would become the archetypal short-story form for many writers in the
following decades. This attraction for the surprise-inversion had been
slowly intensifying ever since the Civil War. It was born, perhaps, with
Thomas Bailey Aldrich's "Marjorie Daw" in 1873 and was nurtured by
Frank Stockton's "The Lady, or the Tiger?" in 1882. With the emergence
of *The Odd Number* the literary public judged Maupassant as a master
and, erroneously, a champion of the form. In the years after 1890, the
adjective *Maupassantian* came in America to stand for an odd assort-
ment of fictional qualities—brevity, sexuality (or, as some charged,
pornography), gothicism, madness—but the most enduring was the
curious assumption that all of Maupassant's plots depended upon last-
minute surprises.[7]

---

quotes this passage from an August 1890 edition of *Critic*: "Guy de Maupassant . . .
has been a marked influence on the younger generation of writers. He has taught them
what can be done with very little plot by one who has a mastery of the art of story-
telling." See Pattee, *The Development of the American Short Story: An Historical
Survey* (1923; reprint, New York: Biblio and Tannen, 1975), 310.

5. Sturges's translations appearing in *Modern Ghosts*, ed. George William Curtis
(New York: Harper and Brothers, 1890) were "The Horla" ("Le Horla") and "On the
River" ("Sur l'eau"). Translations of five other continental writers also appeared in
the anthology.

Harper and Brothers later attempted to capitalize on the popularity of *The Odd
Number* by issuing a sequel; see *The Second Odd Number*, translated by Charles
Henry White, introduction by William Dean Howells (New York: Harper, 1917). Failing
to attract significant notice, this second edition of thirteen stories was soon eclipsed
by other contemporary translations of Maupassant.

6. The other translations are "The Piece of String" ("La Ficelle"), "La Mère
Sauvage" (Sturges did not translate the French title), "Moonlight" ("Clair de lune"),
"The Confession" ("La Confession"), "On the Journey" ("En voyage"), "The Beggar"
("Le Gueux"), "A Ghost" ("Apparition"), "Little Soldier" ("Petit Soldat"), and "The
Wreck" ("L'Epave").

7. For a brief survey of the legacy this reputation left to twentieth-century American

In effect, Maupassant influenced a generation of American writers who depended too heavily upon the tastes of his translations. Basically, this response was twofold. First, for several writers of the early 1890s, "The Necklace" confirmed a technique that hitherto they had considered or had already been practicing. Second, early in the next century, budding writers came to the short story after the surprise-inversion had already become an idée fixe in various literary circles and a criterion of acceptance for many American editors of major periodicals.

Two literary volumes appearing over a decade apart best typify these differing receptions. By virtue of his temperament and his personal experience with tragedy, Ambrose Bierce had already adopted the surprise-inversion in his fiction by the time Harper and Brothers released *The Odd Number.* In Maupassant's short stories, Bierce found a fellow iconoclast, who sharpened his handling of form in his own fiction. In addition, the success of *The Odd Number* possibly paved the way for his *Tales of Soldiers and Civilians* (1891).[8] Beyond the turn of the century, William Sidney Porter (O. Henry) would grasp the surprise-inversion as his supreme aesthetic truth.[9] Starting with his initial volume on New York life, *The Four Million* (1906), Porter would eventually usurp the title of master of the "trick ending" by repeating the form ad nauseam. The guiltiest of those who embraced a principle too tightly, Porter would become the target of ridicule in literary circles after World War I. His (and the form's) descent into disfavor would spill over into America's more resolute dismissal of Maupassant's status as an artist. Ironically, the sins of the child were visited upon his parent.

---

writers (as diverse as Sherwood Anderson, John Dos Passos, Theodore Dreiser, Ellen Glasgow, H. L. Mencken, and William Carlos Williams), examine Artine Artinian, *Maupassant Criticism in France, 1880–1940, with an Inquiry into his Present Fame and a Bibliography* (Morningside Heights, N.Y.: King's Crown, 1941).

8. In his preface to the volume, Bierce noted the difficulty he had in securing a publisher for the project; see Ambrose Bierce, *Tales of Soldiers and Civilians* (San Francisco: E. L. G. Steele, 1891), 3. M. E. Grenander reports that the American edition was actually issued on 28 January 1892, the same day as its British release (which was retitled by an editor as *In the Midst of Life: Tales of Soldiers and Civilians*); see *Ambrose Bierce* (New York: Twayne, 1970), 58. The list of stories in the British version slightly differs from the American edition. Hereafter, I shall refer to the volume using its British title, which Bierce himself came to prefer.

9. For a clarification of the proper spelling of Porter's middle name, see Gerald Langford, *Alias O. Henry: A Biography of William Sidney Porter* (New York: Macmillan, 1957), 261n. I shall not amend in this chapter another commentator's preference for "Sydney."

Maupassant and Bierce

Earlier in the century, Charles Baudelaire found that by critiquing the fiction and poetry of Poe and the paintings of Delacroix he reaffirmed and clarified his own aesthetic theories. Similarly, Ambrose Bierce already possessed a well-ordered approach to fiction before he first encountered Maupassant, yet in the Frenchman he discovered someone who shared his vision of a mocking universe whose calling card was a devastating irony. *The Odd Number* likely enlightened Bierce about his own formula for the short story: an effective marriage of the descending helical with the surprise-inversion.[10] In tandem, these structures foredoomed each Bierce protagonist to confront a crisis alone, only to have chance or whim cast an unexpected final twist. The bizarreness underscoring death and ruination as assembled in the short stories of *In the Midst of Life* serves a twofold purpose. First, it attacks the neoromanticism of fin-de-siècle America concerning the Civil War and of war in general.[11] Second, in implying parallels between death in combat and in civilian life, Bierce not only provides his audience with the means

10. Cathy N. Davidson discusses at length the anagnorisis component of Bierce's turning points, labeling them with a term borrowed from Joycean criticism: epiphany. She also sees a three-stage process in Bierce's stories that anticipates my notion of a descending helical. In his initial confrontation with a potential crisis, the Bierce protagonist reacts "automatically." The second stage comes into play when conventional responses fail, necessitating a "heightened awareness" that is likewise doomed. The final descent of the psyche forces the "painful acknowledgement of one's own limitations"; see Davidson, *The Experimental Fictions of Ambrose Bierce* (Lincoln: University of Nebraska Press, 1984), 24–45.

Grenander sees a similar three-staged psychological fall in Bierce's central characters: (1) "an intellectual awareness of a dangerous situation"; (2) "an emotion of fear, deepening to terror, and frequently thence to madness"; and (3) "a tremendous heightening and acceleration of sensory perceptions"; see "Bierce's Turn of the Screw: Tales of Ironical Terror," *Western Humanities Review* 2 (1957): 257–64, reprinted in *Critical Essays on Ambrose Bierce*, ed. Cathy N. Davidson (Boston: G. K. Hall, 1982), 211 (hereafter cited as *Critical Essays*).

11. H. L. Mencken sympathetically describes Bierce's "cynical delight" in war as a phenomenon which became for him "a sort of magnificent *reductio ad absurdum* of all romance. The world viewed war as something heroic, glorious, idealistic. Very well, he would show how sordid and filthy it was—how stupid, savage and degrading"; see Mencken, *Prejudices*, 6th ser. (New York: Knopf, 1927), excerpted in *Critical Essays*, 62.

Lawrence I. Berkove qualifies Mencken's assessment somewhat by suggesting that Bierce could hate war "intellectually, but not emotionally"; see Berkove, *Ambrose*

by which to apprehend the true horrors of war, he condemns all significant human experience: only death, which inevitably robs man of his dignity by ending his illusion of free will, is meaningful.

More than a year before the publication of *The Odd Number*, Bierce was already experimenting with the formula that he would employ repeatedly in his Civil War tales. Starting with "One of the Missing" on 11 March 1888, the San Francisco *Examiner* published various pieces by Bierce as part of its Sunday supplement. Evidently, his contributions were well received: the editor quickly began to place them at the lead position on the first page of the supplement, and a Bierce short story or essay soon appeared approximately twice a month. Although personal problems eventually reduced his rate of production and editorial changes moved his stories to less prominent columns, Bierce still managed to compose a sizeable number of pieces by 1891, from which he would cull more than a dozen to form the backbone of the various editions of *In the Midst of Life*.

From the very first, Bierce's conception of a short-story formula gravitated toward the dramatic and the shocking. The descending helical allowed him to explore aspects of literary impressionism—especially of how a crisis intensifies and dilates the individual's consciousness. Since it was bantered about as a minor challenge to the entrenched American realistic school of the day, impressionism in fiction likely had appeal for the iconoclastic Bierce, especially in support of his war against the literary tastes of W. D. Howells.[12]

On the other hand, the surprise-inversion technique suited Bierce's temperament even more.[13] Of course he may have developed

---

Bierce: A Braver Man Than Anybody Knew (Ann Arbor: Ardis, 1981), excerpted in *Critical Essays*, 137.

12. In any event, perhaps it was a Bierce tale more than Hamlin Garland's notion of *veritism* that influenced the battle scenes in Stephen Crane's *The Red Badge of Courage*.

13. Several critics have recently defended Bierce against the charge that he became a second-rate writer by relying too often on trick endings. For example, see F. J. Logan, "The Wry Seriousness of 'Owl Creek Bridge,' " *American Literary Realism* 10 (Spring 1977): 101–13, reprinted in *Critical Essays*, 195–208. On this matter, Grenander comments: "Bierce was not above using this artificial device. But in his best stories, the irony lies not in a self-conscious coyness on the part of the narrator, but in a certain relationship between a given character and the incidents of the plot" ("Bierce's Turn of the Screw," 211).

For a discussion of Bierce's preference for the short story (versus the novel), see Grenander, *Ambrose Bierce*, 78–79.

his approach to the form by studying examples from contemporary and past masters of the short story, but his understanding seems more founded upon and reinforced by his personal experience. He treated the tragedies in his life as culminating shocks that suspended reason, leaving an aftermath devoid of meaning, during which he donned a stoical mask. For Bierce, the severity of his war experience, the breakup of his marriage, and the grotesque circumstances that surrounded his son Day's suicide after a gun battle over a woman— all supported his vision that life's meaning can be reduced to its isolated, almost farcical moments of defeat.[14] In his short stories, Bierce seldom carries a plot beyond this point; any appendix would ultimately prove superfluous and perhaps would threaten to dismiss his insights by rendering them sentimental. Thus the surprise-inversion structure focuses our attention upon horror and ironical futility.[15]

In his first story in the *Examiner* series, Bierce immediately grasped the essentials of short-story form. "One of the Missing" uses structure to achieve effects that would prove common to the Bierce agenda: (1) to re-create an individual's fear so horrifically that it challenges the audience's simplistic notion about war, (2) to invoke the metaphors of family rift and suffering to comment upon the historical meaning of the Civil War itself, and (3) to portray death as the result of a ludicrous and unpredictable chain of causes.[16]

The story centers on the plight of Private Jerome Searing, a scout for Sherman's army during 1864. Bierce engineers a wild series of coincidences to entrap his protagonist. Searing is dispatched beyond

14. Following the example of earlier biographers, Berkove believes that Bierce's war ordeal formed the basis for his skepticism, which eventually guided him toward his own brand of stoicism (*Ambrose Bierce*, 137, 140–43). For a detailed account (relying mostly upon contemporary newspaper accounts) of Day Bierce's death in July 1889, see Paul Fatout, *Ambrose Bierce: The Devil's Lexicographer* (Norman: University of Oklahoma Press, 1951), 170–77. Conflicting reports exist on the extent of Bierce's grief over the matter; Carey McWilliams gives the fullest account in *Ambrose Bierce, A Biography* (New York: Boni, 1929), 193–94. Fatout reports that Bierce recovered sufficiently by September to resume his journalistic duties.

15. Oddly enough, Bierce eventually found that the epigram allowed him to capture more of this pessimistic spirit than the short story, manifesting itself in the perversely inspired definitions collected in *The Devil's Dictionary*. Grenander notes this trend also (*Ambrose Bierce*, 79).

16. Davidson notes that "[e]piphany frequently precedes extinction" in a Bierce text; see *Experimental Fictions*, 33.

the picket line to spy on Confederate positions where he witnesses "the rear-guard of the retiring enemy." Rather than reporting this intelligence immediately, he yields to his impulse (conditioned by his military training) to harass a retreating troop column as a sniper. Nestled in a war-damaged farm building, he prepares his Springfield rifle, but Bierce's concept of fate prevents the soldier from firing:

> But it was decreed from the beginning of time that Private Searing was not to murder anybody that bright summer morning, nor was the Confederate retreat to be announced by him. For countless ages events had been so matching themselves together in that wondrous mosaic to some parts of which, dimly discernible, we give the name of history, that the acts which he had in will would have marred the harmony of the pattern. (B1, 2:76)

From here, Bierce immediately retreats his narrative by twenty-five years and traces at length the life of a Confederate artillery captain and the coincidental experiences that destined him to be at that battlefield:

> As it fell out, [he], having nothing better to do while awaiting his turn to pull out and be off, amused himself by sighting a field-piece obliquely to his right at what his mistook for some Federal officers on the crest of a hill, and discharged it. The shot flew high of its mark. (B1, 2:77)

The errant cannonball strikes and collapses the building in which Searing hides. Whim, chance, a directionless and unfathomable universe—all conspire to doom the private.

At this point, Bierce launches into a descending helical that details how Searing's fear becomes a psychic cancer. The collapsed building has pinned and immobilized him. Although distressed at first, the soldier expects the Union army will soon advance and thereupon rescue him. He gradually becomes aware, however, that the explosion had placed his Springfield out of reach, the muzzle of which was "aimed at the exact centre of his forehead." The dread induced by the hair-triggered weapon gradually sharpens an ache in his brain; obviously his imagination creates the sensation of a head wound before the fact. As his fear expands geometrically, so apparently does his awareness of time:

> No thoughts of home, of wife and children, of country, of glory. The whole record of memory was effaced. The world had passed away—not a vestige remained. Here in this confusion of timbers and boards is the sole universe. Here is immortality in time—each pain an everlasting life. The throbs tick off eternities. (B1, 88)

After an agonizing succession of such eternities, he resolves to discharge the rifle (by using a board to nudge the trigger) and end his suspense.

Here, three unexpected revelations end the story. First, Jerome Searing does die but not in the way he or we anticipated. The weapon had already discharged when the building fell. What killed the private was his horror, which could only be relieved by death. Thus, the nonexistent bullet becomes superfluous. Second, the soldier's body is discovered by his brother, a lieutenant in charge of a skirmish mission. But Jerome Searing's ordeal had so disfigured his appearance through emotional self-torture that his own brother does not recognize him, treating the body perfunctorily as just another war victim.[17] Third, the officer ironically misjudges how long the soldier has been dead. The lieutenant estimates a week, which symbolically corresponds to the excruciating eternity the private had imagined. Bierce, however, has the brother note the times when "he heard a faint, confused rumble, like the clatter of a falling building translated by distance" and later when he discovered the body (B1, 2:91). Only twenty-three minutes separated these events.

Together, these three revelations sharply requalify our comprehension of the story and, hence, of war. Like other successful surprise-inversions, the text takes on differing interpretive attributes on a second reading. As in our first encounter with his plight, Searing remains doomed, but our subsequent readings reveal more precisely the physiological and mental devastation caused by terror. Bierce portrays man as ultimately hapless, a creature who, oddly because

---

17. The distortions in family relationships caused by war would become a favorite theme for Bierce in his other Civil War tales. For example, examine his "A Horseman in the Sky" or "The Mocking-Bird."

of his intelligence, can respond inordinately to a dilemma—in this case, exaggerating fear until it becomes an obsession. In essence, Bierce challenges our self-confidence in discerning the capacity of man. War places individuals beyond the limits of reasonable expectations. The "good soldier," long resigned to the possibility and perhaps the inevitability of his death, nevertheless is caught unaware by a prankish universe, which casts him in circumstances that melt his resolve and rob him of his humanity. Therefore, our second reading focuses our attention upon the intensity of man's imagination, laying bare how he hastens his own degeneration.

In all, seven Civil War texts destined for the final version of *In the Midst of Life* (each pursuing similar interpretive avenues) appeared in the pages of the *Examiner* before the November 1889 publication of *The Odd Number*. Most of these employed surprise-inversion structures. For example, in "A Horseman in the Sky: An Incident in the Civil War" (14 April 1889), we learn of the symbolic toll a West Virginian volunteer must pay for falling asleep at his post: to prevent an enemy officer from reporting the Union position, the sentry fires his musket, spooking the rider's horse to bolt over a cliff. At the end of the text, the soldier tells the corporal of the guard that the Confederate was his father. Bierce re-echoes this theme of families torn asunder by war in "The Affair at Coulter's Notch" (20 October 1889). Ordered by a Union general of dubious integrity, an artillery captain overcomes his reluctance and engages in a gunnery duel with a Confederate battery situated near a plantation. Captain Coulter performs heroically, continuing the barrage despite injury and exhaustion. After the battle is won, however, we discover the officer cradling his dead wife and child amid the ruins. The plantation was the one he had forsaken because of his ethical convictions.[18]

Obviously, then, Bierce had committed himself to the trick-ending format well before reading Maupassant's work. Nevertheless, evidence suggests that *The Odd Number* did have an impact on the American.[19] If nothing else, it likely confirmed the potency of his

18. Other texts and publication dates include: "A Son of the Gods: A Study in the Historical Present" (29 July 1888), "Chickamauga" (20 January 1889), "A Coward" (later retitled "One Officer, One Man") (17 February 1889), "The Coup de Grâce: An Uncanny Occurrence in the Chicahominy Woods" (30 June 1889).

19. One probable antecedent for Bierce was Poe, which most students of Bierce concede; the most thorough treatment of this relationship is Arthur M. Miller's "The Influence of Edgar Allan Poe on Ambrose Bierce," *American Literature* 4 (1932): 130–

own approach to the short story. The textual revisions Bierce eventually incorporated in subsequent editions of In the Midst of Life suggest that Maupassant's example clarified for him some of the elegant nuances of the structure. This refinement likely inspired Bierce to demand of himself tighter control of his materials in the tales composed in 1890 and 1891. I also suspect that Bierce may have sought other Maupassant texts than those in The Odd Number. The juxtaposition of military against civilian experiences with horror in In the Midst of Life seems to borrow a Maupassantian organizing principle for short-story collections. In any event, the popularity of The Odd Number at least partially paved the way for the final editorial acceptance of the Bierce volume.[20] It may even have facilitated its critical success.[21]

Bierce undoubtedly knew about the Sturges book. He may have been instrumental in having the Examiner publish one of its translations ("In the Moonlight") on 10 August 1890. A more interesting inference can be developed from one change Bierce felt compelled to make between the newspaper and the book version of one short story. Originally, "One Officer, One Man"—which Bierce did not include in In the Midst of Life until the collection was republished

---

50. Since Maupassant borrowed from Poe also, I suspect that the Frenchman's example reiterated Poe's aesthetic lessons for Bierce.

20. A number of early critics noted various artistic similarities between Bierce and Maupassant. In 1911 Frederic Taber Cooper proclaimed that Bierce was "a sort of American Maupassant" despite the iconoclast's claim that he saw little worth in contemporary foreign fiction; see "Ambrose Bierce: An Appraisal," Bookman 33 (1911): 471–80, reprinted in Critical Essays, 31, 36. Shortly after, a critic for the New York Evening Post favorably compared Bierce's terse short stories on war with Maupassant's; significant portions of this review were cited in "Another Attempt to Boost Bierce into Immortality," Current Opinion 65 (September 1918): 184–85, reprinted in Critical Essays, 50. Walter Neale identifies the cited critic as Percival Pollard in Life of Ambrose Bierce (New York: Walter Neale, 1929), 283.

Pattee notes briefly similarities between Maupassant's "Le Horla" and Bierce's "The Damned Thing" (1893) but judges the latter as cold and hence inferior (Development of the American Short Story, 305). Haldeen Braddy mentions the same parallel without any further development in "Ambrose Bierce and Guy de Maupassant," American Notes & Queries 1 (1941): 67–68. Fatout sees the same possibility (Ambrose Bierce, 202–3). In Buried Caesars: Essays in Literary Appreciation (1923; reprint, New York: AMS, 1970), 49–51, Vincent Starrett sees parallels between Bierce's "A Horseman in the Sky" and Maupassant's method.

21. Critics have long debated whether or not Bierce's volume met with critical success in 1892. McWilliams presents a strong case for the possibility that he secured his fame in America as well as in Great Britain (Ambrose Bierce, 211–12).

in volume 2 of his *Collected Works* in 1909—had been titled "A Coward" (on 17 February 1889). Although Bierce likely composed and published the tale before he knew of Maupassant, it has remarkable parallels with "Un lâche," which Sturges translated under the same title: "A Coward." By the time Bierce included his "A Coward" in *Can Such Things Be?* (1893), he had changed the title to "One Officer, One Man" and later kept the new title when he transferred the tale to the *In the Midst of Life* volume in his *Collected Works* in 1909.

In the Bierce tale Captain Graffenreid suffers the same cancerous fear that destroys Signoles in the Maupassant story.[22] Structurally, both texts pursue identical paths. They trace in descending helical fashion the psychological degeneration imposed upon a mind when imagination fills the lull before an anticipated test of courage (in one case, a duel; in the other, a battle). Paradoxically, both Signoles and Graffenreid end their maniacal dwelling upon the possibility of death by committing suicide, attesting to the power the mind ultimately holds over all horror in the human condition.

After years of administrative duties far from the war front, the inexperienced Graffenreid takes a field command and finds himself impatiently waiting for a battle to commence, wanting to prove his valor to his doubting peers and the men under him: "His spirit was buoyant, his faculties were riotous. He was in a state of mental exaltation and scarcely could endure the enemy's tardiness in advancing to the attack." At the front line, however, his fear intensifies at the whistle of a Confederate cannonball, "a hideous rushing sound that seemed to leap forward across the intervening space with inconceivable rapidity, rising from whisper to roar with too quick a gradation for attention to note the successive stages of its horrible progression!" When he shows his panic, the soldiers near the captain laugh derisively, which further alienates him. Thus sealed hermetically, his fear circles viciously; all of his preconceived notions about himself and war fail. Every event heightens anxiety. Sporadic sniping by the Confederates has little effect upon the integrity of the Union line, but the only man hit by this rifle fire falls dead right next to Graffenreid, forcing him to examine every gory nuance of what he feared most. Even recognizing his true enemy—

22. For a full discussion of the helical aspects in "Un lâche," see Chapter 2.

"The delay was hideous, maddening! It unnerved like a respite at the guillotine"—does not bring about relief or reconciliation (B1, 2:200, 201, 206).

Hearing the clamor of battle begin on the far right flank, Graffenreid loses control of "the whole range of his sensibilities." An idle thought while contemplating his sword provides him with the means by which to escape his dread. He remembers the classical Roman method for "heroic" suicide. At this point, the narrative point of view shifts from the captain's mind to a sergeant's who, standing behind the officer, "observed a strange sight." His attention drawn to Graffenreid's odd preparatory movements, the sergeant "saw spring from between the officer's shoulders a bright point of metal which prolonged itself outward, nearly a half-arm's length—a blade!" Bierce symbolically twists the captain's sword one more turn by ending the text with the corps commander's report on the battle: ". . . owing to the enemy's withdrawal from my front to reinforce his beaten left, my command was not seriously engaged. My loss was as follows: Killed, one officer, one man" (B1, 2:207).

Bierce's choice to retitle his story *In the Midst of Life* using its ironic four last words may indicate that he had indeed read *The Odd Number* and felt uncomfortable with the obvious parallels between the Maupassant story and his own. Based upon the dates involved, I do not think it possible that Bierce had read "Un lâche" before composing his tale—otherwise, why use a title that would bolster a charge of plagiarism? Nevertheless, confronted with the established popularity of Maupassant's story, Bierce probably sought to place some distance between it and his own by the emendation.[23]

At the very least, he certainly found in Maupassant a brother artist whose cynical vision of life matched his own and who made clearer his understanding of short-story structure. This had one minor effect on the tales he had already written. Bierce revised these texts between their newspaper and book versions using a Maupassantian principle: avoid revealing so much in the course of a plot that it dilutes the impact of the ending. For instance, in "One Officer, One Man," Bierce subsequently deleted the first line from the original version—"I shall break down! I shall break down!"—a declaration

---

23. The story was originally collected in *Can Such Things Be?* (1893); Bierce did not transfer it to *In the Midst of Life* until *Collected Works*.

that lessens the vividness of our impression of the captain's psychological descent because with it we anticipate each stage of it rather than immerse ourselves into his consciousness. Even the change of title succeeds in removing the author's prejudgment of his protagonist's cowardice, forcing us the audience to form our own opinion.

Some of Bierce's alterations owe even greater debt to a pristine notion of the surprise-ending structure.[24] In the original version of "One of the Missing," Bierce had divided the narrative concerning Jerome Searing's officer-brother into two parts—the first placed roughly one-third of the way in the text (right after the farm building collapses on the private), the second passage concluding the story. This construction separates the lieutenant's two time observations with the long passage on the musings of the entrapped Private Searing, a narrative distance too great for the reader to make the necessary interpretive associations. By relocating the first section to the end of the text, as he does in the *Collected Works* version of the story, Bierce has to effect an awkward retreat in narrative time, but he ensures our cognizance and our surprise over how much a mind can crowd into a short moment.

This tightening of his control over structure benefited even more the construction of the tales composed after *The Odd Number* reached the public. Above all else, Bierce seemed to strive for more incredible narrative tricks in the endings of these stories—much as if in reading Maupassant, Bierce had rededicated himself to shocking his audience; as if he had reaffirmed that his purpose as a short-story writer was to attack his reader's smug intellectual security. His post-1889 Civil War tales certainly achieve this aim.

Of the four *In the Midst of Life*–bound war stories published in the *Examiner* after November 1889, the most effective and historically successful is "An Occurrence at Owl Creek Bridge," published on 13 July 1890.[25] The lessons he learned from Maupassant and from his own previous fictional experiments gave Bierce the proper

24. For a testimonial to Bierce's intense editing of his *Collected Works*, see McWilliams, *Ambrose Bierce*, 297, 305.

25. The other texts and dates are: "Dramer Brune, Deserter: A War Memory of the Cumberland Mountains" (later retitled "The Story of a Conscience") (1 June 1890), "James Adderson, Philosopher and Wit" (later retitled "Parker Adderson, Philosopher") (22 February 1891), and "The Mocking-Bird: A Story of a Soldier Who Had a Dream" (31 May 1891).

insight into the well-wrought surprise. In addition to destroying our confidence in our own ability to read a text, such an ending redirects rather sharply the interpretive thrust of the plot. The tale becomes, then, a vicious and sweeping attack upon the audience's complacency and staid expectation of sentimentality.[26] In "Owl Creek Bridge" we empathize and even identify with the main character as he flees for his life. The nearer he comes to succeeding, the greater our wish that he elude his pursuers and reach the security of his home. And Bierce gives us just enough narrative rope so that we ultimately can hang ourselves intellectually.

Ironically, the object for our sympathy bears all the social labels that should arouse our hostility toward him. Peyton Farquhar is a Southern plantation owner, an avowed secessionist and slaveholder, who for dubious reasons had thus far evaded military service. The story begins with Farquhar already caught by Union forces and about to be hanged as a spy and saboteur. Initially, we view the scene rather dispassionately as Bierce describes the perfunctory action (though with grisly undertones) of the execution ceremony. The regimented pace of the proceeding immediately alerts us that time has been mystically slowed down. Gradually, Bierce shifts the narrative focus from a realist's position (that is, describing the scene from an external point of view) to a literary impressionist's, in which we enter the mind of the doomed Farquhar as he too notes how time has dilated:

> And now he became conscious of a new disturbance. . . . a sharp, distinct, metallic percussion like the stroke of a blacksmith's hammer upon the anvil. . . . Its recurrence as regular, but as slow as the tolling of a death knell. He awaited each stroke with impatience and—he knew not why—apprehension. The intervals of silence grew progressively longer; the delays became maddening. With greater infrequency the sounds increased in strength and sharpness. They hurt his ear like the thrust of a knife; he feared he would shriek. What he heard was the ticking of his watch. (B1, 2:31)

---

26. Davidson likewise notes Bierce's aggressive intentions directed at his reader: "This contiguity of narrative and interpretation [as well as] his trick endings . . . cue the reader to the ways in which Bierce works to minimize the distance between writer and reader, to extend the meaning of the narrative into the reader's life, and, finally, to assault the silence beyond the text" (*Experimental Fictions,* 55).

Bierce continues this playing with fictional time after the rope around Farquhar's neck "breaks" and he effects his "escape."[27] The violence of his struggle awakens his instinct for life:

> He was now in full possession of his physical senses. They were, indeed, preternaturally keen and alert. Something in the awful disturbance of his organic system had so exalted and refined them that they made record of things never before perceived. . . . He had come to the surface facing down the stream; in a moment the visible world seemed to wheel slowly round, himself the pivotal point . . . (B1, 2:38)

This obvious expansion of time sets up how our egos will be ironically subverted: Bierce clearly places throughout the tale sufficient clues about how the human mind reacts in a crisis, but we misinterpret their meaning because we are mired in our superficial and sentimental reading of the text.[28] In other words, we are shocked at the end to discover that time has indeed dilated, but it has done so far beyond the limits of what we imagined. After we suffer with the prisoner in his long, arduous ordeal in fleeing across the Alabama countryside, just when we share his joy as he reaches his home and wife (the symbols of his assured freedom), Bierce abruptly returns the narrative to the bridge:

> As he is about to clasp [his wife] he feels a stunning blow upon the back of the neck; a blinding white light blazes all about him with a sound like the shock of a cannon—then all is darkness and silence!
>
> Peyton Farquhar was dead; his body, with a broken neck, swung gently from side to side beneath the timbers of the Owl Creek bridge. (B1, 2:44–45)

27. Many critics have considered how Bierce manipulated time, particularly in this short story; for an example, see Eric Solomon, "The Bitterness of Battle: Ambrose Bierce's War Fiction," *Midwest Quarterly* 5 (1963–64): 147–65, reprinted in *Critical Essays*, 187–88.

28. In his close reading of "Owl Creek Bridge," Logan details how allusions to Shakespeare's *Henry IV, Part I* provide clues that would allow us to see through Farquhar's self-delusion ("Wry Seriousness," 198–200). Davidson notes less eclectic clues such as a throbbing neck and the loss of sensation in his feet that the prisoner feels as he "flees." She correctly concludes that "the physical reality of death finally begins to replace the psychic reality of imagined flight" (*Experimental Fictions*, 53).

Only here do we truly witness how desperately men cling to life. The entire lengthy narrative of the escape existed only in the single moment just before the hangman's rope did its work.[29]

Like Maupassant, Bierce asserts his authorial dominance over his audience by using such a structure.[30] The magnitude of the surprise challenges us to abandon our romantic delusions, leaving us agape over the extreme manifestations of human imagination. Because Farquhar needed impending death to heighten his sensibilities and to reveal to him that life merits celebration, we begin to question our ability to discern meaning in our own diurnal experience. The success of Bierce's attack upon our values not only renders us dumbfounded but also imprints the tale in our memory—an artistic aspiration, albeit a shallow one, that Bierce shared with Maupassant.

Maupassant's impact upon Bierce may have had a larger context than merely clarifying the American's concept of structure in his revisions and new compositions. I suspect that Maupassant's example may have guided Bierce in organizing In the Midst of Life. Maupassant's 1885 collection Contes du jour et de la nuit (Stories of day and night) explored the shared gothic symbolism between the subconscious horror of night and the conscious horror of day. Bierce similarly attempts to synthesize two superficially disparate phenomena in his volume. Evidence does not exist to prove that Sturges's translation inspired Bierce to seek original texts such as Contes, but circumstantial events suggest at least the possibility. Bierce had published some of the In the Midst of Life–bound civilian stories years earlier.[31] In the Examiner run, however, no civilian story destined for the collection found its way into a Sunday supplement until December 1889, a month after the publication of The Odd Number. From this sequence, I reconstruct the following scenario: Bierce's infatuation with the aesthetic spirit he discovers in The

29. Logan believes that this revelation represents Bierce's struggle to systematize his philosophy: "it is a speculation on the nature of time and on the nature of abnormal psychology, particularly on processes of abnormal perception and cognition" ("Wry Seriousness," 196).

30. For a discussion of Bierce's distaste for inattentive readers, see Logan, "Wry Seriousness," 196–97.

31. In Ambrose Gwinett [sic] Bierce: Bibliography and Biographical Data (New York: Burt Franklin, 1935; reprint, 1968), 7, Joseph Gaer reports that "A Holy Terror" (published in the "Civilian" section of Tales) first appeared in The Wasp on 23 December 1883.

Odd Number compels him to read more Maupassant, leading the American to texts such as *Contes* in which he encounters Maupassant's synthetic approach to arranging stories in a volume. This insight reminds Bierce of his previous compositions about civilian experiences with horror that would counterpoint his recent tales in the *Examiner* about the Civil War. Not only this, he also resumes writing such stories to supplement the civilian half of his upcoming volume.[32] Granted, such speculation without sufficient support strains credibility; it does nonetheless diagram how fond both authors were of pursuing a metaphysical conceit by yoking (almost violently) two separate aspects of the human condition in order to demonstrate the omnipresence of horror in it.

The parallels between the soldier and civilian tales are clear and obviously deliberate. For example, "A Watcher by the Dead" explores the physically disfiguring effects of intense horror, much in the manner of "One of the Missing."[33] In the latter, Lieutenant Adrian Searing fails to recognize his own brother after Jerome's ordeal. In the other story, after their practical joke goes awry, two men misidentify the horror-transformed appearances of their victim and their co-conspirator. Jarette, a gambler willing to accept any wager, agrees to sit alone by a "corpse" in an abandoned house throughout a night. One of the three perpetrators, William Mancher, plays the role of the corpse. As in a typical Bierce plot, the terror invoked by the stillness of the night overcomes Jarette's reason in descending-helical fashion. Bierce breaks off the narrative perspective at that point with the "body" moving and the dupe's primal fears coming to the surface.

The narrative shifts to the perspectives of Harper and Helberson—Mancher's fellow jokesters. Fearing the worst, they go to the abandoned house and find it the object of police and public scrutiny. There they encounter two spectacles. The first is a man maniacally struggling to flee, whom Harper "recognizes" as Jarette: "His eyes, wild and restless, had in them something more terrifying than his

32. The following "Civilian" stories were published in the *Examiner* after November 1889: "The Watcher by the Dead" (later retitled "A Watcher by the Dead") (29 December 1889), "The Man and the Snake" (29 June 1890), and "The Boarded Window: An Incident in the Life of an Ohio Pioneer" (12 April 1891).
33. From title through plot to psychological insight, "A Watcher by the Dead" resembles Maupassant's "Auprès d'un morte."

apparently superhuman strength. His face, smooth-shaven, was bloodless, his hair frost-white." Inside the house is a body, presumedly Mancher's: "The face of the body showed yellow, repulsive, horrible! The eyes were partly open and upturned and the jaw fallen; traces of froth defiled the lips, the chin, the cheeks" (B1. 2:304, 306). These images confirmed Harper and Helberson's previous anxieties: they had already conceded that a frightened Jarette might kill Mancher.

Bierce completes the surprise-inversion format by having Harper and Helberson, who had both fled the country in fear of prosecution, meet the live Mancher by chance years later, after their return to America. As Mancher dispels their confusion, Bierce simultaneously clarifies for us the potential that horror holds for destroying life or violently altering its quality. (Though still living, Mancher himself had been driven insane by the experience.)

In essence, the civilian section of Bierce's volume rebuts the message of the war section. Considered alone, the tales of the Civil War seem to confront our romantic notions about heroism and other human conduct in battle. The civilian texts, however, suggest that we can find counterparts in our contemporary experience. Thus, war does not represent a horrible aberration from life; instead it acts only as a catalyst, crowding many such occurrences within a brief time span and a confined space. In other words, to imagine the terrors of war, we need only to seek the horror around us—the grim report one finds in a newspaper about a murder, the sordid testimony one hears in a police court, the unexpected curves that chance throws into our own lives. For Bierce the violent shock of his son's death likely synthesized his brother-against-brother memories about the Civil War with a darkening vision of the world around him during the 1880s and 1890s. In this respect, he would find in Maupassant not only a blueprint for style and organization but also—given the Frenchman's Schopenhauerian gloom—a kindred soul.

In his own way, then, Bierce envisioned *In the Midst of Life* partially along the borders that American literary naturalists would try to map out later in the decade. His surprise endings usually had twists that revealed how much men were victimized by forces outside their control. And, as practiced by a Crane, a Norris, a Chopin, a Dreiser, or a London, Bierce's inherent pessimism would incorporate both the biological and environmental sources for deterministic phenomena in his fiction. Events as diverse as a Private Searing's inability to control his instinctual fear and the pot shot taken by his whimsical enemy doubly condemn him. Both the individual and a bizarre universe conspire to abet self-destruction. Viewed together, the stories of In the Midst of Life almost postulate man's unconscious yearning for suicide. In the surprise-inversion format, however, Bierce's protagonists finally realize this lifelong pursuit only at the moment of impending death. Thus, for Bierce such tumultuous insight cannot enrich an individual's life—it becomes merely the last ironic twist of fate's knife.

Maupassant and O. Henry

In the Ohio State Penitentiary from 1898 to 1901, prisoner number 30664 began his first significant experiments as a short-story craftsman. Having the benefit of witnessing America's decadelong fascination with the trick-ending text, the ambitious, budding author William Sidney Porter (O. Henry) had a ready blueprint to construct his early efforts in fiction. Maupassant's example did take hold during the 1890s, as the commentator for the August 1890 edition of the Critic noted.[34] Thus, whether or not Porter read Maupassant during the 1890s (which does, however, seem likely), his perusal of contemporary American fiction would have introduced him at least at second hand to the Frenchman's structural precepts. While neither he nor any other biographer addresses whether Porter read Maupassant any earlier, C. Alphonso Smith notes that late in his life, Porter "kept a copy of De Maupassant always at hand."[35] This

34. See the quotation in note 4 above in this chapter. In O. Henry (William Sydney Porter) (New York: Twayne, 1965), 138, Eugene Current-Garcia summarizes Graves Glenwood Clark's unpublished master's thesis, "The Development of the Surprise Ending in the American Short Story from Washington Irving Through O. Henry" (Columbia University, 1930). In tracing the historical development of the surprise ending in American literature, Clark states that Porter added little to the form already perfected by writers such as Edgar Allan Poe, Bret Harte, Frank Stockton, Ambrose Bierce, and Thomas Bailey Aldrich. He identifies seven paths the trick ending may take: "[1] the hoax and practical joke, [2] the anti-conventional or distorted revelation of events, [3] the paradoxical or antithetical disclosure, [4] the manipulation of psychological concepts, [5] the double reversal, [6] the problem close, [and 7] disclosing sudden proof of the tyranny of habit or of environment." Of these variations, Clark asserts only the last was a Porter innovation.

35. O. Henry Biography (Garden City, N.Y.: Doubleday, Page, 1916), 83.

edition was likely one of the several editorially butchered translations commissioned and published by M. Walter Dunne under
various editions starting in 1903.[36]
Despite its quality, this "complete" set of Maupassant's works in
English rekindled Maupassant's presence in the minds of American
critics. When his publishers distributed advertising circulars for *The
Four Million* that invited comparisons between Maupassant and
their new author, critics quickly accepted their proposition both to
praise and condemn O. Henry's tales in that and subsequent volumes. In the following, note how the reviewer presumes Maupassant's usefulness as a standard and how Porter measures up to it:

> The conventional paragraph of exploitation issued by the
> publishers speaks of one or two stories of the collection
> having a terror and grimness that is suggestive of Maupassant.
> Now we are accustomed to that sort of thing. It comes to us
> every day. It used to exasperate us, but of later years it has
> only bored. In this instance, however, we wish to record the
> very extraordinary fact that these stories of O. Henry's, to
> which reference is made, actually do suggest Maupassant.
> Beyond this we need say nothing.[37]

Soon, such analogies became so commonplace that one reviewer
entitled his sampling of contemporary criticism regarding O. Henry
"A Yankee Maupassant."[38]
Eventually, several critics balked at the prospect of proclaiming O.
Henry's genius by establishing his aesthetic debt to a foreigner, and
so argued for the American's superiority: "His work has been compared with de Maupassant's. But this is not fair—he is not like de

36. For an account of what was likely a publishing con game at the turn of the
century, see Francis Steegmuller, *Maupassant: A Lion in the Path* (New York: Grosset
and Dunlap, 1949), 355–59. Steegmuller's assessment ended the "authoritative"
status the Dunne edition had enjoyed for over forty years; however, its legacy still
inexplicably continues: the 1985 Avenel edition of *The Complete Stories of Guy de
Maupassant* reprints the ten volumes of short stories from the 1903 translation.
Among other dubious practices, Dunne included sixty-five stories not written by
Maupassant as part of his "complete works." Ironically, the only "Maupassant story"
that Smith attempts to compare to a Porter tale is one of these bogus texts (*O. Henry
Biography*, 208).
37. "Chronicle and Comment," *The Bookman* (New York) 23 (June 1906): 365.
38. *Current Literature* 45 (1908): 518–20.

Maupassant except in the remarkable cleverness and brilliancy with which his plots are worked out; but in his expression, in his individuality, and in his humor, he is pure American."[39] Later, in commenting on *Heart of the West* (1907), Henry James Forman added: "Cattle-king, cowboy, miner, the plains and the chaparral—material of the 'dime novel,' but all treated with the skill of a Maupassant, and a humor Maupassant never dreamed of."[40]

Shortly after Porter's death, critical assessments about his quality versus Maupassant's grew less favorable. In a review of Porter's posthumously published volume *Sixes and Sevens*, focusing attention especially upon "Makes the Whole World Kin" an anonymous critic comments:

> Now, this is a story which we can imagine being told, in his lighter moods, by the European writer to whom O. Henry has so frequently been compared. But whereas Maupassant, relying on the innate humor of the idea, would have told his story soberly, we have in O. Henry the "rapid fire" manner of a newer day. Almost every line has its grip, and every sentence has its surprise. In other words, manner strives to be more extravagant even than matter.[41]

By 1916, such attacks became more frequent and sweeping. Katherine Fullerton Gerould called O. Henry a "Pernicious Influence" on literature who "did not write the short story [but] wrote the expanded anecdote":

> In a short story you should get life in the round, as you do in Maupassant's short stories. From seeing how people act in certain circumstances which are described you should be able to imagine how they would act in any other circumstance.
>
> It's not a matter of length. In the very shortest of Maupassant's stories you find the people etched in so clearly that you know them; you know how they would act whatever extraneous conditions might enter. But you do not find this to be the case in O. Henry's stories; you know how the people acted in

39. Gilman Hall, "Tarkington and O. Henry," *Everybody's* 17 (October 1907): 576.
40. "O. Henry's Short Stories," *North American Review* 187 (1908): 783.
41. "Current Fiction," *The Nation* (New York) 93 (1911): 493.

one set of circumstances, but you have no idea how they would act at any other time.

Therefore, in this respect it seems to me that Maupassant has moral significance, and O. Henry has none.[42]

During his life, however, Porter felt uncomfortable with the critics' continual assessment of the similarity between his stories and Maupassant's. At one point, he testily commented: "I have been called . . . the American De Maupassant. Well, I never wrote a filthy word in my life, and I don't like to be compared to a filthy writer."[43] This statement is interesting for two reasons. First, it indicates the status of Maupassant's reputation in America, especially after rumors about his satyric personality had spread and the Dunne editions had placed more of his sexually oriented stories before an English-speaking audience. Second, it demonstrates the smoke screen that Porter tried to place between him and Maupassant. Seeking to establish himself as an original and self-reliant writer, he attempted to divert critical notice away from techniques in structure and to direct it toward the subject of Maupassant's naturalistic use of sexual instincts in his writing, with which Porter shared little inclination.

Whatever his practical motives, however, Porter's borrowing of the surprise-inversion did cultivate editors and audience alike in his bid to establish himself in the literary marketplace. In addition, it provided him with a pattern to mass-produce stories when his need for money increased during his last ten years. More important, however, his writing gave him a psychological avenue to escape from his own difficulties. Whereas he could not cope with the bizarre twists in his own life, he could control fate in his fictional universe. This was a diversion with which his readers could sympathize and often vicariously share.

Oddly, Porter ultimately used the trick ending to project a universe somewhat along the lines of the naturalist's philosophy. In a preponderance of his tales, human intention often does not contribute directly or sufficiently to effect a result. Even when

42. Reported in Joyce Kilmer, "Is O. Henry a Pernicious Literary Influence?" *New York Times Magazine*, 23 July 1916, p. 12. Gerould echoed similar though briefer sentiments in her "The American Short Story," *Yale Review* n.s. 13 (1924): 642–45.

43. Smith, *O. Henry Biography*, 83.

that end had been (or would have been) initially desired by a protagonist, events out of his control rather than his volition bring it about. On several occasions a character suffers an ignoble fate that tallies with Bierce's notion of determinism. Many other O. Henry plots lead a character (and the reader) toward sentimental, almost idyllic, achievements. In doing so, though, the author reduces good fortune, like bad, to the mere product of coincidence.

This is where Porter departed from the American naturalists who preceded him. He agreed with them that man was at the mercy of a chaotic and, at times, brutish world, that his belief he could manipulate his destiny was pretentious and absurd, that the accidental interplay among uncontrollable internal and external causes created effects that often seem in retrospect ironical and overwhelming. But Porter also examined the flip side of determinism that most early literary naturalists ignored. For him the causal chain that yoked an array of instincts and environmental occurrences could, and often did, lead to fortunate outcomes. Thus, rather than the naturalist tendency to present human endeavor with consistent and broad pessimistic brush strokes, the O. Henry fictive world (as painted in most of his stories) disintegrates into a canvas spotted by an ambivalent pointillist. In a typical O. Henry collection, the stories in which some measure of happiness is achieved often outnumber those in which a protagonist suffers ignominy, defeat, or death; the aggregate impact of the former, however, seldom dominates their darker counterparts. Thus, all degenerate into a hodgepodge where good and evil are both products of chance.[44] By implication, Porter does not even allow man's ego the luxury of imagining that universal laws conspire to defeat his aspirations.[45]

44. Current-Garcia mentions one aspect of this ambivalence in interpretive import. Depending upon which stories he chooses, a critic could support either a Marxist thesis that O. Henry intended to ridicule the social failure in capitalism or a more conservative one that he "offer[ed] a complacent, if sometimes cynical, approval of the status quo" (O. Henry, 100–101).

45. Kent Bales suggests a relationship between Porter's use of literary structure and his parodic intent: "Parody . . . ceases to be simply the indulgent or satirical mocking of literary or other art forms. It becomes a passkey to the world of forms, and perhaps as well an instrument for registering the pressures exerted upon those forms by the realities of the contiguous but directly unknown realms of natural, social, psychological, and perhaps even spiritual force"; see "O. Henry: 1862–1910," American Writers:

Consequently, Porter did not employ the surprise-inversion formula, as did Bierce and Maupassant, to assault his audience's confidence in reading; the O. Henry trick could just as likely arouse sentimental delight as horrify us with a violent, last-second correction of our misperception of a plot circumstance.[46] Rather than an instrument of artistic attack, then, Porter transformed the surprise-inversion into a personal psychic defense mechanism. I suspect that Porter gravitated toward abrupt conclusions, particularly in his sentimental tales, because continuing such a text would have meant returning his protagonists to the diurnal, commonplace, in some cases poverty-stricken existence that oppressed them when the story began. As the pen name O. Henry became a mask to disguise the embittered and ashamed William Sidney Porter, embezzler and ex-convict, the surprise-inversion story lifted him, if only for a moment, out of his continual lament over his own life. If reconciliation with one's self, if happiness with one's lot, if pleasure in attaining a goal could only be sustained in brief interludes, then so be it. O. Henry the romantic did not have to deal with aftereffects. He need only end with a character's realization of achievement or change. Thus, the typical O. Henry tale celebrates escape—sometimes from physical confines, sometimes from social restraints, often from self-delusion—invariably stealing an illusionary insightful and resplendent moment away from reality.[47]

Porter's concept of story structure developed in two stages. Initially, he experimented with form during his first significant efforts to write marketable stories while still a prisoner at the Columbus, Ohio, prison. Although these fourteen texts were even-

---

A Collection of Literary Biographies, supp. II, part 1: W. H. Auden to O. Henry, ed. A. Walton Litz (New York: Charles Scribner's Sons, 1981), 406.

46. Regarding previous full studies of Maupassant's influence on Porter, I have not been able to locate Crystal Ray Ross's Le Conteur américain O. Henry et l'art de Maupassant (Strasbourg: Imprimerie Strasbourgeoise, 1925). Bibliographer Richard C. Harris describes the content of Ross's book as consisting of six sections, one of which treats the parallels between the authors; see Harris, William Sydney Porter [O. Henry]: A Reference Guide (Boston: G. K. Hall, 1980), 95.

47. B. M. Ejxenbaum suggests that Porter was deliberately not realistic because he wanted to inspire an intellectual and not an emotional response in his reader; see O. Henry and the Theory of the Short Story, trans. I. R. Titunik (Ann Arbor: University of Michigan, 1968; originally published in Russian, 1925), 23. For reasons given later in this chapter, I disagree with this assessment.

tually scattered among seven different collections, they share enough traits to merit considering them as a group, especially as several of them explore the sentimental origins of altruism.[48]

Whereas Porter drew upon the diversity of his own experiences and acquaintanceships as source material for these early apprentice efforts, he mastered his short-story formula and focused his attention by the time he issued *The Four Million*, his second published book-length work but in truth his first significant volume.[49] In it he suggests how much and how often coincidence, accident, and whim determine success, complacency or tragedy. Amid the nostalgia for the simple but antiquated values, despite the racial bigotry and ethnic slurs in authorial voice, and even with contrived plots that often bleach personalities into caricatures, O. Henry's repetitive use of form succeeds in *The Four Million* in presenting a unified vision of New York City. His continual and insistent use of the trick ending does quickly deflate its effect so as to lessen our surprise in the latter stories in the volume, but each successive "revelation" leads us from buoyant through ambiguous to heart-rending fates.[50] The common link of form among these disparate ends invites us to juxtapose phenomena as different as the poignancy in mutual self-sacrifice and the ironic circumstances underscoring the suicides of two people, the

48. To the twelve originally identified by Smith in his *O. Henry Biography* (170), Langford added two more texts *(Alias O. Henry*, 137), all of which follow: "Whistling Dick's Christmas Stocking," "Georgia's Ruling," "An Afternoon Miracle" (originally "The Miracle of Lava Canyon"), "A Medley of Moods" (also titled "Blind Man's Holiday"), "Money Maze," "No Story," "A Fog in Santone," "A Blackjack Bargainer," "The Enchanted Kiss," "Hygeia at the Solito," "Rouge et Noir," "The Duplicity of Hargraves," "The Marionettes," and "A Chaparral Christmas Gift." Current-Garcia's brief comment that "The Enchanted Kiss" "employs a sequence of weird dreams vaguely reminiscent of de Maupassant to dramatize the contrast between illusion and reality" *(O. Henry*, 85) suggests that Porter may have read some of his stories by 1900.

49. Although composed of stories originally published individually, his first volume, *Cabbages and Kings* (1904), attempts to coordinate the texts so that the collection approaches the structure of a novel. I omit discussion of *Cabbages and Kings* here because although it does employ the surprise-inversion, it also integrates other literary techniques that Porter quickly abandoned.

50. In his sympathetic reading of O. Henry, Current-Garcia nevertheless notes this fatal stylistic flaw: "In sheer quantity O. Henry's surprise endings are therefore impressive, though qualitatively too many of them are so patently contrived that the sophisticated reader soon tires of the guessing contest which their anticipated discovery interposes between him and the author" *(O. Henry*, 138).

cumulative effect of which weakens our faith in the capacity individual faith has to sway our destiny.

One common pattern among the fourteen stories Porter wrote while in prison shows desires being satisfied in convoluted and unpredictable ways. In the beginning of a typical text, he quickly establishes a plight and a protagonist's hope for his future, but then has his hero apparently fail in striving for that end. At the brink of the precipice, however, a surprising twist rescues the hero, which ironically fulfills the original desire. Obviously, Porter's own situation contributed to this implicit faith in the future. The distress he felt in his past and present left him with only one avenue for escape. These stories tell us that Porter could imagine escaping from the humiliation he felt over his incarceration by blindly trusting that a whimsical universe would lead him to some sort of personal salvation.[51]

On an allegorical level, Porter probably equated his own life with "Cricket" McGuire's in "Hygeia at the Solito."[52] Porter's own spiritual malaise became physically manifested in McGuire's tuberculosis and poverty.[53] The "exfeather-weight prize-fighter" and jack-of-all-dubious-trades finds himself broke and stranded in Texas, whose climate the New Yorker had hoped would alleviate his condition. An altruistic cattleman, Curtis Raidler, takes pity on the slowly dying man so obviously out of his element in this environment (which perhaps parallels Porter's thoughts about his own existence in prison). Taking McGuire back to his ranch, Raidler tries to make life comfortable for him, but in return the

51. Smith offers much testimonial evidence concerning Porter's reaction to prison life. The biographer states that Porter exited prison "a changed man. Something of the old buoyancy and waggishness had gone, never to return." Smith even suggests that Porter's choice for a new career as a writer, who creates his product in isolation, was motivated by his desire to keep private "his secret" (O. Henry, 146–67). Langford gives a similar account of Porter's state of mind during and after prison, suggesting that his writing became his primary means of psychological escape from his anxiety (Alias O. Henry, 132–37).

52. "Hygeia at the Solito" was first published in the February 1903 issue of Everybody's and was subsequently collected in Heart of the West.

53. Current-Garcia mentions but does not elaborate on the autobiographical nature of the story (O. Henry, 82). Porter's knowledge of consumption was obviously the result of his pharmacological duties while a prisoner. Langford quotes at length from a Porter letter that describes an epidemic and the appalling conditions for treatment at the Columbus penitentiary (Alias O. Henry, 135).

city man "instituted the reign of terror at the Solito Ranch. For a few weeks McGuire blustered and boasted and swaggered before the cowpunchers who rode in for miles around to see this latest importation of Raidler's. He was an absolutely new experience to them . . . like a being from a new world" (H1, 159). Although two months of coddling by Raidler and the ranch hands feed his ego, McGuire complains of feeling weaker, which eventually arouses in his benefactor suspicions of fraud.

This signals the end of Raidler's conscious impact on the welfare of his self-adopted charge. He had wanted to palliate McGuire's physical plight, perhaps even to cure it. When he gives up the quest, coincidence takes control of matters. Raidler sends a doctor to see McGuire. The physician pronounces him "sound as a new dollar," but Porter withholds vital information about the examination so that he can set up his trick ending. Needless to say, Raidler (as well as the reader) feels certain that McGuire shams his symptoms. Seeking vengeance, the cattleman forces the New Yorker to work off the cost of indulging him for so long. At this juncture, Porter conveniently dispatches Raidler by having him attend to a family matter in Alabama.

When the cattleman finally returns home, we learn along with him of the perverse irony of events. When Raidler intended to do good, his careful forbearance only worsened the indeed ill McGuire. In contrast, by consigning his patient to live and work outdoors riding the range to tend the herd, Raidler unintentionally immerses McGuire into a climate and exercise routine that cures him. Raidler then finds out that the doctor had examined the wrong man. Thus, rather than killing the Irishman with kindness, Raidler is manipulated by someone else's mistake to set into motion circumstances that achieve the goal he initially wanted. Not only that, the work ethic of range life brings about a spiritual revolution in McGuire, who forsakes his "something for nothing" bravado while earning the respect of his new peers.

Our accumulated impression of Raidler, then, is of a pawn who presumed he could rule like a king. He could only imagine simple causal relationships. In his self-image as the Good Samaritan, he reduces his altruistic syllogism to the point that intention alone suffices in effecting a cure. Life and its unpredictability prove to be more complicated, though. Man's powerlessness, however, does

not doom him or render his life meaningless. Raidler's last sensations are relief that his revenge did not kill McGuire and wonder
that it instead helped to drive the disease from his lungs. Raidler
was foolish to believe his actions could be meaningful, but ultimately even that flaw also becomes insignificant. Gone from the
surprise-inversion technique was Maupassant's probing for the
jugular—only his irony remained.

In another early story, Porter constructed the central metaphor
for his future canon. As he did frequently, he used the tale's title
not to preidentify a vital character or locale but to provide his
readers with an interpretive key, which in itself violates the
realist's (and thus Maupassant's) credo of noninterference in the
audience's judgment of a text. Thus, the title "The Marionettes"
does not refer to any specific aspect of the plot but instead
establishes a conceit that directs our attention to the inability of
the characters to control their lives. All indeed become puppets
to coincidence, tragedy, and their own ingrained values. As in
many of his future efforts, Porter could not suggest who or what
controls the strings. He could only marvel at fate's bizarre manifestations.

The pivotal figure in "The Marionettes" is Charles Spencer
James, a sort of a cut-rate Professor Moriarty, a licensed physician
who in his clandestine night life leads a gang of burglars.[54] In the
beginning, Porter carefully shades the darker side of the doctor's
soul, chronicling his latest exploit, which netted the thief an $830
share of a $2,500 haul. Already, Porter allows us to see a depth in
the physician's true character. Our vision as readers is thus superior to that of the trusting society of New York City, who can only
see Doctor James's "good citizenship, his devotion to his family,
and his success as a practitioner" (H1, 974). Even the physician's
black bag becomes only a veneer of symbolic respectability; inside
it lies his booty and the instruments of his criminal trade.

Porter thus presents James as a manipulator, a cynic who defies
social laws and even fate itself. And at first he does appear to win
by successfully duping the police and protecting his secret. Unexpectedly, however, a medical crisis interferes with his criminal

54. First printed in *Black Cat* during April 1902, "The Marionettes" was collected
in the posthumous volume *Rolling Stones* (1912).

schemes. Recognizing him as a doctor by his bag, a servant beseeches James to follow her to the Chandler home where the husband lies dying after suffering a heart attack. Here, Porter presents us with the other pole of James's soul. He is a competent physician, capable of acute observation, rapid diagnosis, and accurate medical decisions. His sympathies quickly fall to Amy Chandler, as he notes her bruises and concludes that her husband had recently beat her. Consequently, his attempt to maintain control of all about him becomes directed at easing the wife's distress over the impending death of her spouse.

With both faces of his protagonist fully exposed, Porter then has fate present James with a tempting dilemma after he has been left alone to tend to his patient. The dying man utters: "The money— the twenty thousand dollars." The thief presumes that cash had been secreted in the room: "There arose in Doctor James's brain and heart the instincts of his other profession. Promptly, as he acted in everything, he decided to learn the whereabouts of this money, and at the calculated and certain cost of a human life" (H1, 978). The nitroglycerin he had employed earlier that night to crack a safe ironically has a medical use. Although it will inevitably hasten Chandler's death, the diluted chemical does manage to revive him sufficiently for a short, lucid conversation.

Fate again turns the tables for the doctor. His patient's reference to money was a regret about gambling away his wife's entire inheritance. James had committed murder (by causing Chandler's premature death) for no material profit. His greed, which could only be satiated by securing the twenty thousand and vanishing into the night, was misled and thus defeated by chance.

That same randomness in the permutations of life had simultaneously aroused his instinctual sentimentality. Ascertaining from the servant that Amy Chandler now faced destitution, the doctor bestows upon her the $830 from his previous activity that night, fabricating that Rob Chandler had bequeathed it so that she could "carry out his last request": "That was that you should return to your old home, and, in after days, when time shall have made it easier, forgive his many sins against you." The physician's altruistic "lie fanned into life one last spark of tenderness where she had thought all was turned to ashes and dust"; on that note James leaves without even claiming any gratitude for services rendered (H1, 983).

Controlled by the taut strings of fate, the intentions of marionette James flip-flop so many times that we can only see his final act as a momentary gesture to a suppressed romantic impulse rather than a decisive commitment to pursue more socially acceptable goals. In essence, the interplay between internal and external factors guided the doctor's belated but effective charity. Nevertheless, our surprise at his kindness does not elevate his act beyond that of a whim.[55] Thus, even at this early developmental stage of his writing career, Porter was already shackling himself to a form that failed to penetrate human motivation with any substantial theoretical foundation. By diluting the aggressive potential of the surprise-inversion, as found in a Maupassant or a Bierce text, Porter meandered his way in describing the human condition, depending upon plot tricks that evoked sensations of irony and delight but no profound and consistent insight.

Such a limited vision often flatters its subjects. It tends to exaggerate the importance of commonplace events. It celebrates the significant moment that must be experienced by the individual but that also arouses his neighbor's empathy. Thus, when Porter applied his technique to render thumbnail fictional sketches of New Yorkers in the short stories that were eventually collected in The Four Million (1906), his readers found the portraits pleasant and usually complimentary, feeding their metropolitan ego especially concerning the mythology of dynamism and diversity associated with their city.[56] The surprise-inversion does suit the extent of the typical city-dweller's curiosity about his neighbors: he usually remains interested in a stranger's story until the punch line is reached, after which he reduces his impression into an ironic tile to add to his mosaic conception of a colorful city. The

55. Langford has a differing interpretation, placing "The Marionettes" among eight stories written in prison that posited "the vindication of a character who has in some way forfeited his claim to respectability or even integrity," a view which has obvious implications for Porter himself (Alias O. Henry, 150).

56. Langford lists a few samples of negative reviews of Heart of the West, O. Henry's next published volume, in which several critics objected to the author's apparent abandonment of "little old New York" for source material (Alias O. Henry, 212). I suggest that these Gotham readers were rankled by the notion that the O. Henry formula for insight could be applied elsewhere.

Four Million provides us with twenty-five such tales, each of which tries to substantiate how Gotham customs, privileges, plights, and circumstances promote chance events not possible elsewhere in the world.[57]

O. Henry had a subtler purpose, though. Of all his short-story collections, *The Four Million* has perhaps the strongest structural integrity linking the individual tales. Several are among the best in Porter's career because he completed them after his apprenticeship but before the erosion of his enthusiasm. He loosely arranged the volume in descending order of geniality—from blissful revelations to pessimistic and, at times, self-damning resignation.[58] Along the way, the repetitive use of form fuses the diversity of New York phenomena. Porter orchestrates matters even further by planting parallel stories at intervals in the volume, each isolating a differing manifestation of the randomness in human existence. The sum total of these insights equals zero: if happenstance brings a dilemma to a happy conclusion in one corner of New York, it will be balanced by a failure in another case with similar circumstances.

The majority of the initial stories in *The Four Million* portray New York dwellers as quaint and, in several instances, quite heroic, an impression Porter tries to capture at a poignant moment. For example, in the second and sixth stories of his volume, he details with sentimental relish one splendid aspect in the daily struggle against poverty: mutual self-sacrifice. Both "The Gift of the Magi" and "A Service of Love" follow the same pattern.[59] In

57. By Current-Garcia's count, O. Henry eventually wrote 125 New York stories, which he and his posthumous editors distributed over six volumes (*O. Henry*, 96, 175n).

For a discussion of the sources of Porter's conceptions for New York City, see Martin B. Ostrofsky, "O. Henry's Use of Stereotypes in His New York Stories: An Example of the Utilization of Folklore in Literature," *New York Folklore Quarterly* 7, nos. 1–2 (Summer 1981): 41–64.

58. Bales notes this same descent of spirit throughout the volume. He proposes that "The Gift of the Magi," "Mammon and the Archer," and "The Furnished Room" provide an internal framework for the collection that permits the reader to perceive this transformation ("O. Henry," 408).

59. Current-Garcia notes the similarity between the two stories, but he does not analyze their parallels (*O. Henry*, 104). In *Cheap Rooms and Restless Hearts: A Study of Formula in the Urban Tales of William Sydney Porter* (Bowling Green: Bowling Green State University Popular Press, 1988), 39–44, 106, Karen Charmaine Blansfield identifies both "Magi" and "Service" as belonging to the same subcategory of Porter's

each, a young couple confront a difficult choice placed upon them by their scant means. Each spouse secretly sacrifices something dear to him or her for the sake of the other. At the surprise conclusion, both husband and wife discover each other's covert unselfishness and how their individual efforts canceled each other out. Nonetheless, Porter proposes that the spirit of sacrifice permeates true love: the satisfaction a husband and wife gain from such insight renders meaningless any initial desire for material or cultural gain. The surprise-inversion form abets such a didactic intent for it concludes the texts at the moment of blissful discovery. In both stories, to continue the narrative would have meant to return each couple to the poverty that ruled their lives, which would dim their recent illumination. Apparently, Porter could celebrate revelation but could not deal with its possible inadequacy to provide any sustained relief from circumstances increasingly desperate.

The most celebrated of his tales, "The Gift of the Magi," needs no extended summary here.[60] Basically, we follow Della Young's quest to procure a perfect Christmas gift for her husband despite their reduced means. To buy a platinum fob for her husband's prize possession—his grandfather's gold watch—the wife parts with hers: she sells her long hair to a wig maker. The plot hinges upon Porter's withholding until the conclusion the parallel activities of the husband, James, who concurrently sells his watch to purchase for his wife an expensive comb set. Here, the author intrudes his voice to pronounce judgment:

And here I have lamely related to you the uneventful chronicle of two foolish children in a flat who most unwisely sacrificed for each other the greatest treasures of their house. But in a last word to the wise of these days let it be said that of all who give gifts these two were the wisest. Of all who give and receive gifts, such as they are wisest. Everywhere they are wisest. They are the magi. (H1, 11)

---

more frequently used plot pattern. Essentially, both texts depend upon the two protagonists working at "cross purposes." Blansfield gives in tandem a close reading of both texts.

60. "The Gift of the Magi" was written originally for the New York Sunday World Magazine, 10 December 1905.

In essence, this improbable simultaneous proof of love creates an elegant conclusion that outweighs the sum of the individual gifts. Had, for instance, Della surrendered her hair while James did nothing commensurate, we would focus upon the materialistic nature of the event, judging her to be impulsive, doting, unpractical and, at times, petty. The shock of Porter's final plot twist drives such evaluations from our immediate thoughts and leaves us with the significant irony that only coincidence can inspire.[61]

The thematic companion story to "The Gift of the Magi"—"A Service of Love"—accomplishes the same interpretive effect, but Porter somewhat undermines the exaltation in the final discovery by making the sacrifices in it more substantial.[62] Della and James from "Magi" are slightly altered in "A Service" to Delia and Joe, but rather than prizing material objects, the Larrabees value music and painting.[63] Granted that their pursuit of art seems pretentious, especially as described by Porter's interested narrator, whose assessment becomes accentuated by the story's thematic refrain: "When one loves one's Art no service seems too hard" (H1, 24). Overwhelmed by financial problems, both husband and wife make sacrifices that each tries to hide from the other (and, for the moment, the reader) through elaborate and creative lies. The wife pretends to give music lessons; the husband, to sell his watercolors and sketches. In truth, both work in different parts of the same laundry. Not only were both willing to forgo their art for the sake of their partner's love of art, they both tried to cover up their activities to avoid arousing guilt in their spouse.

Like Della Chandler's loss of her cherished hair, Delia Larrabee also pays a physical price. She suffers a severe burn on her hand from a hot iron, which likely threatens her career as a pianist. Despite all the dreams that circumstances force them to relin-

61. Current-Garcia isolates Porter's essential thrust in the story as the "fundamental value in ordinary family life. Unselfish love shared, regardless of the attendant difficulties or distractions—this is the idea repeatedly implied as a criterion in his fictional treatment of domestic affairs. If such love is present, life can be a great adventure transcending all drabness; if it is absent, nothing else can take its place" (O. Henry, 116).

62. The New York Sunday World Magazine published "A Service of Love" on 8 January 1905.

63. Blansfield also notes the similarity in names between these stories (Cheap Rooms, 106).

quish, the Larrabees nevertheless find something more meaningful, as Delia amends their oft-repeated maxim to just: "When one loves." The coincidences of simultaneous yet independent sacrifice and both finding employment at the same workplace are contrived to elicit the reader's surprised delight at the end. The artistic future for husband and wife seems uncertain, but this short-story form does not compel Porter to deal with such unpleasant considerations. When compared with the ultimately pointless gifts the Youngs gave to each other, Delia and Joe Larrabee's private concessions of aspiration seem relatively more tragic. Because of the economic difficulty of surviving amid its confines, New York City tends to starve the artistic impulse, leaving love as the only significant means for escaping an unpalatable reality.

Although the emotional decline in interpretive circumstances between "Magi" and "Service" is slight, it does suggest Porter's tendency to arrange his texts in *The Four Million* according to their place in descending order of psychological response. Other parallel texts in the collection trace more precipitous differences. "Springtime à la Carte" and "The Furnished Room" both describe the experiences of someone who comes to New York City to find a lost love. The pattern, which Porter would repeat in other New York stories, is rather simple.[64] Because of circumstances and accidents of fate, a couple find themselves lost to each other amid the environs of the city. One of the lovers is invariably a stranger to New York, and his or her search for the other is made difficult by its diversity, complexity, and enormity. Chance always intervenes to bring the two together again, although not always in the way they originally desired. In "Springtime à la Carte," it remedies the problem created by a lost letter. In "The Furnished Room," it coordinates the separate deaths of the lovers after each loses hope. The final twist in each story emphasizes how irony defies yet perhaps also depends upon overcoming incredible odds.

In "Springtime à la Carte" the narrative unfolds events from the point of view of Sarah, the object of Walter Franklin's search.[65]

64. See, for instance, "No Story" in *Options* (1909). As distinguished from "cross purposes," Blansfield places both "Springtime" and "Furnished Room" in the "cross-paths" subcategory, again treating each text in depth (*Cheap Rooms*, 48–51).

65. The story was first issued in the *New York Sunday World Magazine* on 2 April 1905.

Porter begins his portrait of the woman using conventional details that have some clues carefully planted to germinate the surprise ending. Even her mundane profession, a typist with insufficient skills to be a secretary, contributes to the story's happy resolution. Having become engaged to farmer Franklin the summer before, Sarah returned to the city to await his arrival for their marriage the following spring. When March arrives, the apparently negligent Walter does not. One of her piecemeal jobs, to type copies of the changing bill of fare for a local German restaurant, painfully reminds her of her lover's broken promise. One of the vegetable dishes—dandelions with hard-boiled eggs—recalls images of Walter's token for his proposal of marriage the previous year: "[In the] shaded and raspberried lane that Walter wooed and won her[, he had] woven a crown of dandelions for her hair." The menu item causes her to cry uncontrollably as dandelions symbolized for her "the harbingers of spring, her sorrow's crown of sorrow—reminder of her happiest days" (H1, 60, 61).

Porter, however, does not play fair with the reader. He withholds relevant information until the surprise revelation at the end. Up until the conclusion, we do not know that Sarah had recently moved, informing her fiancé by a letter, which was never delivered. Franklin wanted to keep his pledge but was stymied after failing to find his bride-to-be at her previous residence. But fate's bizarre machinations step in. In one of the twenty-one menus she composed, Sarah had subconsciously substituted during her outburst "Dearest Walter, with hard-boiled egg" for "Dandelions, with hard-boiled egg." Improbability reigns tyrannically over a typical reader's demand for some plausibility: Walter walks into the one eatery in all of New York where the one slim chance for success exists, and he is given the only menu that could assure it.

Evaluated in isolation, "Springtime" seems to prove that Porter had an irresistible impulse toward sentimentality. Regardless of the dictates of probability, true love must triumph. When the story is compared to its sister text, "The Furnished Room," however, Porter's superficial mawkishness loses some of its sweetness.[66] One of the darker tales in *The Four Million* (and in the entire O.

66. The *New York Sunday World Magazine* originally printed the story on 14 August 1904.

Henry canon), "The Furnished Room" presents a search that ends grimly. Unlike most of his stories where readers share the protagonist's sense of discovery, Porter permits only the audience to witness the full circumstantial irony in the death of an unnamed young man. Chance denies the protagonist not only knowledge of his lover's fate but also the curious twist in his own. As the penultimate tale in the volume, "The Furnished Room" forms the last rung as we descend O. Henry's ladder from exaltation to despair.

The final hours of the victim complete our sensation of whimsical tragedy. After five months of exhaustive searching for Eloise Vashner, "a fair girl" with professional aspirations in musical theater, her lover succumbs physically and emotionally before the futility of his quest. New York itself erects an impassable obstacle: "He was sure that since her disappearance from home this great, water-girt city held her somewhere, but it was like a monstrous quicksand, shifting its particles constantly, with no foundation, its upper granules of to-day buried to-morrow in ooze and slime" (H1, 100). Weary and apparently almost penniless, he engages a cheap tenement room on the lower West Side. With the remnants of his will, he questions his new landlady, Mrs. Purdy, as to whether she had ever seen Eloise. Purdy responds in the negative, possibly duplicitously.

Intent upon renting the room, the landlady does not tell her new lodger about the fate of the previous inhabitant: probably known by a stage name to Purdy, Eloise Vashner had committed suicide in it (as we find out only at the text's end). All traces of her existence there had been obliterated save one—"the strong, sweet odor of mignonette," her favorite scent. Whereas his frustration before arose in coping with a city so large, he now grows exasperated in failing to trace the origin of the vestigial perfume in a space so small. Further inquiries of Purdy lead him further astray from the truth. As the odor fades, so does his hope, which provokes him also to take his own life by gas asphyxiation.

The crash of all the pertinent facts upon us at the end impresses us with only the coincidental irony in the parallel deaths. Unlike a Maupassant text, a Porter surprise-inversion does not force us to reinterpret a text upon second reading. The trick revelation only punctuates what Porter has already led us to ascertain about a character's personality.[67] Discovering that his lover ended her life in the same furnished room does not alter our original pity at his plight or our resignation at his death. True, we as readers missed on first perusal the true significance of a few incidents along the way, but Porter hides most of the substantial clues. Thus, after almost fifteen years of impact on American fiction, Maupassant's concept of the surprise-inversion formula survived, but his intentions in employing it had not.

Both the above sets of parallel texts from The Four Million suggest the overall ambivalent undertone in the collection's philosophical import. In effect, Porter hoodwinks his readers by loading the volume with flattering portraits meant to appeal to a New Yorker's mythologically based self-identity. After feeding this ego, the author sneaks in subtle, darker versions of situations with which his audience has already empathized. By the end of the volume, we come to recognize how insignificant men and women are in controlling their own fate. Chance alone is the precipitating determinant of individual and collective destiny. If our lives prove fortunate, we are not to be congratulated. If our lives prove disastrous, we are not to be blamed. Unlike Maupassant, who hinted that human beings must suffer in a decaying universe, O. Henry proposed that men and women must contend in a stagnant one.

In other words, as a unified work The Four Million reads as if it were a reluctant admission that chaos rules the world. The author's responsibility then becomes to select and describe the most curious of chance happenings—in the case of this collection, twenty-five interesting occurrences amid the collective wealth of human experience that distinguishes New York. Ultimately, these parallel stories that explore contrasting consequences of chance reduce to a philosophical nullity. Gone from the surprise-inversion is Maupassant's Schopenhauerian bleakness, a view shared by Bierce. Gone from the form is the Frenchman's penchant for assaulting his reader's confidence and sensibilities. In Porter's hands, only its mandated skeleton of last-minute inverted vision remained. By the time of Porter's death in 1910, the form was reduced to just a recipe that several short-story-writing cookbooks

67. I disagree with Ejxenbaum's judgment that O. Henry employs trick endings so successfully that an audience is compelled to reinterpret the entire text (O. Henry, 21).

proclaimed as the highest goal in literary art.[68] Late in his career, even Porter employed the formula almost by rote. Little wonder that O. Henry in himself comprised the single most important standard from which many modernists later rebelled.[59] And as his literary status ebbed, so did Maupassant's because of the errone-ous assumptions made by critics and other literati about the history and purpose of the surprise-inversion story.[70]

68. At the end of his history of the genre, Pattee launches into a diatribe about the attempt to "codify and promulgate" the short story "as if it were an exact science," challenging the notions of textbook authors like Charles R. Barrett and Robert W. Chambers; see Pattee, *Development of the American Short Story*, 364–68 for his discussion and 377–78 for his bibliography of such works. Many early twentieth-century-fiction textbook writers offered O. Henry as their model, particularly in his use of the surprise ending. Blansfield borrows a portion of her plot-pattern taxonomy from one such work: Blanche Williams's *A Handbook on Story Writing* (New York: Dodd, Mead, 1920).

69. Current-Garcia gives the fullest account of the decline in Porter's literary reputation, noting the hallmarks of (1) the continual and thorough attacks on the trite quality in Porter's works by critics like Pattee and H. L. Mencken; (2) the dismissal of his importance by Sherwood Anderson and his disciples; and (3) the trashing of Porter's "The Furnished Room" by Cleanth Brooks and Robert Penn Warren in their influential *Understanding Fiction* (New York: Holt, 1943); see Current-Garcia, *O. Henry*, 137, 163–65. In *O. Henry: The Legendary Life of William S. Porter* (Garden City, N.Y.: Doubleday, 1970), 236–37, Richard O'Connor gives a similar account but also adds a few comments about O. Henry's treatment in academic circles.

70. Curiously, despite his challenge to Porter's status as an artist, Pattee praises him for being "more original" than Maupassant (*Development of the American Short Story*, 361).

4

Maupassant and Chopin

Not all American pupils of Maupassant succumbed so totally to the allure of the trick ending. The most attentive of his readers during the 1890s, Kate Chopin, found in his work a springboard for her own artistic maturity on a variety of levels, including structural diversity. Unlike most of her fellow disciples, who relied perhaps too heavily upon the tastes of Maupassant's English translators, Chopin used her fluency in French to explore firsthand the teachings of the master. As a consequence, she could break through the barriers of his American reputation and witness the true breadth of his literary skill. This reading impelled in her own work a growing freedom to deal with human sexuality, a commitment to encapsulate the essence of the human experience, and a preference to eschew conventional plot, or at least what she perceived as the norm in American letters.[1] At first, like many novice writers, she occasionally imitated

1. Regarding Maupassant's impact on sexuality in Chopin's fiction, Per Seyersted writes: "When [Maupassant] spoke so secretly to her it was undoubtedly because he

what she admired. Eventually, however, her understanding of short-story form sparked a measurable perceptual revolution.

She never resigned herself to the unrelenting cynicism of Maupassant, but as she experimented with more complicated structures, she retreated from the sentimentality that characterizes several of her earlier stories. Although Chopin could not abandon her Romantic leanings totally, by the end of her career she balanced such impulses with a fatalistic vision. One impetus for this perceptual change may be Chopin's study of the Maupassantian descending-helical story. In fact, the epistemological impact of her comprehension seems to affect more than Chopin's helically structured texts. It often imbues her later work with various shades of deterministic human regression. Generally, Chopin did not present falls so precipitous as those experienced by Maupassant's characters, but more and more her stories began to deal with the maddening aspects of existence. Like a good teacher, Maupassant and his canon gave Chopin a framework for self-study; like a good student, she exploited his example to discover more possibilities for her own voice.

Chopin's appreciation for Maupassant is not difficult to establish. She acknowledged his influence at length in an unpublished essay (drafted in 1896). Starting in 1894, she undertook translations of eight Maupassant short stories, planning to publish six of them together in book form. She sometimes tacked a loose or an exact English translation of a Maupassant title at the head of her own efforts; for example, "Regret," "The Kiss," "A Morning Walk," The Awakening. In rare instances, she directly transposed a Maupassantian plot to her locale. "A Very Fine Fiddle," for example, has remarkable, almost imitative, parallels to "Les Bijoux." Once, Chopin even managed to work a reference to the Frenchman in "A Family Affair." Together these prima facie details indicate that Chopin examined Maupassant more acutely than was common in America during her time.

Since 1969, all the major students of Chopin have acknowledged this literary relationship.[2] In that year, Per Seyersted published his

discussed with such frankness the hidden life of women"; see his *Kate Chopin: A Critical Biography* (Baton Rouge: Louisiana State University Press, 1969), 101.

2. In *Kate Chopin* (New York: Ungar, 1986), 19, Barbara C. Ewell summarizes the typical assumptions made by modern critics of Chopin's work: "What Chopin learned from Maupassant is evident in her stories: her own clear prose; her pointed use of details; the solid, authentic folk that populate her fiction. She also adapted—and

landmark critical biography and his edition of her collected works. The latter included a second draft of her essay "Confidences," in which she explores aspects of writing in a tone that seems more self-clarifying than expository.[3] The only author she praises in the piece is Maupassant, which she does at length:

> About eight years ago there fell accidentally into my hands a volume of Maupassant's tales. These were new to me. I had been in the woods, in the fields, groping around; looking for something big, satisfying, convincing, and finding nothing but—myself; a something neither big nor satisfying but wholly convincing. It was at this period of my emerging from the vast solitude in which I had been making my own acquaintance, that I stumbled upon Maupassant. I read his stories and marvelled at them. Here was life, not fiction; for where were the plots, the old fashioned mechanism and stage trapping that in a vague, unthinking way I had fancied were essential to the art of story making. Here was a man who had escaped from tradition and authority, who had entered into himself and looked out upon life through his own being and

---

used effectively—the surprise ending, for which Maupassant is most often remembered. But what seems to have most impressed Chopin was not so much his technique as his clear spirited commitment to a unique vision of life."

There have been several attempts to trace thematic and symbolic parallels between Maupassant and Chopin stories. For example, see Pamela Gaudé, "Kate Chopin's 'The Storm': A Study of Maupassant's Influence," *Kate Chopin Newsletter* 1 (Fall 1976): 1–6. In *Kate Chopin* (New York: William Morrow, 1990), Emily Toth notes how Maupassant's "Solitude" contributed to Chopin's "The Night Came Slowly" and how " 'Suicide' anticipates *The Awakening* in its description of 'a solitary existence left without illusions' " (272).

Seyersted compares at length Maupassant's "La Reine Hortense" and Chopin's "Regret," and later notes the debt of *The Awakening* to several Maupassant short stories (*Kate Chopin,* 125–30, 137–38, 143). Eliane Jasenas attempts to water down Seyersted's assertion by delineating how Chopin diverged from Maupassant's themes; see "The French Influence in Kate Chopin's *The Awakening,*" *Nineteenth-Century French Studies* 4 (1976): 313–14.

3. Three drafts of this essay are known to have existed. The first has been lost. The second, from which I now quote, was composed in September 1896 and was never published. The final draft was retitled "In the Confidence of a Story-Writer." Composed in October 1896, the essay did not reach print until the January 1899 issue of the *Atlantic Monthly.* Chopin excised the long passage on Maupassant from this third version. See the editor's notes in *The Complete Works of Kate Chopin,* ed. Per Seyersted (Baton Rouge: Louisiana State University Press, 1969), 1029–30.

with his own eyes; and who, in a direct and simple way, told us what he saw. When a man does this, he gives us the best that he can; something valuable for it is genuine and spontaneous. He gives us his impressions. Some one told me the other day that Maupassant had gone out of fashion. I was not grieved to hear it. He has never seemed to me to belong to the multitude, but rather to the individual. He is not one whom we gather in crowds to listen to—whom we follow in procession—with beating of brass instruments. He does not move us to throw ourselves into the throng—having the integral of an unthinking whole to shout his praise. I even like to think that he appeals to me alone. You probably like to think that he reaches you exclusively. A whole multitude may be secretly nourishing the belief in regard to him for all I know. Someway I like to cherish the delusion that he has spoken to no one else so directly, so intimately as he does to me. He did not say, as another might have done, "do you see these are charming stories of mine? take them into your closet—study them closely—mark their combination—observe their method, the manner of their putting together—and if you are ever moved to write stories you can do no better than to imitate." (C1, 700–701)

Unfortunately, the following two pages of manuscript have been lost. Seyersted speculated that Chopin may have given specifics to clarify her previous abstractions.[4] In the next surviving page of the manuscript, Chopin had already moved on to other topics, indicating her intention to treat various artistic matters (related by their impact upon her artistry) rather than an attempt to compose an extended panegyric devoted solely to Maupassant.

Chopin's declaration seemingly establishes her first encounter with a Maupassant work in 1888. There exists some evidence that she may have been in error. Lafcadio Hearn had already begun publishing translations of Maupassant short stories in the New Orleans *Times-Democrat* before Chopin had left Natchitoches Parish to return to St. Louis in 1884. There is no documented proof that she read a New Orleans newspaper while living in northern Louisiana during 1883 and 1884.[5] In assuming the reins of her late

4. *Kate Chopin*, 51.
5. Although Seyersted notes Hearn's translations, he does not assert that Chopin

husband's business, however, she had to have kept abreast of financial affairs in the city, thus making it at least possible that she
perused some of Hearn's translations in his "French Forum" column.
Hearn's tastes corresponded to Chopin's, at times. In 1886, Hearn
translated Maupassant's "Solitude" and wrote an accompanying
essay praising it. Probably unaware of Hearn's efforts after she left
Louisiana, Chopin later admired the same story so much that she
tried her own hand at translating it. Before 1884, however, it seems
likely that at best she only glanced at Hearn's column and then
promptly forgot about it as business and family responsibilities
engulfed her life, especially her aesthetic pursuits.

For me, it seems more likely that the volume Chopin examined
"[a]bout eight years ago" was Sturges's *The Odd Number*. Her
uncertainty about the year makes the 1889 collection a possibility.[6]
Although her fluency allows the possibility that a volume in French
found its way from Paris to her hands in St. Louis, the popularity of
The Odd Number in America makes it probable that she encountered
the book through a recommendation, a review, or her browsing in a
bookstore.[7] My evidence for such an assertion is circumstantial. As
was the case with many of her American peers, Chopin's conception
of Maupassant's literary structures seemed initially limited by
Sturges's selections in *The Odd Number* and *Modern Ghosts*. Interspersed amid her early, linearly anecdotal, local-color stories are a
few surprise-inversions, including her most famous short story,
"Désirée's Baby." Unlike the dogmatic repetitions practiced by
Bierce and Porter, however, Chopin exercised restraint in employing
the form. In her first volume of short stories, *Bayou Folk* (1894), only
four of the twenty-three texts end with an unexpected twist.

Several explanations for Chopin's judiciousness occur simultaneously. First, early in her career she immersed herself in the American local-color movement, adhering to the advice of theorists who
lauded the unadorned anecdote. Therefore, her introduction to Mau-

---

read them. Later, however, he suggests that she may have encountered Maupassant
before 1888 (*Kate Chopin*, 42, 51).

6. Seyersted apparently assumed that Chopin's entire knowledge of Maupassant
came from a single volume, which he found impossible to identify (206). He did
concede, however, that Chopin may have been "careless with dates" (*Kate Chopin*,
120).

7. Toth hints that Chopin's literary circle in St. Louis introduced her to Maupassant
(*Kate Chopin*, 181, 205).

passant had to compete with other literary considerations. Second, unlike some of her contemporaries, she evidently recognized the artistic self-defeat in juxtaposing late surprises in text after text. Finally, an examination of Chopin's shifting openness toward depicting sexuality in her fiction, the darkening of her vision of the human dilemma, and especially her increasingly diversified approach to fictional structures suggests that the decisive impact that Maupassant had on her artistic vision may not have occurred in 1888 or 1889 as she claimed in "Confidences."

Structurally, her early works (before 1893) consist mostly of linear causal chains supplemented by a few contrast stories.[8] Her initial imitations of Maupassantian form lie chiefly in the sporadic surprise-inversion tale and in her fondness for the commentary coda at the end of a linear text. In 1893, however, Chopin began to refrain from the straight anecdote to experiment more and more with helical and sinusoidal structures. Taking this change as a sign of a revitalized and more intense interest in Maupassant, I suspect that Maupassant's recent death (and the public speculations accompanying it) stimulated her to examine his work again. Sometime between 1893 and 1895 she began to scrutinize the canon in its original language.[9] Together, the seven Maupassant short stories that she translated by 1896 indicate that she would have to have perused at least six different volumes of his work. Her intention to collect six of these in a book under the title *Mad Stories* suggests that her recent insight had sufficient depth to fathom a major Maupassant theme.

In essence, what Chopin describes in "Confidences" is not the flood of impressions triggered by a single volume read eight years earlier; instead, she responds to her recent meticulous and comprehensive reading. The demands for proper translation obviously compelled her to examine various Maupassant texts with greater care. Despite her disclaimer at the end of her comments on Maupassant in "Confidences," this undertaking guided the next step in her artistic evolution, especially her capacity to fuse structure with theme. Unlike the limited implied lessons of *The Odd Number* in

8. In his analysis of Chopin's first novel, Bernard J. Koloski sees a diptych-like structure marked by a "well conceived succession on contrasts"; see "The Structure of Kate Chopin's *At Fault*," *Studies in American Fiction* 3 (1975): 89–91.

9. Seyersted cites William Schuyler's 1894 article in *Writer* that attests to Chopin's intense interest in Maupassant during that year (*Kate Chopin*, 89).

1889, which provided Chopin with a few alternatives to the fictional anecdote, the expansive teachings contained in the Maupassant canon clarified her understanding of simple forms and introduced her to more challenging ones. The quality of Chopin's reexamination of Maupassant during the 1890s depended upon her achievements as a practicing writer. With at least four productive years behind her, she had developed a substantive personal standard by which to evaluate and appreciate Maupassant. In effect, she reacquainted herself with his short stories at a time when she sought tighter control of her own materials. Amid his panorama of forms, she found no literary dogma but a credo by which she could assert truth as she saw it, including the darker depths of human experience, which she sometimes seemed reluctant to tackle explicitly in her early fiction.

Even if Chopin had a more profound encounter with Maupassant's works during the mid-1890s, I still do not think she intended to mislead her readers deliberately in "Confidences" about the chronology of the matter. She likely believed that her recent endeavors in translation merely confirmed the vague literary impressions she had held for years. Her early short stories would not substantiate such a claim, particularly in light of the paucity in structural variety. The fervor of her impressionistic evaluation in "Confidences" has an immediacy to it that suggests a fresh rather than a stale remembrance. For example, she cherished Maupassant's example because it did not demand imitation. (I suspect that the next sentence in the missing portion of the manuscript may have dealt with how Maupassant's work encouraged his disciples to diverge from the practices of the master.)

No aspect of the essay suggests an ongoing scrutiny of the Maupassant canon more than her defense against the charge that he "had gone out of fashion." Perhaps responding out of frustration in failing to get *Mad Stories* published, Chopin assumed the offensive, taking a tack that several twentieth-century literary schools would popularize: that artistic endeavor is an exclusionary process. Tapping into her experience in life and as an artist, the Maupassant short story for Chopin "appeals to me alone." Although she confronts the likelihood of her self-delusion, she sustains it as a useful fabrication, for it justifies the soul as the source for literary inspiration. Thus, she could follow Maupassant's lead in dealing with copulation in

her fiction, but also liberate herself from the ribaldry of his metaphors and the cynicism in his delineation of the motives underlying
sexual relationships—because both outlooks did not reflect her
values. Whereas Maupassant invariably tinted irony with a bemused
futility, Chopin began to imbue it with a similar sense of human
tragedy but with little humor. Maupassant's fictional assaults upon
the world that surrounded him did not compel Chopin to choose the
same targets and the same weapons. His influence was more inspi-
rational than substantive. Even his use of form was suggestive rather
than prescriptive. It merely confirmed patterns of literary perspective. It remained for Chopin to explore them herself so that she
could blaze her own path.

The Early Stories

As indicated above, an analysis of form in Chopin's early short
stories indicates that Maupassant's work may not have been so
decisive as she wanted to remember. Like many of her local-color
predecessors, she pursued, for the most part, simple linear structures
during her formative years. At one extreme, she composed elemental
anecdotes such as "Boulôt and Boulotte" (1891), "The Bênitous'
Slave" (1892) and "A Turkey Hunt" (1892)—all with plots so unadorned that they verge on retreating from fiction back to the expository essay. These three vignettes, along with other simple accounts,
impose the backbone on her short-story collection *Bayou Folk*. Apart
from a shared interest in presenting a remote region to a sophisticated eastern audience, these anecdotes about Natchitoches bear
slight resemblance to Maupassant's ambivalence about the people of
Normandy. Even at his most simple, Maupassant never composed so
uncomplicated a linear text. These little excerpts of life in the bayou
by Chopin owed their form immediately to local-color precepts but
fundamentally to an older American literary tradition. Earlier in the
century, Washington Irving and later Nathaniel Hawthorne had in-
termingled contemplative essays with fictional texts in their book-
length collections.

   In *Bayou Folk*, such texts contribute to the mosaic background of
Louisianian customs and behavior. For the American audience of

the 1890s, Chopin reveals an alien world not too strange or unpleasant to witness. At times, the circumstances in an anecdote would have probably struck a reader as charming, poignant, or sentimental: returning from purchasing new shoes, four children establish a social hierarchy in microcosm; clinging to his memories of security and loyalty in a slave past, a servile old black man is rescued by providence and human kindness from confinement in an institution; a black child with symptoms of autism finds three missing turkeys when the rest of a household cannot. In these simple stories, Chopin does not employ structure to attack manners, behavior, or customs as Maupassant was wont to do. The initial reticence to take a criticizing social perspective dominates the atmosphere of *Bayou Folk*. On one hand, it confirms Chopin's early adherence to local-color principles. On the other, it suggests that while Maupassant's works did have a measurable impact upon her writing after 1889, they did not yet dominate her artistic conceptions.

Even within linear structures, however, Chopin soon realized the potential of the short story to fathom and, perhaps at times, to purge her emerging artistic discordance with aspects of the human condition. In 1893, for example, "In Sabine" testifies to the patriarchal injustices of marriage. Chopin's immediate source for her story may have been an early edition of Hamlin Garland's *Main-Travelled Roads*. In many ways the circumstance and denouement of "In Sabine" resemble a condensed transposition of Garland's "A Branch Road" to a northern Louisiana setting; Chopin even parallels Garland's linear causal-chain approach to form.[10]

In truth, no one incident dominates our perception of the text. Each event logically precipitates a consequence, which in turn leads to another. Even Grégoire Santien's rescue of 'Tite Reine from the squalor of her life and prospects fails to assert its prominence over the rest of the story; although the flight takes the woman's husband, Bud Aiken, by surprise, Chopin amply prepares her audience for such an eventuality.[11] She juxtaposes the image of Santien's wistful memory of 'Tite Reine's past existence (before she eloped) and that

10. Regarding Chopin's awareness of Garland's works, she praised his literary manifesto, *Crumbling Idols*, in a 6 October 1894 review in *St. Louis Life*; for the text of the essay, see *C1*, 693–94.

11. " 'Tite Reine," the wife's nickname, is a dialect corruption of the French for "little queen."

of the marriage-worn woman who now stands before him in Sabine parish. Her once "saucy black coquettish eyes" had become "larger, with an alert, uneasy look in them" (C1, 326, 327). Her subsequent confession to Santien confirms the impression of a degenerating spirit, which triggers his resolve to save her from Aiken. The text concludes with Santien's guileful machinations to effect a safe escape, which fulfills the reader's sentimental expectation.

Although Chopin pursues a frequent Maupassantian theme, cuckoldry, she sides more with Garland's sympathetic attitude than the Frenchman's cynical leanings. She does, however, portray the "victim," Aiken, in satirical light. By story's end, he comes off as dense enough and brutal enough to deserve the loss of his wife to another man. Ironically, Santien tricks Aiken by mimicking his gruff manners. The husband believes that his new companion extended his stay to pursue friendship with him.

All told, "In Sabine" exploits sentimentality in a manner typical of nineteenth-century melodrama, progressing linearly to the happy conclusion that the audience wants. Consequently, the assault upon the then-popular notion of the inviolable sanctity of marriage becomes just one point integrated within a fictional continuum. Curiously, one relationship between a man and a woman becomes displaced by another, which tends to reduce the cognitive importance of both upon the reader. The demands of the text's linear structure thus divert attention from the social issue at hand, a diffusive literary tack seldom followed by Maupassant.

Nevertheless, there are marked Maupassantian aspects to Chopin's early fiction. In a few instances, Chopin apparently tried to transpose a Maupassant plot to an American setting and circumstance. One possible instance of this is suggested by the parallels between "Les Bijoux" and "A Very Fine Fiddle" (1891). Although other means of access were available, Chopin would likely have first read "Les Bijoux" in one of the several editions of the collection *Clair de Lune*.[12] In "A Very Fine Fiddle," Chopin converts Maupassant's symbol-laden jewels into a rare musical instrument. As M. Lantin believed his wife's *bijoux* to be costume, Fifine undervalues her

12. Chopin probably used the same collection as a textual source for her translation of "La Nuit." For an analysis of "Les Bijoux," see Chapter 2.

father's violin, which the author hints has the quality of an Amati or a Stradivarius.[13]

With the plot hinging upon the discovery of the true value of the instrument, Chopin follows the contrast technique of "Les Bijoux." Again, the circumstances for the revelation have parallel points. Like Lantin's plight, poverty compels Fifine to sell the fiddle, hoping to get meal money. To her surprise three city musicians give her a glossy new violin and more money than she expected for her father's worn fiddle. The inartistic daughter revels over what she will do with the windfall, but her father cannot accept the swap emotionally. The old violin had the power "to drown [his children's] cries, or their hunger, or his conscience, or all three" (C1, 149).

In "Les Bijoux" Lantin reaped riches at the expense of his fond memories of his dead wife. In Chopin's story Cléophas mourns a similar perceptual loss. After bowing his new violin, he tells his daughter: "It's one fine fiddle; an' like you say, it shine' like satin. But some way or udder, 't ain' de same. Yair, Fifine, take it—put it 'side. I b'lieve, me, I ain' goin' play de fiddle no mo' " (C1, 150). Chopin applies Maupassant's notion of how materialism overwhelms more abstract but more vital human values to a question she often considered: the survivability of artistic sensibilities in a hostile environment. Beginning with Paula Von Stoltz in "Wiser Than a God" and ending with Edna Pontellier and Mademoiselle Reisz in *The Awakening*, she presents an interesting array of accomplished and prospective artistic figures whose endeavors, whether destined for success or failure, mandate substantive personal costs. The aggressive and apparently tone-deaf Fifine elevates her financial worries over her father's crude but accurate appraisal of the old violin's value, which he measures not by money but by its ability to reflect his soul. Ultimately, it is in this commitment to fathom the dilemma of the artist (a question that seldom interested Maupassant) that Chopin rescues "A Very Fine Fiddle" from being solely a simple transposition of "Les Bijoux."

Like several of her peers among American short-story writers, Chopin felt early in her career the literary power underlying Mau-

13. Her father, Cléophas, recalls "dat *Italien* w'at give it to me w en he die, 'long yonder befo' de war" (C1, 149; italics in original).

passant's surprise-inversion texts. Although she never committed herself to this plot form with the absolute allegiance of Bierce, she too succumbed to the allure of Sturges's suggestive collection. She experimented with inversion structures as early as 1891, and continued to use the form well beyond her reconversion to Maupassantian literary values following his death. I suspect that, aside from imitative stories such as "A Very Fine Fiddle" and "Doctor Chevalier's Lie," texts employing surprise endings establish the primary impact of Maupassant's writings upon Chopin that she herself would have recognized prior to 1893.

Of course, Chopin's most successful inversion story is her famous "Désirée's Baby" (1892).[14] This early attempt adheres to an essential Maupassantian principle in invoking such a structure: the surprise ending should not introduce a new issue but instead amplify with great force a theme that pervades the whole text. For instance, Mathilde Loisel's discovery of the necklace's worthlessness, although it shocks us, merely reasserts the vulnerability of her pride. Likewise, the revelation of Armand Aubigny's black ancestry in "Désirée's Baby" offers us an ironic and precipitous conclusion; nevertheless, Chopin's final twist still continues her account of the devastating costs racial prejudice demands in Southern society.[15]

Although she maintains a naturalist's stoical voice in describing Désirée's plight, Chopin still manages to convey the unfairness inherent in the way social values determine individual behavior. Her method begins with an account of the initial bliss in the Aubigny marriage. In it, the foundling Désirée believes her life complete; her husband similarly benefits: "Marriage, and later the birth of his son had softened Armand Aubigny's imperious and exacting nature greatly," so much so that his treatment of the blacks he employs becomes noticeably less tyrannical (C1, 242).

As he grows, the child whose existence promises domestic happiness then becomes a center for discord. The suspicion and then the

14. The impact of Maupassant's technique on "Désirée's Baby" has been noted by various critics since Seyersted's 1969 biography, which comments: "in its taut compression and restrained intensity it is more like a story by Maupassant, and the surprise ending, though somewhat contrived, has a bitter, piercing quality that could not have been surpassed by the master himself" (Kate Chopin, 94).

15. Ewell notes perceptively: "Like the best of her mentor Maupassant's work in this mode, the ending not only inverts our expectations but seems inevitable in doing so" (Kate Chopin, 70).

admission that their baby has black blood erects an immovable social wall between the couple. Observing the bigoted premises that control American society, Aubigny first displaces his anxiety by reverting to his mistreatment of his black workers. The mystery of his wife's past, which formerly his love for her had deemed as inconsequential, now haunts his imagination. When the distracted Désirée confronts him, he reacts "coldly," ultimately demanding that she leave his home. Given the conventions of Louisianan class structure, Aubigny's choice is inevitable. Nevertheless, this environmental determinism does not prevent the reader from casting the husband in the role of a villain, especially given that his victim is the far more sympathetic Désirée, about whom the author evokes even more pity from her audience by the wife's mystery-shrouded probable suicide.[16]

Thus far, the plot has progressed insightfully, provokingly, but linearly. Even the concluding scene at first seems to sustain the reader's expectations: Aubigny's burning of Désirée's possessions superficially completes his attempt to erase her "crime" against him by immolating all tangible traces of her memory. In this pursuit, however, he finds and reads a "part of an old letter from his mother to his father":

> "But, above all," she wrote, "night and day, I thank the good God for having so arranged our lives that our dear Armand will never know that his mother, who adores him, belongs to the race that is cursed with the brand of slavery." (C1, 244, 245)

This twist opens several interpretive avenues. If we assume that Aubigny here reads the letter for the first time, we can conclude that Chopin, like several of her contemporaries, believes in a destiny manifesting itself through chance. Egotistical man struggles against this uncaring universe only to perceive irony in his existence. In Aubigny's case, his discovery compromises his original solution to disown wife and child. A second interpretive possibility arises if one makes a differing assumption: that Aubigny had known of the

---

16. Note, however, that Désirée also reacts prejudicially. Rather than arguing that her husband accept the situation, she tries to defend herself against the charge.

letter for a long while, that he perused it one last time during the last scene before consigning it to the obliterating bonfire. If true, we must assess Aubigny to be even more calculating, desperate, and despicable than we earlier believed.

Whichever the case, the letter shocks us into rethinking our understanding of the text. As in Maupassant, we find in a second perusal of "Désirée's Baby" a number of statements with double meanings. At one point during Désirée's excited attempt to comprehend, she notes all her Caucasian features, including: "Look at my hand; whiter than yours, Armand" (C1, 243).[17] The second and subsequent readings confirm the depth of the text's assault upon our analytical pretensions, yet the trick has not altered the main subject of the piece. Instead, it intensifies our apprehension of the consequences of racism.[18] Given this unity and the astonishment aroused in us by the conclusion, it is no wonder that "Désirée's Baby" survived through the first half of the twentieth century in literary anthologies when the rest of Bayou Folk (and the Chopin canon) resided forgotten on dusty library shelves.

17. For a fuller treatment of how Chopin foreshadows the conclusion by strewing imagery throughout the text, see Robert Arner's "Pride and Prejudice: Kate Chopin's 'Désirée's Baby,' " Mississippi Quarterly 25 (1975): 135.

18. In both "Pride and Prejudice," 135 and "Kate Chopin," Louisiana Studies 14 (1975): 54, Arner proposes the prejudicial nature of Chopin's imagery in associating the traditionally negative connotations of darkness with Aubigny and the positive counterpart of whiteness with Désirée. Ewell assesses the difficulty of fixing Chopin's stand in her fiction on racism: "Of course, Chopin's association of black with Satanic evil and the discovery that the cruel villain of the piece is Afro-American reveals her continuing ambivalence about race. Even so, her portrayal of the senseless destruction that arises from unexamined pride and fears comments powerfully on the ironic, wasteful nature of prejudice" (italics in original; Kate Chopin, 71–72).

Several critics believe that the prejudice against women imposed by men overshadows racism in the story. For example, in "The Man-Instinct of Possession: A Persistent Theme in Kate Chopin's Stories," Louisiana Studies 14 (1975): 278, Peggy Skaggs suggests: "In the ironic reversal which ends the story, . . . Chopin indirectly but clearly points out that male possessiveness, even more than racism perhaps, causes the tragic end of Désirée and the child." I do agree with this point, but I cannot accept Skaggs's subsequent opinion (in Kate Chopin [Boston: Twayne, 1985], 26) that Armand Aubigny "would not have been destroyed" had the truth surfaced. For me, the husband's ritual burning of his mother's letter suggests that he could not tolerate life if his secret was revealed to the public.

Upon noting Chopin's distaste for the marriage of social issues and fiction, Cynthia Griffin Wolff suggests that in lieu of "dissecting" slavery Chopin "limits herself almost entirely to the personal and the interior"; see "Kate Chopin and the Fiction of Limits: 'Désirée's Baby,' " Southern Literary Journal 10 (Spring 1978): 127–28.

Even during and after her rediscovery of Maupassant and other story structures, Chopin never put aside the surprise-inversion. Unlike many of her competitors, she avoided presenting the form frequently—at most, only two such stories in a single year. No doubt, she shared with Maupassant the fear that artistic indifference could arise out of excessive indulgence in one theme or in one structure. And likely she realized the maxim that her surprise-inversion stories would have greater impact if her readers did not associate the literary practice with her. Also, given that "trick" stories flooded the American periodical marketplace during the 1890s, Chopin may have shied away from them in her effort to assert her own literary presence.

In her later stories—such as "The Story of an Hour" (1894), "The Blind Man" (1896), and "The Locket" (1897)—Chopin employs various techniques early in the text to deceive the reader about the truth of a circumstance. For example, "The Story of an Hour" begins in medias res, with an erroneous report of a railroad accident, which, however, we have little cause to mistrust: "Knowing that Mrs. Mallard was afflicted with a heart trouble, great care was taken to break to her as gently as possible the news of her husband's death" (C1, 352).[19] Confirmed by two telegrams, the report of Brently Mallard's death in a train wreck immediately merges our perspective with his wife's. As a consequence, we become privy to Mrs. Mallard's complex moment—manifesting itself schismatically between her public mourning and private revelry.

In the guise of a false report, chance arouses in the woman a renewed interest in her own life, complete with the fantasy of a glorious future. Alone in her bedroom, she feverishly contemplates her victory as an individual, although directing no malice toward her "deceased" husband. The progression of her exaltations culminates as she repeats almost maniacally a whispered declaration: "Free! Body and soul free!" (C1, 354). As Maupassant was wont to do, Chopin presents us with an uncensored account of emotions and desires that a human being often hides from others—and sometimes suppresses within himself.

With Brently Mallard's unexpected arrival home, Chopin attacks

---

19. Ewell notes the physical and spiritual duality in the woman's "heart trouble" (*Kate Chopin*, 89).

several notions in concert. First, Louise Mallard's death by heart attack (from shock) suggests the untenability of her new conceptions. Obviously, her husband's return symbolizes to her a return to the prison of marriage. If individual freedom with a potential to achieve depends upon the death of another, however, the quality of such a release seems questionable. The surprise of her husband's appearance compromises the first premise in her earlier self-reevaluation, the initial syllogism in her causal chain to independence. With this link proved false, the entire argument collapses, paralleled by her physical collapse, which in their postmortem her doctors call the "joy that kills."

Second, as is typical in an inversion story, the perceptive powers of the reader are challenged by the concluding twist. Here, Chopin attacks our propensity to accept without sufficient proof the validity of declarative statements. As was the case in "Désirée's Baby" and in other similarly structured stories, "facts" are rendered impotent by the inadequacy of all communication and by our tendency to presume rather than discern. The author challenges her audience not with Maupassant's desire to affront but more with the air of a corrective to lazy reading habits—to jolt us into necessary caution. She also prepares us for a second reading of the text that will differ perceptually from our initial encounter. In "The Story of an Hour" we become engrossed by the ascending spirit in Louise Mallard's meditations. (The bird analogy suggested by her name is certainly no accident.) We approach subsequent readings, however, with the foreknowledge of the story's end, which scores her private elation with futility and impending tragedy. Essentially, the multiple interpretive possibilities of these Chopin texts parallel the implications inherent in the works of her exemplar, Maupassant. As much as any other influence early in her career, the demands of the surprise-inversion seem to draw Chopin out of an artistic complacency, making her more prone to recognize worthy social and behavioral targets and to attack them through her fiction.

The Translations

Chopin's adroit understanding of Maupassant's inversion structures may have played a part in her desire to study his work more closely after 1893. Probably several other circumstances contributed as well. As suggested above, Maupassant's death (and the rumors accompanying it) likely renewed Chopin's curiosity about him. Quite possibly, she had been sporadically adding to her library volumes of his short stories and his novels since 1889. Finally, after four productive years of writing, she felt that she had matured beyond a apprenticeship and so began to seek sophisticated models to refine her literary technique.

At the center of Chopin's reexamination were her eight translations of Maupassant short stories: (1) "A Divorce Case" ("Un cas de divorce"), composed 11 July 1894; (2) "Mad?" ("Fou?"), 4 September 1894; (3) "It?" ("Lui?"), 4 February 1895; (4) "Solitude" ("Solitude"), 5 March 1895; (5) "Night" ("La Nuit"), 8 March 1895; (6) "Suicide" ("Suicides"), 18 December 1895; (7) "For Sale" ("A vendre"), 26 October 1896; and (8) "Father Amable" ("Le Père Amable"), 21 April 1898. Her biographer reports that she intended to publish the first six of these in a collection entitled *Mad Stories*, but the publishers of *Bayou Folk*, Houghton Mifflin, rejected her proposal, effectively ending the project. Of the eight translations, only three would reach print during Chopin's lifetime. In 1895 *St. Louis Life* published "It?" and "Solitude." Three years later, the St. Louis *Republic* printed "Suicide."[20] The eight stories were likely culled from the following Maupassant volumes: (1) *Clair de lune*, (2) *L'Inutile Beauté*, (3) *Le Petite Roque*, (4) *Les Soeurs Rondoli*, (5) *Mademoiselle Fifi*, and (6) *Monsieur Parent*. This in itself suggests that Chopin had access to at least six of the fifteen major collections authorized by Maupassant, which equates to knowledge of more than eighty-five stories in their original language. Of course, she may have read even more than such evidence suggests. Certainly her criteria for selection were quite focused: she usually picked only one title in a volume for translation, never more than two. Thus, it remains quite possible that certain Maupassant collections yielded no material that satisfied her aims in the project.

The title of her proposed collections, *Mad Stories*, indicates the essential thrust of her interest. For Maupassant, insanity was dynamic, which usually demanded descending-helical forms in his

20. Seyersted reports the publication dates in *Kate Chopin*, 234. Thomas Bonner, Jr., reprints all eight translations in *The Kate Chopin Companion* (Westport, Conn.: Greenwood, 1988), 179–224.

fiction. In each of the eight texts that Chopin chose to translate, Maupassant invoked such a structure. Thus, in pursuing one thematic approach to Maupassant's works, she also must have absorbed insight on an alternative way to shape a story, one she had yet to learn to master. Sturges had already handled Maupassant's archetypal text of this literary formula—"Le Horla"—in *Modern Ghosts*. Chopin's omission of this horror tale may indicate that she avoided redoing what was already available in English (save for the already forgotten efforts of Lafcadio Hearn). More important Chopin sensed in these Maupassant texts a movement of life that she herself had lately felt. In her fiction she would seldom match Maupassant's cataclysmic pessimism; but starting in 1894 she delved more and more into a darker perspective of humanity.

For the most part, the translations have merit. An examination of the extant manuscripts indicates that Chopin completed each effort in one rapid sitting. The paucity of emendations and deletions suggests that she seldom struggled over words.[21] Her fluency allowed her to overcome the simpler problems of translation, although on occasion she made puzzling choices. (For example, her selection of "It?" for Maupassant's title "Lui?" fails to convey his intent to anthropomorphize the narrator's imagined apparition.) Sometimes, she avoided easy English substitutes for French cognates by applying more imaginative but less precise synonyms, which may be attributable to a desire to stamp her own stylistic imprint on each text. Other aspects of the translations bear out this speculation. Like most of contemporary translators, she would silently combine two or more fragmented French paragraphs into a single English one. She was not above substantively changing the format of a passage, including altering a Maupassant dialogue sentence into third-person narration. And when a Maupassant passage seemed too bare for her, Chopin fleshed out her English equivalent.

Nevertheless, the translations do largely succeed in conveying the essence of Maupassant's intent. Chopin may have found her swift method of completing each transcription was conducive with the helical flow of the story, almost as if the psychological descent engrossed her so much that she felt compelled to record first impressions to capture a text's dynamic progression.

21. Calling it a great weakness, Skaggs attributes Chopin's "reluctance to revise" to her desire to capture Maupassant's spontaneity (*Kate Chopin*, 69).

This procedure did not prevent Chopin from practicing reasonable care in her work. The surviving manuscripts demonstrate her competence and thoroughness.[22] Ironically, the only two of these works to be printed in St. Louis Life during 1895 possibly suffered heavily at the hands of compositors and under the demands of editors In the first piece published, "It?", several passages are overly condensed. Compare Maupassant's original with its St. Louis Life counterpart:

> Et pourtant mes idées et mes convictions n'ont pas changé. Je considère l'accouplement légal comme une bêtise. Je suis certain que huit maris sur dix sont cocus. Et ils ne méritent pas moins pour avoir eu l'imbécillité d'enchaîner leur vie, de renoncer à l'amour libre, la seule chose gaie et bonne au monde, de couper l'aile à la fantaisie qui nous pousse sans cesse à toutes les femmes, etc., etc. Plus que jamais je me sens incapable d'aimer une femme parce que j'aimerai toujours trop toutes les autres. Je voudrais avoir mille bras, mille lèvres et mille . . . tempéraments pour pouvoir étreindre en même temps une armée de ces êtres charmants et sans importance. (M1, 1:869)

> My ideas and convictions on the subject of matrimony have suffered no change. I still consider legal mating a folly. More than ever do I feel myself incapable of confining my love to one woman. I long for a thousand arms, a thousand lips, that I might hold in one embrace a very host of those beings at once so charming and so insignificant.[23]

Given the tenor of Chopin's translating competence evident in the extant manuscripts, two explanations are possible. Either Chopin yielded to an editor's demand to reduce her copy or the editors themselves applied a blue pencil.

The second piece printed in 1895, "Solitude," suffers even more. In her issue of St. Louis Life, Chopin corrected more than a dozen errors made by the typesetter, who produced nonsensical prose. For

22. The manuscripts for "It?" and "Solitude" have been lost.
23. "It?: From the French of Guy de Maupassant, by Kate Chopin." St. Louis Life, 23 February 1895, p. 12.

example, Chopin wrote: "A cool breeze was blowing, and a legion of stars besprinkled the black heavens like powdered gold." Her "heavens" was a reasonable choice for Maupassant's "ciel." Either working in haste or unable to read Chopin's handwriting, the typesetter substituted "leaves," rendering the sentence idiotic. The parade of similar errors in the short, two-column piece destroys its quality.[24] Although Seyersted and Toth do not report that Chopin reacted angrily over the matter, her displeasure seems possible. She did not offer another of her Maupassant translations to St. Louis Life, nor did she publish any other type of work in it during the remainder of its short existence.[25] Indeed, Chopin's corrections assert her intention to present Maupassant as accurately as her powers permitted to her American audience.

Her six selections for Mad Stories suggest that she had a thematic aim as well. Substantively and structurally, her proposed collection is remarkably uniform. All six follow Poe's and Maupassant's model for the descending helical. All present someone, usually the narrator, in the throes of creeping insanity. In each case, mental dissolution stems from a philosophical notion that is skewed from common belief. "Fou?" depicts one man's inability to accept his own hypnotic powers. "Un cas de divorce" offers journal excerpts of a tormented husband who cannot resolve the distinction between poetic and sexual love. In "La Nuit" Maupassant charges his prose with a highly metaphoric account of a pedestrian who falls prey to a hopelessness instilled by a silent and empty Paris in the dead of night. In "Solitude" Maupassant's protagonist theorizes on the intractable and irreducible alienation of all men and women, to which his listener, the narrator, vacillates in judging whether his friend reasons from insanity or wisdom. This cognitive dissonance has echoes in "Lui?" in which a letter correspondent's fear of solitude embodies itself in an imaginary spirit, prompting him to get married. The helical aspects of a man reacquainting himself with his own past in "Suicides" comment upon the negative proclivities inherent in self-contemplations.

24. Chopin's copy of her translation in St. Louis Life is in the possession of the Missouri Historical Society.

25. Toth reports that during 1897 Chopin did publish in the St. Louis Criterion, "the new incarnation of St. Louis Life." Sue V. Moore, Chopin's friend and editor of Life, no longer controlled the periodical, however (Kate Chopin, 284).

One motivation for Chopin's choices likely derived from the popularity in America during the 1890s of fiction depicting ghosts and dementia. By the time she had assembled enough material for a book, however, Chopin found that although such themes were popular among publishers, Maupassant himself was not. Perhaps Houghton Mifflin's rejection of the project signaled a personal omen for her. In effect, the publisher dismissed a writer with whom she partially identified, whose influence upon her was indelible. This episode represented an early manifestation of her later alienation from the literary mainstream, which ironically paralleled the theme of solitude in the texts she chose to translate.

Descending Helicals and the Later Stories

Chopin's close scrutiny of Maupassant guided her in her movement away from the external, literal realism of the American local-color movement and toward the psychological realism practiced by writers such as Stephen Crane and Frank Norris. On the whole, a strong empathic bond exists between writer and protagonist in Chopin's later stories. The descending-helical structure provided her with one apparatus by which to delve more deeply into the private sanctions of the soul, particularly her own. Although she would touch upon the subject of madness on occasion, Chopin also explored the helical's ability to illustrate other human experiences. Maupassant also recognized the potential diversity for the form, which may have induced Chopin to try one more translation in 1898. "Le Père Amable" is a chronicle of dispossession, a theme that she pursued more and more during her career, from an overt case in "Dead Man's Shoes" (1895) to the more subtle and insidious encroachment upon individuality by social mores in The Awakening.

Another and more profound manifestation of helicals within the Chopin canon was her recurrent interest in sexual awakening. Rather than Maupassant's often satiric (and satyric) portrayal of this subject, Chopin approached it without an overt moral perspective, much in the manner practiced by the literary naturalists of her day. Like those peers, however, she still manages to shape her text in a way that evokes pessimism in the reader. This response owes its sense of human degradation to the structural effects of a descending helical. Although she reduces their prominence in favor of a story's sexual theme, Chopin does make use of Maupassant's devices in portraying progressive insanity. For Chopin, sexual urges do not in themselves precipitate madness, but they do nudge an individual toward suspending his volition. In a typical story human will battles against an ever-strengthening sexual instinct, resulting in an ebb-and-flow pattern within a character's ability to control his own life. This variation of the helical echoes the structure of "Le Horla."[26] For Chopin, however, sexuality is not madness, but maddening. Rather than the abrupt decay of the human spirit that so interested Maupassant, Chopin explored the little falls with which all must contend. In other words, she avoided dealing with the bizarre extremes of human behavior, but still employed Maupassant's techniques in her depictions of more common people.

In "A Vocation and a Voice" (1896) Chopin pits a boy's sense of security arising from his deep faith in Catholicism against his pubescent lust for a vagabond woman. In refusing to give the boy's name in the first nine sections of the twelve-part story, Chopin attempts to universalize his interpretive significance. Although the boy's sexual maturity will have specific persons and events to mark its progress, the author raises all the signposts of the community's place in his experience. Unlike a Maupassant protagonist the boy will not be driven irrevocably insane by his inability to resolve the cognitive dilemma presented by the clash between piety and carnality. But his behavior becomes increasingly motivated by desperate impulses, resulting in moments of temporary madness driven by lust.[27]

Chopin carefully establishes the boy's relative innocence at the start of the story. She notes the still effeminate lilt in his voice. Although "an alien member" of a foster home, he feels a superficial contentment with his place in the community. The foundation for this sensation, the author hints, is a social order imposed by Catholicism.

26. See Chapter 2 for a fuller discussion of this pattern in "Le Horla."
27. In "The Boy's Quest in Kate Chopin's 'A Vocation and a Voice,' " *American Literature* 51 (1979): 270–76, Peggy Skaggs traces the analogies of dynamics between "A Vocation and a Voice" and *The Awakening*, which are related to my notions about descending helicals.

While religion suffices for a small hermetic world, however, it fails to prepare the boy for experiences beyond the parish. Sent alone by his guardian on an errand, he becomes lost both geographically and morally. The new vistas presented by a foreign neighborhood attract his aesthetic curiosity, while loosening the underpinnings of his faith, albeit marginally at first:

> There were a dozen boys or more of the neighborhood who would serve Mass as ably as he, and who could run Father Doran's errands and do the priest's chores as capably. These reflections embodied themselves in a vague sense of being unessential which always dwelt with him, and which permitted him, at that moment, to abandon himself completely to the novelty and charm of his surroundings. (C1, 521)

Coterminous with questioning the limitations placed upon his youth, the boy's latent sexual drive is softly kindled by a literal and figurative spark. His hunger—both physical and multifariously symbolic—compels him to leave the road to follow an odor of frying bacon and brewing coffee. In a secluded spot, he encounters an itinerant woman trying to put out a fire that threatens her tent and wagon. This situation immediately produces in the boy a desire to protect her, as he rescues her from the danger. When the young woman, nicknamed Suzima, invites the boy to travel the countryside with her and her companion, a brutish mule driver named Gutro, the boy accepts, thus forsaking his past in favor of the allure of an adventurous and uncertain future. Subconsciously, he is also attracted to Suzima, though his body cannot yet respond to this sensation. In effect, her duality elicits cognitive dissonance in both the boy and the reader, as Arner explains:

> Suzima possesses two names and two identities. As Susan, she is the civilizing and cohesive force underlying society, the pure maiden, the chaste, somehow holy woman who supplants the Catholic Virgin. But as Suzima, the dark mysterious maid of the Orient (itself a symbol of sexuality), she represents passion, lust, the destructive power of sexual attraction.[28]

---

28. Arner, "Kate Chopin," 83–84.

As the boy immerses himself in his new world, he undergoes the glandular changes of manhood, which are manifested in a variety of ways. Physically, his soprano voice begins to crack. He finds himself more and more in competition with Gutro, which at one point threatens to end in a knife fight. Suzima herself becomes the center of his thoughts.

Similar to Maupassant's exploration of human sexuality, Chopin strives for realism in her account by dealing with the boy's natural self-doubt. His difficulties with his own sexual awakening find a temporary respite through the revival of his faith. When the journeyers decide to settle in one place for a while and pursue more socially acceptable lives—Suzima had been a fortune-teller and Gutro sold herbal medicines—religion reenters the boy's life. He becomes intimately acquainted with a village priest, and he resumes performing the duties of an altar boy. For the moment, the moral demands of Catholicism overshadow the allure of Suzima—so much so that the boy worries how the villagers will perceive her gruff sensuality. When Gutro and Suzima decide to pull up stakes, however, the boy again, though this time more reluctantly, forsakes organized religion in order to follow her.

Back on the road, the sexual ties between the woman and the boy become more overt. Seeing her bathe nude incites a compulsion in him that is not satisfied until they subsequently copulate. Later, when a drunken Gutro threatens to beat Suzima, the boy defends her with a knife. Her intervention saves Gutro from serious harm, but the boy becomes "pale and confused" by his own murderous rage. Once again he finds himself increasingly not in control of his actions: from leaving a secure environment for reasons he himself cannot fathom, through succumbing to animalistic sexual urges, to impulsively yielding to hatred. For Chopin, the helical pattern stripped the cloak of civility from the baser human drives.

The boy leaves the vagabonds and resumes his journey through lost territory. Encountering the gilded cross of a monastic school, he joins the religious order, assuming the name of Brother Ludovic, to escape the primeval experiences of his recent past. After several years he becomes a stirring example of devoutness and purity to all in his new world. Still haunted by his past, though, he singly undertakes the task of erecting a stone wall around the institution as a barrier against everything external to it.

Despite his vows, however, religion again only provides him with brief respite from his intensifying sexuality. When Suzima passes by in her wagon one day, he

> sprang upon the bit of wall he had built and stood there, the breeze lashing his black frock. He was conscious of nothing in the world but the voice that was calling him and the cry of his own being that responded. Brother Ludovic bounded down from the wall and followed the voice of the woman. (C1, 546)

His last "fall" is from a more precipitous edge than those of the past. Each time he yields to the allure of Suzima, he forsakes a greater intellectual commitment. The first time he does so, the innocent boy feels that he only surrenders a spot in a world that can survive without him. Later, when the vagabonds attempt to settle for a spell, the boy develops a deeper appreciation for Catholicism and, in the process, plants communal roots that were more difficult to sever. Finally, Brother Ludovic attempts to conduct his life according to religious dogma that excludes all secular pleasures. Probably reflecting Chopin's own revaluation of religion, Ludovic's fall from his own conception of grace suggests an inverse correlation between the degree of one's faith and the ability to cope with life. Consequently, by chasing after the promise of Suzima, Ludovic affirms his own humanity.[29]

Not all of Chopin's helicals abridge Maupassant's original conception of their proper thematic use in fiction. In fact, her story "The Godmother" manages to add a provocative twist to the form. The primary focus of the text is upon a woman's physical and spiritual descent as she tries to extricate her godson from his criminal predicament. Simultaneously, Chopin includes an account of the godson's parallel dissolution within the progression of the plot. Although Maupassant on occasion did trace a symbiotic fall in the fortunes of two characters (compare "Le Modèle"), he seldom attempted such a

29. Patricia Hopkins Lattin suggests that Chopin follows a Hawthornean brand of transcendentalism in the matter. By "learning to accept and live with the potential evil of his heart, [Ludovic becomes] humanized by his 'fortunate fall' [and achieves full] possession of selfhood"; see Lattin, "The Search for Self in Kate Chopin's Fiction: Simple Versus Complex Vision," *Southern Studies* 21 (1982): 223, 227.

tack in a helical story, especially in his madmen's narratives. Consequently, Chopin's innovative revision suggests that she, like Maupassant, conceived that her improvement in literary skills partially (and yet necessarily) depended upon her ability to manipulate more complicated short-story structures viably.[30]

In "The Godmother" Chopin subtly targets one aspect of the parental instinct. When her godson, Gabriel Lucaze, commits murder, his "Tante" Elodie connives with paradoxical heroism to protect him from the authorities. Driven by a maternal love that blinds her to Lucaze's sins, she sees deception as her only alternative. Elodie concocts a lie to give her godson an alibi and then undertakes a perilous night-journey to alter evidence at the murder scene. She acts with what society would deem a noble motivation, but its consequence ultimately dooms both her and Lucaze, thus in retrospect undercutting the rightness of her behavior.

True to formula, Chopin establishes Elodie's conservative sense of family security as a plateau from which to carve the precipice. Having an affable appeal to young people, Elodie favors Lucaze over the others who frequent her home. Chopin hints that her protagonist has heretofore enjoyed the benefits of an implicit motherhood without having to brave its travails. In her physical description of Elodie, the author notes with metaphoric emphasis: "There were many lines in her face, but it did not look care-worn" (C1, 599). At the close of one evening, however, young Lucaze alters the conditions that permit his godmother's pleasure in innocuous doting. Responding to her query, the impatient godson chides her:

> Now, Tante Elodie, . . . It is always "where are you going?" "Where have you been?" I have spoiled you. I have told you too much. You expect me to tell you everything; consequently, I must sometimes tell you fibs. I am going to confession. There! are you satisfied? (C1, 598)

30. "The Godmother" has not enjoyed a good reputation among Chopin's modern critics. The most generous is Arner: "The result is not great art—the reader has the feeling that Mrs. Chopin is contriving too many events, in some cases merely for the sake of an additional turn of the screw—but it is a story which demonstrates again Mrs. Chopin's interest in the extremes of emotion under pressure and in the unpredictable and unexpected" ("Kate Chopin," 95). I maintain that in portraying a psyche in decay, Chopin, like Maupassant, was justified in exploiting unusual circumstances in order to delineate a psychological truth.

The ensuing exchange induces a sleepless anxiety in the woman, a psychological sparking of a moral concern that eventually will consume her spiritual essence.

When Lucaze subsequently murders a man in hot blood and then confesses his crime to Tante Elodie, she asserts her domineering personality in dealing with the matter, overriding her godson's inclination to give himself up. Her instructions to him almost sound as if she were trying to rewrite reality:

> You 'ave not killed the man Everson, . . . You know nothing about 'im. You do not know that he left Symund's or that he followed you. You left at ten o'clock. You came straight in town, not feeling well. You saw a light in my window, came here; rapped on the door; I let you in and gave you something for cramps in the stomach and made you warm yourself and lie down on the sofa. (C1, 603)

Realizing that her false witness in itself would not extricate her boy, Elodie immerses herself further in his sin by becoming an accessory after the fact. Before the body is discovered, she surreptitiously visits the murder cabin, recovering Lucaze's knife and falsifying clues to suggest that robbery, rather than rage, was the motive for the crime. Her efforts do succeed in masking Lucaze's guilt from society. Nevertheless, both she and her godson collapse under the weight of their sins into a nihilistic existence.

Elodie's psychological fall derives from her inability to accept change. As she believed that the emancipation of slaves failed to benefit their lot in the world, she likewise clings to her prelapsarian memory of her godson. But his suffering from unabsolved guilt renders her reestablished conservative order an illusion obvious even to herself. Lucaze gives up on his ambitions for a career and a marriage, and takes to drink with self-destructing fury. His often-ill godmother "appeared to be shrivelling away to nothing" (C1, 612). Their conspiracy ironically drives them apart. After an awkward, anguished-filled, final meeting, Elodie hears news about her godson only through mutual acquaintances. Her desire to maintain her relationship with him only succeeds in alienating him forever.

At the vanishing point of the helical, Lucaze dies, almost mercifully, in a horse-riding accident. When the report of his death arrives, Tante Elodie "sank deeper down into the rocker, more shrivelled than ever." In effect, she herself succumbs to what for her is tantamount to utter madness—despondent alienation. At a wedding party when she heard about her godson's fate, "Tante Elodie did not seem to want [to] go in doors [sic] again. . . . She stayed there alone in the corner, under the deep shadow of the oaks while the stars came out to keep her company" (C1, 614).

Thus, despite forgoing Maupassant's implied recommendation that helicals be narrated in the first person, Chopin still manages to convey the structure's psychological dimensions through dialogue and allegorical images. With such devices she distills Maupassant's pessimism and reflavors it with her metaphoric personal vision. More than other concerns, Chopin's employment of helicals in her canon after Maupassant's death suggests that as she rethought her attitudes toward life, religion, sexuality, and art, she arrived at negative conclusions that paralleled Maupassant's belief that every individual may ultimately yield to the inherent degradation of existence. Like Tante Elodie, we may exert much energy to elude a futile solitude, but an inviolable universal current relentlessly washes us out to a forlorn and enveloping sea.

Sinusoidals and the Later Stories

Obviously, given her more intense interest in the Maupassant short story after 1893, Chopin discovered other types of useful structures besides descending helicals. Assuming that she had examined at least six Maupassant collections, then she had to witness the entire panorama of his experiment in form. In some cases, this rereading seems to have clarified the philosophic and interpretive implications of structures with which she was already familiar, particularly the contrast story (compare "The Storm"). More important, she encountered fiction such as "L'Inutile Beauté" (in Maupassant's collection of the same title) that introduced her to the thematic subtleties imposed by the sinusoidal text. Whereas helicals sustained her shift toward disconsolation, sinusoidals seemed to have sharpened her appreciation of human irony, which in effect acted as a counterbalance to the despair in her other works.

Although Chopin employed such a structure in a story written in October 1893 ("At Chênière Caminada"), two more years would elapse until she remolded the sinusoidal to reflect her own artistic perspective. She composed her first important work using this form, "Madame Martel's Christmas Eve," during 1895, toward the end of her translation project.[31] Cruder than her later efforts, "Madame Martel's Christmas Eve" still establishes one departure point from Maupassant's conception of the form. Unlike her predecessor's compulsion to interject degradation or, at best, ambivalence into a character's ironic return to a past circumstance or value, Chopin tended to soften the effect by underscoring it with a suggestion of qualified progress. On the whole, as Chopin traveled amid more difficult psychological waters late in her career, she seemed to treat the sinusoidal story more and more as the last remaining port for her latent Romanticism.

"Madame Martel's Christmas Eve" follows the essential Maupassantian pattern: a tripartite text divided into a parallel beginning and ending, with a romantic interlude between. The widow Martel's self-imposed solitude, to which society acquiesces, dominates the thematic progression of the text. The author begins by carefully noting all the accouterments of mourning, from the "fine, black-bordered cambric handkerchief" to the paralyzing self-pity suffered by her protagonist (C1, 473). In effect, Mme. Martel's inability to reconcile herself to the death of her husband after six years "make[s] a luxury of grief." With an ambivalent mixture of motives—desiring to respect their mother's apparent preference and seeking a more cheerful atmosphere to celebrate the season—all three of the woman's children find holiday refuge away from home. And Mme. Martel completes the inescapable gloom of her Christmas Eve by dismissing the servants. As one might expect, that most powerful of stimuli to the imagination—solitude—forces the woman to experience again the madness of mourning as a "thousand recollections crowded upon her" (C1, 474).

Heralded by the distant sounds of a Christmas party, the romantic interlude of the text plunges the widow into a desperate ploy to end her loneliness quickly. The music simultaneously exacerbates her

31. Interestingly, Seyersted believes that Maupassant's "Lui?" partially inspired the composition of "Madame Martel's Christmas Eve" (Kate Chopin, 210).

inquietude and reminds her that her youngest daughter, Lulu, is a guest at a neighbor's party. Seeking companionship to palliate a grief grown intolerable, Mme. Martel sets out to bring her daughter back, blindly anticipating that Lulu's presence will restore some of the gaiety of past holidays. As she walks, nature itself validates the promise of her proposed remedy: "The moon had grown brighter. It was not so misty now and she could see plainly ahead of her and all about her" (C1, 475).

Ultimately, Mme. Martel's insight on the redemptive powers of love prove to have some merit; but the initial response of society, symbolized by the reaction of Lulu and her fellow guests to the widow's unexpected arrival, punctures the filmy bubble of her hope. Too young to fathom her mother's motives, the daughter begs for permission to remain. Realizing that her presence injects a somber element into the festivities, the widow politely rejects the superficially solicitous offers to stay. Her feverish quest fails; she returns home to the isolation that once seemed self-indulgent but that has now grown into an egotistical prison guarded by society's indifference.

The final section of the story initially repeats with a vengeance the symbolic costs of grief elaborated on by Chopin's omniscient narrator before the interlude. Mme. Martel's despair intensifies, for now she can see no avenues to escape it—save perhaps insanity. Indeed, Chopin deceptively suggests that her character approaches the verge of madness: upon the widow's return home, her vestigial memories of her husband apparently materialize bodily into his favorite chair. The apparition turns out to be her adult son, Gustave, who, to her amazement, now remarkably resembles her husband.

Citing his own need as reason for canceling his plans in order to be with his mother (despite his perception of her wish to be alone), Gustave confirms to a degree Mme. Martel's insight on the necessity of love. She acknowledges that the past will continue to haunt her; but although companionship cannot cure grief, it can serve as a balm, especially in alleviating some of the nostalgic ills brought on by the season. Her home remains a psychic prison, but the temporary addition of another inmate, one who paradoxically will continually remind her of her husband, tempers the horror in the confinement. For Chopin, the slight progression in the sinusoidal story's ironical though necessary return in the conclusion to the original plight suggests the capability of the human spirit to purge from itself the maddening aspects of life. Few Maupassant characters possessed such abilities.

As was Maupassant's experience, Chopin found that a sinusoidal text demanded length as well as complicated substructures in each of its three sections. One of her last efforts, "Charlie" (1900), bears all the earmarks of a confidently employed formula. At the center of the author's story resides the importance of place. In "Madame Martel's Christmas Eve" Chopin locates the first and concluding sections of the text in the protagonist's home, while the interlude allows the bereaved widow to escape for a moment her prison of self-denial. In "Charlie" the text begins and ends with its central character trying to contend with the differing demands home life makes upon her. To permit readers to measure Charlie's maturation, the interlude that demarcates these changing roles must necessarily take her away from her country home and place her in metropolitan New Orleans.

The narrative causes for Charlie's alternate banishment and restoration to home involve parallel incidents. In both turning points, Chopin signals significant change through violent accidents suffered by the men in Charlie's life. First, the girl mistakenly shoots the arm of Firman Walton, a young businessman from the city, who later becomes the object of her infatuation but subsequently marries her older sister. The second inflection point in the plot occurs when her father loses his arm in a mishap on his farm. The interpretive difference between the arm wounds lies in their severity. In recovering from his relatively slight injury, Walton figuratively indicates that he has no need for an assertive and unvanquished companion like Charlie. On the other hand, Laborde (her father) becomes, in effect, emasculated by his misfortune, which creates a void in the handling of his business interests and thus allows his daughter's latent management skills to come to the surface.

These two events trisect the text. The first section details, in quasi–descending-helical fashion, how tomboy Charlie rebels against the staid conformity of her sisters and the prim demands of her tutor. Her every act brings her reluctant father closer to deciding to send her away to a private school to instill discipline. After the mishap with Walton precipitates Charlie's "exile," the interlude traces an important episode in the girl's social development. The substructure in this section resembles a contrast text. At first, the new student tries to reassert her independent ways, but this behavior only serves to accentuate her loneliness. Upon her classmates' discovery of her one talent, poetry, Charlie finds that she appreciates her new comradeship. In fact, her personality permits her to maneuver in her new world—so much so that she soon assumes some authority over it.

When her father's accident necessitates her return home, she discovers that her status in the family parallels what she experiences before her banishment. Everyone tolerates her solitude. Plans are made for all Laborde's children—from marriage through travel to schooling—save for Charlie. Through a contrast substructure again, the third section represents the final significant stage of her understanding and acceptance of social responsibility. The turning point within the conclusion comes when Charlie learns of her sister's surprise engagement to Walton. Although the news does not kill it entirely, Charlie's romantic enthusiasm does suffer a blow. She realizes that she cannot let her well-being depend on the whim of another. Her self-sufficiency signals that she can assume the business reins for her broken father; in effect, she becomes a substitute "right arm" for him. Later, when a childhood friend broaches the possibility of developing their relationship into something stronger, Charlie assents—but in doing so, her now confident will, not her infatuated impulses, assumes control of the situation. Her independence has traveled around a full Möbius strip; rather than providing her father with only an indulgent delight, it now becomes an economic and emotional necessity for him.

Even Chopin's novel The Awakening (1899) owes some of its success to her earlier experiments in the short story.[32] Like Hawthorne's The Scarlet Letter before it, The Awakening somewhat represents a compilation of the author's short-story canon—especially in the matter of form.[33] Overall, the novel has a sinusoidal

32. Seyersted believes that Chopin derived the title and primary circumstance of The Awakening from Maupassant's "Réveil." He also suggests that "Solitude" and "Suicides," two stories that Chopin translated, contributed to the novel's original title and surviving theme—A Solitary Soul (Kate Chopin, 137–38, 143, 147). Jasenas expands upon Seyersted's ideas using the same texts ("French Influence," 313–15).

33. Borrowing from Sylvia Saidlower, "Moral Relativism in American Fiction of the Eighteen Nineties," Diss., New York University, 1970, 440, Skaggs offers a differing scheme to understand the novel's structure: "[Edna Pontellier's] 'awakening' progresses simultaneously with [Adèle Ratignolle's] pregnancy; thus the structure of the

structure. Each of the three sections in the text again depends upon place. Contrasting with Chopin's usual approach in her short stories, though, the interlude takes place at Edna Pontellier's home (both her husband's house and the cottage she later rents for herself) in New Orleans. Instead of this intervening segment, Chopin ascribes the aspect of externality to the framing sections, which take place at the resort Grand Isle.[34] Each part of the novel has its own substructure, but the descending helical in the interlude seems to dominate the spirit of the whole text.[35] The changes in locale are heralded by almost identical events: the two instances when Robert Lebrun leaves Edna Pontellier. The first time he is a man unable to deal with his infatuation; the second, he is one who cannot accept the social consequences of becoming a paramour.

While instructive on a number of minor interpretive levels, treating The Awakening as a sinusoidal text offers a possible explanation for Pontellier's suicide, an incident that baffles some critics by its ambiguity, which some see as being in conflict with the novel's philosophic flow.[36] Chopin's conception of the sinusoidal differed from Maupassant's in that she often imposed relative improvement in a protagonist's return to a previous place and circumstance. In "Madame Martel's Christmas Eve" and "Charlie," both central char-

novel is related to the basic, natural rhythm of the human gestation cycle" (Kate Chopin, 89, 121).

34. Thomas Bonner, Jr., has already suggested that The Awakening has three parts, each marked by its geographical setting. Rather than deal with the interpretive consequences of his finding, however, he studies image and thematic patterns; see "Kate Chopin's At Fault and The Awakening: A Study in Structure," Markham Review 7 (1977): 10–14.

35. In his recounting of Chopin's reputation in the twentieth century, Seyersted judges that Cyrille Arnavon's landmark essay "Les Débuts du roman réaliste américain et l'influence française" (in Romanciers américains contemporains, ed. Henri Kerst, Cahiers des langues modernes I [Paris: Didier, 1946], 9–35) was the first to associate "Maupassantian pessimism" with Chopin's novel.

36. For a concise history of this controversy among critics, see Suzanne Wolkenfeld, "Edna's Suicide: The Problem of the One and the Many," in The Awakening: An Authoritative Text, Contexts, Criticism, ed. Margaret Culley (New York: Norton, 1976), 218–221. George M. Spangler, for one, deems Chopin's conclusion "unsatisfactory because it is fundamentally evasive"; see "Kate Chopin's The Awakening: A Partial Dissent" Novel 3 (1970): 249–55; excerpted in Culley, 186–89 (quote is on 186). Opposing Spangler's charge that Chopin's characterization is inconsistent, Wolkenfeld proposes that Pontellier's suicide was not a conscious but a subconscious decision, representing "a regression to the animality of infancy." She finally completes her quest for identity by "her union with the One in the sea" ("Edna's Suicide," 222–23).

acters become more aware of their place in their families. The texts end with each woman more resolute, more tolerant, and, measured against her earlier life, more content.

The Awakening, however, concludes with the heroine's dissociation from family and friends. Nevertheless, Chopin may not have been able to redirect the sentimentality inherent in her conception of sinusoidal texts. Consequently, the interpretive ambivalences in Pontellier's choice for death seem structurally dictated by the author's subconscious attitudes about fictional structures. Chopin does present the incident in quasi-mystical light, for in Pontellier's quest for self-possession, death becomes preferable over returning to her social plight. In other words, the pattern of struggling individuals achieving limited success in past sinusoidal texts became too ingrained in Chopin for her to dismiss her own philosophical perspective so easily. Consequently, structure dictates that Pontellier's return to Grand Isle, the scene of her first awakening to the possibilities of self, must accentuate in some manner the protagonist's spiritual ascent. Obviously, such a thesis cannot in itself explain the critical dilemma presented by the novel's conclusion, but it may find a place in concert with a dozen other factors in helping us understand the multiple complex artistic reasons underlying the suicide.

Thus, despite the pessimism Maupassant's descending helical seems to have induced in Chopin's literary practices during the mid-1890s, by the end of the decade her struggle to assert the precarious but extant rewards for perseverance kept the darker impulses in check. As a result, the second wave of Maupassant's influence upon her flowed back to the sea, for she could not accept the destructive implications of a sinusoidal's cognitive dissonance. Instead, she had to reconceptualize the philosophical dimensions of such structures to accommodate her temperament and artistic perspective.

5

Maupassant and James

Although Henry James knew Guy de Maupassant during the 1870s, he did not consider the Frenchman as a serious artist until the 1880s, and he did not try his hand at imitating a Maupassant literary principle until the 1890s. The middle decade of the three found James attempting to reconcile Maupassant's image as a rake with his obvious talents as a writer of short fiction. When events and his aesthetics allowed him to do so during the 1890s, James began to entertain Maupassantian precepts for the short story, particularly in two ways to structure a plot. Despite the popularity of such stories, James avoided the surprise-inversion. For the most part the *contrast* became his structural ideal. Even when inspired by a Maupassant surprise-inversion plot, James would invariably rearrange incidents to reconstruct an interpretively rich contrast.

Initially reluctant to consider it as a form that captured any valid aspect of the human experience, James eventually experimented also with the descending helical. James's protagonists do not suffer the same mental doom as a Maupassant madman-narrator. Nevertheless, they do parallel their French cousin in that (1) they endure some loss of intellectual control and (2) alternative interpretations of events in effect double the reader's vision. Thus, like Maupassant, James tried to impregnate a text with Gestalt-like devices to produce cognitive dissonance. Unlike Maupassant, however, he employed the technique to explore the more subtle transformations of personality. Life did not make one absurdly insane—it was just maddening. For James, the capacity of man to reflect was his hedge against such extremities of intellectual doom. In the end, then, he transformed Maupassant's principle so completely that indeed it became truly his own.

The Reluctant Disciple

On a personal level, James's memory of Maupassant took on significance after the latter's death, which in the long run exceeded the realities of the past. During his Paris excursion (after the publication of his first novel, *Roderick Hudson*), James was introduced by Ivan Turgenev into Gustave Flaubert's circle during the winter of 1875–76. In his letters from France to family and friends, James conveyed his high regard for Turgenev and especially Flaubert, but he quickly dismissed their disciples.[1] Maupassant existed apparently as among the most minor of satellites, lumped into that scornful abbreviation for irrelevance—*etc.* On 24 January 1876, James wrote to his mother:

> I also spent a Sunday afternoon again at Flaubert's with his *cénacle*: E. de Goncourt, Alphonse Daudet etc. They are a queer lot, and intellectually very remote from my own sympathies. They are extremely narrow and it makes me rather scorn them that not a mother's son of them can read English. But this hardly matters, for they couldn't really understand it if they did. (J2, 2:20)

1. Besides Maupassant and Turgenev, some of the notables that assembled at Flaubert's Sunday gatherings included Alphonse Daudet, Edmond de Goncourt, J. K. Huysmans, Hippolyte Taine, and Emile Zola. A dozen or so more minor figures were among the regular guests.

Maupassant's name does not appear in any extant James correspondence for that winter, but in a 3 February 1876 letter to William Dean Howells, James expanded on the nature of his discomfort, which he discreetly glossed over with his mother:

> . . . at [Flaubert's] house I have seen the little *coterie* of the young realists in fiction. They are all charming talkers— though as editor of the austere *Atlantic* it would startle you to hear some of their projected subjects. The other day Edmond de Goncourt (the best of them) said he had been lately working very hard on his novel—he had got upon an episode that greatly interested him, and into which he was going very far. *Flaubert*: "What is it?" *E. de G.*[:] "A whore-house de province." (*J2*, 2:23; italics in original)

As his biographer recounts, Maupassant, tiring of his position as a governmental clerk, attended Flaubert's weekly get-togethers mostly "to qualify himself for the greater freedom of a writer's career." Although other regulars thought of Maupassant as "modest, quiet and self-effacing," he almost assuredly contributed his fair share to the ribald conversation every Sunday.[2] Years later, in 1912, James mentioned one such fantastic anecdote with a recall so delicate that his description becomes mired in imprecision. Prompted by Edmund Gosse's essay on Algernon Swinburne in the October 1912 *Cornhill Magazine*, James offered the following tease in the middle of a letter congratulating his friend on the publication:

> Distinct to me [is] the memory of a Sunday afternoon at Flaubert's in the winter of '75–'76, when Maupassant, still *inédit*, but always "round," regaled me with a fantastic tale, irreproducible here, of the relations between two Englishmen, each other, and their monkey! A picture of the details of which have faded for me, but not the lurid impression. Most deliciously Victorian that too—I bend over it all so yearningly . . . (*J2*, 4:630)

2. Francis Steegmuller, "Flaubert's Sundays: Maupassant and Henry James," *Cornhill Magazine* 163 (1948): 124, 126.

Gosse replied immediately, hoping that James would relent and offer some of the details. Gosse had heard two versions of Maupassant's lurid tale. In one, Swinburne's servant, jealous of his master's pet monkey, "hanged the Monkey outside the master's bedroom window, and then rushed out and drowned himself." Characteristically, Swinburne "raised a marble monument not to the Page, but to the Monkey." In the other version, Swinburne supposedly "killed and roasted his own pet monkey as a feast for Maupassant."[3]

In his reply on 17 October 1912 James acknowledged that the first story was the one that Maupassant told him. His expanded account confirmed his original suspicion about his faulty memory for its details. His "corrections" to Gosse's understanding were tenuous at best—such as: "some thin ghost of an impression abides with me that the 'jealousy' was more on the Monkey's part toward him than on his toward the Monkey." Interestingly, James explained why that past remained so indistinct to him, which fixes how insignificant he thought Maupassant in 1876: "I didn't in the least know that M[aupassant] himself was going to be so remarkable; I didn't in the least know that I was going to be." Maupassant's anecdote was, for James, just in keeping with the climate of the circle: " 'Here they are at it!'—I remember that as my main inward comment on Maupassant's vivid little history; which was thus thereby somehow more vivid to me about *him*, than about either our friends or the Monkey" (J2, 4:630–32; italics in original).

In essence, James's initial impression of Maupassant was more like that of a second-string athlete engaging in prototypical masculine locker-room banter than that of a fellow artist.[4] Only the Frenchman's subsequent accomplishments and fate would alter the expatriate's opinion of him. Eventually, the mention of Maupassant's name would occasionally trigger James's treasured memory of "a golden blur of old-time Flaubertism." One private *altar of the dead* James tabulated for himself honored each member of Flaubert's circle upon his death. His candle of "mourning" for Maupassant in 1893 became a poignant reminder of how far removed in the past

3. Portions of Gosse's 16 October 1912 letter are reprinted in J2, 4:631n.
4. Steegmuller speculates that James and Maupassant—"two of the decidedly lesser figures at the gathering"—would have naturally gravitated toward each other because of their *inferior* status within Flaubert's circle ("Flaubert's Sundays," 127–28). I have found no evidence to support Steegmuller's suspicion.

1876 Paris seemed for him. By 1912, he would marvel and be dismayed that he was "the last survivor of those then surrounding Gustave Flaubert" (*J2*, 4:632).

The metamorphosis of James's qualified appreciation for Maupassant coincided with the latter's emergence from his literary cocoon. After Flaubert's death in 1880, James initially had little direct contact with the master's disciples. But he did read their literary efforts avidly. Based upon his professed admiration for "Boule de suif," James, I suspect, became aware of Maupassant as writer from early on, starting with the Zola conclave's collaborative volume, *Les Soirées de Médan* (1880). Scholars Leon Edel and Adeline R. Tintner list thirteen Maupassant books that James had in his library or was known to have once possessed: *Au soleil, Bel-Ami, Clair de lune, Contes de la bécasse, Des vers, L'Inutile Beauté, Mademoiselle Fifi, Miss Harriet, La Maison Tellier, Sur l'eau, Une vie, La Vie errante,* and *Yvette*.[5] Elsewhere, Edel documents that James procured *Une vie* and *Contes de la bécasse* while in Boston during the summer of 1883 and testifies that "all the books show signs of having been carefully read," including marginal notations on "descriptive passages."[6] Judging from his 1888 critical assessment of Maupassant, James obviously also read the novel *Pierre et Jean* and possibly the short-story collections *Monsieur Parent, La Petite Roque, Les Soeurs Rondoli,* and *Le Horla*. Of course, James also kept track of Maupassant's production through literary organs such as *Gil Blas* and *Le Gaulois*. He obviously read "Histoire d'un chien" in the latter journal because the story was never printed elsewhere during the 1880s. Interestingly, when he composed his long essay about Maupassant, James relied in part on his library but also upon his memory. He incorrectly remembered the title of "Histoire d'un chien" as "Un Chien." A more glaring error happened when he mistakenly substituted the synonym "Le Collier" for "La Parure." Consequently, I suspect that James never saw Maupassant's *Contes du jour et de la nuit,* the volume that included the story.[7]

5. See "The Library of Henry James, from Inventory, Catalogues and Library Lists," *Henry James Review* 4 (1983): 179. I have arbitrarily excluded from this list a subsequent edition of "Boule de suif" because its 1908 publication date falls outside the period covered by this chapter.

6. Leon Edel, *Henry James,* 5 vols. (Philadelphia: Lippincott, 1953–72), 3:172.

7. See *J3*, 535–36. James finally got the title of "La Parure" correct when he briefly discussed the story in one of his New York Edition prefaces (*J3*, 242–43).

Because of his unique interests, social opportunities, and literary acumen, then, Henry James became the only American during his time willing and able to confront fully the irreconcilability of Maupassant the artist with Maupassant the man. During 1885 Maupassant's literary production became a recurring subject for James in his correspondence. To journalist-editor Theodore Child, then residing in Paris, he wrote: "I also languish for a new volume of Maupassant; there has [been] none since *Yvette*—full three months ago!" (13 May [1885]; *J2*, 3:88). When his correspondent sent him the just-published *Bel-Ami* in reply, James recorded his ambivalence to "Maupassant's ineffable novel" in his thank-you note:

> I fell upon and devoured [it] with the utmost relish and gratitude. It brightened me up, here, for a day or two, amazingly. It is as clever—as brilliant—as it is beastly, and though it has very weak points it shows that the gifted and lascivious Guy *can* write a novel. . . . *En somme, Bel[-]Ami* strikes me as the history of a Cad, *by* a Cad—of genius! (*J2*, 3:91; italics in original)

Already, fascination was intermingling with moral misgiving in James's effort to rate Maupassant's achievement on a rigid aesthetic scale.

Complicating matters for James was Maupassant's excursion to England during 1886. Afraid that James would not remember him, the Frenchman obtained a letter of reintroduction from their mutual friend (and James's early disciple) Paul Bourget. Little is known about what transpired that August. Reputedly, Oscar Wilde once related an anecdote concerning an incident in a restaurant. With transparent sexual designs, Maupassant supposedly demanded that James introduce him to a succession of female patrons. Each time, the flustered host professed not knowing the woman in the Frenchman's sights. After five such prudent refusals from the American, Maupassant testily observed that James did not "seem to know anybody in London."[8]

T. M. Segnitz has already pointed out this lapse in James's memory. He interestingly notes that while *collier* translates as *necklace*, *coller* translates as *to paste*; see "The Actual Genesis of Henry James's 'Paste,' " *American Literature* 36 (1964): 219.

8. Francis Steegmuller believes the anecdote might be true, judging that it would be in character for Maupassant to play such a perverse joke on his American friend;

Apparently, Maupassant's initial reason for contacting James was his anxiety over his deficiencies in the English language. With the multilingual James, he had at least a capable translator to help cultivate British acquaintances, both artistic and female. But the self-respecting James was intentionally not very effective in securing the latter, which soon made him socially superfluous for the Frenchman. Maupassant wrote to his traveling companion, Joseph Primoli, that "Monday we will have several agreeable ladies, it would seem—plus Henry James."[9] For the host, though, Maupassant's visit became a strong memory, especially their August 12 dinner in Greenwich with Primoli, George du Maurier, and Edmund Gosse. James would briefly recall the affair in a letter to Gosse almost thirty years later, but no other evidence survives regarding the subjects discussed that day (J2, 4:698).

In one sense the Maupassant of 1886 elicited the same response in James that the latter had experienced in 1875. As then, James remained uncomfortable with his guest's pursuit of life's bounty. Save for the venereal price he now had to pay, Maupassant's self-serving interests and behavior were only an intensified manifestation of the amorality among Flaubert's disciples a decade earlier. This time, however, James had to juxtapose the fascinating artifacts of the now-published writer against the indelicacies of the man, creating an artistic dilemma for James that he would never put to rest.

One early fruit of this internal conflict of aesthetic perception was James's incisive discourse "Guy de Maupassant," which first appeared in the March 1888 issue of the *Fortnightly Review* and was reprinted in *Partial Portraits* later that same year.[10] The American's inspiration for the piece must have been severalfold. First, their recent liaison surely made Maupassant an appropriate, accessible, and viable subject for James to include among his recent series of articles about contemporary Continental literati. James's interest in the *conte* prompted him to keep current with Maupassant's produc-

---

see *Maupassant: A Lion in the Path* (New York: Grosset and Dunlap, 1949), 242. Edel concurs with Steegmuller's assessment; see Edel, *Henry James* 3:173. The source for the Wilde story is Vincent O'Sullivan, *Aspects of Wilde* (New York: Henry Holt, 1936), 206.

9. The original letter has not been published yet; Edel provides a translated passage from it in *Henry James* 3:173.

10. In a 27 March [1888] letter to Theodore Child, James complained that he had received only twenty-three pounds for the piece (J2, 3:229).

tion of fiction. Also, his friend's recent publication of the short novel *Pierre et Jean* seemed to recapture, in James's estimation, the literary prowess apparently lost in Maupassant's previous volume, *Mont Oriol*—enough so as to elicit genuine admiration in the delighted reviewer for the Frenchman's talents as a novelist.[11] This dimension had emerged only lately in Maupassant's career. In effect, for James the quality of *Pierre et Jean* dismissed all of Maupassant's previous attempts at the novel as ineffectual, substandard, or trite.

In his essay, James invoked a potent metaphor to fix his response to Maupassant as artist:

> . . . his point of view is almost solely that of the senses. If he is a very interesting case, this makes him also an embarrassing one, embarrassing and mystifying for the moralist. I may as well admit that no writer of the day strikes me as equally so. To find M. de Maupassant *a lion in the path*—that may seem to some people a singular proof of want of courage; but I think the obstacle will not be made light of by those who have really taken the measure of the animal. (*J3*, 529; italics mine)

The path represented to James cultivation, advancement, the ability to meditate, morality, and faith; the lion, instinct, amorality, the embodiment of the indiscriminate brutality inherent in nature— hence the civilized moralist's embarrassed silence before its primitive presence. Maupassant became a symbolic lion in a potent literary sense. His genius lay in uncalculated verbal paintings—the beast does not ponder its prey before pouncing. This limitation denies such an artist the ability to elaborate upon his talent in any form save its direct expression; thus, "[i]n short, as a commentator M. de Maupassant is slightly common, while as an artist he is wonderfully rare" (*J3*, 522). As a natural consequence of such a claim, James dismissed for the most part Maupassant's preface to *Pierre et Jean* while proclaiming that the novel itself approached perfection.

11. In an earlier letter to Gosse, dated 24 April [1887], James had critiqued *Mont Oriol* unfavorably: "*Mont Oriol* has the supreme quality of *life*—but I don't think it is *du meilleur Maupassant*. . . . It has no idea—no *donnée*—except the smutty one of the water operating on the sterility of the young wife through the *robinet*—(I won't use a plainer English word though in connection with water it would be exact) of the young lover. And that has served many times" (*J2*, 3:181; italics in original).

James's assault upon the imprecision and banality of the critical precepts in the preface in effect confirms the undeniability of the lion. His actions alone matter. For James, Maupassant's innate reliance upon sensual description created passages brilliant in their simplicity. Thus, through the implausibility of his success, the instinctual artist (the lion Maupassant) poses a conundrum for his contemplative peer (a cultivated James who had helped to clear the path through the jungle). In essence, Maupassant does not belong in the literary world inhabited by James, but the natural majesty and sensual splendor of the beast fascinate us. For all of his savageness, then, we, as well as James, admire him despite ourselves. Therefore, for all his "indecency," "cynicism," and "pessimism," Maupassant must be confronted: "The situation would be simpler certainly if he were a bad writer; but none the less it is possible, I think, on the whole, to circumvent him, even without attempting to prove that after all he is one" (J3, 529).[12]

The route around the lion was fraught with vital hazards in logical commentary for James. On one hand he had to acknowledge and reluctantly praise Maupassant's leonine quality of literary brevity. Ultimately, though, the critic had to condemn such restrictiveness. In fact, James at one point challenged how brief Maupassant's brevity really was. Maupassant, according to James, "would probably urge that the right thing is to know, or to guess, how events come to pass, but to say as little as possible about them." Despite his friend's professed desire to hide "psychology," James noted that Maupassant practiced otherwise, albeit with overly reductive insight: "If the sexual impulse be not a moral antecedent, it is none the less the wire that moves almost all M. de Maupassant's puppets, and as he has not hidden it, I cannot see that he has eliminated analysis or made a sacrifice to discretion" (J3, 529–30).

Nevertheless, this impulse for poetic sparseness manifests itself in honed passages that excite our imagination. It also sustains Maupassant's upper hand over short stories, which for James "deserve the first place in any candid appreciation of his talent[:] they represent him best in his originality, and their brevity, extreme in some cases,

12. In *The Literary Criticism of Henry James* (Athens: Ohio University Press, 1981), 141–43, Sarah B. Daugherty judges that the Maupassant essay marked a crossroad of criticism for James: "Maupassant's perspective clearly was not James's; but then again, the critic was past the point in demanding that it should be."

does not prevent them from being a collection of masterpieces." Thus, the tales of Normandy, the theme that James enjoyed most amid Maupassant's works, are wrought with such sensuous precision that the reader fathoms the peasant's "caution, his canniness, his natural astuteness, his stinginess, his general grinding sordidness [and his] quaint and brutish dialect" (J3, 534, 537).

But Maupassant had no "window" for morality. This blind spot arose not out of consciously formulated artistic scruples, as Maupassant claimed, but resulted, according to James, from a fundamental moral ignorance in the Frenchman. To forge "a legitimate way round" the embarrassing presence of the lion, then, James concluded that "Maupassant has simply skipped the whole reflective part of his men and women—that reflective part which governs conduct and produces character" (J3, 547). The very impulse that channeled Maupassant's perspective into its most appropriate outlet, the short story, coincidentally denied him his place among "the first artists," consigning him to the secondary rank of "valid artists"—undismissible, compelling, but not distilling the essence of high art. Maupassant's ignorance of Jamesian reflection allowed him to wrap his prose more tightly around a text's significant point. Indeed, excessive digression might have buried the moment so deeply that it would prove difficult to unearth for even the most erudite reader.

Such aesthetic methods were too restrictive for James, who had loftier ambitions for himself. Foremost among these was that even in the shortest of his stories James seldom confined anagnorisis to an isolated, fleeting significant moment. When revelation was the focus of a piece, it rarely descended upon characters or readers in a blinding flash of insight, as Maupassant and his heirs sometimes practiced. Instead, realization creeps upon us like successive waves encroaching upon a beach during an incoming tide. Consequently, James treasured the longer Maupassant texts where anagnorisis was dilated. He could appreciate such brief efforts as "Petit Soldat" and "La Parure," but in his final analysis they indicated only momentary perfections. Texts that approached the length of a novella, however, were singled out for praise. Many of them employ a sinusoidal structure, a complicated formula that James likely found more to his tastes, as in "Boule de suif" or "L'Héritage." In a way, such texts prepared James to compliment *Pierre et Jean*, within which he saw Maupassant's meaningful departure from literary primitivism toward incorporating valid reflection in order to ascend one rung on the ladder of aesthetic prowess. Structurally, *Pierre et Jean* parallels the sinusoidal lines of its short-story predecessors.

Curiously, several of the texts with which James found severe fault in his literary portrait of Maupassant fall into a single form: the descending helical. He especially abhorred "Le Horla," citing it as a mere imitation of Poe. Given his later experimentation with the supernatural in his fiction of the 1890s, James's opprobrium here marks an unexpected starting point to measure Maupassant's influence upon him. The popularity of "Le Horla" and other similar supernatural-madmen texts early in that decade obviously caused James to reevaluate his stance. Starting with "Sir Edmund Orme" and culminating with "The Turn of the Screw," he would emulate the pattern of his French friend's texts. James would do so, however, with apparent theoretical consistency. He likely assumed that Maupassant's protagonist in "Le Horla" was incapable of contemplating the horrific decline of his own psyche. In contrast, James's heroes and heroines can battle using their intellect to mitigate the personal effects of such gothic circumstances.

What caused James to recant somewhat his position on the interplay among the devices of the mad narrator, the descending helical, and the supernatural? Perhaps, in his slow, progressive, agonizing death, Maupassant himself provided his critic with a case sufficient to prove the validity of such a perspective. Paul Bourget kept James apprised of Maupassant's deterioration in the asylum.[13] James knew some of the details of the illness as early as 1891, when he wrote Robert Louis Stevenson: "The Frenchmen are passing away—Maupassant dying of locomotor paralysis, the fruits of fabulous habits, I am told. *Je n'en sais rien;* but I shall miss him" (30 October 1891; *J2*, 3:362). When death finally claimed Maupassant in 1893, James wrote to newspaperman William Morton Fullerton on July 14:

13. There is a remote possibility that James visited the institutionalized Maupassant. In the August 1925 issue of the *Cornhill Magazine*, "Sigma," the pseudonym for the notorious Julian Osgood Field (according to Steegmuller), claimed that James made repeated trips to the asylum, all of which had deleterious effects on the dying Maupassant. Steegmuller correctly labels the account as bogus; see *Maupassant*, 412–13, for the excerpt and Steegmuller's reaction. One aspect of this story does have a ring of truth: James often rallied in support of a sick acquaintance, as he later would with Stephen Crane. Nevertheless, I agree with Steegmuller's doubt; for one thing, Maupassant's doctors did not permit him any visitors in the last stages of his illness.

> No, I'm not a brute for having failed so long to thank you . . .
> for the touching two words you had the friendly thought of
> sending me when the indignity that life had heaped upon
> poor Maupassant found itself stayed. . . . I don't know what
> prevented my wiring you a crystalline tear to drop on Mau-
> passant's grave. Or rather, I do. Everything prevented it, in-
> cluding the fact that my tears had been already wept; even
> though the image of that history had been too *hard* for such
> droppings. (*J2*, 3:419; italics in original)

The progression in Maupassant's physical decline had induced an
equivalent emotional descent in James, perhaps leading to a subsequent, reluctant agreement that descending helicals do accurately
describe some human experiences.

A second factor compelling James's self-reassessment was Jonathan Sturges's translations. It seems probable that James's article in
the *Fortnightly Review* at least partially inspired his young friend to
undertake the project. Most of Sturges's selections for *The Odd
Number* seem to bear out James's insights in his essay. James felt
comfortable and perhaps flattered enough to compose a prefatory
essay for the short-story collection. (James first published the introduction in *Harper's Weekly* on 19 October 1889, two weeks before
the volume's date of issue.) This preface was less ambitious than the
Fortnightly article. In it, James assumed the role of apologist to
convince readers to divorce their American provincialism and read
foreign, especially French, literature. In extolling Maupassant's merits and faults, James echoed tersely his previous observations and
proclamations, focusing primarily on (1) Maupassant's deft portraits
of Norman peasants, (2) the precision of his prose style, and (3) the
limitations placed upon our appreciation by his cynicism, his occasional cruelty, and his reliance on exclusively sensate depictions.

The translator's contributions for the subsequently published
Modern Ghosts, however, were made apparently despite James's
printed objections. The Poesque "Le Horla" and "Sur l'eau" likely
sparked a spirited debate between mentor and protégé during their
frequent conversations in London. *Modern Ghosts*, nevertheless, was
among the first rumblings of the avalanche of supernatural fiction
that descended upon the United States during the 1890s. During this
same time James's confidence was shaken by his apparent inability

to secure a comfortable position in the literary marketplace, so shaken that he curtailed his novelistic impulses for almost a decade in order to pursue other, more hopeful artistic avenues.[14] A writer with so many self-misgivings may have gravitated (within aesthetic reason) toward whatever currently attracted popular tastes. Thus, despite earlier declarations, James felt it necessary to reexamine the public impact of "Le Horla" so as to gain sufficient insight to recapture his lost audience. As with most of his compromises, however, James would reformulate this French source for inspiration so radically that it eventually became truly his own literary invention.

In his search for a new literary self, however, James tried to incorporate in his works an approach that he believed fundamental to Maupassant's genius. The stylistic criterion he came to associate with Maupassant more that any other was *brevity*. He could not have seized upon a principle more antithetical to his inclinations. But during the early 1890s he was at times a writer committed to explore uneasy paths to assemble a larger audience. The reception of Sturges's volume likely proved to the analytical James that success lay in achieving the simplicity the public seemed to crave. Initially, James conceived of "brevity" in light of a manner of exposition; that is, descriptive passages stripped of as much reflection as possible. Later, he came to understand that brevity also entailed the numerical limitation of themes and even premises within a text.[15] In addition, I think that James's subconscious treatment of structure in the short story changed, aiming for greater simplicity.

James may have striven for these qualities in his "Guy de Maupassant" essay itself. A letter from his brother William suggested that "[i]n your Maupassant [essay] you used that author's own directness more than is your wont, and I think with great good effect. If you keep on writing like that I'll never utter another cavil as long as I live!"[16] As he entered and survived his own artistic experiments

14. James's artistic difficulties during the 1890s are discussed throughout volumes 3 and 4 of Edel's landmark biography.

15. In agonizing over the difficulties in meeting a 10,000-word limit of a story, James surmised (in a notebook entry dated 8 September 1895) that he had to restrict the plot itself: "I must try [the short story] on the basis of rigid limitation of subject. That is, I must take, and take only, the single incident" (J4, 130).

16. Cited in Steegmuller, *Maupassant*, 397.

during the 1890s, James often chastised himself and his work in progress with buzzwords such as "brevity" and "à la Maupassant." Although he invoked in his notebooks the name of his friend more than any other writer during the decade, James's entries suggest that Maupassantian principles were not central to the formulation of any single plot but instead acted as corrections to his expansive inclinations.

The first invoking of Maupassantian brevity in James's journal came while he mapped out a plot sequence for The Tragic Muse: "Oh, spirit of Maupassant, come to my aid! This may be a triumph of robust and vivid concision; and certainly ought to be." Obviously, James aimed for descriptive economy in his novel, having in mind, I think, the simple prose of Pierre et Jean than of any short story. By February 1889, he found himself failing to meet this principle and tried to renew his vow:

> I have undertaken to tell and to describe too much—given my data, such as they are—one of the reasons being that I was afraid of my story being too thin. For fear of making it too small I have made it too big. This, however, is a good fault, and I see my way out of it. Variety and concision must be my formula for the rest of the story—rapidity and action. . . . I have very interesting things to relate, but I must only touch them individually. A la Maupassant must be my constant motto. I must depend on the collective effect. (J4, 45, 48; italics in original)

By 1893 James found the principle of prose economy so constricting, possibly the product of his frustration in trying to accomplish it in The Tragic Muse, that he rebelled in the privacy of his journal: "God knows how dear is brevity and how sacred today is concision. But it's a question of degree, and of the quantity of importance that one can give. That importance is everything now. To try and squeeze it into a fixed and beggarly number of words is a poor and a vain undertaking—a waste of time." Yet, as he contemplated starting a new short novel, James recalled the recently deceased Maupassant's accomplishment: "There are excellent examples of the short novel— and one that has always struck me as a supremely happy instance is poor Maupassant's admirable Pierre et Jean. . . . I want to do

something that I can do in three months—something of the dimensions of *Pierre et Jean*" (J4, 77–78). Thereafter, though, James never
juxtaposed the name of Maupassant against any preliminary
sketches for a novel.[17]

Instead, as James turned temporarily away from the novel and
toward the short story during his artistic digressions in the 1890s,
the term *Maupassant* became more useful as a stylistic reminder. In
his 1891 preliminary musings for "The Real Thing," James appended a self-imposed restriction to the intentions he described
earlier in his journal: "But in how tremendously few words I must
do it. This is a lesson—a *magnificent* lesson—if I'm to do a good
many. Something as admirably compact and *selected* as Maupassant" (J4, 57; italics in original). A similar yoking of Maupassant to
a blueprint for a new story occurred earlier, in 1890, in a notebook
entry for the plot that eventually evolved into "Europe." And the
spirit of Maupassant would be reinvoked in James's meditations in
his journal about "Glasses" in 1895 and "The Tree of Knowledge"
in 1899. The fact that James needed to remind himself periodically
about this stylistic goal indicates that fundamentally it remained
difficult for him to pursue it.

The culmination and apparently the last of James's efforts to
assimilate Maupassantian principles occurred in the short story
"Paste." After a decade of toying with such notions, James finally

17. James occasionally invoked the symbol of Maupassant by name in his fiction.
In his preliminary sketch for "Europe," he planned to include a Maupassant volume
as part of the "atmosphere" of the central character's library (J4, 55). By the time he
published the tale in 1899, he had discarded this notion.

In *The Wings of the Dove*, Susan Stringham reads Maupassant. In *The Ambassadors*, Lambert Strether recalls the spirit of Maupassant at a moment when he
experiences sensual liberation. A few critics have suggested that a James novel owed
a partial debt to some Maupassant work. For instance, Charles R. Anderson argues for
the impact of Maupassant's literary impressionism upon *The Ambassadors*, citing
Maupassant's friendship with Claude Monet, Monet's painting *La Seine à Vetheuil*,
and Maupassant's "Mouche" as significant contributors to the pictorialness of certain
scenes in the novel; see Anderson, *Person, Place and Thing in Henry James's Novels*
(Durham: Duke University Press, 1977), 279–80. In *The Novels of Henry James* (1961;
reprint, New York: Hafner, 1971), 218–19, 438n., Oscar Cargill argues that Maupassant's "En famille" had a significant impact on *The Spoils of Poynton* and, less
confidently, that *Pierre et Jean* and *Forte comme la morte* seem to anticipate the
"alternating points of view" in *The Golden Bowl*. Adeline R. Tintner disagrees with
Cargill's assessment and suggests instead that Maupassant's "Qui sait?" had more of
an influence on *Poynton*; see *The Book World of Henry James: Appropriating the
Classics* (Ann Arbor, Mich.: UMI Research Press, 1987), 225–30.

resorted to direct imitation, twisting the premise of "La Parure." Even then, though, James found that the prose economy necessary to produce a surprise-inversion was impossible for him to achieve. His need to meditate and reflect through prose became too strong of an enemy to such a stylistic value. He was about to enter what F. O. Matthiessen has labeled his "major phase," abandoning in the process his quest to attain popularity using Maupassantian literary methods. The Frenchman ceased to symbolize an active aesthetic principle and was consigned to the netherrealm of nostalgia.

In sum, during the 1890s James studied, employed, and developed two structural precepts practiced by Maupassant. First, from "The Real Thing" through "Glasses" to "Paste," James increasingly adjusted himself to the notion of how descriptive terseness affects the sequencing of a plot, insights that allowed him to hone the shape of a contrast story. Second, at the same time, James repudiated an artistic value that he had professed in his 1888 essay. In experimenting with the "ghost story" during the 1890s, James had to incorporate elements he previously judged an inferior deviation by writers from Poe to Maupassant himself. One aspect of this critical retreat involved the descending helical—the form best suited to trace the inevitable succumbing of a man's soul to dark psychological forces. James's handling of structure in most of his supernatural tales—such as "Sir Edmund Orme" and "The Turn of the Screw"—departed from his friend's example, mostly through softening the mental dissolution suffered by a protagonist and through enhancing a narrator's reflective powers.[18] In essence, James strived to convey in such texts not gloom or pessimistic finality but instead a sense of weariness and resignation. For him the pure Schopenhauerian impulse simply would not do.

James and the Contrast Story

During the 1890s the short-story form that James employed the most was the contrast. Apparently, his concepts of Maupassantian brevity

18. Other stories by James—such as "The Real Right Thing" and "The Friends of the Friends"—adhere to the same pattern.

dictated that he reduce plot to a simple fictional premise involving an isolated comparison between characters or of situations. The impact that Maupassant had upon these stories seemingly increased with the passing of the decade. Initially, James borrowed the most complex variation of the contrast formula, applying it to wholly original plots or to those derived from sources other than Maupassant. As James channeled more of his energies into short-story production, he took inspiration more directly from Maupassant's tales themselves, eventually so much so that several Jamesian efforts composed during the late 1890s involved the mere transposition of a premise underlying a well-established *conte*. Ironically, the same pressure for diversity that compelled Maupassant to borrow from a variety of sources during his most prolific period began to affect James also.

There would be one self-imposed proviso to such gleanings for inspiration, though: James would use premises from Maupassant's surprise-inversion stories—likely because their shock value made them more memorable to the American—but he consistently diluted their structural impact by converting the plot sequence into a contrast.[19] This necessity for positioning the turning point of a text elsewhere results from James's preference for meditative fiction. A reflective man is seldom caught completely unsuspecting, for he has already anticipated all relevant possibilities. He may marvel at a remote chance event manifesting itself, but he cannot be shocked.

During his planning for "The Real Thing" in 1891, James had Maupassant very much in mind.[20] After outlining characters and plot in his notebook, James assessed the difficulties his temperament might present in completing the tale. Among other matters, he

19. Ora Segal arrives at a somewhat similar conclusion in treating James's "Madame de Mauves": "the final twist [in James's story] does not reverse the central point (or even moral) of the fable" (as a Maupassant ending would); see *The Lucid Reflector: The Observer in Henry James' Fiction* (New Haven: Yale University Press, 1969), 28–29.

20. I cannot agree with Tintner's assessment that "The Real Thing" was inspired by "Mlle. Dardenne," a story once attributed to Maupassant but since excised from the canon. Tintner's notions are based upon her reading of one of the bogus editions in English of Maupassant's complete works, published in 1902. (See Chapter 3 for a fuller discussion of the textual problems in these editions.) While she is aware of the apocryphal nature of the text, a story first attributed to Maupassant in 1902 (which is certainly the earliest that James could have read it) could not have influenced the composition of "The Real Thing" in 1891; see *Book World*, 222–23.

worried that in striving for brevity he could strip too much meat off the bone to sustain the effort: "Frankly, however, is this contrast enough of a *story*, by itself? It seems to me Yes—for it's an IDEA—and how the deuce should I get *more* into 7000 words?" (J4, 56; italics in original). The author's meditation suggests that "The Real Thing" exists at the bare minimum necessary to survive as a Jamesian fictional endeavor. Such economy demanded maintaining "a very short pulse of rhythm" and "the closest attention to detail," which could be achieved by energetic prose summaries and avoiding "lateral development." As a consequence, the simple juxtaposition of a contrasting dyad must be adhered to rigidly. His preference in the novel to digress fruitfully had no place in such a confined textual space. For James, the tale proved to be an experiment not only in form but in his own character as well, for the experience of dealing with such limitations promised to be "a magnificent lesson." With one eye to the future, then, James distilled his intention in the concluding fragment to the notebook entry: "Something as admirably compact and *selected* as Maupassant" (J4, 57; italics in original).

The essential contrast in "The Real Thing" juxtaposes the ineffable unsuitability of the Monarchs as artist's models against the annoying aptness of two social inferiors who provide the same service.[21] One can only suppose that James selected his subjects along the same line as Maupassant's adherence to the precepts of realism—not only to write about what you know best but also to exploit your own ambivalent response to your subject. James admired the Normandy stories the most because in them Maupassant could not subdue his caustic condemnation of the Norman character while he defended its spirit. James's equivalent experience arose out of the English, Continental, and, occasionally, American societies he observed and participated in with diurnal relish. The short story, then, becomes useful as a medium to deal with types—the gadfly, the fop, the swanks—interesting enough to caricature in a short text but insufficient to sustain any symbolic weight throughout an entire novel.

The Monarchs of "The Real Thing" mark a standard by which James's audience could perceive its illusions about itself. Major and

---

21. For James's account of his original inspiration for the plot (after a conversation with George du Maurier), see J1, 18:xx–xxi.

Mrs. Monarch arouse a modicum of pathos in the narrator-artist (or really -illustrator) of the text. The husband and wife believe and practice a multitude of questionable virtues emblematic of Victorian society. Their dilemma begins, continues, and ends with how to project their pride amid ever-declining circumstances. Their means reduced by a bad investment, they petition for work as models, which in itself threatens their social standing. The naiveté of the two about such a profession surfaces quickly when they illogically approach a landscape painter for their initial assignment. Referred to the narrator, the neophyte models presume that the reality of their more comfortable past would more than adequately prepare them to project such affluence in the present. Initially out of a sense of charity, later because of a growing aesthetic commitment, the narrator uses them both for various projects, including a make-or-break assignment to illustrate the first volume of a variorum edition of a newly renowned author.

Juxtaposed against the Monarchs are the cockney Miss Churm, an accomplished artist's model, and the immigrant Oronte, a newcomer who, unlike the Monarchs, proves to be useful. By their mannerisms, speech, and values, they both earn the immediate enmity of the Monarchs, who assume that people of such inferior social status could not serve as patterns for elegance and graceful fictional characters. Ironically, Churm and Oronte stimulate the illustrator's imagination better than his high-bred alternatives. The narrator's view of his regular models is plastic enough that he can mold them into whatever social roles a project demands. Meanwhile, his drawings of the Monarchs prove to be, at times, taxing and only net him the rebuffs of critical peers and editors.

Essentially, the structure of "The Real Thing" depends upon the relative status between the competing set of models. In and of itself, there is no superficially identifiable turning point in the text, especially one that signals a notable change in the fortune of the Monarchs. Ostensibly, one significant event has already occurred before the text picks up the plot, that is, when they squander their financial security. At the other end of the story, where the Major and his wife will end up finally remains only a subject for our conjecture, for both the author and his narrator seem temperamentally incapable of forecasting it. James could only measure a small segment of the Monarchs' fall from social grace.

The point of contrast in the text is a relative one—when the declining Monarchs cross social levels with the ascending Churm and Oronte. Servitude becomes the symbolic activity that fixes this cultural flux. At one point in the text, the demeanor of the Monarchs so overwhelms the narrator that without thinking he asks Churm to serve tea, which she does but later "surprised me greatly by making a scene about it." Subsequently, after the narrator finally confesses to the Monarchs that he has no use for them, the desperation of the Monarchs prompts them to tidy up the studio and to administer to the needs of even the once inferior Churm so as to convince him of their worth as servants; but the still modest means of the illustrator (as well as his embarrassment for them) make such employment impossible.

Through the contrast, then, we witness a curious phenomenon: the fluidness of social position. Maupassant used such a demanding structural variant sparingly, preferring more simple contrasts that focused upon events that even superficial examination would reveal as significant.[22] James wanted to train a subtler eye in his audience so that it too could discern the meaning of nuances in diurnal life. For James, the short story imposed even greater limitations on his aesthetic perspective than did the novel.

This contrast may suggest on a symbolic level James's changing attitudes about his status as artist. Initially, the narrator of "The Real Thing" does mention briefly his artistic hopes, but as he confronts more and more the mercenary side of his profession—illustrating advertisements and books—such lofty self-references diminish in frequency. One way to consider the interpretive meaning of the models is that the Monarchs represent James's faltering commitment to the tenets of pure realism. The demands of the public—to which James tried to cede some ground in the 1890s—influenced him to pursue other, less comfortable literary avenues that required, at times, different aesthetic values. Thus, one deficiency of James's narrator in the story is his penchant to draw a figure substantially larger, in effect, than the posing model. The practice worked well with the diminutive Oronte, but the illustrator had to temper his pen so as not to proportion the major as a "brawny giant."

22. Maupassant did occasionally use this variant of the contrast; for example, see "En wagon" in M1, 2:478–84.

When the narrator finally forsakes the Monarchs, he simultaneously forgoes absolute realism. Instead he transforms what he sees (Churm and Oronte) into images that the public believes to be realistic. But the narrator, and hence James, lets go of his past aesthetic value only reluctantly: "my friend Hawley repeats that Major and Mrs. Monarch did me a permanent harm, got me into false ways. If it be true I'm content to have paid the price—for the memory" (J1, 18:346). Perhaps, like his narrator, James eventually came to see himself in his shifting of aesthetic gears during the early 1890s no longer as an artist but as an illustrator given more to meeting the tastes of the audience.

As James acclimated himself to the pace of producing short stories during the decade, hints of Maupassant's influence surfaced here and there in his productions. Even Maupassant's death seemed to inspire James to create. Although the plot itself hears little resemblance to the Frenchman's life, "The Death of the Lion" (1894) recalls in its title the metaphor James applied in his essay six years earlier, placing it now in the context of the tragic conclusion of his friend's life.[23] Interestingly, the author names one minor character Guy Walsingham, which proves to be the pseudonym for a woman among whose works is the suggestively titled "Obsessions." The name Guy would occasionally reappear among James's literary output during the decade, including the play Guy Domville and the short story "Paste."

Eventually, James borrowed more than just precepts for construction from Maupassant. Several of his works elaborate on premises that Maupassant had already explored a decade earlier. In most cases, James obviously did not have a text before him to imitate. Likely, he worked from a sum impression of themes, expanding and remolding a situation to fit into his perspective. Perhaps in trying to imitate Maupassant's spirit, James had to gravitate to pursuing similar subjects. Perhaps facing the grind of mass-producing stories, especially those of the 7000- to 10,000-word length, which he found easier to "place" with editors, James consciously or subconsciously reworked his friend's plots as a means of developing new material. Perhaps in an effort to master the genre, James resorted to emulating

23. Edel suggests that Constance Fenimore Woolson's recent death also contributed to James's struggle to rationalize in "The Death of the Lion"; see Henry James, 3:373.

Maupassantian texts in order to grasp more tightly the subtle and, at times, elusive nuances of the short story.

Whatever the case, James arrived at final drafts that increasing suggest similarities with Maupassant's plots. At first, James's inspiration was faint but extant. In his notebook entry of 26 July 1895, he recorded his preliminary ideas for a new short story. Observing "a very little woman . . . on the top of an omnibus," James immediately recalled the spirit of his recently deceased friend: "A little idea occurred to me the other day for a little tale that Maupassant would have called *Les Lunettes*, though I'm afraid that *The Spectacles* won't do" (J4, 125). The "little tale" would eventually approach 20,000 words and would be called "Glasses" when published in the *Atlantic Monthly* for February 1896.[24] James's musing about the title and his subsequent solution indicate that he had well in mind Maupassant's preference for identifying a text's central metaphor through its title. This concept ought not to be surrounded with adjectives or other interpretive modifiers that might interfere with a reader's ability to discover meaning for himself.

Although James did not continue to allude to Maupassant while tracing out his ideas for "Glasses," the tale's debt to the Frenchman goes beyond the brevity of its title. The premise of the story—how a woman's infirmity affects her prospects for love, marriage, and security—harkens back to several Maupassant efforts. In fact, "Glasses" mutes the severity but expands the treatment of a major theme from "Le Modèle" (1883).

Structurally, "Le Modèle" is a loop, barely two thousand words in length. Openly professing his inspiration from Daudet's "Les Femmes d'artistes," Maupassant traces an artist's relationship with his mistress. The text begins with a superficially poignant scene where Jean Summer administers to his crippled wife at a resort. Then the narrative loops back into the past before their marriage to recount their stormy relationship, Summer's attempt to break it off, the whimsical suicide attempt by his mistress, and the guilt-inspired marriage that resulted. The cynicism underlying the tale surfaces in the comments made to the narrator by an onlooker, who is privy to the truth of the couple's history:

24. In settling matters for the publication of the tale, James demonstrated how acutely aware he was that he far exceeded his initial length limitations; see Edel, *Henry James*, 4:145.

[Les femmes] sont toujours sincères dans une éternelle mobilité d'impressions. Elles sont emportées, criminelles, dévouées, admirables, et ignobles, pour obéir à d'insaisissables émotions. Elles mentent sans cesse, sans le vouloir, sans le savoir, sans comprendre, et elles ont, avec cela, malgré cela, une franchise absolue de sensations et de sentiments qu'elles témoignent par des résolutions violentes, inattendues, incompréhensibles, folles, qui déroutent nos raisonnements, nos habitudes de pondération et toutes nos combinaisons égoïstes. (M1, 1:1104)

([Women] are always sincere amid a perpetual riot of impressions. Yielding to elusive emotions, they are fiery, criminal, loyal, admirable, and vile. Without meaning to, without knowing it, without understanding why, they lie continually; and because of this, despite this, they are absolutely devoid of feeling and sentiment, which they evince in violent, surprising, incomprehensible, mad decisions that disconcert our logic, our well-weighed social customs, and all our selfish arrangements.)

Obviously, James would never have accepted the flagrant cynicism of this confused assault upon the motives of women. Nevertheless, his perspective in "Glasses" would pursue a similar direction but not go so far. For example, the physical problem of his heroine, Flora Saunt, would not be totally self-inflicted but instead the result of a collective disregard for the practicalities mandated by nature. Her failing eyesight, correctable if she heeds her oculist, has a devious catalyst: her vanity. Trying to find security by landing a rich husband, Saunt believes her facial beauty to be her passport, and the opinions and behavior of her acquaintances bear this out. Thus, the hideous spectacles that render her face plain become for her a necessity that must be either dispensed with or kept secret. The latter strategy fails when her perspective groom, Lord Iffield, unexpectedly catches her wearing her glasses. Yielding to the tastes of society, then, she tries to manage without them, which secures her engagement to Iffield but also contributes manifestly to her subsequent blindness.[25]

25. In treating the importance of light symbols in the story, Granville H. Jones

In developing his idea from "Le Modèle," James rearranges relationships, fragments one character into several, and expands each's role. Unlike the original, the artist figure in "Glasses" is not the victim of circumstances but becomes the interested narrator—the observer of the social tragicomedy. He sees the folly of the players involved, including his own, but his condemnation of people and situations deliberately lacks the decisive bite of Maupassant's pessimism. Jean Summers is split into Lord Iffield and the more sympathetic Geoffrey Dawling; meanwhile, the cynical commentator of "Le Modèle" has a worthy counterpart in Mrs. Meldrum, who always chastises while attempting to fathom motivations.

Despite his alterations, James arrived at a similar insight about the strange possibilities in human relationships. Although more protracted, Saunt's choice is just as desperate as the model's. The crippling effects of the model's suicidal fall created a bond sufficient enough to compel Summers to marry her even though he did not love her. James redirects this impulse somewhat: Saunt's blindness ends her hopes to marry Iffield, yet it also endears her more so to Dawling. Impoverished by her pursuit for a husband, dependent because of her condition upon the kindness of others, Saunt, with the help of Meldrum, seems to lapse into a convenient marriage to Dawling—motivated on her part by something less than love; on his, by love corrupted by pity.

Because of its length, the structure of "Glasses" is rather diffuse, as several forms contend unsuccessfully at the same time. James apparently wanted the heroine's blindness to come as a surprise to his audience, but he laces most of the text with the suspicions and fears of especially Dawling and the artist-narrator; these hunches anticipate rather explicitly the eventual outcome of such behavior. Thus, the reflective character of James's prose makes constructing a surprise-inversion rather difficult for him.[26]

---

assesses that Flora Saunt "is utterly unconcerned about the moral implications of her choice, as indifferent to them as fate was to her, she likely feels, when she was marked indiscriminately to be blind. . . . Her obsession, on the other hand, does limit her perception and awareness"; see *Henry James's Psychology of Experience* (The Hague: Mouton, 1975), 62.

26. In defending the story's value, George Bishop notes the traditional view "that its rather trite ending lacks punch"; see "Shattered Notions of Mastery: Henry James's 'Glasses,' " *Criticism* 27 (1985): 348.

James also wanted to build his tale in the form of a loop. He begins the narrative with:

> Yes indeed, I say to myself, pen in hand, I can keep hold of the thread and let it lead me back to the first impression. The little story is all there, I can touch it from point to point; for the thread, as I call it, is a row of coloured beads on a string. None of the beads are missing—at least I think they're not: that's exactly what I shall amuse myself with finding out. (J5, 9:317)

Here, James had a valid definition for a loop: have the conclusion ready and then tell the tale with it in mind. Thus, the progression of "coloured beads" will appear complete and logically ordered for the reader. But this introductory statement deals with the form of presenting a text and not with its fictional manifestation. A proper loop (in Maupassant terms) would have begun with a decisive moment and then retracted into the past to elaborate on how such an event came about. Without such an initial scene, "Glasses" has more of a descending-helical structure, where events form a causal chain to an inevitable end. However, the sensation of relative satisfaction felt by the concerned principals in the story—that the best has been made from a bad situation—somewhat moves the text away from the descending helical because it does not strike the final emotional coup that often ends such accounts.

The one story form that survives fairly well in "Glasses" is the contrast.[27] The plot is fraught with intended comparisons. They begin with characterization: the demanding Iffield versus the aspiring Dawling; Saunt versus the bespectacled and practical Mrs. Meldrum, whose appearance anticipates what the young woman dreads. The text itself is directed neatly through one incident. The first half of the story presents Saunt as she avoids and worries about the disfiguring prospects caused by her vision problems. Visiting a toy store, she has to don her glasses to observe the intricacy of a toy, an action she tries to hide from Iffield, who is distracted elsewhere. Despite her precautions, the nobleman, the narrator (who acciden-

---

27. Bishop sees a differing structure for the story: "four tableaux and their accompanying sub-scenes" ("Shattered Notions," 355). The inflection point I discuss would fall between tableaux 2 and 3 in Bishop's scheme.

tally witnessed the scene), and we get our first glimpse of the effect the glasses have upon her beauty:

> Lord Iffield had already seized her arm; with a violent jerk he brought her round toward him. Then it was that there met my eyes a quite distressing sight: this exquisite creature, blushing, glaring, exposed, with a pair of big black-rimmed eyeglasses, defacing her by their position, crookedly astride of her beautiful nose. She made a grab at them with her free hand while I turned confusedly away. (J5, 9:340)

After this scene the rest of the text delineates how this new image affects everyone. The woman is essentially the same as she was in the first part of the story, but the reaction of everyone to her, including her own, alters. After first publishing an announcement of their engagement, Iffield subsequently withdraws his offer and from the scene. Saunt still avoids wearing her glasses whenever possible, no longer because of a vague apprehension. The toy-store incident provides her with a precise illustration of their impact upon her physical charm and her evaporating hopes. Even the narrator succumbs to the pictorial memory of that incident; he no longer seeks her out to model for his paintings.[28]

In organizing such comparisons, James enables us to discern the unavoidable folly in human behavior. The conspiracy of values shared by all drives one woman to blindness and everyone else to acts that are cruelly negligent, unduly sentimental, or dangerously self-sacrificing. This interplay aims for a Maupassantian perspective but with a softer edge. James strives to be more the reporter than the critic. Thus, we as readers approach the text not with the curious but dismissing cynicism of Maupassant but with an appraising and,

28. In "The Myopic Narrator in Henry James's 'Glasses,' " *Henry James Review* 4 (1983): 191–93, Sharon Dean attacks the narrator-artist's ability to perceive, arriving at a similar conclusion to the one I suggest for the illustrator in "The Real Thing." In judging the artist in "Glasses," however, Dean remains unforgiving: "At the end of the tale, the narrator could have acted on his insights . . . and shown some signs of growth, but he does not."

Bishop interestingly suggests that James's choice to call the tale "Glasses" rather than the more restrictive "The Glasses" directs us to examine how everyone in the story perceives rather than to focus upon Saunt's problem alone ("Shattered Notions," 348ff.).

like Dawling and the narrator, pitying interest. Consequently, the structural contrast in "Glasses," more clear-cut than in "The Real Thing," guides us to judge the bizarre incidents of fate with a kinder and, hence for James, more perceptive eye. This aesthetic approach demanded explicit detail to highlight each nuance properly. As a result, James found his perspective still too expansive for the reductive discipline necessary for a good Maupassantian short story. To learn more, James had to imitate the *conte* more closely.

The last and fullest efforts to mimic Maupassant's criteria would come at the end of the decade. As James himself later attested in one of his New York edition prefaces, "La Parure" directly inspired the premise for "Paste" (1899):

> The origin of "Paste" is rather more expressible, since it was to consist but of the ingenious thought of transposing the terms of one of Guy de Maupassant's admirable *contes*. . . . It seemed harmless sport simply to turn [the premise of "La Parure"] round—to shift, in other words, the ground of the horrid mistake, making this a matter not of a false treasure supposed to be true and precious, but of a real treasure supposed to be false and hollow: though a new little "drama," a new setting for my pearls—and as different as possible from the other—had of course withal to be found. (J1, 16:x; italics in original)

As in other cases during this last phase of his debt to Maupassant, James seized upon a surprise-inversion text, likely because the shock of the ending made the plot memorable for him. He remembered succinctly but fully the impact of the final twist: "[The Loisels] obliterate [their debt] all to find that their whole consciousness and life have been convulsed and deformed in vain, that the pearls were but highly artful 'imitation' and that their passionate penance has ruined them for nothing" (J1, 16:x).[29]

In his transposition, however, James found that he could not or should not duplicate the effects of a surprise-inversion. He could not guide his readers toward perceptual catastrophes that dismiss

29. James's memory fails him in one detail: the necklace in Maupassant's story was made of diamonds, not pearls.

human motivation and endeavor in one sweeping stroke of the author's pen. Unlike the unsuspecting Loisels, the characters in James's tale, because of their ability to imagine alternate realities, anticipate the true value of the supposedly paste necklace. In other words, their penchant to reflect pre-empts the possibility of forming a plot as a surprise-inversion. James shifts emphasis in story structure to befit a contrast text. For him, revelation of truth was only part of his aim. The changes in perception evoked by such knowledge had greater interpretive significance. By virtue of its attempt to explain a turning point, this structure mitigates the perceptual severity of such change, a consequence that suited James well. His delicate pen preferred to detail the finest gradations of human insight.

Strangely enough, Maupassant had already anticipated the direction of James's transposition. "La Parure" itself reversed the circumstances of Maupassant's earlier story "Les Bijoux."[30] As is "Paste," "Les Bijoux" is a contrast text that allows us to realize consequences before any character does. The perceptual dilemma of M. Lantin in "Les Bijoux" resembles greatly that of Arthur Prime in the James story. In the former, the protagonist gradually discovers the genuineness of what he believed to be his late wife's costume jewelry, forcing him to surmise her secret sexual escapades for profit. As truth loots Lantin's treasured memory of its security and ability to sustain him, the genuine pearls in the "paste" necklace owned by Arthur Prime's recently deceased mother force him to confront an image he needs to deny. The pearls, cleverly hidden in a box of worthless trinkets, threaten the sanctity of the reputation of his mother, a former actress who had married a clergyman.

30. Starting with Steegmuller (Maupassant, 207–8), many scholars have already commented on this oversight.

Segnitz argues, I think without adequate foundation, that James had "Les Bijoux" firmly in mind while composing "Paste" ("Actual Genesis," 216–19). For one thing, James did not leave any clue to substantiate such a claim. Also, in his attempt to reverse the situation in "La Parure" completely, James had to arrive at a premise similar to the one in "Les Bijoux," a causal chain that suggests coincidence more than conscious design.

On the other hand, Tintner interestingly notes the presence of theater imagery in both "Les Bijoux" and "Paste," which suggests the possibility that James indeed had the former text at least subconsciously in mind while composing his version (Book World, 231–32).

The contrast structure in each text allows us to compare the effect of such knowledge on a character. For Lantin, the new perspective ends his self-indulgent idolizing of his wife's memory, replacing it with a resigned, distrusting attitude toward all women, which leads him into another marriage with a troublesome but faithful wife. On the other hand, Arthur Prime does not change his outward stance. Even after testimony and other conclusive evidence to the contrary, he still proclaims the jewels to be false and, thus, his mother innocent of any social impropriety. We can only guess at what has occurred within the inner man because his cousin Charlotte's and not his reflections are ultimately the focus of James's little study. We do know from their mutual acquaintance, Mrs. Guy, that he sold the necklace, which adds a touch of deceit and hypocrisy to his attestations late in the story, when he ends his relationship with Charlotte rather than risk hearing her version of the matter. Thus, we are not presented with a radical change in behavior but instead have our insight into motivation redirected toward a sympathetic yet slightly cynical appreciation.

Rather than toward the character most afflicted by the truth, James trains our eyes toward an interested observer of this little social farce. Charlotte Prime is the first to speculate about the true monetary worth of the necklace. It is she who has to deal with her cousin's indignant dismissal of such a possibility. When he lets her have the jewels (as a keepsake of her dead aunt) to prove their worthlessness, she shows them to the more worldly Mrs. Guy, who immediately apprises her young friend of their genuineness. This marks the turning point. Since Mrs. Guy is not a gemologist, Charlotte cannot be absolutely sure about the assessment, but in her own mind, the niece shifts her suspicions about the pearls being real from possible to probable.

The most interesting contrast set up by the text of "Paste" is the relative change in Charlotte's attitude toward her acquaintances. In the beginning of the story she is a naive, trusting governess—in essence, a stock character one can find strewn throughout nineteenth-century British fiction. In the face of her lying cousin's stubborn proclamations at the end of the story, however, the governess grows more skeptical about her world. Her doubt even spills over into her relationship with Mrs. Guy, as she is tempted to reject the account of how the woman managed to procure the necklace for herself.[31] Thus, "Paste," the text in which James had Maupassant mostly in mind, comes perhaps the closest in arriving at a Maupassantian perspective: that living life itself is disillusioning.

James may have read "Les Bijoux" in *Gil Blas* during 1883, but I see no evidence that he remembered the story when he composed "Paste," despite the fact he did own one of the editions of *Clair de lune*, the volume in which Maupassant included the short story. Therefore, even if "Les Bijoux" could, at most, inspire James only subconsciously, the many contrast stories he encountered while reading Maupassant could still evoke a Maupassantian attitude. Likely remembered because of Sturges's popular translation, "La Parure" became a model that could be easily manipulated to suit James's more subtle temperament. His decade-long experiments in fiction to unearth the secrets of his friend's *contes* finally reached fruition. "Paste" does not represent James's best effort in the short story, but it does mark the closest he could come to "brevity." Even at this relative terseness in prose, though, he still could not control the reflective component in his style.

How antithetical such a practice was to James is demonstrated in one plot aspect of a story contemporary to "Paste"—"The Tree of Knowledge" (1900). This tale seems to have owed a partial debt to Maupassant's "Regret," first published in 1884 and later reprinted in *Miss Harriet*, a volume James likely read.[32] Again, he tried to tame the magnitude of Maupassant's premise. At the turning point of "Regret," the sixty-two-year-old Paul Saval discovers that if he had pressed his infatuation with the wife of his friend Sandres during a memorable picnic decades ago, she would have "cédé," a confession that crystallizes for him all the vague sensations of personal disappointment and futility in his life. The shock of realization, enhanced by the story's contrast structure, condemns the protagonist to a

31. Jones proposes a *fortunate-fall* interpretation of Charlotte Prime's experience: "Selfless she is, but she is no ninny: she reacts, learns, and decides on the basis of her new knowledge that she could not and cannot compromise her principles. The responsibility for the consequences of her morality she accepts—even though it is synonymous with a kind of renunciation. Her innocence is lost, but her integrity is intact" (*Henry James's Psychology*, 93).

32. James did incorporate the spirit of his friend while planning for the story in his notebook. In a brief record for one aspect of the plot, he tagged his proviso: "Practical on the rigid Maupassant (at extremest brevity) system" (*J4*, 184).

hermetic despondence in which he must contemplate for the remainder of his existence fate's last ironic twist of the knife.

James likely felt compelled to subdue such a premise, that is, the consequences of knowledge that comes too late. Again, he reworked the contrast point in the plot so that it would confront the reader less than its counterpart in "Regret." As Madame Sandres coyly perceived Saval's love for her from its inception, so did Mrs. Mallow in "The Tree of Knowledge" know about Peter Brench's secret love and sacrifices for her. The fifty-year-old Brench finds himself also in love with the wife of his "friend," Morgan Mallow—a devotion that forces Brench to equivocate in commenting about the husband's inferior abilities as a sculptor. Brench's relationship with the couple is fragile, sustained mainly by the critic's disciplined silence.

The turning point in the story involves the aesthetic education of the Mallows' son (and Brench's godson), Lancelot. To maintain the status quo, Brench tries to persuade the young man to continue his studies at Cambridge rather than go to Paris, realizing that in France Lance Mallow would discover sophisticated artistic values. This intellectual revolution would lead him to see the fallacies in his father's statues. Such knowledge would threaten the precarious bonds between all the principals. Despite Brench's advice, Lance does go to France and cultivates what the godfather feared most, a critical eye superior to his father's talent.

Structurally, the youth's intellectual attainment separates the reticent, speculating Brench of the first half of the text from the resigned, ascertaining Brench of the final part. The godson's testimony that his mother "had always, always known" about her admirer's love allows Brench to see a different nuance to his past. Unlike the dismally vanquished Saval, Brench, at Lance Mallow's suggestion, applies the word "wonderful" to his plight, but he does shade it with regret in his final shared thought: "It might have been at the futility Peter appeared for a little to gaze. 'I think it must have been—without my quite at the time knowing it—to keep *me!*' he replied as he turned away" (J1, 16:190, italics in original). His conclusion is indeed the logical end to the progression of the plot. Although James may have been trying to construct a dramatic revelation *à la Maupassant*, the reflective nature of his prose pre-empted this last revelation. Thus, rather than an unexpected twist, we anticipate the small but measurable change in Brench's life. The textual contrast suggests that his relationship with the Mallows will continue as before, only now with a touch more of conscious awkwardness. In the Jamesian perspective, only such experiences were worth describing. At the end of the 1890s, he found that his instincts had been correct at the beginning of the decade: that such psychologically adept portraitures were best encapsulated in the form of a contrast. Even in the brief confines of the short story, James still needed to trace a significant perceptual change in a speculating character.

James and the Descending Helical

This fundamental component—reflection—to a Jamesian text was one reason why he initially dismissed Maupassant's descending helical texts as inferior. The narrator of "Le Horla" speculated about every supernatural possibility to explain his plight, but he could not see his own emerging paranoia. In 1888, when he wrote his Maupassant essay, James could not accept such a limitation upon the mind, and he certainly could not imagine its total dissolution. That sort of character belonged in a tale by someone like Poe, a *poeta non grata* for James and his literary circles. Therefore, in his biographical-critical essay, James could treat such a story like "Le Horla" only as a mere imitative effort, continuing a gothic vision that was flawed in its original conception, rather than as a literary product that arose from Maupassant's own experiences.

Consequently, as James turned his energies toward the short story during the 1890s, descending helicals were at the bottom of the list of Maupassantian models to be studied. As I have suggested earlier, however, several happenings combined to change James's mind: (1) the popularity of "Le Horla" in *Modern Ghosts*; (2) the growing market for ghost tales in American magazines during the 1890s; (3) the renewed interest in especially abnormal psychology by American writers during the decade; and (4) the justification of such a fictional perspective given by the circumstances surrounding Maupassant's death. Obviously, the last of these proved to be the most significant. James himself attested to the length of his grieving over Maupassant in a 1893 letter—that by the time of his friend's death, "my tears had been already wept" (J2, 3:419). The American's ability to sympathize allowed him to measure the stages of Maupassant's demise. This protracted sense of grief gave him the framework to compare loosely the cumulative effect of his own spiritual distress with Maupassant's physical pain.

James composed what his biographer Leon Edel has called the first "full-blown Jamesian tale of the supernatural" in 1891, after Sturges's success with "Le Horla" and after Maupassant had been already confined in an asylum.[33] "Sir Edmund Orme" began a series of efforts along such lines that would eventually include tales such as "The Friends of the Friends" (1896) and "The Real Right Thing" (1899), but ultimately James's temporary impulse for the ghost story culminated in "The Turn of the Screw" (1898).[34]

Like a typical descending helical by Maupassant, most of these Jamesian ghost tales take an important turning point in a character's life and dilate it throughout an entire text. Each stage of relative mental aberration, manifesting itself in the degree to which a protagonist believes in the reality of ghosts, is carefully positioned one degree below its predecessor. However, the loss of sanity in a James character is seldom so precipitate as that experienced by a Maupassant madman-narrator. Thus, the Jamesian ghost story does not end with a raving lunatic awaiting an inevitable death but with, in effect, someone who has only suffered a significant but not devastating decline from psychological grace. To establish these finer shades of difference in character development, then, James had to elaborate more on nuances so as to give the reader sufficient data to measure the alpha and omega of a protagonist's personality. As his experiments with such fiction continued in the 1890s, James increasingly found Maupassantian "brevity" impossible under such conditions. The "insanity" that James traced threatened not to end life in a whirlwind of destructive passion but to qualify the security and enjoyment a protagonist has in his or her ability to observe.

A contrast story, James's usual structural formula for his short

33. See Leon Edel, ed., *Henry James: Stories of the Supernatural* (New York: Taplinger, 1970), 141.

34. Analyzing an early notebook entry by James, Edel believes that James first conceived the essential plot of "Sir Edmund Orme" in 1879 (J4, 10). Obviously, the sparsely published Maupassant could not have had any impact on this original premise. I would argue that Maupassant's descending-helical texts contributed to James's development of the idea.

stories during the decade, could note this downward change in attitude, but the descending helical allowed him more room to explore subtle manifestations. And since James came to the ghost tale in 1891 after a long interval of avoiding such a theme, his reflective nature likely inspired him to make it a full study, to construct as complete a picture as his intellect permitted him to envision. Two stories mark significant points along James's developing conception of the descending helical: (1) "Sir Edmund Orme," the text in which James tested the waters of such a textual structure, and (2) "The Turn of the Screw," which represents James's vision on such matters developed to its fullest.

James begins "Sir Edmund Orme" with a strategy that, although certainly not invented by Maupassant, his friend frequently employed to introduce a madman narrative: a brief passage composed by a "narrator" not involved in the main story itself. In essence, the author tries to substantiate how such a manuscript—obviously meant only for private consumption—came to be public. Given his bizarre temperament and experiences, such a protagonist would seem unlikely to offer his manuscript for publication. Therefore, this preface establishes (in a fictional sense) the legitimacy of the central narrative, which tricks us into believing that we are indeed privy to thoughts not meant to be read.

The single paragraph that introduces the reader to "Sir Edmund Orme" casts a curious interpretive pall over the text that follows. It states that the tale's ingenue, Charlotte Marden, died in childbirth a year after her marriage, a fact that has little to do with the story of the supernatural events that surrounded her engagement.[35] And not only that; apparently, the author of the ghost tale has also died more recently, for the narrator talks about taking possession of his acquaintance's effects. Despite this seeming flaw in integration, these declarations prepare us for the descending pattern of the main narrative, about which James probably expects a modicum of incredulity among his readers. Thus, he warily attests to the powers of the protagonist to report truthfully about the ghost in his and his dead wife's past:

35. Jones believes that in facilitating the marriage, the ghost "has led the narrator and Charlotte into a painfully brief love affair. The revenge of Sir Edmund Orme is [only then] complete" (*Henry James's Psychology*, 105).

I can't, I allow, vouch for his having intended [the manuscript] as a report of real occurrence—I can only vouch for his general veracity. In any case it was written for himself, not for others. I offer it to others—having full option—precisely because of its oddity. Let them, in respect to the form of the thing, bear in mind that it was written quite for himself. (J1, 17:367)

Like Maupassant, James wanted to paste a transparent sheet of realism over his surrealistic prose painting.

James does include in "Sir Edmund Orme" a character that suffers a fate that could be found in a Maupassant story. Mrs. Marden, mother of Charlotte, feels the full force of the presence of Sir Edmund Orme's ghost. As her child begins to entertain eligible young men, Mrs. Marden must relive her own guilt over forsaking Orme—whom she did not love but who did love her—for Marden, whom she subsequently married. The spurned Orme's suicide does not affect the widow until after her husband's death. The intermittent appearance of her lover's ghost obviously becomes a tangible manifestation of her guilt in choosing love rather than following the dictates of social propriety. Like a Maupassant protagonist, Mrs. Marden suffers from an increasing sense of sin, so much so that only death can and does relieve her burden.

But Mrs. Marden's inability to deal with her past is not the primary focus of the text. James distances us from her perspective by having an interested, unnamed narrator relate the central story. This narrator, who will become Charlotte's fiancé, shares Mrs. Marden's sensations but on a smaller scale. As he courts Charlotte, he too sees Orme's ghost. Slowly, he grasps the situation and its implications, and, in doing so, he can sympathize with the mother. He too undergoes a gradual perceptual decay, which he has more resolve to withstand. Despite the descending spiral of the plot, though, his end is not death but an engagement to Charlotte.

James painstakingly details each stage of his narrator's growing awareness. Initially, he discovers Mrs. Marden's distress but cannot see any cause for it. After he falls in love with her daughter, however, he too observes the figure of Orme, although he first does not realize that he sees a ghost (believing instead that the dark man is just another suitor for Charlotte). His vision is altered after Mrs. Marden informs him of what Orme really is and is further corrupted when the woman tells him, in piecemeal fashion, about the history between Orme and herself. Each new fact immerses him more into a reality distorted by this past.

His commitment to oppose the ghost reflects his conscious effort not to succumb to its symbolic meaning, which threatens the quality of his prospects with Charlotte. To ameliorate the effects of Orme, he takes on the role of Mrs. Marden's confessor, which does temporarily relieve her of her burden. Ironically, though, this kindness (based in part on self-interest) contributes symbolically to the mother's death. In her recent past, she had survived in part because of this guilt and its consequence for her daughter's future. The sound sleep she could finally enjoy after sharing her secret with the narrator presages the subsequent permanent therapy of death.

Out of the spiraling entanglement forced by the ghost's presence, the narrator emerges with a less idealistic vision of love. The constraints faced by Mrs. Marden so long ago qualify his own relationship with Charlotte. Mrs. Marden chose to sacrifice the interests of Orme so that she could pursue her own by marrying another man. But the presence of the apparition suggests that a bond existed between them with which she could not consciously deal. In other words, had she waited, she might have fallen in love with him.

Charlotte does wait and thus grows to love the narrator. Initially, although his infatuation was immediate, she was more at ease with coquettish games than with a serious suitor. When the narrator tried to press matters, she grew flustered, asked him to wait, but did not reject him. As Orme symbolically appears to the narrator after he subconsciously realized his passion, so does the ghost manifest itself to Charlotte after she finally requited her suitor's affections. Her response is not a passionate one; her chief reason for accepting the proposal is because "you are good to me." Interestingly, she agrees to a type of marriage that her mother had shunned, which vindicates the spirit (in the dual sense of the word) represented by Orme.[36] She

36. Jones interprets Charlotte's actions in a positive light, suggesting that she "has proven trustworthy and has surrendered her selfish aloofness." This choice dispels the spirit of Orme, easing her mother's conscience enough to allow her to die "peacefully": "Although Charlotte has lost her innocence, she has gained insight into responsibility and honor and love" (Henry James's Psychology, 105). Such a perspective would obviously deflect the trajectory of a descending-helical text; Jones himself, though, later notes how Charlotte's subsequent death negates all the positive overtones in her accomplishment.

never knows, as the narrator does, that her vision is a ghostly one, nor does she discover the full import of Orme's meaning.

Only the narrator survives with any comprehension of the temporally far-reaching consequences of Charlotte's decision. With the unexpected death of Mrs. Marden and Charlotte's simultaneous promise to marry him, the narrator finds that the ghost with all its symbolism has exited his life; but, as the preface promises, he will soon face his own haunted past after Charlotte's death. In coordinating Mrs. Marden's demise, the narrator's own experience with the ghost, and his probable response to Charlotte's death (which, the preface hints, caused him to withdraw in a manner similar to Mrs. Marden's seclusion), James suggests that life itself may be composed of a series of such small perceptual shocks that darken one's vision. Like the narrator, however, we struggle against such decline, using our intellect, rather than resign ourselves to the psychic whirlpool as did Maupassant and his characters.

This relatively early Jamesian ghost story does falter in one Maupassantian precept for the descending helical. There does exist an element of cognitive dissonance in what characters see and believe in "Sir Edmund Orme," but James does not unduly tax his audience's imagination by interjecting substantial doubt about the authenticity of the ghost. We do not see a hysterical or paranoic narrator *à la Poe ou Maupassant* but a composed tactician, who witnesses the ghost prior to Mrs. Marden's confession to him. The uninformed Charlotte's subsequent vision of Orme seems to confirm the rationality of her future husband. Of course, the chance exists that the lover, writing long after the incident, may remember the sequence and the facts of events incorrectly. In his guilt and grief over his dead wife, he may have imagined that he saw the ghost before Mrs. Marden explained its significance. And somehow, in a manner not known to the narrator, the mother may have conveyed her hysteria regarding Orme to her daughter. Unlike future supernatural tales, however, James in "Sir Edmund Orme" did not provide sufficient clues in the text to support such an alternative reading.

Nevertheless, James found intriguing this strategy of constructing a text that supports two vastly conflicting interpretations. Ultimately, I think that his understanding of Maupassant's brevity incorporated such a textual goal. Throughout his career he had striven to interject cognitively dissonant situations with which his characters had to cope, but he presented these perceptual dilemmas to his readers only on limited levels. We always had a capable, mediating first- or third-person narrator to guide our apprehension. In shuttling back and forth between lucidity and insanity, however, Maupassant's madman-narrator allows us no quarter for interpretive certainty. While he does provide ample evidence of his schizophrenia, we become so immersed in his vision that his account of a ghost seems genuine. The power of such a text to evoke simultaneous yet conflicting interpretations would have seemed to James to be a method of retaining a densely complex text despite the prose confines of the sort of short story that editors and the public craved.

Thus, during the 1890s this literary potential plus his growing interest in abnormal psychology likely inspired James to experiment with the descending helical despite his earlier dismissal of "Le Horla." The fruition of this exploration was "The Turn of the Screw." With so many James critics having already argued every aspect of the issue, I need not elaborate on the multiple readings provided by the governess's narrative.[37] Basically, the debate boils down to two main probabilities: (1) that the governess imagines the ghosts of Peter Quint and Miss Jessel because of her hysterical infatuation with a man she has only met briefly twice and because of her misdeveloped maternal instincts; or (2) that the ghosts she witnesses are real ones, capable of destroying all by their evil portent. James abets our dual vision as readers by bringing into question all evidence that might corroborate the governess's story. For instance, does the housekeeper, Mrs. Grose, indulge the imagination of an obviously distressed woman? James suggests such a possibility but does not confirm it. Whether she lacks the sensitivity or the sympathy to perceive the ghosts, Grose still manages to create an interpretive tension in us. If we constitute the governess's peers, we would remain a hung jury.

The impish Miles does much to enhance our distorted vision. His nocturnal wanderings suggest a valid presence of Peter Quint, a conclusion that the governess readily accepted; but the child's intelligence and love for games offer us an alternative scenario: a

---

37. In *The Turn of the Screw: Bewildered Vision* (Boston: Twayne, 1989), 8–15, Terry Harte offers a brief history of the controversy (which was fueled by Edmund Wilson's 1934 revisionist reading of the story); the remainder of Harte's treatise explores the irresolvable cognitive dissonance inherent in the tale.

prank that takes advantage of his guardian's naiveté. Whatever the case, both interpretive possibilities reach a climax when, with the urgency inspired by the perception (or, if you will, the illusion) of impending doom, the governess tries to wrest the soul of Miles from the clutches of Quint. More so than in any other text by James, in "The Turn of the Screw" our vision teeters between docilely accepting a supernatural explanation of a phenomenon and psychoanalyzing a character's emerging insanity. Whereas Maupassant would ultimately distribute textual weight to allow us to settle upon the descent of a human mind—as in "Le Horla"—James precariously balances these alternative interpretations, thus more effectively achieving the Gestalt perceptual conundrum.

James's improvement of Maupassant's techniques for the descending helical goes beyond just the perceptual. The story's title itself attests to the distortion of vision that follows it: a screw rotated one half-turn may appear the same, but in reality it has been inverted and has penetrated a surface one thread deeper. Even the cryptic clue in the title alerts us, in a Maupassantian manner, about the conceit in the piece. It may be no accident that after the initial article, the initial letters for the remaining words in the title spell TOTS. Indeed, our attention should be centered upon how all in the story corrupts our image of Miles and Flora.

More substantively, James introduced a twist to Maupassant's practice of justifying the existence and presentation of a "madman's manuscript" through a fictional preface. In the narrator's prelude to the governess's account, he recalls the circumstances of hearing it read by Douglas. This multiple distancing of the reader from the central story is obviously reminiscent of traditional gothic devices used in Victorian novels as early as *Wuthering Heights*. Confined by the rules of prose and image economy for the short story, however, Maupassant would seldom set up such a complicated system of three or more narrators. And his "sane" narrator, as mere presenter of another secret journal, would almost never intrude his opinions into his subject's account. Oftentimes, his preface would not exceed two compact paragraphs, and only occasionally would he tack a terse sentence at the conclusion of the encapsulated text.

In "The Turn of the Screw," however, we find ourselves guided by a long prelude that subtly immerses us in the mood and the problems of the governess's story. Through this introduction, the pall instilled by death immediately casts our eyes and hopes downward. The narrator informs us that both the governess and Douglas are dead, which in itself creates a pseudogothic temporal distancing between our present and the events in the core story. This separation may reflect the psychological makeup of James at the time. In experiencing the madness gradually induced by syphilis, Maupassant could portray its manifestations in his fiction more directly than his old friend could. James had to rely upon observation: the essence of his own thought processes did not capture the complex emotional state of the governess. Instead, his portrait was the product of witnessing phenomena with which he found difficult to empathize but could sympathize. This foreign behavior pattern in his intellectual spirit forced him to create an extra narrative layer between himself and his hysterical subject. The length of the preface itself indicates that the rational mind must be eased, rather than cast headlong, into such psychological pits.

James's major debt to Maupassant in "The Turn of the Screw" is, however, structural. The initial sentence in the governess's manuscript confirms symbolically the general trajectory of her experience: "I remember the whole beginning as a succession of flights and drops, a little see-saw of the right throbs and the wrong" (J1, 12:158). In each successive roman-numbered section of her manuscript, the governess chronicles a new stage of her gradual descent into desperation. For example, in the opening two sections (1) she confesses to Mrs. Grose her infatuation with her employer; (2) she becomes distressed at learning that Miles had been summarily dismissed from his boarding school for an unspecified reason; and (3) right after that, she is told that the children's former governess died under mysterious circumstances. All this gossip might have been treated as random dismissible impressions, but the governess tries to discern the truth that underlies all she witnesses. Thus, these three incidents combine to form the initial premise for a vicious causal chain.

Degree by degree, James manipulates the text so that his heroine, fighting for her own stability all the way, slowly succumbs to the horror in the history and the present dangers of her environment. She first sees Peter Quint not as a ghost but as an intruder, arousing her alarm on a practical level rather than an imaginative, supernatural one. After Mrs. Grose's identification, the governess entertains the notion that Quint was an apparition, from which she extracts a suspicion regarding his evil designs about her charges, Miles and Flora. Each successive encounter with a ghost (curiously, Quint and Jessel never materialize together) pushes the protagonist into increasingly hysterical reflections, desperate plans, and bizarre behavior. Flora's meeting with Jessel by a lakeshore, Miles's nightly travels under his sister's attentive vigil, and all the other strange occurrences are arranged to take the governess one rung downward each time on the ladder to an irrational hell. The final confrontation between her and Quint, during which they engage in a spiritual tug-of-war for the soul of Miles, thus becomes the inevitable target of the plot's trajectory.[38]

As in "Sir Edmund Orme" we are not privy to the thoughts of the being condemned to death by such quasi-supernatural events, as we would be in a Maupassant text. Instead, our own identity is merged into that of the intimately entangled observer—the governess—as she fights for control over the doomed victim, Miles. In sum, we share the growing desperation and perhaps the frenzy of the governess in her sympathy with the evil fate that awaits the children. James could only deal with the maddening transitions of individual perspective. He could not envision through a reflective first-person narrator the ultimate, prolonged destruction along such a mental path; he could only witness such events and report their manifestations. Maupassant saw such possibilities in his own life and thus could assume a fictional guise that dealt directly with their perceptual consequences; James saw such possibilities in his friend's life and death and thus could only hypothesize about their emotional effects through employing an interested narrator who suffers sympathetic pains, who must cope with a decline in her own sensibili-

38. In a 9 December 1898 letter to H. G. Wells, James outlined the concise unity he demanded of his own talents in integrating the governess into the story, borrowing in his analysis standards and terms Maupassant accepted and practiced: "Of course I had, about my young woman, to take a very sharp line. The grotesque business I had to make her picture and the childish psychology I had to make her trace and present, were, for me at least, a very difficult job, in which absolute lucidity and logic, a singleness of effect, were imperative. Therefore I had to rule out subjective complications of her own—play of tone etc.; and keep her impersonal save for the most obvious and indispensable little note of neatness, firmness and courage—without which she wouldn't have had her data. But the thing is essentially a pot-boiler and a *jeu d'esprit*" (*J2*, 4:86).

ties, but who survives by virtue of her intellect. Even if, as Douglas attests, the governess is doomed to a subsequent death, we cannot witness it because such a scene would be irrelevant to James's aesthetic sensibilities.

Thus, after toying with the descending helical for almost a decade, James did what he had always done with any literary, artistic, or philosophical influence in his career: he manipulated a principle so delicately but so thoroughly that his use of it seems more original than borrowed.[39] In other words, Maupassant's values do exist in the tapestry of James's artistic consciousness, but they have been interwoven into a pattern that contains a thousand other artistic threads. Thus, any debt to Maupassant for the structure of "The Turn of the Screw" could not be for James an isolable, conscious one.

As exquisite as "The Turn of the Screw" is, there have not been many attempts by American writers of quality to imitate it. In addition, James's intentions for his fiction were too expansive to become the predominate standards for the twentieth-century short story. I believe that when he returned to the novel at the turn of the century, he confirmed (by implication) that this rhetorical preference made composing the terse Maupassantian conte very difficult for him. Among the items in his relatively slower production of short fiction after 1900, only a few seemed to be written with Maupassant in mind. In "Paste," "The Tree of Knowledge," "Europe," "The Turn of the Screw," and "The Real Right Thing," he had carried his friend's notions for fiction as far as he could take them.

Here, in the twentieth century, short-story writers who have learned from James seemed to read his novels for inspiration more often than his shorter fiction. In critical circles, it is assumed, even among James's enthusiasts, that his quintessential principles are more likely found in his major novels than anywhere else. In most of the important critical treatises, his short stories are usually treated only in passing references. Hence, James's flirtation with the Maupassant conte and nouvelle during the 1890s did not establish any

39. In discussing structural elements in The Golden Bowl, Daniel Mark Fogel proposes that the novel is built around a "spiral ascent," which, in a loose fashion, inverts the principle of the descending helical; see Henry James and the Structure of the Romantic Imagination (Baton Rouge: Louisiana State University Press, 1981), 85–137.

profound legacy for succeeding generations of writers. Save for "The Turn of the Screw" and an occasional appearance in a college literary anthology, such stories are not usually considered part of the essential American canon. For the most part, the longer of the Maupassant-influenced texts are not even among James's best novellas, especially among those still read regularly today.

Thus, James's artistic acknowledgment of the diversity possible in the Maupassant *conte* (that is, beyond that of the surprise-inversion) has remained in relative obscurity during this century. The other witness to this fuller vision of Maupassant's ability, Kate Chopin, had just as little effect on modern literature until her rescue from obscurity during the late 1960s. In consequence, our vision of Maupassant and his American impact has been restricted to the trick-ending short story and its use by writers we consider relatively inferior, such as Ambrose Bierce and O. Henry. Perhaps this history illuminates some flaw in the American character—that we hold doggedly to first impressions because we lack the vitality to search for fundamental truth.

Afterword

In critiquing the Introduction to this book, my friend Martha Turner commented on a competing duality in my thesis, the interweaving of the theoretical approach to fictive structure with historical trends in the history of a genre. In the heart of the book itself, I interlace a third fiber: biographical impulses that strengthened the dynamics of a literary historical moment within the confines of short-story form. And, along the way, I managed to graft other threads of influence. In retrospect, I am relieved that the safeguard of my limited imagination avoided assembling a more complex argumentative weave.

In essence, the multiple strands of seven structures of fiction, three decades of international literary history, and five very different literary lives became inextricably twisted in my vision of short-story history. I could not divorce literary history from fictional form. To pluck one thread was to risk unraveling the entire fabric.

The Fates foreordained a curious life for the short story around the turn of the century. The chord of its existence spun by Clotho weaved a nation's misperception of artistic intent with its celebration of personal insight. Maupassant—instinctive lion of economical prose, unconscious fuser of irreconcilable tenets by Schopenhauer, Poe, Mérimée, Flaubert, Turgenev, and Zola, unwitting compiler of nineteenth-century short-story forms—became, in America's meager perception, the proponent and supreme practitioner of a narrow conception of the *conte*: terse in prose and plot, structured to shock readers, celebrating the moment of devastating discovery. Of all the personalities and beliefs extant in the Maupassant canon, the majority of American writers seemed to prefer the geocentric-chronocentric-egocentric artist—that is, the being who tended to ignore or

minimize the complexities of the external world by confining himself to fictional accounts that isolated a place, a moment, a self.

Within the three decades measured by Lachesis (from the appearance of "Boule de suif" to the death of O. Henry), the practice of the
short story had to conform to the exigencies of American culture.
Disinherited by Manifest Destiny from the promise of democracy,
confused by the price exacted by the Industrial Revolution, frightened by the political and social turmoil of the 1890s, several key
American writers and editors sought temporal escape by opting for
this Maupassantian, narcissistic self-image. Stressing the significant
moment in their stories, they highlighted change and insight without
care about aftereffects. Thus, forms such as the surprise-inversion
gave American story writers the necessary contrivance to steal illusions of personal meaning. By disregarding posteriority, as they
misunderstood their master to have practiced and commended, they
escaped the philosophical burdens of projecting the effects of discovery. On a larger scale, the dynamics of turn-of-the-century American society were so confounding that few could anticipate national
destiny; therefore, writers such as Bierce and O. Henry chose fictive
structures that precluded any worry about the future. In effect,
choice of form allowed them to construct less rigorous ontologies.

By severing the chord of life so early for several principal figures,
Atropos also curtailed the time span for this critical transition of the
short story. With concern for consequence related to the American
subconscious, short-story writers indulged themselves with their
delusions of vestigial truth. The suggestive symbolism provided by
the career and death of Maupassant himself may have encouraged
this interpretive bias in America. Despite the progressive threat of
syphilis, Maupassant often chose to celebrate the present in his
contes, almost as if he could displace anxiety over death with
exaltation of insight. Curiously, his fate—artistic (a decade's worth
of feverish publication), social (an attraction for hedonism), and
physical (a premature death)—anticipated the lives of several subsequent American writers. Besides Chopin and O. Henry, Stephen
Crane, Frank Norris, Harold Frederic, Paul Dunbar, and the Harvard
poets come to mind. In effect, the artistic need to distill time, place,
and self into a moment of discovery ironically paralleled the brevity
in this era of American letters.

Furthermore, the egocentricity of the American writer, with all its eccentricities, found expression in end-oriented stories, especially in the structures popularized by the Maupassant translations. As with the postimpressionists' idiosyncratic use of color and form, the story writer's employment of surprise-inversions contributed to a national literary movement too philosophically heterogeneous to call properly a school. Thus, when recollecting antebellum fiction, subsequent figures such as Sherwood Anderson, Gertrude Stein, and Ernest Hemingway reduced Bierce's cynicism, Bunner's sentimentality, and O. Henry's human ironies to a common base of textual structure. Form proved an easier authority to rebel against. Accepting earlier circumscriptions of his importance, the writers of the 1920s likewise dismissed Maupassant. I suspect, however, as with most revolutionaries, that they secretly aspired to achieve what they openly attacked. We have passed the centennial of Maupassant's death, yet his meaning for twentieth-century American fiction still needs critical illumination. As the generation of the 1890s was wont to do, I dwell on the significant moment, ignoring the future but blindly trusting that it will arrive.

Works Cited

Alvado, Hervé. *Maupassant ou l'amour realiste*. Paris: La Pensée Universelle, 1980.

Anderson, Charles R. *Person, Place and Thing in Henry James's Novels*. Durham: Duke University Press, 1977.

"Another Attempt to Boost Bierce into Immortality." *Current Opinion* 65 (September 1918): 184–85. Reprinted in *Critical Essays on Ambrose Bierce*. Ed. Cathy N. Davidson. Boston: G. K. Hall, 1982. 50.

Arnavon, Cyrille. "Les Débuts du roman réaliste américain et l'influence française." In *Romanciers américains contemporains*. Ed. Henri Kerst. Cahiers des langues modernes I. Paris: Didier, 1946.

Arner, Robert. "Kate Chopin." *Louisiana Studies* 14 (1975): 11–139.

———. "Pride and Prejudice: Kate Chopin's 'Désirée's Baby.' " *Mississippi Quarterly* 25 (1975): 131–40.

Artinian, Artine. *Maupassant Criticism in France, 1880–1940 with an Inquiry into his Present Fame and a Bibliography*. Morningside Heights, N.Y.: King's Crown, 1941.

Baldeshwiler, Eileen. "The Lyric Short Story: The Sketch of a History." In *Short-Story Theories*. Ed. Charles E. May. Athens: Ohio University Press, 1976. 202–13.

Bales, Kent. "O. Henry: 1862–1910." In *American Writers: A Collection of Literary Biographies*. Supp. II, part 1: *W. H. Auden to O. Henry*. Ed. A. Walton Litz. New York: Charles Scribner's Sons, 1981.

Bancquart, Marie-Claire. *Maupassant conteur fantastique*. Archives des lettres modernes [63]. Paris: Minard, 1976.

Beachcroft, T. O. *The Modest Art: A Survey of the Short Story in English*. London: Oxford, 1968.

Berkove, Lawrence I. *Ambrose Bierce: A Braver Man Than Anyone Knew*. Ann Arbor: Ardis, 1981. Excerpted in *Critical Essays on Ambrose Bierce*. Ed. Cathy N. Davidson. Boston: G. K. Hall, 1982. 136–49.

Besnard-Coursodon, Micheline. *Etude thématique et structurale de l'oeuvre de Maupassant: Le piège*. Paris: A.-G. Nizet, 1973.

Bierce, Ambrose. *The Collected Works of Ambrose Bierce*. Vol. 2: *In the Midst of Life: Tales of Soldiers and Civilians*. 1909. Reprint. New York: Gordian, 1966. (B1 in text)

———. *Tales of Soldiers and Civilians*. San Francisco: E.L.G. Steele, 1891.

Bishop, George. "Shattered Notions of Mastery: Henry James's 'Glasses.' "
    Criticism 27 (1985): 347–62.
Blansfield, Karen Charmaine. Cheap Rooms and Restless Hearts: A Study of
    Formula in the Urban Tales of William Sydney Porter. Bowling Green:
    Bowling Green State University Popular Press, 1988.
Bonner, Thomas, Jr. "Kate Chopin's At Fault and The Awakening: A Study
    in Structure." Markham Review 7 (1977): 10–14.
———. The Kate Chopin Companion. Westport, Conn.: Greenwood, 1988.
Braddy, Haldeen. "Ambrose Bierce and Guy de Maupassant." American
    Notes & Queries 1 (1941): 67–68.
Brooks, Cleanth, and Robert Penn Warren. Understanding Fiction. New York:
    Holt, 1943.
Bunner, H. C. Made in France: French Tales Retold with a United States
    Twist. New York: Keppler and Schwarzmann, 1893.
———. Short Sixes: Stories To Be Read While the Candle Burns. New York:
    Keppler and Schwarzmann, 1891.
Cargill, Oscar. The Novels of Henry James. 1961. Reprint. New York: Hafner,
    1971.
Chambers, Ross. "La Lecteur comme hantise: Spirite et Le Horla." Revue des
    sciences humaines, no. 177 (1980): 105–17.
Chessex, Jacques. Maupassant et les autres. Paris: Editions Ramsay, 1981.
Chopin, Kate. The Complete Works of Kate Chopin. Ed. Per Seyersted. Baton
    Rouge: Louisiana State University Press, 1969. (C1 in text)
———. "It?: From the French of Guy de Maupassant, by Kate Chopin." St.
    Louis Life, 23 February 1895, p. 12.
"Chronicle and Comment." The Bookman [New York] 23 (1906): 365.
Conrad, Joseph. Notes on Life and Letters. Garden City, N.Y.: Doubleday,
    Page, 1921.
Cooper, Frederick Taber. "Ambrose Bierce: An Appraisal." Bookman 33
    (1911): 471–80. Reprinted in Critical Essays on Ambrose Bierce. Ed.
    Cathy N. Davidson. Boston: G. K. Hall, 1982. 28–38.
Croce, Benedetto. European Literature in the Nineteenth Century. Trans.
    Douglas Ainslie. New York: Haskell House, 1967.
Culley, Margaret, ed. The Awakening: An Authoritative Text, Contexts,
    Criticism. By Kate Chopin. (New York: Norton, 1976).
"Current Fiction." The Nation [New York] 93 (1911): 493–94.
Current-Garcia, Eugene. O. Henry (William Sydney Porter). New York:
    Twayne, 1965.
Daugherty, Sarah B. The Literary Criticism of Henry James. Athens: Ohio
    University Press, 1981.
Davidson, Cathy N., ed. Critical Essays on Ambrose Bierce. Boston: G. K.
    Hall, 1982.
———. The Experimental Fictions of Ambrose Bierce. Lincoln: University
    of Nebraska Press, 1984.
Dean, Sharon. "The Myopic Narrator in Henry James's 'Glasses.' " Henry
    James Review 4 (1983): 191–95.
Dollerup, Cay. "The Concept of 'Tension,' 'Intensity,' and 'Suspense' in
    Short-Story Theory." Orbis Litterarum 25 (1970): 314–37.
Donaldson-Evans, Mary. "Beginning to Understand the Narrative 'Come-On'
    in Maupassant's Stories." Neophilologus 68 (1984): 37–47.

———. "The Last Laugh: Maupassant's 'Les Bijoux' and 'La Parure.' " *French Forum* 10 (1985): 168–73.

———. *A Woman's Revenge: The Chronology of Dispossession in Maupassant's Fiction.* Lexington, Ky.: French Forum, 1986.

Dugan, John Raymond. *Illusion and Reality: A Study of Descriptive Techniques in the Works of Guy de Maupassant.* The Hague: Mouton, 1973.

Dumesnil, René. *Guy de Maupassant.* Paris: Armand Colin, 1933.

Edel, Leon. *Henry James.* 5 vols. Philadelphia: Lippincott, 1953–1972.

———, ed. *Henry James: Stories of the Supernatural.* New York: Taplinger, 1970.

———. "Jonathan Sturges." *Princeton University Library Chronicle* 15 (1953): 1–9.

———, and Adeline R. Tintner. "The Library of Henry James, from Inventory, Catalogues and Library Lists." *Henry James Review* 4 (1983): 159–90.

Ejxenbaum, B. M. *O. Henry and the Theory of the Short Story.* Trans. I. R. Tutunik. Ann Arbor: University of Michigan, 1968. (Originally published in Russian, 1925.)

Ewell, Barbara C. *Kate Chopin.* New York: Ungar, 1986.

Fatout, Paul. *Ambrose Bierce: The Devil's Lexicographer.* Norman: University of Oklahoma Press, 1951.

Fogel, Daniel Mark. *Henry James and the Structure of the Romantic Imagination.* Baton Rouge: Louisiana State University Press, 1981.

Forestier, Louis, ed. *Contes et nouvelles.* By Guy de Maupassant. 2 vols. Paris: Gallimard, Editions de la Pléiade, 1974 and 1979.

Forman, Henry James. "O. Henry's Short Stories." *North American Review* 187 (1908): 783.

Frye, Northrop. *Anatomy of Criticism: Four Essays.* Princeton: Princeton University Press, 1957.

Gaer, Joseph. *Ambrose Gwinett [sic] Bierce: Bibliography and Biographical Data.* New York: Burt Franklin, 1935. Reprint. 1968.

Galantière, Lewis. Introduction to *The Portable Maupassant.* New York: Viking, 1947.

Gaudé, Pamela. "Kate Chopin's 'The Storm': A Study of Maupassant's Influence." *Kate Chopin Newsletter* 1 (Fall 1976): 1–6.

Gerould, Katherine Fullerton. "The American Short Story." *Yale Review,* n.s. 13 (1924): 642–45.

Grenander, M. E. *Ambrose Bierce.* New York: Twayne, 1970.

———. "Bierce's Turn of the Screw: Tales of Ironical Terror." *Western Humanities Review* 2 (1957): 257–64. Reprinted in *Critical Essays on Ambrose Bierce.* Ed. Cathy N. Davidson, Boston: G. K. Hall, 1982. 209–16.

Hainsworth, G. "Pattern and Symbol in the Work of Maupassant." *French Studies* 5 (1951): 1–17.

Hall, Gilman. "Tarkington and O. Henry." *Everybody's* 17 (October 1907): 576.

Harris, Richard C. *William Sydney Porter (O. Henry): A Reference Guide.* Boston: G. K. Hall, 1980.

Harte, Terry. *The Turn of the Screw: Bewildered Vision.* Boston: Twayne, 1989.

Hearn, Lafcadio. *The Adventures of Walter Schnaffs, and Other Stories by Guy de Maupassant.* Tokyo: Hokuseido [1931].

———. *Saint Anthony and Other Stories by Guy de Maupassant.* New York: Boni, 1923.

Henry, O. [William Sidney Porter]. *The Complete Works of O. Henry.* Garden City, N.Y.: Doubleday, 1953. (H1 in text)

Ignotus, Paul. *The Paradox of Maupassant.* London: University of London Press, 1967.

James, Henry. *The Complete Notebooks of Henry James.* Ed. Leon Edel and Lyall H. Powers. New York: Oxford University Press, 1987. (J4 in text)

———. *The Complete Tales of Henry James.* Ed. Leon Edel. Philadelphia: Lippincott, 1964. (J5 in text)

———. *Henry James Letters.* 4 vols. Ed. Leon Edel. Cambridge: Harvard University Press, 1974–84. (J2 in text)

———. *Henry James Literary Criticism: French Writers, Other European Writers, The Prefaces to the New York Edition.* Ed. Leon Edel and Mark Wilson. New York: Library of America, 1984. (J3 in text)

———. *The Novels and Tales of Henry James. New York Edition.* 24 vols. New York: Charles Scribner's Sons, 1907–9. (J1 in text)

———. *Partial Portraits.* 1888. Reprint. Ann Arbor: University of Michigan Press, 1970.

———. Preface to *The Odd Number.* By Guy de Maupassant. Trans. Jonathan Sturges. New York: Harper, 1889.

James, William. *The Varieties of Religious Experience.* 1890. Reprint. New York: Dolphin, n.d.

Jasenas, Eliane. "The French Influence in Kate Chopin's *The Awakening.*" *Nineteenth-Century French Studies* 4 (1976): 312–22.

Jennings, Chantal. "La Dualité de Maupassant: Son attitude envers la femme." *Revue des sciences humaines,* no. 144 (1970): 559–78.

Jensen, Gerald E. *The Life and Letters of Henry Cuyler Bunner.* Durham: Duke University Press, 1939.

Jones, Granville H. *Henry James's Psychology of Experience.* The Hague: Mouton, 1975.

Kilmer, Joyce. "Is O. Henry a Pernicious Literary Influence?" *New York Times Magazine,* 23 July 1916, p. 12.

Koloski, Bernard J. "The Structure of Kate Chopin's *At Fault.*" *Studies in American Fiction* 3 (1975): 89–95.

Langford, Gerald. *Alias O. Henry: A Biography of William Sidney Porter.* New York: Macmillan, 1957.

Lattin, Patricia Hopkins. "The Search for Self in Kate Chopin's Fiction: Simple Versus Complex Vision." *Southern Studies* 21 (1982): 222–35.

Lerner, Michael G. *Maupassant.* New York: George Braziller, 1975.

Logan, F. J. "The Wry Seriousness of 'Owl Creek Bridge,'" *American Literary Realism* 10 (Spring 1977): 101–13. Reprinted in *Critical Essays on Ambrose Bierce.* Ed. Cathy N. Davidson. Boston: G. K. Hall, 1982. 195–208.

Lohafer, Susan. *Coming to Terms with the Short Story.* Baton Rouge: Louisiana State University Press, 1983.

Matthews, Brander. *Pen and Ink.* New York: Longmans, Green, 1888.

————. "The Philosophy of the Short Story." *Lippincott's Magazine* 36 (1885): 374.

————. *The Philosophy of the Short Story.* New York: Peter Smith, 1901.

Maupassant, Guy de. *Contes et nouvelles.* Ed. Louis Forestier. 2 vols. Paris: Gallimard, Editions de la Pléiade, 1974 and 1979. (M1 in text)

————. *The Odd Number.* Trans. Jonathan Sturges. Intro. Henry James. New York: Harper, 1889.

————. *The Second Odd Number.* Trans. Charles Henry White. Intro. William Dean Howells. New York: Harper, 1917.

————. *Yvette and Other Stories.* Trans. Ada Galsworthy. Preface by Joseph Conrad. London: Duckwork, 1904.

May, Charles E. "The Unique Effect of the Short Story: A Reconsideration and an Example." *Studies in Short Fiction* 13 (1976): 289–97.

McWilliams, Carey. *Ambrose Bierce. A Biography.* New York: Boni, 1929.

Mencken, H. L. *Prejudices.* 6th ser. New York: Knopf, 1927. Excerpted in *Critical Essays on Ambrose Bierce.* Ed. Cathy N. Davidson. Boston: G. K. Hall, 1982. 61–64.

Miller, Arthur M. "The Influence of Edgar Allan Poe on Ambrose Bierce." *American Literature* 4 (1932): 130–50.

Moger, Angela S. "Narrative Structures in Maupassant: Frames of Desire." *PMLA* 100 (1985): 315–27.

————. "That Obscure Object of Narrative." *Yale French Studies* 63 (1982): 129–38.

Neale, Walter. *Life of Ambrose Bierce.* New York: Walter Neale, 1929.

O'Connor, Richard. *O. Henry: The Legendary Life of William S. Porter.* Garden City, N.Y.: Doubleday, 1970.

O'Sullivan, Vincent. *Aspects of Wilde.* New York: Henry Holt, 1936.

Ostrofsky, Martin B. "O. Henry's Use of Stereotypes in His New York Stories: An Example of the Utilization of Folklore in Literature." *New York Folklore Quarterly* 7, nos. 1–2 (Summer 1981): 41–64.

Pattee, Fred Lewis. *The Development of the American Short Story: An Historical Survey.* 1923. Reprint. New York: Biblio and Tannen, 1975.

Poe, Edgar Allan. "Review of *Twice-Told Tales.* By Nathaniel Hawthorne." 1842. Reprinted in *Great Short Works of Edgar Allan Poe.* Ed. G. R. Thompson. New York: Harper and Row, 1970.

[Pollard, Percival]. "Another Attempt to Boost Bierce into Immortality." *Current Opinion* 65 (September 1918): 184–85. Reprinted in *Critical Essays on Ambrose Bierce.* Ed. Cathy N. Davidson. Boston: G. K. Hall, 1982. 48–52.

Ross, Crystal Ray. *Le Conteur américain O Henry et l'art de Maupassant.* Strasbourg: Imprimerie Strasbourgeoise, 1925.

Saidlower, Sylvia. "Moral Relativism in American Fiction of the Eighteen Nineties." Diss. New York University, 1970.

Schasch, Nafissa A.-F. *Guy de Maupassant et le fantastique ténébreux.* Paris: Librairie A.-G. Nizet, 1983.

Segal, Ora. *The Lucid Reflector: The Observer in Henry James' Fiction.* New Haven: Yale University Press, 1969.

Segnitz, T. M. "The Actual Genesis of Henry James's 'Paste.' " *American Literature* 36 (1964): 216–19.

Seyersted, Per. *Kate Chopin: A Critical Biography.* Baton Rouge: Louisiana State University Press, 1969.

Skaggs, Peggy. "The Boy's Quest in Kate Chopin's 'A Vocation and a Voice.'"
    American Literature 51 (1979): 270–76.
———. Kate Chopin. Boston: Twayne, 1985.
———. "The Man-Instinct of Possession: A Persistent Theme in Kate Cho-
    pin's Stories." Louisiana Studies 14 (1975): 277–85.
Smith, C. Alphonso. O. Henry Biography. Garden City, N.Y.: Doubleday,
    Page, 1916.
Solomon, Eric. "The Bitterness of Battle: Ambrose Bierce's War Fiction."
    Midwest Quarterly 5 (1963–64): 147–65. Reprinted in Critical Essays
    on Ambrose Bierce. Ed. Cathy N. Davidson. Boston: G. K. Hall, 1982.
    182–94.
Spangler, George M. "Kate Chopin's The Awakening: A Partial Dissent."
    Novel 3 (1970): 249–55.
Starrett, Vincent. Buried Caesars: Essays in Literary Appreciation. 1923.
    Reprint. New York: AMS, 1970.
Steegmuller, Francis. "Flaubert's Sundays: Maupassant and Henry James."
    Cornhill Magazine 163 (1948): 124–30.
———. Maupassant: A Lion in the Path. New York: Grosset and Dunlap,
    1949.
Stringham, Susan. Person, Place and Thing in Henry James's Novels. Dur-
    ham: Duke University Press, 1977.
Sturges, Jonathan. The First Supper and Other Episodes. New York: Dodd,
    Mead, 1893.
———, trans. The Odd Number. By Guy de Maupassant. Intro. Henry James.
    New York: Harper, 1889.
Sullivan, Edward D. "Maupassant and the Motif of the Mask." Symposium
    10 (1956): 34–41.
———. Maupassant the Novelist. Port Washington, N.Y.: Kennikat, 1972.
———. Maupassant: The Short Stories. London: Edward Arnold, 1962.
Tintner, Adeline R. The Book World of Henry James: Appropriating the
    Classics. Ann Arbor, Mich.: UMI Research Press, 1987.
Tolstoy, Leo. "Guy de Maupassant." In The Novels and Other Works of Lyof
    N. Tolstoï. Vol. 20. Trans. Aylmer Maude et al. New York: Charles
    Scribner's Sons, 1900. 477–500.
Toth, Emily. Kate Chopin. New York: William Morrow, 1990.
Vial, André. Guy de Maupassant et l'art du roman. Paris: Librairie Nizet,
    1954.
Wallace, A. H. Guy de Maupassant. Boston: Twayne, 1973.
White, Charles Henry, trans. The Second Odd Number. Intro. William Dean
    Howells. New York: Harper, 1917.
Willi, Kurt. Déterminisme et liberté chez Guy de Maupassant. Zurich: Juris-
    Verlag, 1972.
Williams, Blanche. A Handbook on Story Writing. New York: Dodd, Mead,
    1920.
Wolff, Cynthia Griffin. "Kate Chopin and the Fiction of Limits: 'Désirée's
    Baby.'" Southern Literary Journal 10 (Spring 1978): 123–33.
Wolkenfeld, Suzanne. "Edna's Suicide: The Problem of the One and the
    Many." In The Awakening: An Authoritative Text, Contexts, Criti-
    cism. Ed. Margaret Culley. New York: Norton, 1976. 218–24.
"A Yankee Maupassant." Current Literature 45 (1908): 518–20.

Index

Aldrich, Thomas Bailey, 118 n. 34
"Marjorie Daw," 101
Anderson, Sherwood, 4, 21 n. 14, 102 n.
7, 137 n. 69, 219
Aristotle, 5, 65–66
Poetics, 5, 66

Baudelaire, Charles, 1, 49, 103
Bierce, Ambrose, 10, 102–18, 122–23,
129, 143, 150, 215, 218–19
"The Affair at Coulter's Notch," 108
"The Boarded Window," 116 n. 32
Can Such Things Be? 110, 111 n. 23
"Chickamauga," 108 n. 18
Collected Works, 109–10, 111 n. 23,
112
"The Coup de Grâce," 108 n. 18
"The Damned Thing," 109 n. 20
"A Holy Terror," 115 n. 31
"A Horseman in the Sky," 107 n. 17,
108, 109 n. 20
In the Midst of Life, 102–4, 108–9,
111–12, 115, 117–18
"The Man and the Snake," 116 n. 32
"The Mocking-Bird," 107 n. 17, 112 n.
25
"An Occurrence at Owl Creek
Bridge," 112–15
"One of the Missing," 104–8, 112,
116, 118
"One Officer, One Man," 108 n. 18,
109–12
"Parker Adderson, Philosopher," 112
n. 25
"A Son of the Gods," 108 n. 18

"The Story of a Conscience," 112 n.
25
*Tales of Soldiers and Civilians. See
Bierce, Ambrose, In the Midst of
Life*
"A Watcher by the Dead," 116–17
Bourget, Paul, 178, 183
Brontë, Emily
Wuthering Heights, 211
Bunner, H. C., 2–3, 219
Made in France, 2
Short Sixes, 2–3

Chekhov, Anton, 4, 10, 46, 64, 66
"The Kiss," 66
Child, Theodore, 178, 179 n. 10
Chopin, Kate, 10, 117, 139–72, 215, 218
"At Chênière Caminada," 167
The Awakening, 140, 141 n. 2, 149,
159, 160 n. 27, 170–72
Bayou Folk, 143, 146–47, 152, 155
"The Bênitous' Slave, " 146–47
"The Blind Man," 153
"Boulôt and Boulotte," 146–47
"Charlie," 169–72
"Confidences," 141–42, 144–45
"Dead Man's Shoes," 159
"Désirée's Baby," 143, 150–52, 154
"A Divorce Case" (trans.), 155
"Doctor Chevalier's Lie," 150
"A Family Affair," 140
"Father Amable" (trans.), 155, 159
"For Sale" (trans.), 155
"The Godmother," 163–66
"In Sabine," 147–48

"It?" (trans.), 155–57
"The Kiss," 140
"The Locket," 153
"Mad?" (trans.), 155
Mad Stories, 144–45, 155–56, 158
"Madame Martel's Christmas Eve,"
    167–69, 171–72
"A Morning Walk," 140
"Night" (trans.), 155
"The Night Came Slowly," 141 n. 2
"Regret," 140, 141 n. 2
"Solitude" (trans.), 155, 157–58
"The Storm," 166
"The Story of an Hour," 153–54
"Suicide" (trans.), 155
"A Turkey Hunt," 146–47
"A Very Fine Fiddle," 140, 148–50
"A Vocation and a Voice," 160–63
"Wiser Than a God," 149
Conrad, Joseph, 7, 8 n. 13
Coppée, François, 80
Crane, Stephen, 109 n. 12, 117, 159, 183
    n. 13, 218
Croce, Benedetto, 96

Daudet, Alphonse, 174
"Les Femmes d'artistes," 193
Delacroix, Eugène, 103
Dos Passos, John, 102 n. 7
Dreiser, Theodore, 102 n. 7, 117
du Maurier, George, 179, 190 n. 21
Dunbar, Paul, 218

Field, Julian Osgood ("Sigma"), 183 n.
    13
Flaubert, Gustave, 1, 35 n. 34, 46, 96, 97
    n. 37, 174–77, 217
Frederic, Harold, 218
French, Alice, 2–3
Frye, Northrop, 5
Fullerton, William Morton, 183

Garland, Hamlin, 104 n. 12, 147–48
Main-Travelled Roads, 147
Glasgow, Ellen, 102 n. 7
Goncourt, Edmond de, 174–75
Gosse, Edmund, 175–76, 179, 180 n. 11

Harte, Bret, 118 n. 34
Hawthorne, Nathaniel, 146, 163 n. 29
The Scarlet Letter, 170

Hearn, Lafcadio, 1, 99, 142–43, 156
Hemingway, Ernest, 4, 219
Henry, O., 4, 6, 10, 21 n. 14, 22, 102,
    118–37, 143, 215, 218–19
"An Afternoon Miracle," 124 n. 48
"A Blackjack Bargainer," 124 n. 48
Cabbages and Kings, 124 n. 49
"A Chaparral Christmas Gift," 124 n.
    48
"The Duplicity of Hargraves," 124 n.
    48
"The Enchanted Kiss," 124 n. 48
"A Fog in Santone," 124 n. 48
The Four Million, 102, 124, 129–30,
    133–34, 136
"The Furnished Room," 130 n. 58,
    133–36, 137 n. 70
"Georgia's Ruling," 124 n. 48
"The Gift of the Magi," 130–32
Heart of the West, 120, 129 n. 56
"Hygeia at the Solito," 124 n. 48, 125–
    27
"Mammon and the Archer," 130 n. 58
"The Marionettes," 124 n. 48, 127–29
"A Medley of Moods," 124 n. 48
"Money Maze," 124 n. 48
"No Story," 124 n. 48, 133 n. 64
Options, 133 n. 64
Rolling Stones, 125 n. 52
"Rouge et Noir," 124 n. 48
"A Service of Love," 130, 132–33
Sixes and Sevens, 120
"Springtime à la Carte," 133–34
"Whistling Dick's Christmas
    Stocking," 124 n. 48
Howells, William Dean, 16 n. 8, 101 n. 5,
    104, 175
Hugo, Victor, 1

Irving, Washington, 146

James, Henry, 1–2, 4, 9–10, 16 n. 8, 43,
    97 n. 37, 98 n. 39, 100, 173–215
The Ambassadors, 187 n. 17
"The Death of the Lion," 193
"Europe," 187, 214
"The Friends of the Friends," 188 n.
    18, 205
"Glasses," 187–88, 193–99
The Golden Bowl, 197 n. 17, 214 n. 39

"Guy de Maupassant," 179–83, 185.
   See also James, Henry, *Partial
   Portraits*
Guy Domville, 193
Introduction to *The Odd Number*
   (Sturges), 184
"Madame de Mauves," 189 n. 19
Partial Portraits, 1, 16 n. 8, 97 n. 37.
   See also James, Henry, "Guy de
   Maupassant"
"Paste," 187, 193, 199–202, 214
"The Real Right Thing" (1899), 188 n.
   18, 205, 214
"The Real Thing" (1891), 187–93, 198
   n. 28, 199
Roderick Hudson, 174
"Sir Edmund Orme," 183, 188, 205–9,
   213
The Spoils of Poynton, 187 n. 17
The Tragic Muse, 100, 186–87
"The Tree of Knowledge," 187, 202–4,
   214
"The Turn of the Screw," 183, 188,
   205–6, 210–15
The Wings of the Dove, 187 n. 17
James, William, 84 n. 26, 185

London, Jack, 117

Mallarmé, Stéphane, 1
Matthews, Brander, 3, 100 n. 2
   Philosophy of the Short Story, 3, 100
   n. 2
Maupassant, Guy de, 1–4, 7–10, 11–98,
   99–102, 108–9, 112, 115–21, 123,
   127, 129, 135–37, 139–50, 152–60,
   162–63, 166–67, 169, 171–90, 192–
   96, 199–200, 202, 204–7, 209, 211–
   12, 213 n. 38, 214–15, 217–19. See
   also Sturges, Jonathan, *Modern
   Ghosts* and *The Odd Number*
"A vendre," 155
"Allouma," 61–63
"L'Ami Joseph," 78
"Apparition," 101 n. 6
Au soleil, 177
"Auprès d'un mort," 94, 116 n. 33
"Aux champs," 67–70
"L'Aventure de Walter Schnaffs," 19–
   20
"Le Baiser," 80–81

"Le Baptême," 42
Bel-ami, 177–78
"Les Bijoux," 69–70, 140, 148–49,
   200–202
"Boitelle," 42
"Le Bonheur," 101
"Boule de suif," 7, 46, 85–88, 97 n.
   37, 177, 182, 218
"Châli," 30
"Le Champ d'oliviers," 31–32
"Clair de lune," 101 n. 6, 109
Clair de lune, 148, 155, 177, 202
"Coco," 16
"La Confession," 101 n. 6
Contes de la bécasse, 177
Contes du jour et de la nuit, 115–16,
   177
"Correspondance," 79–80
"Denis," 26
Des vers, 177
"Deux amis," 71–73
"Le Diable," 16
"Le Docteur Héraclius Gloss," 85
"Le Donneur d'eau bénite," 11–14
"La Dot," 17
"En canot," 23 n. 18
"En famille," 85, 187 n. 17
"En voyage," 84 n. 25, 101 n. 6
"En wagon," 192 n. 22
"L'Épave," 101 n. 6
"Farce normande," 16
"La Femme de Paul," 51–54
"La Ficelle," 41, 101 n. 6
"Fini," 42
Forte comme la morte, 187 n. 17
"Fou?" (1882), 37–38, 155, 158
"Le Gueux," 101 n. 6
"L'Héritage," 182
"Histoire d'un chien,' 177
"Histoire d'un fille de ferme," 65 n. 16
"Le Horla," 48, 57–61, 63, 101 n. 5,
   109 n. 20, 156, 160, 183–85, 204–5,
   210
Le Horla, 177
"Idylle," 30
"L'Inutile Beauté," 49, 91–96, 166
L'Inutile Beauté, 155, 166, 177
"Le Lit 29," 47, 73 n. 22
"Le Loup," 40–41, 101
"Lui?" 155–58, 167 n. 31
"Mademoiselle Cocotte," 41–42

Mademoiselle Fifi, 155, 177
La Maison Tellier, 177
"La Mère sauvage," 101 n. 6
Miss Harriet, 177, 202
"Le Modèle," 42, 163, 194–96
Monsieur Parent, 155, 177
Mont-Oriol, 180
"Mouche," 49, 187 n. 17
Notre Coeur, 94 n. 33
"La Nuit," 148 n. 12, 155, 158
"Le Papa de Simon," 12–14
"La Parure," 27–31, 43, 47, 70 n. 18,
   101–2, 150, 177, 182, 199–200
"Le Père," 65 n. 16
"Le Père Amable," 155, 159
"Le Père Milon," 42
"Petit soldat," 101 n. 6, 182
Le Petite Roque, 155, 177
Pierre et Jean, 177, 180, 182, 186–87
"Première neige," 70
"Les Prisonniers," 20–21
"Promenade," 76–77
"Qui sait?" 187 n. 17
"Regret," 73–76, 202–3
"La Reine Hortense," 141 n. 2
"La Rempailleuse," 84 n. 25
"Le Rendez-vous," 82–83
"Réveil," 170 n. 32
Les Soeurs Rondoli, 155, 177
Les Soirées de Medan, 177
"Solitude," 141 n. 2, 143, 155, 157–
   58, 170 n. 32
"Suicides," 36–38, 141 n. 2, 155, 158,
   170 n. 32
"Sur l'eau," 23–26, 101 n. 5, 184
Sur l'eau, 23 n. 18
"Un cas de divorce," 155, 158
"Un coup d'État," 78 n. 23
"Un duel," 17
"Une partie de campagne," 14–15, 18
"Une ruse," 84 n. 25
Une vie, 177
"Un fou," 56–57
"Un fou?" 56 n. 8
"Un lâche," 30–31, 54–56, 101, 110–
   11
La Vie errante, 177
"Yvette," 88–91
Yvette, 177–78

Mencken, H. L., 102 n. 7, 137 n. 70
Mérimée, Prosper, 217
   "Le Vase étrusque," 85
Monet, Claude, 187 n. 17

Norris, Frank, 117, 159, 218

Poe, Edgar Allan, 5–6, 26 n. 23, 37, 39,
   44, 49–50, 53 n. 6, 58, 103, 108 n.
   19, 118 n. 34, 158, 183, 204, 209,
   217
   "The Cask of Amontillado," 49
   "A Descent into the Maelström," 50
   "Ligeia," 49
   "The Purloined Letter," 39
   "Review of *Twice-Told Tales*," 8–9
   "The Tell-Tale Heart," 49
   "William Wilson," 53 n. 6
Porter, William S. *See* Henry, O.

Schopenhauer, Arthur, 67, 94, 96–98,
   117, 188, 217
Shakespeare, William, 114 n. 28
Stein, Gertrude, 4, 219
Stevenson, Robert Louis, 183
Stockton, Frank, 118 n. 34
   "The Lady or the Tiger?" 2, 101
Sturges, Jonathan, 2–3, 205
   Modern Ghosts, 101, 143, 156, 184–
   85, 204
   The Odd Number, 2, 98 n. 39, 100–
   104, 108–11, 115, 143–45, 150, 184
Swinburne, Algernon, 175–76

Taine, Hippolyte, 174 n. 1
Thanet, Octave. *See* French, Alice
Tolstoy, Leo, 15 n. 6
Turgenev, Ivan, 9, 35, 174, 217
   Sportsman's Sketches, 35
   "Yermolay and the Miller's Wife," 35

Wells, H. G., 213 n. 38
Wilde, Oscar, 178, 179 n. 8
Williams, William Carlos, 102 n. 7
Woolf, Virginia, 94
Woolson, Constance Fenimore, 193 n. 23

Zola, Émile, 1, 46–47, 65, 85, 96, 174 n.
   1, 177, 217